THE WAREHOUSE CORONER

THE WAREHOUSE CORONER

THE FENWAY STEVENSON MYSTERIES
BOOK 9

PAUL AUSTIN ARDOIN

For Janice

Not a soul
But felt a fever of the mad and play'd
Some tricks of desperation. All but mariners
Plunged in the foaming brine and quit the vessel,
Then all afire with me.

—WILLIAM SHAKESPEARE, *THE TEMPEST,*

ACT I, SCENE 2

TABLE OF CONTENTS

PART 1

TUESDAY

CHAPTER ONE

THE HIGH-PITCHED SQUEAL OF THE PACKING TAPE DISPENSER rolling over the top of the box sounded both satisfying and obnoxious.

The kitchen was almost done. McVie's plain white dishes from Marks-the-Spot would cost more in moving truck space to get to Colorado than buying a new set once he arrived. Not an argument she wanted to have, though.

Fenway Stevenson stood and stretched. Packing for someone else: her least favorite way to spend a vacation day.

The front door opened, and Craig McVie walked in.

"Office falling apart without you?" Fenway said, looking up. McVie's light blue polo shirt was tight across his muscular chest and biceps; he was dressed lightly for the June afternoon. She stepped over to him, wrapping her arms around his six foot four frame.

"According to my clients? Yes." He kissed her forehead and took a step back, appraising the stacks of boxes. "Wow. You've been busy."

"I didn't expect you to be gone for the whole morning."

Fenway's stomach rumbled—already one-thirty—and she reached down, grabbed the tape gun, and handed it to McVie.

"I didn't either. Thanks for doing all this."

Fenway pointed to a small brown cardboard box on the counter. "Silverware and cutlery in there. Grab the stuff out of the top drawer."

McVie stood still, his mouth turning down at the corners.

Fenway straightened up and put her hands on her hips. "Don't tell me."

"That's why I had to head into the office. My client saw his wife head to Estancia Shore. Apparently, she's taking two beach chairs, and he's suspicious. He wants me there as soon as possible."

"I thought you'd given him everything he needed."

"It's complicated."

It's always complicated. Fenway opened her mouth, then shut it again. No—the reason she liked McVie so much? It *wasn't* complicated. Sure, they'd had a few complicated weeks as he prepared to put his private investigation business into hibernation and move to Colorado to make sure Megan had an easier transition to a new school her senior year, but all his complications were external: his ex, his daughter, his job.

Fenway narrowed her eyes. "There's something else."

McVie's forehead crinkled, then he heaved a sigh. "Payback Systems moved up my start date to this coming Monday."

"That's less than a week away." Fenway leaned against the kitchen counter. "Your apartment won't be ready—"

"I found a cheap extended stay place."

Fenway frowned. "Wait—so that means..."

"I'll need to leave a week earlier than I planned." McVie looked down and shuffled his feet.

Fenway opened her mouth, then closed it again. That would be *this* Friday, not next Friday. She realized she was clenching her fists and relaxed her hands. She wanted to tell him that she'd been counting on that time with him, that she needed those extra seven days so she could balance herself and come to terms with a long-distance relationship.

"I'm sorry," he said. "I tried to tell them I couldn't make it so early, but they insisted."

Warning bells for the job already. But at least she knew he only intended to stay in Colorado a year.

"I guess it's a good thing I came over to help." Had she kept her tone light enough?

"For sure," McVie said. "I had to rent a storage space. I won't be able to get the moving truck any earlier, so I'll have to dump everything in storage for a week."

Her eyes raked the half-packed living room and small dining area. "Guess we have our work cut out for us."

He ran a hand over his face. "You've been so great through this. You don't need to do anything else."

Fenway raised her eyebrows. "What do you mean? If you have to move up your start date, we definitely have a lot to do."

"I can't have you doing all my packing for me."

"You've taken *some* stuff to the storage space by now, though, right?"

"I haven't taken possession of the storage unit yet." Another crease appeared on McVie's forehead. "I have to pick up the keys by three o'clock, but I'll figure something out."

She turned her head to look at the clock on the oven. 1:33 PM. "Your client's wife headed to the beach *today*?"

"She changed her schedule from Thursday. My client said she wants to avoid the tropical storm."

"That stupid storm." Fenway shook her head. "It's all anyone can talk about this week, and I didn't think we got tropical storms here."

"Hardly ever. Five years ago, they got a tropical depression in San Diego."

"And isn't it either supposed to hit south of Santa Barbara or go out to sea?"

"My client's wife went to her psychic." He grinned. "I bet the psychic is right at least as often as meteorologists."

"Even though we'd planned to do nothing but pack, I still wanted to spend the day with you."

"Me too. Maybe tonight?"

"Hang on," Fenway said. "You're going to the beach, taking pictures—*and* you're going to take possession of the storage unit by three o'clock? That's in an hour and a half."

"I'll figure it out."

Fenway blinked. "I'm taking the day off anyway. How about if I go get the keys for the storage unit for you? One less thing for you to worry about."

"No, no, you've done too much already," McVie said. "I'll ask Piper—"

"Don't be ridiculous." Fenway shook her head. "She's getting your business affairs in order before you leave."

"It's fine."

"I'm offering, Craig. Besides, I could use the change of scenery." Fenway held her right hand up at a purposely weird angle. "See? I'm already getting the dreaded 'tape dispenser hand.' Getting out of this apartment will do me good."

McVie sighed. "You're right. I could really use the extra time. I'll call and put your name on the storage space. Let me make it up to you."

"A foot massage later?"

"Are you kidding? With all that you're doing for me, I'll massage *both* feet." McVie grinned.

"It's a good thing you're usually so nice to me." Fenway reached out and put her hand flat on his chest. "And you're cute, too."

McVie smiled. "I can't tell you how much I appreciate this." He exhaled. "Is it okay with you if I move a few things in here before I go on my stakeout? Only for a few hours."

"Move a few things in here? What do you mean?"

McVie took a breath. "I've got a bunch of boxes in the back of the Highlander."

"From what?" Fenway blinked. "Oh. The office."

McVie nodded. "And a couple of chairs. I can't take the Highlander full of boxes to the beach. I won't be able to take pictures with the rear windows blocked."

Fenway narrowed her eyes. "You mean to tell me you've got your Highlander full of stuff and a job to get to immediately?" Fenway rolled her eyes. "You're not superhuman, Mr. Boy Scout. Let's just swap cars."

"You want me to take your Honda?"

"And I'll take your SUV full of boxes. I'm going to the storage unit anyway. Might as well take a few things in." She poked his chest playfully with her index finger. "Not taking the heavy stuff, though. Letting my big, strong, disorganized man do that."

McVie's jaw dropped—he didn't even acknowledge the playful ribbing. "How about you *relax* on your day off?" McVie handed her his keys. "I mean it. The boxes stay in the car. Just pick up the keys and the gate code for me."

Fenway flexed her biceps and lowered her voice an octave. "Me Craig. Me feel sad when girlfriend carry heavy boxes."

McVie rolled his eyes and turned toward the door.

Fenway smacked him playfully on his backside. "Now go on. Grab the Honda key from my purse and get out of here."

He sighed, taking the Accord key fob from Fenway's purse. "You're a lifesaver."

She shook her head. "The things I do for a foot massage."

"Oh, there's a padlock and a key in the glove compartment. I've just gotta change, and then I'm on my way."

She nodded.

He disappeared into his bedroom.

Despite the chaos of this week, McVie was the ideal guy in a lot of ways—not just his looks and his kindness. Their age difference mattered less every day. But he needed to please people, which, especially right now, mattered *more* every day. He worried about

Megan. Yes, she'd been dumped by her boyfriend and ostracized by her social group. Fenway remembered her high school years: tough, though maybe not quite as hard as what Megan was going through. The decision Megan made to move with her mother a thousand miles away the summer before her senior year was drastic. Probably one reason Craig worried about Megan.

That was the problem, though: he prioritized everyone else's wants before Fenway's.

Hang on—that wasn't quite fair. She'd been his priority for most of the time they'd been dating. And she didn't mind—well, *intellectually* she didn't mind—coming in second to his daughter. Emotionally, a different story. But now, for the last week or two anyway, she stood in line behind not only the needs of his daughter, but the demands of his new job, too.

She crossed her arms. After he left, maybe she'd go for a night out with Rachel. Oh—they could go dancing. They hadn't been on a girls' night out in months, not since Fenway had started seriously dating McVie—and Rachel was seeing Deputy Brian Callahan, and that was getting serious too. Once McVie left for Colorado, Rachel had promised they'd go out.

McVie appeared in the archway between the hall and the kitchen. He wore black swimming trunks, brown flip-flops, and a loose aloha shirt. All that was missing was zinc oxide on his nose.

"Headed to a Fortune 500 board meeting, I see," Fenway said.

"I look like a stereotypical undercover cop, but it'll have to do." McVie cocked his head. "Dinner tonight, and maybe breakfast tomorrow?"

Fenway reached for her purse on the kitchen counter. "One thing at a time, cowboy."

———

A Masco Stor-With-Us had recently opened about six blocks away from McVie's apartment. But for whatever reason, probably financial, he'd rented a ten-by-twenty space at Cahill Warehouse Storage in the industrial part of town.

Fenway stopped at Dos Milagros on her way to the storage place. Okay—maybe it was the wrong direction, but she'd at least get an order of lengua tacos before she schlepped boxes and chairs into a dusty storage unit.

She had to step around two Tailwhip electric scooters lying on their sides in front of the entrance. Fenway frowned. When she'd moved to Estancia, the Tailwhip scooters had just started appearing in her old neighborhood in Seattle. She'd ridden them a few times, and she had to admit they were a lot of fun. She could control them like a pro, too.

But in her last month as a nurse at the clinic in Seattle, before she'd moved to Estancia, she'd had to deal with a spate of injuries due to the scooters—everything from people falling off the scooters to pedestrian collisions. One unlucky rider lost control going down a steep hill and broke both arms.

She wanted to kick the Tailwhip out of the way—and immediately felt crotchety. Not quite thirty years old and she acted like an entitled old lady angry at new technology.

Still, the scooters were a scourge on the town. Fenway pulled the scooter off the sidewalk onto the parking strip, then brushed her hands on her trousers, and entered Dos Milagros.

The lunch rush had ended, and the woman who took her order smiled, her eyes weary. Fenway took her number and sat alone at a high-top table. She scrolled social media on her phone while she waited for her order to be ready, drinking half of her horchata out of boredom.

She'd almost always had company at Dos Milagros over the last six months. If McVie wasn't humoring her, she often convinced Rachel or Piper or Dez—once, Patrick—to join her.

Ever since Patrick Appleby had replaced Piper in the county's IT department, Fenway had a strained relationship with him—and Fenway knew the blame was ninety percent hers. Maybe a hundred percent. So two weeks ago, she'd invited him to join her for lunch at Dos Milagros. He'd accepted after thinking it over for about thirty seconds too long.

After she'd ordered her lengua tacos, Patrick had looked at her suspiciously. They'd sat down—at the same table where Fenway was sitting now.

"Have you been to Dos Milagros before?"

"No."

She'd smiled at him and waited for him to say something else. He pulled a paper napkin out of the dispenser on the table and began to fold it, corner to corner, meticulously. He made a hard crease in the napkin with the back of his thumbnail, then opened the napkin and put the corners together in the other direction.

"Lots of different cultures eat tongue," he said, his thumbnail making a second hard crease.

Fenway nodded. "I like the lengua here. It's delicious."

"Probably because tongue is seventy-five percent fat." Patrick looked at Fenway and pushed his glasses up on his nose. "Of course, that's a rounded average. Moose tongue, for example, is higher in fat than cow tongue."

"Did you say moose tongue?"

"Yes, moose tongue. It's a delicacy in Finland. You must peel the skin off and smoke the meat for several hours. The Finns serve it with lingonberry sauce."

"Ah."

He stared at the table for a moment. "It's important to take the center cartilage out of duck tongue before you cook it. Most people call it a bone, but that's wrong."

Fenway cocked her head. "Really? Duck tongue has a bone in it —sorry, cartilage?"

"The cartilage will explode if you cook the tongue without removing it. That's why the cartilage must be removed first."

"I'm not sure I've ever tried duck tongue."

"I tried tongue once. I don't like the texture."

"What kind?"

Patrick blinked at Fenway in confusion.

"Duck tongue? Moose tongue? Armadillo tongue?"

"Oh. Beef tongue." He didn't smile at Fenway's attempt at levity.

Fenway took a sip of her horchata. "You sure know a lot about tongue for not liking it."

"I don't understand why people would eat a meat with such an unappealing texture and flavor. I thought if I researched it, I would uncover information that would make sense."

"And did you?"

"No."

Fenway cleared her throat. "You like video games, Patrick?"

Head back down, concentrating on folding the napkin. "I like *Nest of Spies.*"

Fenway had nodded. "My boyfriend's daughter likes that one too." And so the conversation had been mostly saved.

She shook her head and came back to the present as the woman behind the counter called her number.

After Fenway ate, she walked out into the bright sunshine, sighed, and got back into McVie's SUV.

She looked out the window as she turned the Highlander onto La Crescenta. Almost a year ago, she had driven by these warehouses for a kidnapping case she'd been on.

The heat ran to her cheeks. She'd had an intense make-out session with McVie in the front seat of this very Highlander during that investigation. She cleared her throat and ran a hand through her hair, then exhaled as she turned onto 31st Street at a lime green sign that said *Cahill Warehouse Storage.*

The storage facility on the corner took up three blocks. The fence around the property was utilitarian: chain-link fencing with barbed wire at the top. It gave the facility the look of a prison rather than a homey place to keep extra furniture and boxes of mementos, but since McVie only needed the storage for a week or two, she figured aesthetics didn't factor into his decision-making process.

Fenway parked the Highlander in a visitor space, got out of the car, and walked through a blue metal door with peeling paint marked *Office.*

She entered a waiting area in front of the counter painted lime green to match the sign outside. A beige metal desk stood perpendicular to the counter, its left side flush with the concrete-block back wall. A framed faded poster from a local paper with a "Best of Dominguez County" logo hung on the wall next to the desk.

A light-skinned Black woman of thirty-five or forty stood behind the counter, the landline phone receiver pressed to her ear. "No, Mr. Hardwick, I don't know Seth's whereabouts. He's *your* client, and last I checked, he was no longer my husband. Why don't you check with Miranda?" She tugged on the sleeve of her denim jacket, which looked too warm for a June afternoon. Holding the phone between her ear and shoulder, she pulled her wavy hair back into a ponytail. She wore a cream-colored blouse under the jacket.

Silence for a moment, and the woman caught Fenway's eye and held up a finger. Fenway nodded.

"I don't know what to tell you," she continued. "I wasn't here last night. I could check with Mathis, see if Seth showed up during his shift. But it's not like his precious Corvette was here this morning."

More silence.

"I sure will—assuming I see him first," she said. "Maybe Seth is cheating on Miranda, too. Did you try the Cactus Lake Hotel? If he's seeing a new girl, he might've gone with their hourly rate."

A moment later, she stared at the receiver, then turned to Fenway with a twinkle in her eye. "I guess he hung up."

"You talking to your ex-husband's lawyer? Isn't he supposed to only contact you through *your* lawyer?"

"Sounds like I should have had you on my team during the divorce proceedings." She grinned. "The divorce finalized last week.

So all those rules no longer apply." She folded her hands. "I apologize for the delay. What can I help you with?"

"My boyfriend rented a storage space and needed me to pick up the key."

"Gotcha." She reached under the counter and pulled out a clipboard, then flipped two pages. "Here it is. Craig McVie?"

"That's right."

"Yep, he put a second person down as an authorized user of the storage space. What's your name?"

Fenway pulled her wallet out of her purse and slid her driver's license out. "Fenway Stevenson."

The woman cocked her head. "*You're* Fenway Stevenson?"

"That's right." Fenway braced herself—what newsworthy item from her recent past would the woman bring up?

"I didn't think you'd be so tall."

Fenway blinked.

The woman held out her hand. "Tyra Cahill. Co-owner—" She stopped herself. "Sorry, *owner* of Cahill Warehouse Storage."

Fenway shook it. "Nice to meet you."

Cahill turned to the computer and typed. "Okay, we'll put you in —" She frowned. "No, that one is reserved. Let's see." She clicked the keyboard again. "All right. Space one-twelve. Lower level, around the corner from the entrance." She pulled a drawer open and handed Fenway a form and a code for the gate.

Beginning a lengthy explanation of the rules of the storage facility, Cahill spoke in a tone surprisingly animated for the hundreds of times she must have repeated the guidelines to customers.

Fenway filled out the form, smiling and nodding at appropriate points of the spiel, thinking about how quickly she could finish. The beautiful warm afternoon was perfect for a run; she'd have just enough time to go home, change into shorts, and jog through the monarch butterfly waystation before McVie got back. She hadn't taken that route in a few months.

Breaking Fenway's reverie, Cahill tapped the clipboard. "If you agree to all the terms I went through, sign here, and initial here, here, and here."

"Month to month, right?"

Cahill nodded. "Mr. McVie put on the online form that he'd only need it for the month." She pointed to the form. "Just empty the unit, cancel within thirty days, and we won't charge him again."

Fenway signed and initialed, vaguely hoping she or McVie wouldn't be on the hook for anything she wasn't expecting.

Cahill handed her a small keychain with two round metal keys.

"I don't use my own padlock?" Fenway asked.

"On the smaller units, but not the ten-by-twenties," she said. "Thanks for your business."

Fenway exited the office and walked back to McVie's Highlander. She glanced at the code on the slip of paper in her hand, got in, and drove the Highlander next to the keypad in front of the gate. She was in such a hurry she mistyped it the first time, then took a deep breath and concentrated on pressing the number pad buttons fully. The gate opened with a clank of metal and the swishing of a chain.

She drove through and stopped in front of 112. The space might be too large for what McVie needed, but better to have too big of a space than too small. She got out of the Highlander, walked around to the storage unit door, grabbed the handle, and lifted.

The space yawned before her—ten feet by twenty feet. McVie must have been in a mindset where he still thought he was living a two-thousand square foot house with two other people rather than his post-divorce reality of a nine hundred square-foot two-bedroom apartment. It wasn't *her* money, though.

But the space wasn't empty. A royal blue sleeping bag with gray stripes. A flashlight. A portable toilet. A gallon jug of drinking water. A small red cooler with a white lid. And the smell of the sea and a tang of body odor. She frowned, pulled down the storage unit door, locked the Highlander, and walked to the office.

She opened the door. "Looks like you have some squatters—"

Instead of Tyra Cahill behind the counter, a short Asian woman in her early twenties looked up from the computer. She wore a nametag: *Isabella.*

"Oh," Fenway said. "Sorry—I'm Fenway Stevenson."

Isabella blinked. "The county coroner?"

"Uh, yes."

"I voted for you back in November! It's nice to meet you."

Fenway forced a smile onto her face. "Thanks. Listen, I just took possession of one-twelve from Tyra Cahill, and I wanted to unload my boxes. But it looks like there's someone living there."

Isabella's eyes grew larger. "Oh, I'm so sorry. I was on break— Tyra doesn't usually sign people in. Let's get you into an empty unit." She looked at the computer. "Okay—there's one available the same size, but it's on the other side of the property. Not quite as convenient." She pulled out a site map and a pen and drew an arrow and a circle.

"Not a problem."

"Let me save you some time," Isabella said, handing Fenway the map. "Unit one seventy-six in Building C. It'll be open. You can start loading your stuff into the unit. I'll meet you over there with the keys and the updated paperwork."

"Sounds good." Fenway glanced at the map; Unit 176 was located at the back of the property, but at least it was the same size.

"Give me about five minutes."

Fenway nodded her thanks, walked out of the office, and went back to the Highlander. As she started the engine, she glanced at the clock on the dashboard—she'd be cutting it close if she wanted to get a run in.

She steered McVie's SUV around Building A, then drove another hundred yards past Building B, finally turning the back corner to Building C. Unit 176 sat at the end of the building, with a gate, unmarked on the map, about twenty feet from the edge. Could she and McVie use the gate? It would make moving stuff in a little easier.

Killing the engine and getting out of the Highlander, Fenway walked to the door of Unit 176 and grabbed the handle and pulled up.

The door didn't move.

Fenway closed her eyes and exhaled through her nose. How annoying. Time ticked away—she wouldn't have time to get her run in. Stretching her arms above her head, she relaxed her shoulders. She still had a few minutes before Isabella showed up, so she moved into the sun, getting warmer as she stepped out of the shade.

A moment later, the clicking of shoes on concrete. Isabella turned the corner, a key in her hand. "Sorry," she said, "there's only one key. I'd swap for a unit with two keys, but this is the last of this size we have."

"One key is fine," Fenway said.

"It's open," Isabella said, motioning to the rolling door.

"It's not, actually."

"It isn't?" Isabella frowned. "It should be. Maybe whoever checked this last accidentally locked it and didn't put the key back. I'll have to ask Mathis." She reached out and put the round key into the lock, and the latch popped open.

"What if someone has rented this unit?" Fenway asked. "Maybe it's just not showing up in your system."

"This one isn't rented," Isabella said, lifting the door. "I checked it yesterday."

As the door rolled up, Fenway's nose twitched.

In the middle of the bare concrete floor, an area rug, rumpled, as if it had unrolled. A Persian design of dusky gold and muted navy blue. A wool and silk blend, perhaps.

The door rolled higher.

Expensive brown designer sneakers, worn without socks.

Fitted blue jeans, casual but pricey.

A man, lying on his back. Trim, maybe five foot six.

Then Isabella's shriek.

A bloodstain on the rug, next to the back of the man's head.

CHAPTER TWO

Warning Isabella to stay well back of the body—a directive Isabella complied with immediately—Fenway took her phone out of her purse and called Sergeant Desiree Roubideaux.

"Don't tell me you and Craig are fighting about moving boxes already," Dez said as she answered.

"There's a dead body on the floor of Craig's storage space," Fenway said, "so I don't think we'll be moving a lot of boxes in today."

Dez paused.

"You there?"

"A dead body," Dez repeated. "On the floor of McVie's storage space?"

"I took possession of it about ninety seconds ago." She closed her eyes. "The storage space, I mean, not the dead body. The first space McVie got hadn't been, uh, vacated yet. So I got this one. White male, five foot six, maybe one fifty."

"Any ID?"

"I'm about to examine the body. You're my first call."

"I'll check missing persons," Dez said, "and I'll call Michi."

"Dr. Yasuda is still working?"

"Michi said she wouldn't be home till seven. So yeah, I think she'll still be in the office."

"Great. I'd like you to head over here and help interview the employees. See if they saw anything."

"On my way."

"Bring Mark too. I might need him to help out."

Dez chuckled. "Making sure the short-timer doesn't goof off his last week at work?"

"This is a big facility, Dez. And there's a squatter in one of the units. We'll get more done with more of us here."

"You sound like my mama," Dez said. "Many hands make light work."

Fenway gave Dez the address of the storage facility before ending the call, then took out a pair of blue nitrile gloves from her purse, snapped them on, then knelt next to the body. Although she knew there wouldn't be a pulse, she felt for one anyway.

Keeping one eye on Isabella, Fenway walked back to the Highlander before she remembered that her crime scene kit sat in the trunk of her Accord, not McVie's SUV.

Okay then—she wouldn't have a liver thermometer. The body had cooled—but just by touch, Fenway couldn't tell how much. It wasn't yet at the temperature of the storage space.

She rocked back onto her heels and tried to bend the man's right elbow. Stiff as a board. She leaned to her left and attempted to bend his right knee. Also stiff. So rigor mortis had fully set in— meaning at least six to eight hours since death. Less than twenty-four.

The body could have been placed here any time during the night. Maybe as late as six or seven this morning. Hopefully, Cahill Warehouse Storage had working cameras. There were three in the spaces between the front buildings. She'd look for cameras on this side of the complex.

She checked the man's pockets. Empty.

Now for the wound. She lifted the man's head—more difficult with the neck in rigor—and felt the wound. Odd—the skin was broken in a line, about an inch wide and perhaps an eighth of an inch high. The first thing she thought: his skull had been stabbed, rather than beaten. A single blow.

She felt around a little more. The hole in the skull wasn't a clean stab wound; the area around the wound indented in a bit, and one side of the wound sank deeper than the other.

She peered at the bloodstain on the Persian rug. Head wounds bled copiously, and there wasn't enough blood on the rug for this storage space to be the murder location.

Which meant the body had been moved.

She looked at the bloodstains more closely. Fenway stood, took her gloves off, then turned on the flashlight on her phone. Odd pattern for the bloodstain, as if parts of the rug had been pushed against itself.

She stared at the body for a moment, then nodded. Someone had killed this man, then wrapped his body in this rug and transported it here.

Dead between six and twenty-four hours. A wide net. She turned off the flashlight. Maybe she'd find out more after Dr. Yasuda performed the autopsy.

Fenway glanced up at Isabella, still gripping the round key tightly in her hand and pointedly looking at the fence on the other side of the unit, rather than at the dead body. Isabella had turned a light shade of green.

"You can go back to the office," Fenway said to her gently. "My sergeant will be here soon, and you can give your statement then."

"I need to make sure I can help customers."

"We'll need you to close the office for the rest of the day," Fenway said.

"I—I can't. There are still people who need to pick up keys for their spaces."

"I'm sorry," Fenway said, "but this facility is a crime scene."

"But—"

Fenway held up a hand. "We'll release it as soon as we can, but the medical examiner is on her way. We need to make sure we can secure this site."

Isabella swallowed hard. "Oh, right. Of course."

Fenway watched Isabella turn, totter, then right herself and walk toward the office.

Now for the victim.

No identification. Maybe fingerprints would help determine who the victim was, but as for identifying his killer, still a challenge. Even if the killer hadn't worn gloves, both Fenway and Isabella had put their hands and fingers all over the lock, the handle, and the roll-up door.

She took a careful walk around the perimeter of the storage unit, looking carefully on the ground for any clues. If this space had been well-cleaned before the body arrived here, anything in the unit might have fallen out of the killer's pockets or might have been missed by the victim.

There. By the front of the unit, past where the closed door would be. A smudge of blood. Possibly tracked by a shoe—but there wasn't much of it. And no visible shoe tread.

Fenway shined the flashlight of her phone around some more— and something glinted in the corner. Fenway took a few steps closer and bent down. A screw. A short, hex-head screw, a dark green head; the body of the screw unpainted steel.

She took a step back, then looked at the rails of the roll-up door. No screws were missing.

The gate across from the unit opened, and a silver Ford SUV drove in, turned toward Unit 176, then stopped. Fenway pulled her badge out of her purse and held it up for the driver to see.

A man with deeply tanned skin drove. He sported a mustache and goatee, and had short hair. Late thirties, maybe, although maybe a bit older: his graying temples hadn't reached his beard yet. The woman in the passenger seat had long black hair and large dark eyes. She looked younger than the driver, though her smile lines made Fenway suspect she was also in her late thirties. Her eyes opened wide when she saw the badge.

Fenway saw movement in the back seat, too, and then the rear door opened.

A figure got out: Tyra Cahill.

She took a step closer. "Hi, Miss Stevenson," she said, her eyes raking over the scene in front of her. "I—what's happening?"

"One-twelve wasn't available," Fenway said, "so I went back to the office and got one seventy-six."

"But—" Cahill started, then stared at the open storage door. "What do you mean, one-twelve wasn't available? I don't understand—"

"Looks like a squatter stayed in there."

Cahill set her jaw. "I thought Seth took care of that."

"You knew about the squatter in one-twelve?"

"We've had—uh, people using the storage spaces as residences," Cahill said, fumbling her words. "Well—not really residences. More like hotel rooms. They'd stay one or two nights, tops. But with the extra cleaning fees, and things like—" She stopped, and her eyes went to the rug—and the body on it.

Fenway followed her gaze. "You have information about this particular unit?"

Cahill's eyes glazed over, and her jaw went slack, her mind obviously elsewhere.

"Sorry—Ms. Cahill?"

Cahill snapped back to the present. "I'm so sorry. I'm not used to this."

"I asked if you know about this."

"About what?"

Fenway gestured. "Why one seventy-six showed up in your system as free, but why it was locked—and why there's a dead body in it."

Cahill flinched. "A dead—" She took a few tentative steps closer.

"What did you think?"

"A mannequin, I guess. You see all sorts of weird stuff in storage units." She squinted. "Oh."

"What?"

"Those—those are Seth's shoes."

Fenway remembered the phone call Cahill had been on when she walked into the office. "Your ex-husband?"

"Yes." Cahill turned around and walked to the passenger side of the SUV. The woman inside rolled down the window. "I—" She paused and placed a shaky hand between her clavicles, took a deep breath, then continued. "Something happened. We won't be going to the Harbor Festival after all."

Fenway couldn't hear the woman's response.

"The coroner found a dead body inside that storage unit. I think it's Seth."

Another response Fenway couldn't understand.

"No, no, please don't wait for me. I'll be fine. I can't imagine I'll be able to get away for at least a few hours."

"Sorry," Fenway said, "but if you could ask your friends to pull their car around the front and wait for the police, we'll want to take their statements."

The driver of the car leaned over and said something.

"I suppose," Cahill said doubtfully. "How will I get home otherwise?"

Fenway glanced at the driver and the passenger through the windshield, but the bright sun reflecting off the glass made it hard to see how they reacted. The driver put the SUV into gear, then drove toward the front of the property, turning the corner around the building and out of sight.

"I think we better..." Fenway began, then trailed off.

Cahill had gone back to staring vacantly at the dead body.

Ordinarily, Fenway wouldn't ask someone to identify a spouse so soon after discovery, but she couldn't leave the crime scene, and she didn't want to send Cahill away to compare stories with her friends in the SUV. "You said those were Seth's shoes."

Cahill nodded, almost imperceptibly.

Fenway paused and took a few steps closer to the dead body. "I'm sorry to ask you this, Ms. Cahill, but would you come over here to where you can see the man's face? I'm afraid we need a positive identification."

Tyra Cahill blanched.

"I wish I didn't have to—" Fenway began.

"No, no," Cahill said quietly. "I understand."

She walked slowly to the body. She barely glanced at his face but said, "Yes, that's Seth," before stepping back away from the corpse.

"I'm sorry for your loss," Fenway said. She studied Tyra's face. If Tyra was shaken by Seth's dead body, she didn't show it. "I know this is sudden, but I need a little information."

"Fine." Tyra's voice, tense but firm. No breaking, no crying, no sobbing.

"Can I ask the last time you saw your ex-husband?"

Cahill swallowed hard. "Last night. He—he came over. I wanted him to get the rest of his stuff."

Fenway cocked her head. "Did he have many items at your house?"

Cahill hesitated. "He did. He does, still."

"I'm not sure I understand."

"Well—he came over last night to take several boxes of his possessions, but he showed up in his sports car." She pressed her lips together. "His *two-seater* sports car."

Ah, Tyra had mentioned the Corvette on the phone. "So he couldn't take much."

"Right. He said he planned to borrow a friend's pickup truck, but he didn't."

"Did you argue about it?"

"About the boxes? Or about his girlfriend wrapping him around her finger?"

"Girlfriend?"

Cahill scoffed. "I can't call her anything else without swearing. She's been screwing Seth for at least a year. Maybe more."

Fenway switched tactics. "Is this woman named Miranda?"

Cahill furrowed her brow.

"You mentioned her on the call with your ex-husband's lawyer. When I was in the office earlier."

"Oh." Cahill thrust her chin out and put her hands on her hips. Still no signs of grief. Probably easier to be angry at Seth about cheating than to process his death. The grief might hit Cahill later. "Miranda Duchy. Seth is staying at her place. One of those big Sycorax Hill mini-mansions by the airport." She gritted her teeth before she spoke again. "Miranda got it from *her* rich ex. I don't think she's worked a day in her life."

"I believe I heard you mention that Seth drove a Corvette?"

"Right, because of *course* he'd embrace every stereotype of a mid-life crisis. He bought it brand-new a couple of years ago. Has the speeding tickets to go along with his fragile ego."

"Did he take any boxes last night?"

"*One* box. He took a single box." She swore under her breath.

Fenway softened her voice. "Can you lead me through everything that happened?"

"We talked earlier in the week, and he agreed to come by my place at nine o'clock—" Cahill stopped speaking, furrowed her brow, paced a few steps in each direction, then looked down at the ground.

"Nine o'clock is pretty late to pack a bunch of boxes in a pickup truck," Fenway prodded.

Cahill crossed her arms. "I won't answer any more questions. You can talk to my lawyer."

Fenway took a step back. "I see."

Cahill lifted her head and glared at Fenway. "Am I free to go?"

"We'd like to establish a timeline, and if you saw him last night, you can help us out."

"I won't talk without my lawyer present." Cahill pursed her lips.

When she'd gotten out of the back seat of the Ford SUV, Tyra Cahill had seemed willing to talk—even after she'd seen her ex-husband's dead body. Had something changed?

Cahill might have realized her answers would throw suspicion onto herself. How frustrating—yes, Fenway knew the spouse was the killer most often in these types of murders, but Cahill's reluctance to talk would only delay the investigation.

Still, she would have done the same thing in Tyra Cahill's shoes.

"We'll question your friends," Fenway said, "but you're free to go."

Cahill nodded, turned on her heel, and walked across the asphalt to the vehicle gate the Ford SUV had come in. She turned and reached out, a smaller pedestrian gate opening. She stepped outside the property, then disappeared around a hedge.

Fenway took out her phone and texted Patrick.

> Check DMV records for a Chevrolet
> Corvette registered to Seth Cahill
>
> Ask an officer to go by his residence
>
> If we can't find the Corvette, put out an
> APB on it

Fenway had just hit Send when the three telltale dots of a response appeared. A moment later:

> Corvettes have the SafeBoard system—we
> can track that

Fenway nodded with satisfaction. If they could find the Corvette, maybe they'd find the murder weapon—and get closer to unveiling the killer.

———

A police cruiser arrived a few minutes later, parking in front of the open door. The window rolled down; a trim white man with salt-and-pepper hair and a short beard stuck his head out: Sergeant Mark Trevino, Fenway's other detective.

"Thanks for coming, Mark," Fenway said. "Can you secure the scene?"

"Of course." He glanced at the open door of the storage unit. "Not the way you wanted to spend your afternoon, huh, Coroner?"

Fenway smiled. "At least I'm not schlepping McVie's boxes back and forth." She indicated the body of Seth Cahill, still partially wrapped in the rug. "What's your take?"

Mark got out of the car, roll of police tape in hand, and stood next to Fenway, outside the storage unit, and studied the body.

"Looks like homicide. Bloodstains on the rug, but not as much as I'd expect." Mark pointed at the pattern of the blood next to Seth Cahill's head. "You thinking he died somewhere else?"

Fenway nodded. "Wrapped up in the carpet and brought here."

"The ex-wife's friends are in the office," Mark said. "Did you want to talk with them?"

"The ex lawyered up," Fenway said. "So I'm not sure how helpful her friends will be."

"Only one way to find out." Mark stepped next to the edge of the entrance to the storage unit, affixing the police tape to a horizontal wooden slat on the interior wall.

"Body's in rigor," Fenway said. "So at least six or eight hours, but not more than twenty-four."

"Still a wide range," Mark said.

"I don't have my kit."

Mark walked to the other side of the entrance with the roll of police tape. "De la Garza should be here in about fifteen minutes. She'll have the right tools."

Fenway pointed at the asphalt area in front of the storage unit. "If the killer dumped the body here," she said, "maybe we need to cordon this area off too. Get tire tracks or something."

Mark looked skeptical, pointing to McVie's Highlander. "You're talking about this area here?"

"Well, yes." Fenway stared at the Highlander for a moment. "I'm sure several cars have driven over this asphalt. But the murder happened in the last day, and even if we get ten sets of tire prints, it'll narrow down the vehicles that were here."

"Even with the drizzle overnight?"

Fenway frowned; she wasn't aware of the drizzle. "I suppose that would complicate things." She paused.

"Kav is good at finding tire tracks. I hope Melissa is bringing him." Mark's eyes focused on the asphalt in front of the door, and he pointed. "Are those fibers?"

Fenway stepped forward, then crouched. Several gold and wine-colored fibers. "Looks like they match the Persian rug."

"The killer might have set the body down here before opening the storage unit door." Mark reached down with a small evidence baggie and nudged the fibers into the bag.

Fenway ducked under the tape and knelt by the body, pointing at the back of the head. "Blunt force trauma, but I haven't seen this kind of wound before. A little over an inch long, but only about an eighth of an inch high."

Mark frowned as he tore off the police tape and tied it to an anchor on the opposite wall. "Like a putty knife?"

"Or the edge of a crowbar if you used a stabbing motion instead of swinging it over your head."

"What if you turned it ninety degrees? So it's tall and narrow?"

Fenway furrowed her brow. Mark walked over and stood next to Fenway, then crouched. Fenway put on a new pair of gloves, then knelt and gently lifted Seth Cahill's head to better see the wound.

Fenway exhaled. "Oh, of course."

"What?"

"The claw end of a hammer. That would explain these marks here."

Mark nodded. "That would do it. We'll see what the M.E. says, but it makes sense to me."

Fenway stood. "You sticking around the storage facility, short-timer?"

He smiled. "Only to make sure no one messes with the crime scene. Can't have me getting involved in a case now."

"You won't know what to do with yourself after Friday." She elbowed Mark lightly. "Oh, of course, you'll join Randy onstage this season."

Mark's face fell. "I love my husband, but that would be my ninth circle of Hell." Then he grinned. "However, I will be using my carpentry skills."

"Really?"

"Building sets."

"That's great." Fenway turned. "See you back in the office."

"Sarah said you still haven't RSVP'd for tomorrow night."

Fenway grimaced. Sarah Summerhill had only been hired as Fenway's assistant around the holidays, yet she had knowledge and co-worker rapport like someone who'd been in the position for years. "Sorry, things with Craig have been crazy. Of course I'll be there." She had to remember a retirement present, too. Maybe a gift card to a home improvement store, now that she knew he'd be building community theater sets. A little impersonal, but useful. "Why aren't you having your retirement party on your actual last day?"

"Randy's the lead in *The Paper Sky*. Friday's opening night, and I've got front row tickets."

"Of course. I should go too."

Mark raised his index finger. "One more thing before you leave..."

Fenway raised her eyebrows.

"I gave you plenty of notice so you could replace me," Mark said. "But I don't think you've hired anyone yet."

"Three interviews a couple weeks ago," Fenway replied. "And a front-runner." Deputy Celeste Salvador, in fact. She and another deputy, Brian Callahan, had both passed their detective exams, and she'd interviewed them both—along with another candidate from the neighboring county.

"Fantastic. I wanted to give them more than a day or two of on-the-job training, but anything is better than nothing."

"The hiring process must be held up in HR." Why was replacing Mark like pulling teeth? Fenway had been in this job for a little over a year now, and so much had changed: Rachel's career change from coroner's assistant to public relations director; two mayors had been murdered; Migs passing the bar exam and his imminent departure; McVie losing the election for mayor. She didn't want Mark to leave, either, though she'd been much closer with Dez since becoming coroner.

But the county needed two sergeants reporting to Fenway. Not only had the county had more murders in the past year than the previous decade combined, but the influx of morpheranyl, opioids, and methamphetamines had significantly impacted the community. Overdoses and violent crime had gone up. Fenway might be a popular local figure, with a stellar solve rate on homicides, but her popularity didn't extend to McVie's replacement, Sheriff Gretchen Donnelly, who hadn't been in office at the beginning of the opioid crisis but caught flak for its effects.

Fortunately, this wasn't her first new hire. After Rachel's promotion, Fenway had figured most of the delay in hiring Sarah had been because of the mayor. And Sarah was a fantastic employee. Fenway felt like she knew the hiring system better now: she'd been confident when submitting the job requisition, filling out the online forms, approving the job requirements. It had taken a while, but she'd done it. But Dominguez County's hiring process obviously moved at a glacial pace.

"Oh, and Mark, get a couple of uniforms to sit on one-twelve."

"One-twelve?"

"McVie's original storage unit. Someone stayed in there last night. Or the night before."

"They're not there now?"

"No. But I saw a striped sleeping bag, a camp stove, a portable toilet. Ms. Cahill said that Seth would take care of the squatters they had."

"You're thinking they had a confrontation with Mr. Cahill and killed him?"

"Maybe." Fenway set her mouth in a line. "We'd be remiss if we didn't follow up," she said. "But I don't have any evidence either way."

"Why wouldn't the squatter be a prime suspect?"

"Because that"—Fenway pointed at the rug the dead body lay on—"looks like an expensive rug. I don't expect they'd have wrapped the body up in a twenty-thousand-dollar rug only to dump it in another storage unit."

Mark tilted his head. "This is a storage facility. There must be dozens of rugs in these units. If they killed him, maybe they took his keys, opened one of the other units, grabbed the first thing they saw to wrap a body in—"

"It's a possibility."

"I'll get a couple uniforms here," Mark said. "But if that's what happened, it follows that they took off and left all their stuff behind."

"Probably," Fenway said, "but still—"

"Right. Due diligence." Mark tilted his head. "You know we're a little short-staffed today."

"Call in some uniforms from the Paso Querido station."

Mark nodded. "After the P.Q. uniforms get here, you want me back at the office?"

"Oh." Fenway thought a moment. "Our victim was living at his girlfriend's house. Her name is Miranda Duchy. Interview her. Ask if she knows if Seth had enemies, if he's been acting strange."

"And where she was last night."

"Right." Fenway smiled at Mark, then turned and walked around Building C toward the office, removing her blue nitrile gloves.

Dez stood inside. The driver and passenger of the Ford SUV sat on plastic chairs, with Isabella behind the counter, standing next to a young white man in coveralls with stitching on the left chest that read *Mathis.*

"There she is," Isabella said, pointing at Fenway. "Ask her."

CHAPTER THREE

Fenway turned her head to Dez.

"Miss Chan," Dez said, indicating Isabella, "thinks you want her to close the business today."

"Only until we get everyone's statements," Fenway said.

"We have clients," Isabella said, "and Tyra won't be pleased if our customers can't get to their storage units. Some of them have schedules. They've got other people depending on them."

"We'll get everyone out of here as soon as we can." Fenway shot a look at Dez.

"I've already taken Ms. Chan's statement," Dez said. "She insisted on going first."

The woman and man sitting on the blue plastic chairs looked up expectantly.

"So we should interview..." Fenway glanced at Dez.

"Hope Dunkelman," the woman said.

"And George Pope," the man added.

"We're married," Dunkelman hastened to add. "I didn't take his name."

"Then Mr. Mathis Jericho," Dez said. "Maintenance and land-scaping."

"Gotcha." Fenway glanced at Isabella, whose frown was directed right at Fenway. "Miss Chan, we appreciate the use of these offices for interviews. I'll let you know if we need anything else." She turned to Dez. "Sergeant Roubideaux, why don't you take Ms. Dunkelman into Tyra's office to interview her? I'll talk to Mr. Pope in, uh…"

"We've got a break room in the back," Isabella said.

"Can I go out and get some of my work done?" Mathis Jericho asked.

"Stay in the waiting room, if you don't mind," Fenway said. "We'll be done shortly."

A quick scan of Jericho's face told Fenway that he *did* very much mind.

They needed photos. Fenway pulled her phone out, tapped the camera app on her phone, and quickly took pictures of all four of them: Isabella, Mathis, Hope, and George.

Mathis's frown deepened, but he said nothing.

George Pope stood. Isabella pointed through a doorway to the break room on the left side that Fenway had first assumed led to a closet or a bathroom.

She opened the door, holding it for George Pope. The tiny break room held only a water cooler, a vending machine, and a rectangular café-style table with two chairs pushed against the opposite wall. Fenway pressed her lips together. It would do.

She pulled out the chair farthest from the door and motioned for Pope to sit.

"We were headed to the Estancia Harbor Festival," Pope said as he sat down.

"Who?" Fenway pulled out her notebook and pen from her purse, then sat across from him.

"Oh, sorry. I figured you'd want to know why we were here." He folded his hands together. "Tyra and Hope and me. We wanted to go to the Harbor Festival before the tropical storm comes through. Taking the afternoon off."

"I see." Fenway opened the notebook, turned the pages until she found a blank sheet, and wrote *Harbor Festival.* "You can take the afternoon off like that?"

"Hope's a nurse at St. Vincent's. She doesn't work Tuesdays. Me, I own a custom screen-printing business over on Thirty-Fifth Street. I can take off whenever I want."

"How do you know Tyra Cahill?"

"We've been friends since high school," Pope said. "Hope and me, we started dating junior year, and Hope and Tyra were best friends. She and I married once I got my contractor's license and she finished at Fresno State."

"Hope Pope," Fenway said absentmindedly.

George Pope laughed, his light brown mustache and goatee quivering. "Yeah, I think that's one reason it took so long for her to say yes. I had to propose three times. My father was angry that she didn't take my name, but I wasn't even going to suggest it."

Fenway herself didn't think she'd take her husband's name, should she ever decide to marry. A flash in her head: *Fenway McVie.* The thought caught her off guard. She cleared her throat. "So the three of you have been friends since high school?"

"Just got the invitation for our twentieth reunion."

"How about Seth?"

"Tyra met him at Fresno State. His family lived up in Sacramento."

"They get married right after college?"

"Not till Seth got a job in P.Q. about ten years ago."

"So the three of you became the four of you."

Pope pressed his lips together.

"What is it?"

He blinked, looked at Fenway, and smiled. "Yes. All four of us started hanging out when Tyra and Seth started dating. He didn't really know anyone else in the area."

"And the four of you still hang out?"

"Well, until Seth started disappearing. He'd work late, get home to Tyra at five in the morning, that kind of thing."

"When did that start?"

"A few years ago. About five years after they were married."

"What did you think of that?"

Pope frowned. "Tyra's been my—my wife's best friend for over two decades. He cheated on her—for years. Of course, I didn't like that, but I hardly saw him over the last eight or nine months. I tried not to think about him."

Fenway nodded. "All right. So where were you last night?"

"Uh—home. Hope and I went to dinner around seven. La Cucina Urbana."

Fenway blanched. Terrible food—bland, no spice, no personality. She wrote it down. "When did you get home?"

"I didn't pay attention to the time. Maybe eight thirty. We sat on the sofa, watched a little TV."

"Then you went to bed?"

"Oh—no. Hope got a call while we were watching TV. Maybe nine thirty, nine forty-five."

"Who called?"

"Tyra." Pope swallowed hard and looked down at his folded hands. "Seth had promised to pick up his things, but he showed up in his Corvette, yelled at Tyra, and drove off." He looked up at Fenway, a glint in his eye. "I wouldn't be surprised if he'd been drinking."

Fenway tapped the end of her pen on her bottom lip. "They fought."

"Yeah—but look, they'd fought before. He's a real piece of work."

"Right. You're on Team Tyra."

Pope shifted in his chair. "Uh—I mean, look, you can ask anyone. I think the world of Tyra. Best friend Hope could have. The kind of friend who'd help you b—" He paused.

"Bury a body?" Fenway asked.

"That's just a figure of speech," George said. "I mean, they were real close. Tyra was good to her."

"You know Tyra well?"

"Course I do. Hope and Tyra were roommates for a couple of years before we got married. I had to pass the test." He puffed his chest out. "I was an idiot in high school, but by the time Hope finished college, I'd grown out of my stupidity." He chuckled. "Well, I guess if you ask Hope, she'd say I still have a little of it left." George sighed deeply, then rubbed his eyes with the thumb and forefinger of his right hand. "I'm not nearly as stupid as Seth, though. He didn't treat Tyra very well. I'm glad they got divorced."

Fenway kept silent. Was there more to the story?

Pope hesitated for a moment, then the words rushed out. "He wasn't a good guy. Not just that he cheated on her—I mean, that was bad enough. No, I mean, hiding things from her."

"Besides his mistress."

"Yeah. Getting mixed up in some—" Pope dropped his eyes to the table again.

"In what?"

Pope raised his head and stared at the ceiling. "Tyra didn't have anything to do with his shady activities, all right? But them being married..."

Fenway nodded. Pope didn't want to get his friend in trouble. Fenway had to tread carefully. "This afternoon, we found evidence of a squatter in one of the storage units. Tyra told me she thought Seth would take care of that. Do you know whether this squatter is involved with Seth's 'shady activities,' as you put it?"

Pope scrunched up his nose. "Look, I've heard things, but I don't know anything for sure."

"What did you hear?"

He hesitated. "Drugs."

Fenway nodded, unsurprised. "He was using?"

"Uh—he was *storing* them. Here."

"Oh. How long has this been going on?"

Pope shrugged. "Just a rumor I heard. Maybe I shouldn't have said anything."

"Right." Fenway studied his face. How much did he know? Maybe nothing. "So what happened after Tyra called?"

"She was upset," Pope said. "Hope went to pick her up."

Probably had been drinking, too, though Pope probably didn't want to mention that. Fenway didn't press the issue. "What time was this?"

"About, I don't know, nine fifteen, nine thirty." He pressed his lips together. "You know, I think it was closer to ten."

"And when did they get back?"

"I guess about eleven thirty."

Fenway raised her eyebrows.

"We live by Prospero Park. Tyra's only a fifteen-minute drive away, but Hope figured she'd need to stay with her a while before bringing her to our place. Like I said, Tyra was pretty upset."

"Did she stay overnight?"

"Yeah. Hope convinced her to pack a bag and come stay with us. The house she shared with Seth has some terrible memories."

"You didn't go with your wife?"

"We've been friends for almost twenty-five years, but sometimes they need girl time. Especially through the divorce." He gave Fenway a sad smile. "I'm sure they had a few unkind words to say about Seth. Maybe about men in general. I shouldn't be there for that."

"And what happened after Hope and Tyra arrived?"

"I came out to the living room, and we all had a few glasses of wine. Tyra calmed down enough to go to sleep in our guest room. We were all in bed by one."

"She didn't leave after that?"

Pope shook his head. "I'm a light sleeper. If she'd left, I'd have woken up."

Fenway tapped her pen on the table. She'd have to research

whether Hope was at Tyra's house for that long. Could Tyra have murdered her ex in the fifteen minutes it took for Hope to drive to her house? More importantly, if Tyra and Hope were really the kind of friends who'd help each other bury a body, would Hope lie in order to give Tyra an alibi?

If Fenway had to, she could track the phones of both Tyra and Hope. She'd have to apply for a warrant, so she'd need to find enough evidence to convince a judge.

Pope shifted in his seat.

"All right," Fenway said, "that's all the questions I have for now. Can I get your contact information and address if I have more questions?"

"Of course."

Fenway handed Pope her pen, turned her notebook to a blank page, and pushed it across the small table. Pope wrote his phone number, email address, and mailing address.

They stood, and Pope opened the door and held it for Fenway. Dez and Hope Dunkelman were waiting in the office, and Mathis Jericho sat on the stool behind the workstation, his arms folded.

"Got everything you need?" Dez asked.

Fenway nodded.

Dez nodded at Dunkelman and Pope. "Thank you for your statements. You can go."

"I hope we were helpful," Dunkelman said.

"And I hope you catch whoever did this," added Pope.

As they hurried out the door, Dez stepped toward Fenway, away from Mathis, and lowered her voice. "Where's the ex-wife?"

"Lawyered up," Fenway murmured.

Dez raised her eyebrows. "Think she's involved?"

"Not sure yet. I thought she'd be forthcoming until she wasn't." Fenway set her mouth in a line. "What did Ms. Dunkelman say?"

Dez hooked her thumb over her shoulder at the closing door. "She swore up and down that Tyra Cahill stayed with her all night.

She went to Tyra's house around nine forty-five, calmed her down, brought her back to her house."

"Pretty much what Mr. Pope said, too. Then they all had some wine and went to bed."

"Does that track with what the ex-wife said?"

Fenway bobbed her head diagonally. "She didn't mention spending the night at her friends' house, but she did tell me Seth stopped by at nine last night." Fenway stopped—did Ms. Cahill actually say nine?

"A lot depends on time of death. If the timing is below—what, eighteen hours? Then she's got an alibi."

Fenway didn't mention her doubts about the validity of Hope providing an alibi. Instead, she pulled out her phone and turned to Mathis, still sitting behind the counter. "Okay, we take your statement, then we can get this business open again." Then Fenway paused. "Where's Isabella?"

Mathis pointed through the office window to the front of the building. "Meeting customers at the gate. Telling them to come back once you're all finished."

Fenway nodded and appraised Mathis for the first time. The young man had a few days' worth of stubble on his face and a rumpled navy blue polo shirt. He wore his straight light brown hair in a Beatles mop, except for a cowlick at the top of his head where a lock of his hair puffed up about an inch. His bloodshot eyes showed he'd likely had a rough night and not much sleep.

Fenway flipped the notebook to a blank page.

"Name?"

"Mathis Jericho."

"And you work here at Cahill Warehouse Storage."

"Yeah."

"For how long?" Dez asked.

He looked down at the counter and tapped his foot on the rail of the stool. He wouldn't be forthcoming with much information.

Fenway sighed. "We found the owner of this business dead in—"

"*Former* owner," Mathis interrupted.

"What?"

"Former owner. Tyra got the whole business as part of the divorce settlement."

Fenway nodded. That's right, Tyra had corrected herself from "co-owner" to "owner"; had that been on the phone with her lawyer? "Former owner," Fenway said. "So like any decent investigator, I need to know how long you've worked for the business, how much interaction you had with the own—the *former* owner. Did anyone have any reason to do him harm?"

"None of that is relevant to how long I've worked here."

Fenway raised herself to her full five-ten height. "Maybe you don't understand how this investigation will work." She pointed to the back wall of the office, in the general direction of the crime scene. "In a few minutes, the crime scene techs will be here. They'll be gathering evidence. Taking all kinds of photographs of this property, including your workspace, the parking lot, even your tire treads."

Mathis frowned. "That's a violation of—"

"There's no expectation of privacy when you're on your employer's property," Dez interrupted. Technically, she stretched the truth, but it did apply to checking the tire treads of employees' cars.

"Then," Fenway said, "when that's all over, we'll be going through this company's finances. If we see something about you that doesn't make sense to us, and you haven't cooperated with the investigation, how do you think I'm going to react?"

"I think you should react like I'm innocent until proven guilty." But Mathis knitted his brow, drummed his fingers on the counter, then looked up at Fenway. "Almost two years."

Fenway hesitated. "Is that how long you've worked here?"

"Yeah."

"Can you tell me where you were last night?"

Mathis folded his arms, breaking eye contact. "I was here until nine o'clock. Then I went home, fixed myself dinner, and went to sleep."

"You said Mr. Cahill formerly owned the facility, so do I have it right that he used to be your boss?"

Mathis nodded. "I'd call him a pretty hands-off manager, but he hired me and I reported to him. I mean, he stayed off-property most of the time, and Tyra would assign me jobs and stuff. So she was sort of my boss, too."

"Had you met Mr. Cahill before you started working for him?"

"I dropped out of Nidever U after my freshman year, and I started working odd jobs. I met him then."

"What job was that?"

"Scuba instructor." Mathis chuckled. "Sounded fun. I had pictures in my head of sunshine, boat trips, bikinis—but no, it was boring. And gross. A pool they didn't keep clean, locker rooms with mold—I should have figured that if they'd hire me without the right credentials that they'd be okay skipping a paycheck or two." He cleared his throat.

"And that's where you met Seth?"

"Yeah. He signed up for a scuba class but didn't seem as excited as everyone else. The vacations they were planning, that kind of thing. Seth just wanted the basics. The technical stuff."

Fenway nodded.

"Anyway, we got to talking. He said he needed someone to work at the storage place, and I jumped at the chance to work for a place where my paychecks didn't bounce."

Fenway scribbled in her notebook.

"How well did you know him?" Dez asked.

"Uh, not that well. We'd say hi to each other when we worked together."

"Never outside of work?" Fenway turned another page in her notebook.

Mathis hesitated.

"What is it?"

"Not really. Like, he asked me to do some stuff for him."

"What kind of stuff?" Getting information out of Mathis was excruciating.

"Yard work for his house. Errands on the weekends if he was busy. And I'd go down—" Mathis paused.

"You'd go down where?"

"To, um, to the harbor," Mathis said. "Sometimes he wanted fresh fish as soon as the shipments came in. I'd wait for the, uh, the fishermen. Sometimes get some great seafood right off the boat."

Fenway and Dez exchanged glances; Mathis flinched.

"And he paid you for that?" Fenway asked.

Mathis looked stricken. Ah, off the books. Mathis probably had a few thousand in cash he hadn't claimed on his taxes.

Had Unit 112 smelled like fish? No, not fish, but it did smell like the ocean—but almost everywhere in Estancia smelled like the ocean unless the wind blew differently than normal.

"What do you do here?" Dez asked after a moment.

Mathis shifted in his seat, his shoulders hunched, his eyes darting back and forth between Dez and Fenway. Maybe he wasn't being forthcoming because he felt ganged up on. Usually, having two people conduct an interview gave better results, but Fenway tilted her head in Dez's direction.

Dez pulled her phone out, glanced at the blank screen. "Oh, sorry, I have to take this. Please continue without me." She held the phone to her ear and strode out of the office into the parking lot, the door closing behind her.

Fenway turned back to Mathis. "You were about to tell me about your job duties."

Mathis nodded, his shoulders lowering, his eyes on Fenway. "Maintenance, landscaping, that kind of stuff. I make sure the place looks presentable to clients. Replace light bulbs, make sure the gate works, clean the units after a client moves out."

"Make sure it's clean when a client moves in?" As soon as the words left her mouth, Fenway regretted saying it. Sounded like she was complaining about the squatter.

"I'm sorry," Mathis said. "I was supposed to get your unit ready, but I—I wasn't feeling well this morning, and I didn't check out your space before you got here."

"So you weren't aware squatters were using the space?"

"I wouldn't—" Mathis began, then blinked. "No. I had no idea."

Fenway took a step closer. "I've taken a bunch of classes in criminology, Mathis. Psychology, interviewing witnesses, that sort of thing. I've gotten pretty good at recognizing the signs when people are lying." She tapped the back of her pen against the notebook. "You want to rethink your last answer?"

Mathis shifted uncomfortably. "Seth told me not to worry about it."

"When? Yesterday?"

"No, no," Mathis held up his hands, palms out. "Not recently. Like, when I got hired."

"He's had people staying in these units for *two years?*"

"Not all the time," Mathis said. "Not like they were living there. They needed a place to crash for a few hours, or maybe a day or two." He hesitated. "At least, that's what Seth told me."

He wasn't telling her the whole truth, but he was at least talking.

"You have any idea who these people were? Friends of Seth's?"

"Nope." Mathis couldn't meet Fenway's eyes.

"I bet you figured Seth knew them," Fenway said.

"I think so." Again, no eye contact.

"Tyra," Fenway said carefully, "thought they'd stop staying here once Seth stopped being part-owner. She said Seth would take care of the problem."

Mathis met Fenway's eyes. "I don't know anything about that."

Fenway held Mathis's stare for a moment. "The first place I want to look is at the person who stayed in Unit 112 last night," Fenway said. "Know how I might find that information?"

Mathis dropped his eyes to the counter again. "I wish I could help you."

Fenway crossed her arms. Mathis was hiding something shady or illegal. Drug trafficking, or maybe even human trafficking. Cahill Warehouse Storage might have been a waystation where the people traveling could stay for the night without leaving a paper trail.

And Mathis had sunk up to his eyeballs in it. The only question: how to get him to open up—and not scare him off.

I thought Seth took care of that.

Tyra Cahill's voice rang in her head. Something didn't feel right; had Tyra suspected something illegal? When the judge awarded Tyra the business in the divorce, she'd wanted nothing to do with the shady business deals. She could have convinced Seth to tell his business partners they'd have to find somewhere else to stay. Maybe those business partners didn't like that answer.

Sergeant Mark Trevino had suggested the squatters had a confrontation and killed Seth Cahill. The information from Mathis supported that suggestion—at least as a possibility. Fenway scribbled in her notebook. "Do you know anyone who'd want to hurt Mr. Cahill?"

Mathis shifted his weight again. "Tyra didn't like it when she found out about Miranda."

"Miranda—Mr. Cahill's girlfriend? Miranda Duchy?"

"Yeah. They, uh, started seeing each other right after I started working here. At least, that's when I first saw them together."

"Miranda came to the storage facility?"

"Just when Tyra was out of town."

"Do you know when Ms. Cahill found out about the affair?"

"No."

"Did things ever get violent between Seth and Tyra?"

"Not that I saw." Mathis's eyes darted to the ceiling for a moment.

"What *did* you see?"

"A lot of passive-aggressive talk from both of them, whenever they were in the office together. It got so bad that they'd go into their separate offices and not talk for the rest of the day."

Fenway raised her eyebrows. "Seth still has an office here? Even though he's no longer an owner?"

"He said he was transitioning out. Ms. Cahill didn't like it."

"Can you show me where his office is?"

"Sure."

Mathis opened the back door, which Fenway had assumed led to Tyra's office. Instead, she saw a small hallway. A door on the right side—faint voices could be heard. Dez and Isabella. Dez must have convinced Isabella to agree to an interview and entered Tyra's office through a rear door.

Mathis turned to his left and arrived at another door. He tried the knob: locked. Pulling a keychain out of his pocket, he looked through half a dozen keys before selecting one and sliding it into the lock. It unlocked and Mathis turned the knob, then pushed the door open. He started to enter the office.

Fenway put her arm in front of him. "Sorry, Mathis. We've got to check it out first. Mr. Cahill was found dead on the premises, so we'll need to go through his things and get fingerprints. You'll need to stand on the other side of the doorway until we're done."

"Don't you need a warrant?"

"This is Mr. Cahill's office, right?"

"Uh, yeah."

"Anyone else using it?"

"No."

"Then there's no reasonable expectation of privacy for anyone but the victim. One of the few exceptions noted in *Flippo vs. West Virginia.* So, no, I don't need a warrant."

The office had a small window in the upper corner behind the standing desk, a Scandinavian-style table with two sets of low file cabinets underneath. Pushed against the wall, about six feet in front of the desk, two metal-framed guest chairs were stacked together. A large expanse of concrete flooring lay in front of the desk, about six feet by ten feet. A high armless task chair sat halfway between the window and the desk. No plants or greenery of any kind were in the room. A large but blank dry-erase board hung to the right of the desk. The walls were painted an industrial medium gray, which reminded Fenway of the women's state prison in Hanford.

The desk held a monitor with two cables dangling from the back. A wireless keyboard and mouse sat on the desk as well, along with a pencil cup, a stapler, and a stack of paperwork. Fenway put on fresh gloves as she walked to the desk. She leaned down and leafed through the first few papers; all were invoices that had been stamped with *Paid* and a date from March.

"Very bachelor-pad chic," Fenway said. "No computer?"

Mathis cleared his throat from outside the doorway. "I think he took it home."

"Even though it belongs to the company, and he no longer works here?"

"Sometimes you have to pick your battles. That's what Tyra said."

Fenway crouched and opened the topmost of the three drawers on the left, a short drawer. A squeak of protest from Mathis, but Fenway ignored it.

Pens, paper clips, and on top, a black leather wallet. Fenway unfolded it. Seth Cahill's California driver's license stared back at her from the clear ID pocket. She checked the card slots: several credit cards, a roadside assistance card, three for various stores in the Estancia area. In the cash section, one hundred and seventy-three dollars in bills. She put the wallet back and pushed the top drawer shut.

The half-full middle drawer held hanging folders divided by month; all paper invoices. Easier to organize everything on the computer, but maybe Seth was the kind of person who needed to hold the paper in his hand. Or more likely, customers who still insisted on forgoing paperless billing.

More of the same in the bottom drawer.

Fenway turned her attention to the file drawers on the right. The heavy top drawer was full of cords, cables, adapters, and power strips. The bottom drawer was heavier, and Fenway struggled to pull it open.

A safe.

The door of the safe faced the ceiling, and a numeric keypad showed white numbers on black plastic buttons.

"Did you know Seth had a safe in here?"

"A what?" Mathis said unconvincingly.

Fenway didn't bother calling him out on his misdirection. "Did Seth ever tell you what he put in the safe?"

Mathis hesitated as if he wanted to deny knowing about the safe, then slumped his shoulders. "Papers, mostly," he said. "I saw him, once. He didn't think I saw it, but I did."

Fenway knelt and looked at the keypad. None of the numbers were worn, which would have given her a place to start. "What's Mr. Cahill's birthday, Mathis?"

Mathis screwed up his face. "Maybe sometime in August."

Fenway opened the left-hand top drawer and grabbed Seth's wallet.

"You, uh, planning to be in here a long time?" Mathis asked, trying to sound casual.

"As long as it takes." She unfolded the wallet. On his driver's license: August 7, 1978.

Fenway put the wallet back in the drawer and pushed the numbers on the keypad of the safe: *8778*. A small red light blinked angrily back at her.

She tried again: *0807*. Nope: same angry blinking.

She picked her phone up again.

Maybe it wasn't his birthday at all. Maybe it was—

Oh, of course.

She pulled out her phone from her purse, tapped on the screen, and launched the Photoxio app. She hadn't used it in so long that she had to log in again. Fenway had few followers, which suited her fine. She tapped the *Search* button and typed *Miranda Duchy*.

There she was, a fair-skinned white woman with long, wavy blonde hair, smiling coquettishly over a bare shoulder in her profile picture. The photo looked almost too perfect.

Just a beach girl who loves to see the world.

She had more than forty thousand followers.

And on her profile, her birthday: May 28.

Fenway pushed *0528* on the keypad.

A green light came on and a quiet *click* came from the safe door. Fenway lifted the door and peered inside.

A book.

She reached in and took the book out with her gloved hands. Leather-bound, black with burgundy corners and a burgundy spine. The book, about two or three hundred pages, had a blank cover and spine.

She opened the book.

Rows of numbers and dates—the telltale red and blue lines of a ledger. Abbreviations, gibberish in the line for the descriptions. The first date had been entered almost two years ago, and the entries grouped in bunches: ten or fifteen within the space of a few days, then another ten to fifteen two weeks later. The numbers were large, too: some of the figures were over ten thousand dollars. A couple of them were over forty thousand.

She flipped through the ledger. The bunches of numbers continued on subsequent pages, but not regularly spaced out. Sometimes there were only eight days between groups of entries, sometimes as many as twenty or twenty-five days.

The book was half full, and the last date listed a transaction for $37,251.

The date of the transaction: tomorrow.

CHAPTER FOUR

Fenway looked up at Mathis. "What's happening tomorrow?"

"I—what?" Mathis stuttered.

She lifted the ledger book from her lap and put it on the desk. "I've got a transaction of almost forty grand that Seth Cahill expected to close tomorrow."

"He's not working here anymore. I don't know what transaction that could be."

Fenway stared into Mathis's eyes for a moment, and he cast his eyes down only a moment later. He knew something, but he wasn't about to tell Fenway.

She sat in Seth's chair, shifting her eyes from Mathis in the doorway to the leather-bound ledger on his desk. Fenway—or maybe the forensic accountants—would need to go through the ledger. Maybe Seth was skimming money from his "shady" activities, as Mathis had put it. And, of course, Mark's theory of the squatters killing Seth Cahill if and when he had tried to kick them out.

Soon, sheriff's deputies would be sitting on Unit 112, but the squatter was likely long gone. If the squatter had killed Seth Cahill, they probably left as soon as they'd wrapped the body in the rug and dumped it in Unit 176. Yes, they'd left their sleeping bag and portable toilet and some other items, but their escape would have been considered more important.

If the squatter *hadn't* killed Cahill, though, they could have witnessed what really happened. But they'd have no reason to stick around and get questioned by law enforcement, especially if they thought they'd be suspected of the murder.

The body had been in full rigor, so if the squatter had been the killer—or a witness—they had six hours to escape. Finding them would be difficult, if not impossible.

Dez appeared in the doorway next to Mathis. "I've wrapped up with Miss Chan. You need anything?"

"An evidence baggie big enough for this ledger." Fenway motioned with her head to Mathis. "And Mr. Jericho here—we'll need to talk with him again."

"What for?" Mathis's eyes widened.

Fenway tapped the ledger with a gloved hand. "Once we finger-print the ledger, I'd like you to go through it with our team."

"Why?"

"You may recognize a few of the transactions." Although it might be tricky to get Mathis to admit anything. But Fenway was certain Mathis had knowledge of at least some of the business deals Seth had made and tracked in the ledger.

"I'm just the maintenance guy." A whine of desperation crept into Mathis's voice. "Besides, Tyra's the one who took care of all the money."

Fenway raised her eyebrows. "Really? Tyra oversaw all the money—even though I found this ledger in Seth's drawer in a safe?"

Mathis shifted his weight from foot to foot.

Fenway shot a meaningful look at Dez. Seth obviously had two sets of books. The clean set of financial records that showed the money coming in from the rental units, payroll going out, expenses like utilities, rent, insurance. And then this ledger.

Something pinged in Fenway's head. Maybe the squatter and the hidden ledger *weren't* separated. If Seth had been involved in drug trafficking, maybe the squatter was there *because* of the drug transaction. Fenway didn't have evidence for that, though. She shook her head.

Another scenario: the squatter was an off-book renter. Perhaps the date of the transaction referred to a move-out date of tomorrow—with the payment due at the time of their departure.

Fenway frowned. Not likely at all. Thirty-seven thousand dollars was way too much money for the rental cost of a space like that.

Oh—unless Seth Cahill was taking on a substantial risk by using Unit 112 as a hotel room. And perhaps other units as places for people to stay.

Fenway suppressed a shudder. She'd seen specials on human trafficking: hundreds of children huddled in the back of a trailer, in basements, and yes—even in storage units.

Drug trafficking or human trafficking. With a thirty-seven-thousand-dollar mystery payment, those were the only two conclusions that made any sense.

Dez stepped into the room and handed Fenway a large evidence baggie. Fenway took it and slipped the ledger book inside, then handed it back to Dez.

Dez put the bagged-up book under her arm. "Melissa and Kav pulled up. You want me to walk them back to Unit 176?"

"Yes." Fenway paused. "On second thought, send one of them back to Unit 176, but ask the other to come in here and take fingerprints of this office."

"Will do."

"After the officers get here to babysit Unit 112, you and Mark can head back to the sheriff's office." Fenway turned to Mathis as Dez stepped out. "And Mr. Jericho, we're finished for today, but please stay in the county. We'll need to talk with you again."

"Am I under arrest?" Mathis asked.

Fenway furrowed her brow. Why would he think that? "The ledger. As I mentioned before, we need you to go through it."

"What if I don't know anything?"

Fenway smiled. "You'll still have the gratitude of the coroner's office."

Mathis was quiet for a moment. Then: "Can I get back to work?"

Fenway nodded, putting her hands on her hips. "Again, Mr. Jericho, please keep your availability open."

"Got it," Mathis said. He rushed outside, pushing by Dez, who was coming back in.

"Problem?"

Dez waited until the door closed. "He's lying about his relationship with Seth, you know."

"Right. Seth made Mathis go to the harbor to get fresh fish." Fenway chuckled. "I don't know what he was hiding, but it was something to do with the harbor. Check if there are cameras at the harbor—maybe we can spot Mathis or his car. Find out what he was *really* doing there."

"I'm on it." Dez cleared her throat. "I hate to bring this up," Dez began. "Since you and he are, well—"

Fenway blinked. "Me and Mathis?" Then she got it. "Oh. McVie." He's the one who had rented the storage unit. The squatter in Unit 112 and the dead body of Seth Cahill in Unit 176 were there before either unit had been assigned to McVie. "Does he really need to be questioned? I don't think that's part of the required procedure."

"You think once we make an arrest, the defense attorney won't be asking us if we interviewed the person who rented the unit? No, you're right, it's not strictly necessary, but I know ADA Pondicherry will be asking."

Fenway nodded. "I'll have him go to the sheriff's office."

"Mark will have to interview him. And if Mark thinks McVie is involved in any way, you'll have to recuse yourself."

"That'll give me more time to help him pack," Fenway cracked. Dez had a point: couldn't very well have McVie's girlfriend interviewing him on a murder case. Appearance of impropriety.

Fenway kept staring at the door that had closed behind Jericho.

"What do you think Mathis is hiding?" Dez asked.

"Seth Cahill's activities in the ledger," Fenway said. "All kinds of scenarios spinning around in my head. Nothing concrete, though. Let's see what the ledger can tell us."

Dez tapped her chin. "Ordinarily, I'd get Friedman from the San Miguelito forensic accounting team—"

"Right, but Friedman's on maternity leave. What about Patrick Appleby?"

Dez shook her head. "If the research is attached to a computer, he's almost as good as Piper, but he doesn't make the connections that she did."

A grin crept over Fenway's face.

Dez barked a laugh. "You seriously want to suggest Piper?"

"Why not? She's done it before. And everyone involved with her firing is gone. We can give her a temporary contract until Friedman comes back."

Dez sighed. "Fine, I'll run it by Sheriff Donnelly. If we have the budget, maybe."

"I'll meet you back at the office," Fenway said to Dez.

Dez nodded and walked down the hall.

A buzz on Fenway's phone. A text from Patrick.

> Unfortunately, Seth Cahill's SafeBoard system was disabled Monday night at 10:12 PM

> Last known location: Cahill Warehouse Storage

Fenway frowned. That wasn't good news, either. She scratched her head. Had the killer disconnected the tracking system?

Fenway heard the front door open, then the low sounds of Dez's voice, and then a woman's voice. But it wasn't Melissa. She stood up.

"Hello?" the voice called.

Oh—Tyra Cahill.

"Ms. Cahill?" Fenway called, stepping around the desk into the doorway. Cahill was standing on the threshold between the front office and the hallway.

"Sorry," she said, eyeing Fenway warily. "I forgot why I came to the facility in the first place—I left my earbuds." She looked Fenway up and down. "What are you doing here?"

"Reviewing the contents of your ex-husband's office," Fenway said. "And I'm glad you came back."

"Me?" Cahill stepped into her office for a moment, returning with a tiny black faux-leather pouch in her hand—the earbuds. "What do you want to talk to me for? I told you everything in the back storage unit. You want anything else from me, like I said, set it up with my lawyer."

"How often are you in the office?"

"Every day," Cahill said. "Well, I take Thursdays off. Fridays are when a lot of people show up in the afternoon to move stuff in. All weekend, really."

Fenway turned her next step over in her mind. Should she tell Tyra about finding the ledger? Fenway would be able to gauge by her reaction whether she knew about it. And that would direct her investigation. There were downsides, too: if Tyra *did* know about the ledger, she'd have more time to explain it away. But it might make her panic, make a mistake. Fenway decided to tell her.

"And how often do you go into your ex-husband's office?"

"Since we separated? Almost never. Why?"

"I thought you'd be interested in what I found."

Cahill made a disgusted face. "If it's evidence of his affair, I don't want to know about it."

"It's a ledger."

Cahill almost dropped the black pouch. "What?"

"Looked like a bunch of payments, all in sets of eight or ten. Going back two years." She cocked her head. "Last entry was for more than thirty-seven thousand dollars, but the transaction date was for tomorrow. Does that ring a bell? Some sort of balloon payment made to your company? A large corporation renting a big block of storage units?"

Cahill put a hand on the door frame to steady herself.

"You're the one who runs the finances, right?"

Cahill was silent.

"I wondered if you knew about this ledger. Looks like your ex was taking payments, but I doubt these payments are showing up in your files." Fenway paused. "Thirty-seven thousand dollars seems like something you should be aware of."

Cahill's mouth opened, shut, opened, then shut again. "I didn't —" she began, then took a slow, deep breath. "My lawyer would tell me not to say anything."

How much of Cahill's reluctance to talk was due to caution, and how much did she know? Shadow payments separate from the corporate receipts. People using a storage unit as a hotel room. This screamed illegal trafficking. Even if Cahill had no knowledge about the payments—or whatever the payments were for—as the current owner of Cahill Warehouse Storage, she might think she was criminally liable. Smart of her to lawyer up, though not helpful to Fenway's murder investigation.

Tyra Cahill had started to say she didn't know—probably about the payments—and Fenway was inclined to believe her.

"I'd cancel your plans for tonight, Ms. Cahill," Fenway said. "Why don't you ask your lawyer to meet us at the sheriff's office?"

———

After Tyra Cahill declared that she was quite capable of driving herself to the sheriff's office, she left in a huff, and Kavish Jayakody from the San Miguelito's medical examiner's office walked in, catching the door as Cahill let it go.

He stared after Cahill for a moment, then turned toward the coroner. "Afternoon, Fenway."

"Hi, Kav."

"That the ex-wife?"

"It is."

"She doesn't seem sad or upset about her ex-husband's death."

Fenway shrugged. "We all grieve in different ways. You should know that better than most people."

"She isn't grieving much at all." Kav raised his eyebrows. "You're letting her go?"

"She's meeting us at the sheriff's office with her lawyer."

Kav pointed to Seth's door. "Dez asked me to fingerprint the decedent's office. It's in there?"

"That's right. I bagged up a ledger—found it in a safe in the bottom right drawer under the desk. Dez took it back to the sheriff's office." Fenway shuffled her feet. "Is Melissa with the body?"

"She is. Not much in the way of storage in there. Just the body."

"Wrapped in the rug, yeah."

The front door opened again, and Fenway snapped her head up. It was McVie.

"Craig?"

McVie had changed from his flip-flops into close-toed sneakers, a much better choice for moving boxes for a few hours. He furrowed his brow. "What's going on?"

"There's been—" Fenway began, then caught the withering look from Kav. Yes, McVie was a civilian now, not sheriff. And more than that, he needed to go to the sheriff's office for questioning. "There's been an incident," Fenway said. "We found—uh, *something*—in the storage unit assigned to you. I'm afraid they need to interview you at the sheriff's office."

McVie's eyebrows knotted. "That sounds serious."

"It is."

He nodded grimly. "If it helps, I've been at the beach for the last three hours. A hundred witnesses. I've got a receipt from the root beer float stand."

Fenway almost rolled her eyes. McVie was *such* a Boy Scout—a root beer float, indeed. "You've been on this side of investigations before. Your name is on the contract, so—"

"Right. Covering your bases."

"And since you and I are dating, Mark will have to question you, not me."

McVie frowned. "What happened to my boxes?"

"Still in your car," Fenway replied. "Kind of hard to unload the boxes when—when there's been an incident."

McVie rubbed his forehead. "I have to be on the road Friday."

"If timing is an issue, you'll need to find another storage facility," Kav said. "We can't have you going into a crime scene."

"I'll pull the Highlander around the front," Fenway offered. "We can switch cars back."

McVie grimaced. "I'll really have to find a new storage place?"

"Really," Fenway said.

He sighed. "It's like the universe is against me moving."

Fenway stared at the floor.

After a moment of awkward silence, McVie shifted from foot to foot. "How long will you be?"

"Before meeting you in front with your SUV? Five, maybe ten minutes."

He took his phone out of his pocket as he turned to leave. "Might as well find another storage place."

Fenway nodded as McVie pushed the door open. "You good here, Kav?"

"Sure am. Fingerprinting should take about forty-five minutes."

"We've got McVie's on file, so if he comes up—" A mischievous smile touched the corner of Kav's mouth.

"Very funny." Fenway pointed to the office. "I'm sure I don't need to say this, but pay particular attention to the drawer the safe is in—and the safe itself. If our victim was tracking payments for illegal activity, someone might have tried to get into the safe and take the ledger."

"Sure thing."

Fenway turned and walked out the rear door of the main office. She couldn't see the front parking lot from where she was, but assumed McVie was out there waiting for her.

She walked briskly as she took her phone out of her purse. A few months ago, she'd connected with the human trafficking detective in San Miguelito, but she figured she'd cross off the drug angle first—and she had a way to get in touch with an informant she'd used before. She kept one eye on where she was walking as she scrolled through her contacts. There it was: *Parker Richards*. She hesitated for a moment; had she talked to him since his brother was a suspect in her very first murder case? She stared at his name for a moment. It didn't matter—Parker was the only one she knew who could connect her to someone with the right information. She tapped his name. It rang twice.

"Uh, hello?"

"Hi, Parker. This is Fenway Stevenson with the county coroner's office."

Silence.

"Sorry for calling you out of the blue like this, but I need to get in touch with Zoso."

"I don't do that stuff anymore," Parker said.

"Didn't say you did." Fenway tried to get easy nonchalance sliding into her voice. "I need his expertise on a couple of things."

"Like, his expertise on pills?"

"Background information only," Fenway replied. "Know where I can find him?"

A pause. Fenway could almost hear the gears grinding in Parker's head.

"Okay—uh—what day is this?"

"Tuesday."

"Oh, right." Another pause. "He's got a contact at the Epsilon Zeta Epsilon house."

"On the Nidever campus?"

"Two blocks away. It's on El Tirigo."

"Gotcha."

"Dinner at Eazy-E starts at six. Zoso shows up a little before that."

"Eazy-E?" As the words came out of her mouth, she heard it: E for Epsilon, Z for Zeta. E-Z-E. "Oh—right." She checked her watch; five minutes to five o'clock. She had enough time.

The interview with Tyra Cahill and her lawyer would have to wait. Wouldn't be great to leave them waiting for her, but for an hour or so, they'd be fine.

"Keep my name out of it," Parker said. "I don't want anyone thinking I gave him—"

"I'm not vice, Parker."

"Shit," Parker said, "if you're still the coroner, does that mean another murder?"

"I investigate all suspicious deaths," Fenway said evenly. "And you have my word—I won't mention your name." She turned the corner to Unit 176, the medical examiner's van parked twenty feet in front of the Highlander. "Gotta go. Thanks."

She tapped *End* on her phone screen and stuck her head into the storage unit. Melissa de la Garza was crouching next to the body.

"Hey, Melissa."

"Liver temp is eighty-five degrees Fahrenheit," Melissa said.

"Almost the same as the temperature in here." Fenway looked up to the left. "So time of death is, what, eighteen hours?"

"Yes, a little over eighteen hours." Melissa touched the dead man's forearm and tried to move it. "Though with the temperature fluctuations last night, I'm giving it an hour on each side."

"Full rigor."

"Right," Melissa said. "Seventeen to nineteen hours."

"So time of death is between—" Fenway looked at her phone. "Between ten p.m. and midnight." An hour or two after Tyra had seen her ex pull up in his Corvette.

"Right."

Fenway pointed at the bloodstain next to Seth Cahill's head. "It looks like this rug was used to transport the body."

"Rolled up in the carpet."

"Someone would have to be pretty strong to carry a body rolled up in this rug," Fenway pointed out. "I mean, the rug itself is what, forty or fifty pounds?"

Melissa nodded. "And I estimate Mr. Cahill is about one-fifty."

"So we're looking at someone who can carry two hundred pounds."

"Or drag it. A lot easier to drag a body rolled up in a carpet than carry it."

"He was wrapped in the rug postmortem?"

"I think so," Melissa said. She took two squatting steps to her right until she was even with Seth Cahill's shoes. She put a gloved hand under one ankle and lifted. "Do you see that?"

Fenway crouched and squinted. "What am I supposed to see? Drag marks on the heel?"

"Correct. No dirt. I think he was killed outside, on concrete or asphalt, not on grass or dirt. He was dragged onto the carpet, and the concrete or asphalt scuffed his shoes."

"I don't suppose you could analyze the type of hard surface?"

Melissa laughed. "If you want to wait a month for the analysis, sure, we could get traces out of the scuff marks and tell you the kind of concrete or asphalt it is. I bet we'd find profiles matching ten thousand different locations in Dominguez County."

"I bet the concrete and asphalt will match the walkways and blacktop at Cahill Warehouse Storage?"

"Oh," Melissa said, "you think he was killed here?"

"Mark brought up the theory," Fenway said. "Someone was sleeping in Unit 112."

"You mean like a squatter?"

"That's what I thought at first, but then we found a hidden ledger in Seth's office. One with hundreds of thousands of dollars in payments reported." Fenway rubbed her chin. "Obviously, we suspect illegal activity, probably at this storage facility. And while I don't have any evidence that the person staying in Unit 112 was tied to the records in the ledger, we need to follow that possibility."

"Oh." Melissa furrowed her brow. "What's your best guess so far?"

"Seth lost ownership of this place in the divorce," Fenway mused. "So here's a possibility. He goes to confront the people staying in Unit 112. Maybe he says now that Tyra is in charge, they can't use the facility for their illegal activities anymore. One of them gets mad and kills Seth. Then, using Seth's keys, they find a rug in a storage space here, wrap his body up, leave it in an empty storage unit, then steal his Corvette and drive away."

Melissa shrugged. "The evidence I've seen supports that theory," she said.

"A lot of assumptions."

"You have to start somewhere."

"Oh!" Fenway snapped her fingers. "I found a screw on the floor. A little unusual. Did you see it?"

Melissa nodded. "Dark green head, about three-quarters of an inch. Doesn't look like the kind you buy at a hardware store."

"What other types are there?"

"Commercial. The kind companies order in bulk and use in assembling their stuff. The color of the screw is painted like that to match the color of the product."

"Like furniture?"

"Sure. Folding chairs, lamps, all kinds of things."

"Can you figure out where it came from?"

Melissa shook her head. "Not quickly, anyway. Maybe I can do some research, but it's low on my priority list. Now the victim's sports car, on the other hand..."

Fenway scratched her head. "I've asked Patrick to put out an APB on Seth Cahill's Corvette. If we find someone driving it through San Diego—"

"We might have our killer." Melissa stood. "At least a Corvette sticks out. Someone will find it."

CHAPTER FIVE

Fenway drove the Highlander around to the front parking lot. She passed Unit 112, with Deputy Celeste Salvador standing guard in front. Fenway waved—and Celeste motioned for her to stop.

Fenway rolled down the window. "Everything okay? Did they come back?"

"The squatter who was staying in this unit? I haven't seen anything." Celeste paused, then a pained look came over her face before she spoke—she might have been arguing with herself. "I hate to bring this up, but do you have an update on Mark's backfill?"

"I've submitted everything to HR," Fenway said, "a couple of weeks ago. Haven't heard anything yet."

"Okay," Celeste said, "but Mark's retirement party is tomorrow night at Winfrey's. If you want him to cross-train anyone—"

"Right." Fenway sighed. "That would have been ideal. I'll see what's holding it up."

"No problem," Celeste said coolly, although her jaw clenched. Ugh. A follow-up call to HR would have to go to the top of her to-do list. Fenway had the hometown advantage: Celeste wouldn't have to move, wouldn't have to learn the ins and outs of a new sheriff's office, and was already familiar with both the geography and many of the people in Dominguez County. But If Fenway didn't get the hiring process moving again, Celeste would likely apply to other sheriff and police departments. She had a good résumé—seven years as an officer and straight-A's in her criminology program at Huntington University. And she'd gotten a 95% on the written exam. Someone would jump at the chance to work with her—and Fenway wanted to make it clear to HR that Celeste was at the top of her list.

Fenway nodded. "I'll get to it as soon as I get back to the office. I promise."

Salvador paused.

"What is it?"

"Debbie Farzan—she's in charge of hiring—she leaves at three thirty."

"Oh. Well, okay, first thing tomorrow."

"All right. And—if you could do me a favor?"

"Sure."

"Donnelly is on my back about overtime. If you need me to stick around late tonight, would you clear it with her?"

"Absolutely. And I *will* need you to stick around. Did you have plans?"

Salvador smiled. "Not tonight. And I can use the extra money."

Fenway smiled back, then turned the corner to the exit gate, which beeped at her and gave several metallic clunks before it started opening. Once through, Fenway found herself on a side street, and turned right to go into the front parking lot.

She saw her Accord next to the curb one block up, and McVie pacing on the sidewalk next to it, on the phone, talking animatedly with his free hand. Getting out of the car and locking the doors with McVie's key fob, Fenway walked over to him. He saw her out of the corner of his eye and reached out his free hand, enveloping Fenway in an embrace.

"I can be there in about fifteen minutes." His voice was confident, but a slight undercurrent of nervousness was buried under the surface. "And it's a ten by twenty?"

She wrapped her arms around him and squeezed. She turned her face into his shoulder. He smelled like sunblock and honey with a slight tang of sweat and the barest hint of his cardamom-scented cologne.

"Thanks," he said into the phone. "I appreciate it. Glad I called." He tapped the screen and squeezed Fenway back. "This sucks," he said.

"Maybe you shouldn't go to Colorado."

"I've got to," he said.

She knew why he believed he had to move: Megan in a new school for her senior year. Amy wasn't the most supportive parent. But Fenway had been on the daughter's side of this before. "Part of the reason Megan's moving is to get away from you."

"I know." McVie patted Fenway's shoulder. "And that's okay. I don't have to see her every day, or even every week. Mark my words, though: one day this year, she'll wake up in a panic, and Amy will be off on a business trip or over at her boyfriend's house, and she'll need her dad. And I'll be damned if I won't be there for her."

Fenway squeezed him tighter.

Fenway never got that assurance from *her* father. Nathaniel Ferris: always two thousand miles away, getting married on the weekend of her high school graduation. She knew why, now—and she knew her mother had been a complicated person. Still, Nathaniel Ferris had never *fought* for her. Not the way McVie did for Megan.

Ironic that the very qualities she valued in McVie were the things moving him away from her.

"I don't know how long I'll be."

"Not a problem," McVie said gruffly. "I'll rent the space, then I'll head to the sheriff's office and talk to Mark, then I'll take some boxes."

"You could use some company."

"And Seth Cahill could use someone to find his killer."

Fenway broke from her embrace and looked askance at McVie.

"Oh, don't give me that," McVie said. "I asked Callahan to help me move boxes, and he said he couldn't because he was on the Cahill homicide."

"So he gave you the name of the victim."

McVie patted her shoulder again. "Don't be too hard on him. It's an awkward spot for everyone."

"Celeste Salvador wouldn't have given out our victim's name."

"No, but I didn't ask her to help me move, either."

Fenway elbowed McVie in the ribs. "A clear-cut case of blatant sexism. You don't think women can move boxes."

McVie knotted his eyebrows, then tapped his phone screen a few times before bringing it to his face.

"Hi, Deputy Salvador," he said. "Listen, Fenway had to cancel on me tonight, and I could really use some help with a few of these boxes for the next hour or so. Pizza and beer on me." A pause. "Oh, okay. What case?" He listened intently. "No, no, of course not. Just thought I'd ask. Thanks." He tapped the phone and put it back in his pocket.

"No victim's name," Fenway said. "I should have bet you twenty bucks."

"Not a bet I would have taken," McVie said. "Did Celeste apply for Mark's job?"

"Of course." Fenway looked at McVie out of the corner of her eye. "She bugged me about following up with her."

"Good. Don't sleep on Celeste. She'll be gone if you don't act fast."

"I know. I've done my part—it's hung up in HR."

"Then un-hang it."

Fenway took her phone out and tapped her email app. She tapped the keyboard on the screen, composing a quick message to Debbie Farzan, asking in a couple of short sentences what the status was on the backfill and when she could move forward with her preferred candidate. Looking into McVie's eyes, she melodramatically swooped her finger onto the screen and hit *Send*.

"There it goes," Fenway said. "My email to HR asking for a status update." She patted McVie's chest and took a step back. "Now, isn't there some overpriced storage facility you need to get to?"

McVie grinned and dropped his hand to Fenway's, giving it a squeeze. "There is. Let me know when you're free tonight."

———

Fenway parked under a tree across from the Epsilon Zeta Epsilon house. The old Victorian house had a large banner draped next to the front door: an image of a Black man in a dark leather jacket, hands clasped in front of him, dark wraparound sunglasses on, and a black Chicago White Sox baseball cap on his head. "Eric Lynn Wright," Fenway murmured, staring at perhaps the most famous photograph of the rapper known as Eazy-E. She'd seen about twenty college-aged kids go in and out of the building; they were, without exception, white.

Another white man, perhaps in his mid-twenties, walked purposefully around the corner and strode toward the E-Z-E house. Fenway blinked; instead of the surfer clothing she had seen him in before, the man wore fitted blue jeans and a polo shirt. Fenway squinted.

Zoso.

She barely recognized him without the long waves of hair that fell to his shoulders. Now, he had a short haircut, still blond, cropped close on the sides but fuller on top. He carried a large backpack. Anyone else might have figured he was returning from a study session in the library.

Fenway opened her car door, got out, and shut it behind her.

Zoso's head snapped around at the sound of the door closing, and his eyes narrowed.

"Hey," Fenway said. "It's been a while."

"Sure has." Zoso looked up and down both sides of the street, but no one was there. "I always enjoy seeing you, Miss Stevenson, although I don't always like why you want to talk with me."

Fenway crossed the street and walked up to Zoso. "You're looking great."

Zoso shrugged. "Easier to do business when I don't look like I'm doing business."

Fenway grinned. "I hear that. Let's take a short walk."

"I have a meeting," Zoso said.

"I promise, it'll be short. Around the block. Five minutes, tops."

"I'll be late."

"If you walk with me, I won't look in that backpack."

"You don't have probable cause."

Fenway looked out of the corner of her eye at Zoso. "How do you think I knew you'd be here? You think my source told me you were selling cookies door-to-door?"

Zoso pursed his lips. "Yeah, all right." He tightened the shoulder straps and started walking down the sidewalk the way he came. Fenway followed.

"Cahill Warehouse Storage."

Zoso stopped in his tracks. "I'm not involved with those guys. Who said I was? They're lying—I would *never* get involved—"

Fenway held up her hand. "Just tell me what goes on there."

"First of all," Zoso said. "I don't touch that Nyllie bullshit anymore."

Nyllie? Of course—morpheranyl. Cute street name.

"Nyllie can kill you," Zoso continued. "I'm all for people medicating their cares away. I'm not about medicating your *life* away. Not worth it, man. Someone dies after taking that shit, there's blood on your hands."

"Too much risk of going to jail?"

"Too much risk of me never being able to live with myself again."

"Aww," Fenway said. "A dealer with a heart of gold."

"Shut up," Zoso said, but color rose to his cheeks.

"So you know Cahill Warehouse Storage is involved with morpheranyl. What do they do with it?"

"How should I know?"

Fenway glanced at Zoso's face, then stared straight ahead. "When I asked about the warehouse, you brought up morpheranyl. Clearly, you know something."

Zoso was quiet.

"So what was it? You were working with them, they cut you out?"

Zoso scoffed. "Possum tell you that?"

Aha. She'd touched a nerve.

"I stopped working with them because of Bear."

First a possum, now a bear. "Bear a friend of yours?"

Zoso shook his head. "Was."

Fenway was quiet, staring at the ground, but feeling the steam rise from Zoso's ears. How angry was he about Possum and Bear? How much had he been involved with morpheranyl?

Zoso glanced up and down the sidewalk again, then lowered his voice. "They hold shipments there until the local dealers can come pick it up."

"How does the morpheranyl get into the county?"

"They use blisters."

Fenway cocked her head. "Those big plastic containers attached to the bottom of boats?"

"That's right. Straight outta *Miami Vice*. Cops got so good at checking that shit that no one used them for a decade. Now that the cops aren't checking for them anymore—"

"Got it." Fenway scratched her nose. "Any idea where the boats land?"

Zoso glanced behind him. No one was following them. He lowered his voice. "Maybe you could jog my memory."

Fenway stopped walking. Zoso went a few more steps, then came back.

"What?" he asked.

"You serious?"

"Twenty bucks is gonna kill you? You're keeping me from a business appointment."

"I haven't asked you what's in your backpack."

"I thought you were cool."

"I *am* cool. That's why I haven't asked about your backpack."

Zoso licked his lips. "This stuff should all be legalized. Or at least decriminalized."

"I don't disagree, Zoso." Fenway dropped her arms to her sides. "I've asked for your help, what, maybe three times in the last year?"

Zoso was silent.

"Tell you what," Fenway said. "When you have a chance, stop by the coroner's office at lunch. I'll take you to the best taquería in the county. Maybe the state."

"I can't be seen with you."

Fenway stared at Zoso for a moment, then took her wallet out of her purse, got a twenty-dollar bill and held it in front of Zoso.

Zoso took the bill smoothly. "Look, I just know how they did it last year. Maybe things have changed."

"You can't ask Possum? Or Bear?"

The corners of Zoso's mouth turned down. "Bear's dead."

Oh. "Whatever info you have. Gives me a place to start. What, cigarette boats? Or those homemade pangas I read about?"

They started walking again.

"Maybe in Florida. Not here." Zoso rubbed his chin. "You familiar with the whale-watching tours that go out of Estancia Harbor?"

Fenway nodded. Always busy on the weekends. McVie kept promising they'd whale-watch soon. Now it might have to wait until

McVie came back for a visit—or maybe after Megan graduated from high school. Assuming McVie would come back at all.

"There's a thirty-foot catamaran, double level, that docks there sometimes. The *Ariel*."

"Like the mermaid?"

"I guess. Anyway, last year, that boat'd be gone for days at a time. Never carried guests."

"Okay, the *Ariel* at Estancia Harbor. Is that where they unload the morpheranyl?"

Zoso scoffed. "No way. Too many people coming and going. If they use blisters, someone will notice a guy in a wetsuit and scuba gear pulling packages out of the water."

"So if not in the harbor, then where?"

"They used to use a little area near Belvedere Beach."

Fenway knotted her brow—Belvedere Beach. That sounded familiar—oh, right, the beach off Ocean Highway about five miles north of the city limits. Near her father's former oil refinery. She'd investigated a dead body found in a pedestrian underpass not too far from the beach. "The Belvedere Terrace Hotel is right there."

"Yeah, but the cops were all over that place last year." Zoso snapped his fingers. "Of course—you were the coroner on that case."

"I was." Fenway cocked her head. "I remember seeing a lot of rock formations just offshore. Didn't look like a good place for a boat to drop anchor."

"Not at the hotel. About a quarter mile farther along the coast," Zoso said, "is a little inlet right near Portico Lagoon. No rocks. Seas can get a little rough, but in the inlet, it's calm. Deep. A boat like the *Ariel* could drop anchor, any decent diver could get the stuff out, and the trees all around the lagoon give it good cover."

"You've thought about this a lot."

Zoso chuckled. "Well, no one would ever use it now. The cops got way too close with all the action at Belvedere Terrace last year."

Fenway put her hands on her hips. "So that doesn't really help me much."

"My point is, that's the kind of place you're looking for. Very little traffic, but a way for a vehicle to get in and out. Well hidden, either with trees or underbrush or a cliff—if there's a way to get up and down."

"You sure you didn't hear anything about where they moved their drop-off point? A conversation you walked into? Maybe some reference someone made?"

Zoso thought for a moment. "Possum took me to this place south of Estancia. You know where Puerto Avila State Beach is?"

Fenway thought for a moment. "Right by Vista del Rincón."

"That's the one. There's another beach, almost totally private, maybe half a mile north of there. Deep enough, no big jutting rocks like at Belvedere Beach. Secluded, no public road, so you won't run into anyone. I had no idea how Possum found it, but it would make sense." He tilted his head. "And now that I think about it, the cops never came. We used to drink, run on the beach in the middle of the night, we even made a bonfire once." His eyes glazed over for a moment. "Anyway, there's a fire road you can access from this weird turnoff about a hundred yards before the Vista del Rincón exit from Ocean Highway. Possum used to be involved, so I guess the *Ariel* might be going there. About a hundred feet of sand between the ocean and the fire road. Wouldn't be that hard to carry about two hundred pounds of Nyllie to a waiting car. It'd be like carrying an extra passenger. I bet you could take the whole shipment of Nyllie in one trip."

"As long as they've got someone who gets the morpheranyl out of the blister." Fenway nodded. "Who was the diver when you were part of the organization?"

"They never told me that. But lots of people in Estancia have wetsuits and scuba gear. Hell, you could do it with a snorkel if you were fast enough."

Fenway scratched her head.

"The *Ariel* goes back to the harbor, no drugs, so no worries about inspections. The driver gets back on Ocean Highway, and he's in L.A. in an hour and a half."

"Or back in Estancia," Fenway muttered. In her head, she calculated the distance and time from Vista del Rincón to Cahill Warehouse Storage. "About twenty minutes to Cahill's storage space if you follow the speed limit, right?"

"Sounds about right."

That would limit the time on public roads—make it less likely to get pulled over. "You think the owner of the storage place is in on it?"

Zoso laughed. "I've got no idea. Everything I told you? Old info. Nyllie is getting here by boat, the *Ariel* used to be one of those boats, they used the Portico Inlet for drop-off."

"And it got stored at Cahill."

Zoso grinned. "And that's all I know."

Fenway nodded. "What about *after* the morpheranyl made it to Cahill? Dealers come get it?"

Zoso sighed and cracked his neck. "I can't believe I'm explaining the distribution system to..." His voice trailed off, then he cleared his throat and straightened up. "Well—look, users get patches, pills, stuff like that."

"So once the morpheranyl gets here, they still have to prepare it for use."

"Don't just skip to the last step." He grinned. "The whole process takes time. I mean, the machinery is cheap, and so is the protective clothing, but you've got to process the Nyllie properly. That adds a week, sometimes two."

"How much morpheranyl are we talking about?"

"No idea."

"Humor me."

Zoso stared at the sidewalk and shuffled his feet as they turned the corner. "If they're using a catamaran and storing drugs in the blisters attached to the bottom of the two hulls, I think we're talking about maybe a hundred kilos per trip."

"That doesn't sound like a lot."

Zoso chuckled. "Those patches are like twenty or twenty-five milligrams, and they go for a hundred bucks on the street. You do the math."

"Isn't that about ten times the lethal dose?"

Zoso shrugged. "Those patches give you a measured amount over time. So you stay high for a few days. Yeah, you can get high for cheaper, but you can't *stay* high for cheaper."

Four hundred bucks for a gram—

No, that'd be off by a factor of ten—a gram would have forty patches' worth of morpheranyl, not four. So it's four *thousand* bucks for a gram. A thousand grams in a kilo, and a hundred kilos.

"Millions of dollars," Fenway whispered.

Zoso laughed. "Maybe when all is said and done, but it's not like any one group of dealers is getting that. Split between maybe three different groups and four or five hundred people like dealers, processing, middlemen, transport—"

"And storage."

"And storage," Zoso said. "Still, when I was working with them, I made a lot more than I do now. A number that high? Almost tempting enough for me to get back into the business," Zoso said. "But..."

"Possum and Bear."

Zoso tilted his head up, looking at the night sky. "Heard you did the autopsy on Bear. Day before Thanksgiving."

Autopsy on Bear? Fenway furrowed her brow, then her head snapped up. "Scott Behrens."

"Bear was a great guy," Zoso said. "One of my best friends growing up. The stuff he went through as a kid, he had a hard time with..." Zoso's voice caught.

Fenway remembered. Scott Behrens had looked a lot like

Fenway, skin color, high cheekbones—they could have been siblings.

Zoso shook his head. "Anyway, I won't *touch* Nyllie anymore. Not even for all that cash."

"Where is all this morpheranyl coming from?"

"I don't know. Someone said something once about All Saints Bay."

"Ah," Fenway said. "Bahía Todos los Santos. Ensenada is right there."

"Oh. Mexico. Yeah, that makes sense. I heard the name and thought maybe it was in Oregon or Canada or something." He cleared his throat. "If what I hear is right, most of the Nyllie gets sent to L.A.—almost none of it stays in Dominguez County." Zoso chuckled. "Can't blame them. They don't want to shit where they eat."

"They? You know who they are?"

"Not the guys in charge. Just the two I've seen on the *Ariel.* Calvin is the negotiator and the muscle—well, I guess he goes by Cal. Young, wiry dude, with a thick accent, maybe Scottish or Irish. Sounds like one of those bad guys on those British crime dramas. He's got a rep for flying off the handle. I wouldn't trust the guy, but you don't want to cross him, either. Lowers the breakage, I guess."

"You said two guys."

"There's an old guy who drives the boat, handles the money. Doesn't negotiate terms but holds the cash once they get it." Zoso smiled. "My buddy said he smokes these weird Indonesian cigarettes. Mostly cloves, I guess. Won't tell anyone his name, though."

"Kreteks?"

Zoso gave Fenway a blank look.

"That's what those Indonesian cigarettes are called. Kreteks." Fenway frowned. "Clove cigarettes—kreteks too—are illegal in the U.S."

"Really?"

"Since the ban on flavored cigarettes. About fifteen, maybe twenty years ago."

"How do you know that?"

"I used to be a nurse, remember? Tobacco's bad for you."

"Sure." Zoso coughed, almost as if he'd been smoking. "I guess he buys them in Mexico while everyone else is getting Nyllie."

"They arrive... when?"

"Never a set schedule. They start showing up every other Tuesday at 8:17, either the cops or the competition show up. Not good for business."

"No, I guess not."

"That's all I got."

"Does Cal have a last name?"

"Uh..." Zoso scratched the side of his head where his formerly long blond tresses had been. "Yeah. Hang on. I heard it once." He scrunched up his face. "You seen the dinosaurs right off the freeway on the way to Palm Springs?"

"The dinosaurs?" Fenway cocked her head.

"A weird place. A building shaped like a big brontosaurus. You can see it from a mile away on the interstate. I loved it when I was a kid. My—" He cleared his throat. "My mom used to take me when I was little."

Fenway shook her head as they turned another corner. These houses were all Greek—and the Alpha Tau Xi house had a large palm tree in front. A memory flashed into Fenway's mind. Yes. Her mom had taken her there, too. Maybe Fenway was five or six. Maybe younger. The stairs going up into the side of the dinosaur. Gripping her mother's index finger tightly.

"I've been there," Fenway said. "Out in the desert, east of Riverside."

Zoso snapped his fingers. "Banning," he said.

"What's Banning?"

"The city in the desert with the dinosaur building. And it's the guy's last name."

Fenway nodded. A research task for Sarah back at the office. "So Banning and the boat driver come into town on the *Ariel* with a boat full of morpheranyl, unload it at Puerto Avila, store it at Cahill's storage place. Where do they stay when they're in town?"

"The Four Seasons. Presidential suite."

Fenway blinked.

Zoso laughed. "You really think I know where they stay? Maybe they live in Estancia. Maybe they sleep on the boat."

"Maybe they stay at the storage facility?"

"I guess."

"What would you say if I told you I found a sleeping bag and a portable toilet at Cahill Warehouse Storage?"

"I'd say I'd rather sleep on a boat with an actual bathroom. But that sounds like Cal. Anyway, *someone* has to stay with the Nyllie." They turned the corner again and the E-Z-E house loomed ahead on the right. "Look, I gotta get to my meeting. This better not get back to Cal. Or anyone. No one takes too kindly to me talking to the cops. Even one as hot as you."

Fenway scoffed. "Save your flattery."

"Just remember how helpful I've been," Zoso said. He turned and strode up the path to the house, readjusting his backpack. "If you ever get a call to raid the Greek houses, I hope you'll take that into consideration."

"Yeah, because the coroner's office conducts so many drug raids."

"You know what I mean. You can put in a good word for me."

He really did look like an overeager freshman. Probably worked well for him.

The fire road off Puerto Avila state beach. She looked at the clock on her phone. She still had enough daylight. Maybe enough time before Tyra Cahill and her lawyer would be antsy enough to leave the sheriff's office.

CHAPTER SIX

"Just keep them there for another hour, Dez," Fenway said into her phone as her Accord bumped over the dirt trail, wide enough for a large pickup. "I got another lead."

"You said you were looking for physical evidence," Dez said. "I didn't think it would take you this long."

"I had to go where I thought the evidence was."

"Where'd you go? Tijuana?"

"No, no. I'm just north of Puerto Avila beach, near Vista del Rincón." The road pitched down toward the beach, and a break appeared in the ironwoods and scrub brush about twenty yards on her left.

"That's forty minutes away."

"And I'll be back in an hour." Fenway slowed the Accord to a stop and put the car into *Park*. "Looking more and more likely that Seth Cahill was involved in drug trafficking."

"What?"

"That's why the squatter's belongings were in Unit 112. Someone stayed Monday night. They always stay with the morpheranyl shipment before they get it packaged for use and distribution."

"I'm sorry—what? Did you uncover additional evidence?"

"I had a talk with Zoso."

Dez scoffed. "Zoso? Are you serious? Look, you're the boss, but he's doing his level best to get Norco and Oxy to every anxious student and depressed housewife in a hundred-mile radius—"

"Zoso knows how the operation runs," Fenway said. "Or at least how it ran a year ago. One of the whale-watching boats out of Estancia Harbor, the *Ariel,* was running drugs. Picking up a hundred kilos of morpheranyl in Mexico and dropping the shipment near Estancia. Then a car takes the drugs from the shoreline to Cahill's storage facility. Other people—maybe like the squatter in Unit 112—process the morpheranyl and get it to distributors. Millions of dollars in morpheranyl every shipment."

Dez was quiet for a moment.

"You still there?" Fenway popped the trunk, got out of the car, and shut the door.

"I'm here," Dez said softly. "Is this a conclusion you jumped to, or do you have any evidence?"

"That's why I came to the beach," Fenway said. "To gather evidence. But everything fits. Seth's secret ledger book in that safe. The timing of the payments makes sense with the story that Zoso told me. That's something we can have Sarah research." She opened the trunk and got gloves and three evidence bags from her toolkit.

"Or Patrick Appleby. That's his job."

"Right." Fenway shut the trunk. "Or Patrick. And we have the name of the boat—oh, and the name of one of the smugglers. Calvin Banning."

Dez clicked her tongue. "We can run his name through the system. What'd you say was the name of the boat?"

"The *Ariel.* Like the mermaid."

"A whale-watching boat?"

"Yeah, a catamaran docked at Estancia Harbor. The boat runs from All Saints Bay near Ensenada. Zoso thought it might unload its shipment here in Dominguez County near Vista del Rincón near Puerto Avila Beach.”

“Zoso ‘thought’?”

“He’s never failed me before.” She cleared her throat. “Besides, it’s not like he’s trying to protect his business interests. He doesn’t touch morpheranyl. Killed one of his friends last year.” She took a few steps toward the sand, then kicked off her flats and picked them up, feeling the dry sand between her toes. “I did his friend’s autopsy, right before Thanksgiving.”

“Oh.” A sharp intake of breath from Dez. “I remember that. Nyllie overdose. Kid, about twenty-two?”

“Right. Scott Behrens.”

“I remember.” Dez cleared her throat. “You’d think I’d have gotten jaded enough by now. But yeah, his death. Sometimes you see a kid like that, it gets under your skin.”

Fenway closed her eyes. Scott’s tawny skin had been pallid in death. His teeth had been crooked and riddled with cavities—he obviously hadn’t been taken care of as a teenager. Product of the foster system. Dr. Yasuda had pulled the sheet over his face and told Fenway she’d already contacted someone to make a positive identification.

“Seth Cahill might have pissed off a few people if he used his property to store morpheranyl,” Fenway said. “Mark thinks if Tyra wouldn’t store the morpheranyl any longer, that Seth’s trafficking partners wouldn’t like it.”

“We need to figure out where he was killed,” Dez said. “I’m sending Deputy Salvador over to Seth’s girlfriend’s house—”

“Mark already spoke to Miranda Duchy.”

“Yep,” Dez responded. “But he didn’t ask her if she’s missing a Persian rug.”

“Neither you nor Mark brought Duchy in for questioning?”

“We’re doing it now, Fenway. If you’re so concerned about questioning suspects, then get your ass off the beach and come back to the sheriff’s office.”

"Ten more minutes here, tops." Fenway walked a few feet out onto the warm sand. An untouched, pristine beach, with no sunbathers, surfers, or body-boarders. The waves came in unrushed, unhurried. "Beautiful," Fenway murmured.

"What?"

"The beach. It's gorgeous." Fenway scanned the sand. She'd hoped she could find something to prove that a drug-smuggling boat had been here. Maybe a discarded plastic container that might have held the morpheranyl, marks in the sand from dragging a couple hundred pounds of contraband over the sand. If a catamaran had been up on shore, there could still be two parallel ruts in the sand where the double hull had been.

Or it might be a waste of time. Was it the right beach? Zoso only said that if *he* were the smuggler, this is the beach he would use.

As if reading her mind, Dez spoke up over the clacking of her keyboard. "What exactly are you looking for?"

"I'm not sure," Fenway said. "I thought there'd be signs of the *Ariel* dropping anchor here."

"At least I found the name of the person who rented the dock at Estancia Harbor," Dez said. "Stephan Butler."

"Evan?"

"With an S-T at the beginning. S-T-E-P-H-A- N."

"How very European."

"Arrested for intent to distribute two years ago," Dez said. "Charges dropped. Lack of evidence. He's the majority owner of Trinculo Tours, L.L.C. It's based in Estancia."

"Age?"

"Sixty-one."

"That fits with what Zoso told me." Fenway took a few more steps onto the beach. "How about the other guy—Calvin Banning?"

"Yeah, I entered his name into the system, but it looks like Cal isn't a California resident."

"Heh." Fenway smiled at Dez's wordplay. "Doesn't look like

there's much to see here. I'll do a quick sweep of the beach and then head back."

"You better hurry. There's only so much I can do with a bag of chips and a can of soda."

"Will do." Fenway tapped *End* and looked out onto the stretch of beach. Not a large beach—the sand only stretched about a hundred yards on either side of where she stood. The fire road began about thirty yards from the surf here—it was close to high tide—but about fifty yards further south seemed like a better location for a catamaran to drop anchor.

She walked along the shore, her feet sinking into the wet sand, and hoped she'd get lucky. Maybe there would be a hidden toolkit for getting the blister open. Or a dropped kilo of morpheranyl.

She visually divided the beach into sections until a grid formed in her mind. Up and down the beach: two hundred yards, give or take; thirty yards across at its narrowest point.

Fenway pulled on her gloves—she'd found a new pack in the Accord's trunk—and started walking up and down the beach, trying to be thorough and hurry at the same time. A ticking clock in her head of when Tyra Cahill and her lawyer would walk out of the sheriff's office.

A metal detector would be nice, although maybe it would bias Fenway toward metallic objects when plastic might be—

Hang on.

Halfway buried in the sand, a cigarette butt. Fenway walked over and crouched. She brought her face close to the sand. Very tiny letters in stylized script, almost like the Hindi alphabet.

Sampuriso A.

What had Zoso told her? *My buddy said he smokes these weird Indonesian cigarettes.* The clinic in Seattle sat in the heart of the Indonesian neighborhood, and Sampuriso was a popular brand of kretek cigarettes with the locals. If Stephan Butler were carrying two hundred pounds of morpheranyl in a few blisters under the double hull, he'd be okay with carrying a couple of cartons of illegal clove cigarettes.

She put the cigarette butt in one of the evidence bags. Out here buried in the sand, with the sun beating down, perhaps no DNA would be found on the kretek. But from what Zoso had said, Fenway thought this beach was possibly where the morpheranyl drop could have happened. If she could get the sheriff's office to approve a stakeout, they might get millions of dollars of morpheranyl off the streets. Maybe a few of the dealers, too.

———

"I appreciate you coming down here to talk with us," Fenway said, shutting the door of the interview room behind her.

"Not enough for you to show up on time," Tyra Cahill said. She wore the same outfit she'd had on at the storage facility: a cream-colored blouse under a faded denim jacket. She wore her hair down now, instead of in the earlier ponytail. "And I'm paying my lawyer by the hour."

The lawyer sat in a black pinstripe suit with a bright white dress shirt and a red tie, and gently laid his hand next to Cahill's on top of the table, almost but not quite touching. "I must insist—"

"Right, right," Cahill murmured.

Fenway set down her notebook and file folder on the table and sat across from Cahill and her lawyer.

"Ms. Cahill is distraught by the loss of her ex-husband," the lawyer said.

"I'm so sorry for your loss," Fenway said. She opened her notebook to a blank page and tapped her pencil on the table three times. She'd have to tread carefully. "Ms. Cahill, who would want to hurt your husband?"

"I—" Tyra Cahill stopped, glanced at the lawyer, then when he nodded, she went on. "I'd heard he and Miranda weren't getting along too well anymore."

"Did you see evidence that Miranda was angry enough to hurt him?"

Tyra bit her lip. "I've heard stories."

Fenway scribbled in her notebook. "What kind of stories?"

"I heard she threw a dish at her ex."

Hearsay, and lack of foundation. She couldn't use that. "Anything else?"

Tyra hesitated. She wanted Miranda to be a suspect; Fenway could see it in her eyes. But Tyra shook her head.

"Was Seth seeing someone behind Ms. Duchy's back?" Fenway asked. "Or was *she* seeing anyone else?"

Tyra considered this for a moment. "I wouldn't be surprised. Once a cheater, always a cheater, right?"

"Your husband—"

"Ex-husband," Tyra corrected.

"He ever get violent?"

"Not with me. He wasn't a large man, either. Fit, funny, charming, good taste. But Miranda could bench-press him."

Fenway glanced at Tyra, who could also bench-press Seth. For that matter, Fenway could have too. Tyra was still throwing suspicion onto Miranda. "You won the business in the divorce?"

"That's right. He got the Corvette, I bought him out of the house, and he gets alimony from me."

"Really? You're paying him?"

"I'm getting the business that we both started, so he's getting a percentage." She narrowed her eyes. "I know what you're thinking, but that's what we agreed to so I wouldn't drag things out. Apparently, he and Miranda wanted to get married right away."

From his briefcase, the lawyer produced an ivory-colored card, embossed with fancy lettering. "Save the date" across the top in an elegant script.

"August," Fenway said. "That's soon."

Tyra grunted. "I told you he wanted to get married quick."

"Right." Fenway cleared her throat. "Any issues with the

business?"

Tyra cocked her head. "What do you mean?"

"Well, sometimes divorced couples can do things to each other to, uh, maliciously comply with the agreement. Maybe he sabotaged some client relationships—"

"Hey, now if you're implying—" the lawyer began.

"—and a client might not have taken too kindly to it," Fenway finished, raising her voice.

He clamped his jaw shut.

"For instance," Fenway said, "the squatter in Unit 112. You said you thought Seth had taken care of them. So you knew about them?"

"I knew Seth had been in charge of securing the premises when he and I co-ran the business," Tyra said. "He still had an office onsite. So, yeah, the squatters were still his problem."

"When did his employ at Cahill Warehouse Storage cease?"

"Two weeks ago," Tyra said. "I still had him finishing up a few things around the property."

"Were you paying him?"

Again, a quick glance at her lawyer. Ah, so she was paying her ex-husband cash and not reporting it.

"Did any of the other employees get mad that he wouldn't leave?" Fenway asked, before Tyra's lawyer could shut down the previous question.

"Who—Mathis and Isabella?" Tyra chuckled. "Isabella is just glad to have a full-time job. If Seth is doing anything around the property, it's one less thing Isabella has to do."

"What about Mathis?"

"Mathis is full-time too." Tyra paused. "Though he and Seth were, uh, maybe I wouldn't say 'close,' but the two of them were sort of like work best friends."

Fenway cocked her head.

"I mean," Tyra said, putting her hands flat on the table, "like they covered each other. If Seth had to leave early, Mathis would take his tasks on. And vice versa. They stayed late, making sure the security systems were up to scratch. Would go out for beers when they were done."

Huh. That's not what Mathis said. Fenway would have to ask Mathis about that. "Did you hire Isabella and Mathis?"

"I hired Isabella. She dropped out of UC Riverside last year. We pay better than most of the entry-level positions around here, and the hours are flexible enough for her to go to community college." Tyra leaned back in her chair. "Not that she ever signed up."

"What about Mathis?"

"Hah. He was Seth's scuba instructor." Tyra pulled a hair tie out from her purse. "The training school was in financial trouble. Mathis hadn't been paid in a couple of weeks. I think Seth admired his dedication to the customers. Hired him as soon as the class ended."

That fit with what Mathis had told Fenway. "Did Seth or Mathis ever mention a man by the name of—" She flipped in her notebook. "Calvin Banning?"

Tyra frowned. "Not that I can remember."

"How about Stephan Butler?"

"No one named Stephan that I know."

Fenway tapped her fingers on the table. "How about the name of a boat called the *Ariel*?"

"You mean the whale-watching boat?" Tyra asked. "Seth said he was part investor in it."

Fenway nodded. "Part investor. Interesting."

"Are we almost done here, Coroner?" the lawyer asked. "We waited two hours for you, and now we're discussing whale-watching."

"Almost," Fenway said. "Ms. Cahill, did you recognize the Persian rug in Unit 176?"

"I—uh..." Cahill said, glancing at her lawyer. "I didn't pay much attention to the rug, to be honest."

"Were you aware that Seth kept a separate ledger in a safe in his office?"

"My client still declines to answer that question," the lawyer said.

"Would you like to tell me where you were last night?" Fenway asked.

"My client declines to answer that question as well," the lawyer said, then he stood. "I think we've given you enough of our time. Is my client free to go?"

"Just to be clear, Ms. Cahill, you told me earlier that he came by your place about nine o'clock. Do you have anything to add to that statement?"

"My client," the lawyer said, "told you that he *agreed* to come over at nine o'clock. She never said whether or not he came over."

"You *absolutely* said he was there at nine," Fenway said, leaning forward in her seat toward Tyra Cahill. "You said he showed up in his Corvette. You made a joke about his midlife crisis. I said it would be hard to fit boxes into the Corvette, and you agreed. Now, maybe that wasn't exactly at nine o'clock, but if you won't give me any more information, I'll be putting those notes into my report, and any reasonable person would conclude you were lying to the police—either then or now."

The lawyer took Tyra Cahill's arm and gently encouraged her to her feet. "We're done here," he said.

"Unfortunately," Fenway said, "I'll need to look into your ex-husband's past. His financials, that kind of thing. I'm apologizing ahead of time—it might feel intrusive. Please understand, we have to do it to find the person responsible."

The lawyer held the door open for Tyra Cahill.

She was halfway out the door when she turned to Fenway. "Speaking of Seth's financials, you might want to see who gets his stuff if he's dead." She spun on her heel, and the lawyer followed her out the door.

Fenway sat at the table, flipping through her notebook.

A moment later, the door opened, and Dez popped her head in.

"You okay?"

"Yep. Just thinking. Tyra was lying, holding a lot of information back."

"She was with her lawyer. Of course she was lying." Dez paused. "Do you want us to see if Seth Cahill had a will?"

"Yes."

"My money's on Miranda Duchy getting everything."

Fenway grunted. "Yeah. Tyra said as much."

"This is a lead, Fenway. Why are you so distracted?"

"I need to figure out why Tyra Cahill isn't answering some of my questions."

"I'd think it was obvious."

"Because she killed her ex?"

"Because the wife is always the prime suspect." Dez sat down on a corner of the table. "But she already has the business, which makes it less likely that she has a financial motive."

Fenway chuckled. "Hatred between ex-spouses goes a lot deeper than money. Maybe Tyra was angry about being cut out of the drug business—or angry that it was happening under her nose. That could be why she came in with her lawyer."

Dez nodded. "Then Tyra is lucky that the ledger only has our victim's prints on it."

Fenway looked up. "That was fast."

"We had a direct means of comparison. Still has to go to the lab to be official, but even I could tell after comparing his prints to the ones we lifted from the ledger."

"So, what does that mean?"

"We need to figure out what those payments were for."

"I'd be shocked if they weren't for the storage and distribution of the morpheranyl that the *Ariel* was ferrying to Estancia." Fenway hooked her thumb over her shoulder. "I found a clove cigarette on the beach north of Puerto Avila. Zoso said that the old guy who drives the boat smokes them. I'd bet anything that's where they do their exchange."

"Let me see if I follow," Dez said. "This whale-watching boat—"

"The *Ariel*."

"It goes between Mexico—"

"I'm thinking Bahía Todos de los Santos near Ensenada," Fenway said. "Though that's mostly an educated guess."

Dez nodded. "And picks up a couple hundred pounds of morpheranyl."

"Right. And stores it in a few blisters."

Dez frowned. "A few what? Blisters?"

Fenway held her right hand out, palm up, then curled it into a cup. "Storage containers attached to the bottom of the hull." She put her right hand flat, palm down, over her cupped left hand. "Or both of the hulls, in the case of a catamaran."

"Then it comes by sea to Estancia."

"Right—to a secluded beach only accessible by a fire road."

"How do they get the drugs out of the blister?"

"You go into the water, swim under the boat, and open the storage container. The drugs are in waterproof bags."

"Sounds like you need to hold your breath for a long time."

"Mathis Jericho was a scuba diver. Maybe he taught Seth how to use the equipment. Either of them could have done it."

"Then they carry two hundred pounds of this stuff up to the car parked on the fire road."

"And drive to Cahill Warehouse Storage. Store it until other people pick it up for processing." Fenway tapped her foot. "Here's what I think the process is. The *Ariel* drops off the morpheranyl in the middle of the night. One of the boat workers goes with one of the storage workers to drive it back to the facility. The worker stays in an empty unit that night, probably with the drugs, to make sure nothing happens to it. Then a third party shows up, maybe someone from the packaging and distribution part of this whole thing, and they complete the transaction with Seth Cahill moderating. And taking his cut."

"Okay—that might be a possibility."

"And as Mark said, if something went wrong with the transaction, the person who stayed in the empty unit—the 'squatter,' as we've been calling them—could have had reason to harm Seth Cahill. And if it was someone else, the squatter could be a witness. We figure out who was on the *Ariel*, I bet we get closer to finding our killer."

"Maybe." Dez rubbed her chin. "I'm thinking in another direction."

"What?"

"It's pretty obvious why Tyra Cahill was so evasive."

"Why?"

"Because she probably recently found out about her husband's agreement to store and transport the morpheranyl."

"Why do you say she 'recently found out'? She could have known the whole time."

Fenway shook her head. "With the ledger in Seth's safe, I think he was hiding it from his wife. And as the business owner, she's legally liable."

"This is one of those 'known or should have known' things?" Dez asked.

"Probably. I guess she could argue that since she recently assumed control of the business, maybe she *shouldn't* have known. But no matter what, Tyra's dealing with a Pandora's Box of legal nightmares."

"And it's Seth's fault."

"So the question is, would she have been angry enough to kill Seth?"

Dez shrugged. "People have killed for less."

"That's one theory, anyway. But let's not get carried away." Fenway scratched her head. "Seth was supposed to marry Miranda Duchy, wasn't he? Let's see if he made any other changes in his life that might give someone else motive to kill him."

CHAPTER SEVEN

Fenway called Seth Cahill's insurance agent on her cellphone to see if the decedent had changed anything else—added coverage, changed beneficiaries—but the office had closed for the day. Fenway crossed the street—stepping over another discarded Tailwhip electric scooter—and entered her office, where she typed her notes into the computer for about half an hour.

She'd just opened her email when Sarah opened her office door.

"I'm heading out."

"Make any headway on the background of the boat or of the people who were in it?"

"Just that the *Ariel* has paid for a slip at the Harbor for about two years," Sarah said. "I'll know more tomorrow. You need me to stay?"

Fenway's phone buzzed in her purse. She pulled it out. A text from Mark.

No sign of the Ariel at Estancia Harbor

She held up the phone. "The *Ariel* isn't in dock."

"Maybe on one of those extremely common overnight whale-watching tours."

Fenway chuckled. "With that cigarette I found on the beach, I would think the *Ariel* had made its delivery."

"So you'd expect it to be in dock."

"Yeah."

"Well, look at the bright side," Sarah said. "One less thing to do tonight."

"Hang on," Fenway said. "What if Seth's death messed up the schedule last night?"

"What do you mean?"

"He was killed between ten and midnight. If he'd intended to drive his car down to Vista del Rincón and go diving to pull the drugs off the boat, but he was killed before he could do it—"

"I see where you're going. Seth doesn't show, the boat can't make its delivery, so it might try again tonight."

"Precisely."

"Want me to see if Sheriff Donnelly can put a couple of uniforms on the beach?"

Fenway shook her head. "Not uniforms. We want them to keep out of sight." Her phone rang in her hand. "Talk to Dez about it and see if she can get a team or two to cover the beach tonight. Then you can go home." She tapped *Answer* as Sarah closed the door behind her.

"Hey, Melissa."

"Couple of things you'll want to note," Melissa said. "We reviewed security footage. You can see Seth Cahill drive to the storage facility's parking lot at about ten fifteen last night."

"Does the tape show him leaving the facility?"

"Nope."

"Okay, then, unless he wandered off somewhere on foot, without the camera seeing, sounds like he was killed on the premises. The question is, by whom?"

"Right. And no one else worked that late. The two employees, Isabella and Mathis, both left at nine o'clock, give or take."

"So Seth was alone."

"Well—we don't know."

"Why not?"

"Because about three minutes after Seth enters the office, the cameras go dead."

"Really?"

"Yep. 10:18 PM. We looked at other footage, too. On a handful of days over the last three months, Seth drives up after closing time, goes in, and turns off the recording."

"When do the cameras go back on?"

"Sometimes around two a.m. Sometimes just before the facility opens the day after."

"Who else is at the facility when this happens?"

"Just Seth Cahill. They have alarms and gates, but no overnight security guard."

Probably just for this reason—no witnesses. "You said this has been going on for three months?"

"They only have ninety days' worth of footage."

Fenway rubbed her forehead. "You got the message that we think Seth Cahill was involved in drug trafficking?" If that were the case, maybe Seth Cahill was the one to disconnect the tracking system on the Corvette, too. Hadn't she read a news story last year about a cheating husband whose wife found out because of his car's automatic tracking system?

"Yeah, I got the update."

"If the ledger we found kept track of the drug trafficking payments, maybe we can use it to establish a timeline. Send over the times and dates when the cameras were turned off. I'll cross-reference those with the entries in the ledger. See if the dates of payment match with the days Seth turned off the cameras."

"Will do. You'll get a text in a few minutes."

"Can you do me a favor? Talk to Patrick Appleby in our IT

department. See if he can cross-reference the dates and times of Seth turning off the cameras with any gaps in the Corvette's Safe-Board tracking system, too."

"Sure."

"Thanks, Melissa. I'll talk to you later—"

"Wait—there's one more thing."

"What?"

"Look at this picture."

The phone buzzed in Fenway's hand. She tapped on the screen and a picture of a small video monitor appeared. The images on the monitor were of Seth Cahill's office, from a corner camera in the ceiling. The Scandinavian desk and the high office chair were directly underneath the camera.

She tapped on the top of the screen and turned on the speaker-phone. "The office is empty," Fenway said.

"Right—but look in front of the desk."

"The metal guest chairs?"

"Look what's on the floor *under* the guest chairs."

Fenway blinked.

Dusky gold and navy blue. The Persian rug that Seth's body was wrapped in.

————

The door seemed especially heavy, and Fenway pushed it open with her foot, the bag with a burger and fries in one hand and the large cola, already half-consumed, in the other.

The door banged against something—a stack of large boxes.

"Craig?" Fenway called. She squeezed through the space between the door and the jamb, into the small linoleum-covered foyer of her apartment. The door swung shut behind her.

Stacks of boxes covered her living room and the dining room, as well as one of the two counters in the kitchen.

"Craig?"

No answer. She pulled her phone out. Two missed calls from McVie, but no voicemail. She'd gotten to Baxter's Burgers before they'd closed, and now it was 9:03 PM. There was no way—

She grimaced. Ah, that made sense. Most of the storage places closed at seven or eight. Cahill Warehouse Storage was one of the few in the area—maybe the only one—that stayed open until nine. The facilities in L.A. stayed open later, but the earlier hours—with restaurants, shops, as well as storage facilities—were part of the charm of living in a beachside community like Estancia.

So she'd seen McVie at five o'clock, or maybe just after. He'd had to go to a new storage facility, sign up, pass their credit check, all of that, then interview at the sheriff's office about the body in his storage unit. Obvious that he'd only had time for one or two trips before the facility had closed for the night. But why not leave everything in his apartment? Not only was he leaving town, not only was he subjecting her to the pain of a long-distance relationship, but he'd dumped thirty or forty boxes in her apartment.

An annoying thought struck her. Maybe McVie hadn't been able to get as large of a storage space as he'd needed. Maybe these boxes were the *overflow*. Would these be staying in Fenway's house for the next week until...

She squeezed past two stacks of boxes in the living room and plopped down on the sofa. The coffee table was clear, so she set down her soda and opened the bag. The tang of Baxter's Chipotle Burger sauce hit her nose. She popped a French fry in her mouth. Tasty, though not piping hot anymore. She pulled her burger out, unwrapped it, and took a bite. For not being Dos Milagros, the food was pretty good. For a moment, she could ignore the stacks of boxes.

The door opened.

Through the crack in the door, three more boxes. And McVie's muscular legs.

"Hang on, Craig," she mumbled loudly through a mouthful, putting the burger on the coffee table. She vaulted over the arm of the sofa and reached the stack of boxes behind the door. She pulled on the stack—

Oh, that wasn't happening.

"Sorry," said McVie's voice from behind the stack of boxes in the doorway. "I wasn't thinking with the last trip I made. I put them too close to the door."

"Well, put those down and help me," Fenway said. "It's too heavy for me to move."

After some grunting, McVie set the stack of boxes down next to Fenway's front door, then stepped sideways through the door to get in. He stepped to the side of the stack behind the door, with Fenway on the far side, and they both grabbed the bottommost box and slid the entire stack on the dining room floor until the door could open most of the way.

"There," McVie said.

"How many more trips do you have?"

"I can leave the rest of the boxes in the car for tonight," McVie said. "These boxes have some of my sentimental stuff. Family photos, mostly. I can replace the other stuff."

"Why did you bring the boxes here?"

"You didn't get my voicemail?"

"Two missed calls. No messages."

"I'm so sorry. The reception at the storage place was terrible." He pushed one of the stacks away from the dining room table, closer to the wall. "Landlord wants a walkthrough, and since I'm leaving early, tomorrow was the only day I could schedule it. And the storage place I rented closes at eight." McVie sniffed the air. "That's not Dos Milagros I smell."

"Baxter's. I went to Dos Milagros for lunch."

"Sorry. I really was planning on taking you to a fancy dinner tonight."

"It's okay—I would have had to cancel." She climbed back over the arm of the sofa and picked up her burger. "How was the inter-view at the sheriff's office?"

"Fine. My name was on the rental agreement, but I didn't have anything to do with either the squatter or the dead body." He scratched his chin. "I don't envy Sheriff Donnelly. Everyone is screaming for her head because of the spike in overdose deaths. She'll have to do something dramatic if she wants the town back on her side."

Fenway chewed and swallowed. Ugh, she hadn't savored that bite properly. "So, are you getting these boxes out of my apartment tomorrow?"

"Yes, but first I have to go on another stakeout. The woman I'm supposed to be following has a Pilates appointment tomorrow morning at nine thirty. And I don't know when it will end." He stepped toward the sofa and rested his arm on top of the stack of boxes next to the coffee table. "Besides, I need the money right now. Colorado is a big question mark."

"I get that," Fenway said. She took another bite.

McVie looked at her burger hungrily.

"Have you eaten?" Fenway said with her mouth full.

"Uh—no. Part of the voicemail you didn't get was me asking if we could grab something when you got home."

"Okay. Well, I have some stuff in the freezer. Maybe some leftovers in the fridge. The spaghetti with meat sauce we had the other night."

"That sounds great. You don't mind?"

"Go ahead."

"Thanks." McVie walked around another stack of boxes into the kitchen, around the corner, behind the wall separating the living room from the dining area. The sound of plates clicking together, then of the microwave opening and closing. *Beep beep beep beep,* then a final *beep.* The microwave powered on.

"I have to start on the case early tomorrow," Fenway said, "but I'll take a few boxes over for you in my car before work."

"I appreciate it, but you really went out of your way today. I'll take care of everything tomorrow." McVie took a comically giant step over the sofa arm and sat next to Fenway, then pulled her close and kissed the top of her head.

After McVie got the spaghetti from the microwave, Fenway polished off the rest of her burger. She turned on the TV, then lay down on the sofa, her feet sticking over the far arm of the sofa, the top of her head pressed against the side of McVie's thigh while he ate. She breathed in; a light scent of cardamom, a bit of musky sweat, as he'd been carrying boxes up and down stairs for most of the last two hours. Fenway didn't mind too much.

The next thing Fenway knew, McVie was shaking her awake.

"Hey," he said. "You want me to go?"

"No," she mumbled. "Stay here tonight." She pushed herself to a sitting position. The bowl of spaghetti was empty and the ice in her soda had completely melted. "Is the show over?"

"Yeah."

"What time is it?"

"Ten fifteen." He stood and grabbed the plate. "Want to get ready for bed before I take a shower?"

"Sure." She stood and rubbed her eyes, then walked around the coffee table, shimmied between two stacks of boxes, then walked into the bathroom.

She stared at herself in the mirror. She looked tired. The last couple of weeks—really, the last year—had been trying sometimes. Tonight was no exception.

But compared to a little over a year ago? When she'd been driving back and forth to the hospital where her mother went from bad to worse? Trying to get through her shifts at the clinic?

The work was hard and mentally demanding, but she felt so much more in control. And her father—well, maybe their relationship wasn't perfect, but it was better than it had been since her mother had moved them both to Seattle twenty-one years before.

The fatigue showed in her eyes. She wasn't getting any younger —she'd be thirty this year—but the bags under her eyes were so much less noticeable than they'd been that last week when she'd visited her mother in the oncology ward. Her hair had come in a little fuller, too, and while this latest twist with McVie had—

Oh no. Was that a gray hair?

Ugh. In a curl about an inch and a half above the right side of her forehead. She rolled the hair between her fingers until she isolated it, then squeezed her fingers together and gave a yank.

Fenway stared at the single strand of gray hair in her hand for what seemed like a long time, then she shook her head, grabbed her face cleanser, and turned the faucet on.

———

She fell asleep as soon as she got into bed, and woke with a start again, the overhead light and the ceiling fan on above her. Fenway glanced over at the clock. Not quite eleven. The sounds of water running. McVie was still in the shower—not that unexpected, although he usually didn't shower for this long. It must have been twenty minutes.

She turned her pillow over to the cool side and fluffed it before setting her head down. She parted her lips—they were dry. Water.

She swung her feet out of bed and padded to the bathroom. The door was closed; a little unusual, but maybe McVie hadn't wanted to wake her up with the sound of the shower.. She reached out to grab the door handle.

Locked.

That was odd.

Then she heard it, almost imperceptible under the sound of the water running, the cascading streams of water hitting the bottom of the tub. Fenway furrowed her brow, then she grimaced.

McVie was sobbing.

Fenway straightened up.

How long had he been crying?

Dazed, she walked into the kitchen and took a short glass out of the cabinet, then pulled out the pitcher of filtered water from the fridge. She poured a glass, and the water went down easily; cold, refreshing. She debated pouring herself another, but instead she put the pitcher back into the refrigerator and closed the door. She stood there for a moment, listening carefully, but from the kitchen she could barely hear the water running, never mind any sobbing underneath.

Had she ever seen McVie cry before? She couldn't remember. Not when he'd lost the mayoral election, though that was a tough defeat. He hadn't cried in the past when Fenway cried either, though he'd held her and comforted her. Maybe when Amy had said she'd wanted the divorce? Fenway hadn't been there for that.

Part of her understood. McVie was scared. New town, new job. He didn't know anyone except the ex-wife he hated and the daughter who tried to avoid him. He hadn't really talked to Fenway about how he felt about moving, but it was reasonable to assume he was crying because he was scared about the future—wasn't it? She hoped she wasn't one of those girlfriends who McVie felt he had to hide his feelings from.

Should she comfort McVie about his decision to move? He's the one who wanted it, even though he knew how hard it was for Fenway to trust anyone, knew how she'd never had a romantic relationship that had lasted more than a few months.

He'd made it clear that he valued his relationship with Megan more than his relationship with Fenway. And Fenway had been fine with it. Fine. Really. It made sense; of course it did. Megan was his daughter. Fenway was his girlfriend, and they'd met just over a year ago.

Fenway set down her water glass on the sink and padded past the bathroom door. As she crossed the threshold into her bedroom, she heard the water turn off. She put on the bedside table light on McVie's side of the bed, turned off the overhead light, and lay down, her back to McVie's side.

McVie came in, padding around the bed, smelling of Fenway's

soap. He climbed into bed and turned his bedside light off, turning onto his back.

"You okay?" she asked tentatively.

"Sure. Little stressful today, I guess."

She turned to face him. "Anything you want to talk about?"

A slight hesitation, then a comforting chuckle. "Honestly, I'm just tired."

She scooted closer to him, then rested her head on his shoulder. He shifted so his arm wrapped around her back and he pulled her in to him. "I'm sorry things are so crazy right now."

"I—" Fenway began, but she didn't know what else to say.

For a moment, Fenway lay in the dark, listening to McVie breathe. His breath didn't hitch; there was no clue he'd been crying or emotional. After a minute or two, his breathing slowed and deepened, and his hand slipped off her back.

Fenway shifted herself carefully and wrapped her right arm around his bare chest. She buried her face in his shoulder.

"I wish you didn't have to leave," she whispered, muffled by his shoulder so he couldn't hear. "But you have to, and even though I hate it, it's okay. We might not be okay, but you'll be okay. It's the right thing to do."

If only she believed it.

PART 2

WEDNESDAY

CHAPTER EIGHT

McVie's elbow. "That's yours."

"Hmm?"

"That's your phone. It's Dez."

"How do you—" Fenway pushed herself up. Her phone was on her bedside table, buzzing, the screen bright. *Dez,* the screen yelled.

Oof. 3:17 AM.

She tapped *Answer.*

"Mathis Jericho is on the move," she said. "I'm assembling a team at Puerto Avila beach in forty-five minutes. You're coming with me."

"What? Mathis..."

"Sheriff Donnelly read your notes," Dez said. "Jericho being a scuba instructor, all that info on the *Ariel,* not being in dock. She was skeptical. We convinced her to put a couple of uniforms on Jericho's apartment. Before we could do that, though, Celeste passed by Jericho's apartment. She reported him carrying a wetsuit and scuba gear into his car."

"And Donnelly thinks—"

"That it would be a good idea to be on that beach, given the cigarette you found. It's not hard evidence, and you have to connect the dots. But Donnelly wants to make a bust."

"If we wait, we could nab the distributors, too."

"Yeah, but there's a deadline to meet. Some sort of six-month quota for an SJRD incentive."

Fenway was quiet, searching her brain, but shook her head. "I don't think I've heard of SJRD."

"Smokin' Joints and Rolling Doobies," Dez said, then cackled. "I don't know what it stands for either, but it's a program that pays agencies that get drugs off the streets." She cleared her throat. "Sarah told me. Apparently, a good percentage of the sheriff's office budget is riding on our ability to get this incentive payment. Might be why Donnelly is in such a bad mood. If the sheriff's office doesn't make a big bust soon, they won't get the incentive. There'll be a budget shortfall."

"What about the *Ariel*?"

"Right." Dez cleared her throat. "Donnelly coordinated with the Coast Guard out of Santa Barbara. Spotted a catamaran headed northwest toward Estancia about ten minutes ago. We estimate they'll both get to the beach by four o'clock, maybe a little after."

"So soon after what happened yesterday?"

"Must want to beat the tropical storm."

Of course. The storm was due to arrive in the next day or two. Fenway ran her hand over her face. "I'm on my way."

"You're leaving?" McVie asked.

"Persons of interest arriving in town." Fenway sat up on the side of the bed and rubbed her eyes. "Gotta go meet Dez." She dropped her hands to her sides. "Oh no."

"What is it?"

"Mark's retirement party. It's right after work—and I haven't gotten his gift yet."

McVie rolled toward Fenway and pushed himself up onto his elbow. "Know what you're getting him?"

"He'll be building sets for the community theater. He could use a home improvement gift card."

"Thoughtful and easy," McVie said.

"Just like you," Fenway cackled, then leaned over and kissed McVie's cheek.

"Let me drive you."

Fenway blinked. "I can't let you do that."

"Sorry. Slipped out." He sighed. "I won't be able to offer to drive you after this week."

"Maybe I'll be back in time for breakfast." Fenway stood and stretched. "One last trip to Jack and Jill's."

"Wake me when you get back." McVie gave Fenway a crooked smile. "I don't have to leave until eight thirty."

———

The wind whipped off Rincón Bay, and Fenway put her hands up to her forehead to keep the hair out of her face. She'd shaved her head in L.A. so she wouldn't be recognized, and now she'd let it grow—and after six months, it still wasn't long enough to do anything with, but it *was* long enough to whip into her eyes.

Above, clouds swirled in front of the half-moon. Every so often, it peeked through the clouds, giving Fenway enough illumination in the parking lot of Puerto Avila Beach to see the waves cresting a hundred feet from the lot.

Not much traffic on Ocean Highway at this time of the morning, but a large sedan exited onto the Puerto Avila offramp. Probably Dez's Impala. It turned toward Fenway at the bottom of the incline, and the headlights blinded her for a moment before it passed her and parked next to her Accord.

The window rolled down; it was Dez. "Didn't think you'd beat me here."

"Me neither."

Dez got out of the car and closed the door. "We've got protocol for drug drop-offs like this, but did Zoso give you any clue how this group does things? Who shows up when? How they get the drugs off the boat?"

Fenway gathered her hair, still whipping with the wind, and held it with one hand behind her head. "We talked in hypotheticals, but I figured someone from the storage facility would already be parked near the beach when the boat comes. Then a diver would get the drugs out of the blister. They put it in the car, then one of the boat's men goes in the car along with the driver—back to the storage facility." She shrugged. "If Mathis Jericho was on the move forty-five minutes ago, I'd expect he'd already be here."

"We know he stopped at the storage facility," Dez said.

"What's he doing there?"

"Who knows?" Dez ran a hand over her close-cropped hair. "Maybe that's where he keeps some of his scuba gear."

"Or maybe he switched vehicles," Fenway said. "Anyone keeping an eye on the back gate of the storage facility?"

Dez's eyes went wide. "I'm not sure. We don't have a lot of resources to put on this, and the state isn't sending their resources, either—couldn't mobilize in time." Dez leaned into the Impala through the open window and grabbed her radio, then pushed the call button. "Thirty-three, what's your twenty?"

Callahan's voice crackled through the small speaker. "Still at Cahill Storage. No movement."

"How long has it been?"

"Subject entered the office building at oh-three twenty-seven."

Fenway took out her phone and looked at the time. 4:08 A.M. "That's almost an hour. You think he's still there?"

"Shit." Dez dropped the hand holding the radio to her side and rubbed her forehead with the other. "I bet he's gone. Out the back gate like you said."

"You don't know that for sure—"

"He must be on his way." Dez shuffled her feet. "Or maybe already here."

Fenway motioned with her head toward the freeway. "No one called the DEA or backup?"

"A few officers trekked down the fire road." Dez pointed to the edge of the parking lot, dark and shrouded in bushes, where there was an entrance to the fire road. "Didn't leave the police cars because we don't want to scare off whoever's meeting the boat here."

"We're okay with *our* cars being here? Won't it freak out the perps?"

"Three police cruisers would scare them off, yeah. But this lot isn't visible from the beach."

"How long ago were the cruisers here?"

"When we still had eyes on Mathis Jericho. I'm positive we didn't spook him." Dez lifted the radio to her face. "Thirty-one, update?"

"Nothing to report," Deputy Salvador's voice said through the radio. "No vehicles or pedestrians on the fire road."

Dez frowned. "I thought you said this was the beach."

"It's the beach where I found the cigarette," Fenway said. "It strongly suggests that Stephan Butler was on the beach recently. The cigarette was in good condition. A day old, maybe less."

Dez set her mouth in a line. "We figured they couldn't make their drop-off of the morpheranyl early yesterday morning because Seth Cahill was dead in that storage unit, so they made alternate plans today."

"With Mathis Jericho instead of Cahill," Fenway said, a lock of curly hair flying into her face. "Yeah, I got that. Maybe they post-poned it more than one day." She paused. "Or maybe it's been Jericho all along, and he wound up getting the morpheranyl last night."

"I suppose it's possible," Dez said, "but then why did Mathis Jericho go to the storage facility at three thirty in the morning?"

"Maybe he met with one of his contacts—the 'squatter' who slept in the storage unit." Fenway rummaged in her purse and pulled out a hair tie. "Or maybe he saw Callahan following him and decided to lie low. Or he's pushing it off to yet another night." She tried to put her hair in a ponytail, as tight as she could make it, but it wasn't long enough.

"Maybe he went and got the drugs from the boat last night, then couldn't go to whatever next step it was back at the storage facility because Seth couldn't help him—"

"—because he was dead."

"So he's finishing it up tonight. He might still be at the facility."

"True, except..." Fenway furrowed her brow. "Why isn't the *Ariel* docked?"

"Another trip to Mexico to get more morpheranyl?"

"It's possible." Fenway ran a hand over her face—and was struck by an idea. "If you were in charge of the boat and Mathis had to change the date of the transfer, would you use the same beach as you did last night?"

Dez crinkled her nose. "I think so. It might be a little riskier, but it'd be a damn sight better than figuring out another location."

Zoso's voice in her head. *They used to use a little area near Belvedere Beach.*

Fenway tightened her jaw. "The boat isn't arriving here. We're too far south."

"What?"

"Tell your team to get to the Portico Inlet north of Belvedere Beach," Fenway said. "I'll meet you there."

"The team is on foot. We won't be able to meet you for at least an hour."

"We can't afford to wait, Dez." Fenway took out the Accord's key fob. "If that's where they are, they've been there for a while. I hope they take a long time to get the morpheranyl out of the blister and into whatever vehicle Mathis is driving. If we're lucky, we might get to them before they're all gone."

"You're not going alone." Dez opened the door of the Impala. "My car's faster. Get in. I'll drive."

Dez had been right; the team couldn't get back to the Puerto Avila parking lot, never mind to a separate location, in less than an hour. She radioed for backup, then put the police light beacon on the Impala's roof. Fenway took hold of the grab bar when they hit ninety miles an hour as they raced down the empty freeway.

"Where is this place?" Dez had to raise her voice over the roar of the Impala's engine. "I don't want to get to the side of the highway and then have to look for the way down to the beach for an hour."

"I don't know," Fenway said. "I scouted the location near Puerto Avila yesterday afternoon, but I didn't even think about this place."

"Why not?"

"Zoso said they used to use Portico Inlet, but with all the police action at Belvedere Terrace in November, the drug boats would avoid the area."

"That was almost nine months ago."

"Right." Fenway opened the maps application on her phone and typed in *Portico Inlet*. With any luck, she'd be able to figure out the best way to get down to the beach from the satellite images on the map.

"Hang on," Dez said. "Your contact didn't actually suggest that the *Ariel* could use this beach?"

"No," Fenway said. "But they're not where they were yesterday. Portico Inlet is the only other suggestion I've got."

Dez frowned. "They won't be there."

"Probably not," Fenway said. "But we need to check, anyway."

They passed by the turnoff for Nidever University. The signs of civilization thinned out through this area of the freeway and Dez pushed down the accelerator, the Impala's engine greeting the encouragement with a throaty roar.

"We won't have the team with us," Fenway said. "And we don't know what we're getting into. First sign of trouble—if backup isn't here yet—you get us out of there."

Dez nodded, her grip tight on the steering wheel.

Dez slowed down for the Belvedere Terrace exit, and instead of turning left toward the ocean, she swung the car to the right, then a hard left to get to a frontage road. A rollercoaster ride. Fenway held on to the plastic handle above the passenger window.

"A quarter mile north of the beach?" Dez asked.

"Take the police light off the car," Fenway said. "We don't want to let them see us coming."

Dez rolled down her window, then reached up and detached the light. She handed it to Fenway.

Fenway could barely read the map as the phone jostled up and down with the bumpy ride on the uneven asphalt of the frontage road. "Make a left on Mariposa Reina," she said. "Then we're looking for a road—maybe dirt, maybe gravel, about, uh, maybe a thousand feet after Seafoam Drive."

As they crossed Seafoam Drive, a small, dark sedan sped past them in the other direction, making a right turn. Dez took her foot off the accelerator. "Tell me when you see the turnoff."

"It'll be on the left," Fenway said.

A break in the brush—

"There." Fenway pointed, and Dez turned the steering wheel hard. The headlights illuminated a shallow set of tire ruts in the gravel. "Someone was here recently."

"Let's hope we're not crashing a big party," Dez muttered.

The tire ruts continued, and about five hundred feet later, Dez braked hard. The dark ocean lay ahead, with only about twenty feet of rocks between the ironwood trees and bushes and the tide.

As they emerged from the trees and rolled to a stop, Fenway looked up.

The boat.

The *Ariel* sat in the water, about fifty yards out.

"You were right," Dez said, throwing the Impala into Park.

"No vehicles here," Fenway muttered. "That means the drugs are probably off the boat and in someone's car on the way to Cahill Warehouse Storage."

"Maybe the dark blue sedan that passed us."

"Yep. Get some officers over to the storage facility right away."

Dez picked up her radio. "Fourteen, come in."

A crackle. "Yeah, Dez?" Callahan's voice, bored.

"Stay at Cahill Storage. The boat's already here at Portico Inlet, but no sign of other vehicles. The drug shipment might be on its way to you."

"Copy."

Dez clicked off.

"What do you think, Dez? Wait for backup?"

"Doesn't look like anyone's here."

Fenway peered through the darkness at the boat. No lights. "I'd expect millions of dollars in morpheranyl to be protected by guards. But not now. It looks empty—"

Then Fenway saw movement. A lone man, about five foot eight, standing on the shore, with his back to them, a lit cigarette between his fingers.

Board shorts, gray hair.

"One man." Fenway put her hand on the door handle. "That might be the guy Zoso was talking about. Drives the boat, handles the money. Let's see what he has to say."

Dez opened the door, one hand holding her badge and one hand on the holster of her gun. "Police!" she shouted.

The man turned. Lines in his weathered, deeply tanned face. A scruffy beard on a round face with full cheeks, heavy-lidded eyes.

Fenway opened the door and got out. She scanned the beach for other signs of life. The half-moon had come out from behind the clouds, and Fenway saw no one on the beach. She squinted: a lone dinghy, pulled up on the sand.

Anyone could be hiding in the shadows. Or, if the *Ariel* were in fact a drug smuggling boat, another person—maybe Calvin Banning —might have been on the boat with a gun. Fenway had brought her service weapon with her, but she wouldn't be accurate from this range. Plus, she couldn't shoot who she couldn't see.

Dez already had her handcuffs in one hand. "Sir, please put your hands where I can see them!"

The man raised his hands slowly, his bushy eyebrows knitted.

"Anyone else with you?"

"No."

"How about in the boat?"

"No." He paused. "I haven't done anything wrong."

"Six-oh-two of the California Penal Code," Dez said. "Trespassing on public property after hours." She pointed to his cigarette. "A violation of section five thousand eight point ten. No tobacco products on public beaches."

"And that's an illegal cigarette," Fenway called.

"Sir, you'll need to come with us." Dez strode to the man, handcuffs in front of her.

"What? You've got to be kidding." The man pressed his lips together, throwing his half-finished cigarette on the ground. "Those charges are bullshit—"

"Littering, too," Dez said. "Right in front of me. Is that your boat?" Dez asked.

"Well, yes—"

"Anyone else with you?"

"Not—" he said, then shook his head. "No."

What had he almost said? *Not tonight? Not right now?* So maybe Calvin Banning had been with him yesterday. She flashed to the sedan that had passed them as they crossed Seafoam Drive. Maybe that had been Mathis Jericho, taking Calvin Banning to Cahill Warehouse Storage.

"Do you have identification?" Dez said.

The man hesitated, then nodded. "Front right pocket."

Dez reached up and took the man's right wrist, put it behind his back, then his left wrist, and snapped the handcuffs on. She reached into his pocket and came out with a wallet.

"You're arresting me? For smoking on the beach?"

"The state of California is cracking down on crime committed on public lands at night," Dez said, flipping through the wallet. "Stephan Butler. What are you doing on the beach this late at night?"

"Couldn't sleep. Beautiful night. Thought I'd take the boat out."

"You thought you'd take out a whale-watching boat?"

"I only have the one boat."

Dez patted Stephan Butler down, and from his shirt pocket, pulled out a pack of Sampurisos.

"These are illegal in the United States, Mr. Butler."

"Not to possess. Only to sell."

"Section five-thirteen point one-four," Fenway offered. "I'm afraid you've been misinformed. Possession of flavored cigarettes. Including cloves. Misdemeanor in the fourth degree. Assuming you haven't been convicted before, of course."

"And assuming you're not selling them." Dez grabbed Butler's elbow. "Looks like we're bringing you in."

"I can't believe this."

"We'll take care of your boat, too," Dez said. "The Coast Guard will come and tow it into storage."

Butler grunted.

"Anything about your boat that you want to tell us now? Maybe get ahead of this?"

Butler shook his head.

Dez walked Butler across the rocks. Fenway stepped ahead of her and opened the back door of the Impala.

"Watch your head." Dez put him in the back seat, then pulled the seatbelt around him.

Dez closed the door. "Keep an eye on him."

"Right."

Dez took her radio and walked about twenty yards down the rocky beach, where the sound of the waves drowned out her words. Fenway caught "Coast Guard" and "how long" and a few other snippets. Fenway watched Butler in the back seat of Dez's car. He stared straight ahead, unflinching, unmoving.

CHAPTER NINE

FENWAY BLINKED AT THE COFFEEMAKER DRIPPING ITS NECTAR—
excruciating in its sluggishness. She glanced at the clock on the wall
of the break area: 5:17 A.M. They'd taken Stephan Butler directly to
the interview room next door. Fenway needed the caffeine if she'd
be halfway effective interrogating him.

Dez walked up behind Fenway. "Is it ready yet?"

"Not even close."

"That's okay. Butler can stew while we brew."

Fenway was too tired to smile.

Dez exhaled. "Can't believe the drugs never showed up at the
storage facility."

"Callahan still there?"

"And backup. But no signs of life. They'll stay for another hour
or so, but if no one's shown up by now…"

Fenway watched the coffee drip into the pot. "If the smugglers
moved the drop-off point from Puerto Avila Beach back to the
Portico Inlet, they probably moved the storage location too.
Staying one step ahead of us."

"I wish we'd figured out the new location sooner." Dez looked at Fenway. "You know Deputy Brasserman?"

Fenway shook her head.

"He's got a wetsuit and a snorkel. He just went in the water at Portico Inlet and confirmed it—two blisters attached to each of the *Ariel*'s hulls."

"But no drugs?" Fenway asked.

"He couldn't stay in the water long enough to detach the blisters from the boat. We contacted the Coast Guard, but they won't examine the boat where it's dropped anchor. They can't get a tugboat until noon at the earliest. Gave me a list of the forms we need to submit."

"Gotta love bureaucracy." Oh—and speaking of bureaucracy, Fenway hadn't gotten any updates from HR on the hiring process to backfill Mark. Fenway made a mental note to call HR as soon as their office opened. "So, do you think we can get information out of Mr. Butler?"

"I doubt he'll give us much of anything about the drug smuggling. But we can see what he knows about Cahill. He might give us something if we can make the misdemeanors go away. The maximum sentence is only thirty days in jail, probably less, but if he has something to give up, he just might do it."

"Has he done jail time before?"

"Three months for assault when he was in his early twenties," Dez said. "Arrested a few other times, spent the night in jail—but the charges were always dropped."

Fenway stared as the coffee sputtered from the machine into the carafe. "He won't give anything up on these misdemeanor charges. He knows he'll beat them anyway—he won't spend more than a night in jail."

"Maybe the charges were always dropped because he always had information to give."

"Anything is possible." The dripping coffee had turned into a weak flow. A couple more minutes and they could each have a cup.

Fenway grabbed two mugs from the shelf above the coffeemaker. "Butler knows these charges are trumped up. But I bet he's already figuring he wouldn't get the handcuff treatment for clove cigarettes unless we wanted something."

"So be direct?"

"I don't see why not. He might be thinking there's no way he'll give up info on the drug smuggling. But Cahill's murder? Maybe he'll talk."

They stared at the coffeemaker as the minutes ticked by.

"He won't talk if he had a hand in it," Dez said.

"True." The coffee machine gurgled. Fenway grabbed the carafe and poured herself a cup. She usually added milk or cream, but this morning she was willing to take it black. She filled Dez's mug, too.

Dez grabbed the coffee and took a long sip. "I really shouldn't. Michi says she's worried about my caffeine intake."

"I think your wife can make an exception for a middle-of-the-night arrest." Fenway smiled, then took a slurp, the coffee burning on the way down, and that sensation woke her up. "Okay. Let's head in."

Fenway opened the door to the interview room, and Dez walked in first, taking a seat directly in front of Butler. Fenway sat on Dez's right.

Dez put a recorder in the middle of the table and pushed *Record*. She recited the date and time. "Interview with Stephan Butler." She sat back and spread her arms. "Let's get right to it, Mr. Butler."

"These charges are bogus," Butler said. "Any judge in the county would release me at the arraignment."

Dez tilted her head. "The laws you broke may not be enforced very often, but they are, nevertheless, laws that you broke. Laws that carry certain penalties."

Butler leaned forward. "Exactly what is it you want from me?"

"I believe you're familiar with someone named Seth Cahill."

"Lots of people say they know me. Maybe I took him out on the boat once."

"We found a ledger in Mr. Cahill's office," Dez continued, "that has a list of dates and payments. We believe those payments and dates correlate to shipments of morpheranyl and the storage of that illegal substance."

Butler's eyes lowered to the table. "I don't know anything about that."

"Are you sure? We can correlate the *Ariel*'s whereabouts to the entries in the ledger."

"Means nothing."

"Might be enough for a warrant."

Butler shook his head. "Maybe it is, but I can't tell you what I don't know."

Fenway nodded. She'd expected this. "Mr. Cahill was murdered about twenty-four hours ago," Dez said.

Butler's face registered shock for a half-second, then relaxed into its previous bored look. "I'm sorry to hear that. Doesn't mean I know who he is."

"Law enforcement needs to clean up this county," Dez said, "but I don't work in vice, I work in homicide. I'm interested in who might have been at Cahill Warehouse Storage yesterday between ten and midnight."

"I had nothing to do with any murder."

"Didn't say you did." Dez leaned forward. "Perhaps you had a client who went on a whale-watching tour who wanted to get the late-night session."

Butler shifted in his chair, keeping his eyes down.

"Seth Cahill lost his business to his ex-wife in their divorce," Fenway said. "Perhaps your client wanted to convince Seth to keep their business deal intact. Storage can be so difficult to obtain nowadays."

Butler's mustache twitched.

"It might be unusual to prosecute for crimes such as littering—" Dez began.

"Your discarded cigarette is worth a hundred-dollar fine and eight hours of community service, minimum," Fenway said. "You've littered twice in the last twenty-four hours on two different public beaches."

"Combined with the clove cigarette possession and being on a public beach outside of daylight hours—"

"Like I said before, bullshit charges. Any judge would let me go."

Fenway sat back in her seat, then a light bulb went on in her head. "Plus, you didn't have your anchor lights on."

Butler shrugged.

"Maybe you're right, Mr. Butler," Fenway continued, "and your lawyer could get the charges dropped. But we've already contacted the Coast Guard. They're very interested in a boat that may have been involved in a drug smuggling operation. Our 'bullshit' charges, as you put it, just happen to be enough to tow your boat into harbor and conduct a thorough search."

"And who knows what they'll find?" Dez leaned forward, her elbows on the table.

Butler glanced up, staring daggers at them, worry lines around his eyes.

"Let's say we have you arraigned later today, and the judge releases you." Fenway steepled her fingers. "You're a free man, but your boat's not at the Portico Inlet anymore. If the Coast Guard impounds your boat—" Fenway casually looked over at Dez. "Where's the closest Coast Guard impound? Monterey or Long Beach?"

Butler's face fell. Both were at least two hours away on the highway.

"At any rate, how would you continue to work for your, uh, whale-watching clients?" Fenway asked.

Staring down at the table, Butler grimaced.

Fenway had him. "The good news for you, Mr. Butler, is that we need to fill out a couple of forms before the Coast Guard will tow your boat to Long Beach. And if there's anything I hate more than drug smuggling, it's filling out paperwork." Fenway leaned forward. "But I hate murder more than both, sir. So here are your choices." She held up a finger. "One: you share whatever information you have on Mr. Cahill and his storage facility, then you walk out of here and go back to your boat." Fenway held up a second finger. "Or we go through the motions of this little play. You get arraigned, maybe this afternoon, sit in a cell until then. You spend a bunch of money on a lawyer to get the judge to turn the misdemeanors into a fine. You get released. Then I spend two or three hours filling out stupid Coast Guard forms, so I make sure you spend the next month trying to get your boat out of impound." Fenway sat back in her seat. "What will that do to your income?"

Butler's nose twitched.

"And if the Coast Guard finds anything on the *Ariel*—"

"Yeah, yeah, I got the picture," Butler said through a snarl. "Answer the questions, drop the charges, get me back to my boat, and you won't contact the Coast Guard."

"That's the deal," Fenway said.

Butler glanced from Dez to Fenway, then nodded. "And take these handcuffs off."

"Fair enough." Dez pulled a set of keys out of her pocket, stood and walked around the table, and unlocked Butler's handcuffs.

With the click of the cuffs unlocking, Butler pulled his hands back and rubbed his wrists.

"All right," Dez said. "Now talk."

"Cahill provided my clients with storage solutions," Butler said. "My clients often had a handler for the merchandise."

"This merchandise—" Dez began.

Fenway gave a small shake of her head. "We don't need to know what was being stored." Maybe that wasn't true, but Fenway didn't need to have confirmation of the morpheranyl to find the killer. "Who met you at the boat?"

"Cahill would meet us. Sometimes with that kid."

"Mathis Jericho?"

"I never got his name."

Fenway took out her phone and tapped a few times until she found the photo of Mathis Jericho she'd taken in the office of the storage facility. "This guy?" She turned the screen toward Butler.

"Yeah, that's the guy."

"And Cahill and Jericho would take the, uh, merchandise to their vehicle?"

"That's right."

"Did you go with them?" Fenway asked.

"Not me."

"The other guy went with them?"

No response.

"That makes sense." Fenway put her elbows on the table and rested her chin in her hands. "Here's the way I see it. You stay behind on the beach—someone's gotta stay with the boat, after all—and you wait ten or twelve hours until your client's representative returns to the boat. Then you and the representative leave, and you repeat the process in a week or two."

Butler said nothing.

"So your client's representative is at the storage facility right now?"

"I don't know where he goes, and I don't ask."

"Calvin Banning, right?"

"Never heard his last name."

Dez nodded. "He'll be wondering where you ran off to."

Butler shrugged.

"Did you hear anything about Seth Cahill not being able to continue with his deal to store your merchandise?"

"I—uh, I guess you could say I didn't have direct knowledge of it."

"But?"

Butler hesitated. "I heard Cal talking on the phone yesterday evening when we were on our way."

"You get cell signal?"

"Cal has a satellite phone. He seemed pretty upset."

"Upset enough to kill Seth Cahill?"

"Couldn't say."

"You see Cal get violent before?"

Butler was silent.

"What exactly did you hear?"

"Only Cal's side of the conversation. He got mad—like saying stuff like, 'What did you say?' in a real agitated voice. Once he said, 'We're counting on you for this. If your place doesn't work, you better find somewhere else that does.'"

"Did Cal threaten Seth Cahill after that?"

Butler pressed his lips together.

"We can protect you."

"You have no clue who you're protecting me from."

"You can make that easier for us—"

Butler shook his head. "No. I don't have a death wish."

Fenway shrugged. "Suit yourself."

Dez leaned toward Fenway. "He's given us enough to get Mathis Jericho and Calvin Banning in here. I'll go put an APB out on Mathis Jericho's car."

"Figure out if there's a dark blue sedan tied to either Mathis or the Cahills' business," Fenway whispered back. "We passed a sedan on the road, and I'll bet they were in that vehicle."

"Good thinking." Dez stood and strode out of the room.

"Where were you between ten and midnight last night?" Fenway asked.

Butler hesitated, then dipped his gaze to the recording device in the middle of the table.

"I'm the county coroner, Mr. Butler," Fenway said. "I'm working the homicide of Seth Cahill. That's what I'm concerned about. Not about you dropping anchor at an unauthorized—"

"Then turn off the recorder," Butler said.

"If we don't get your alibi on the recording, Mr. Butler, I can't guarantee that you'll stay off my radar regarding the murder investigation." Fenway sat back. "Would you rather get fined a few hundred dollars for dropping anchor north of Puerto Avila Beach, or would you rather risk getting detained for suspicion of murder?"

Butler placed his hands flat on the table and stared downward. Fenway could almost see the gears grinding in his head.

"If you have an alibi," Fenway said, "you might as well tell me now."

"Between ten o'clock and midnight on Monday, right? I was in the *Ariel*. On the way to a beach in Dominguez County."

"Can you get more specific?"

"At ten o'clock? Probably somewhere south of the Channel Islands. Midnight, we'd gotten closer. Point Comenzio, maybe. I wasn't paying a lot of attention to the time."

"You said 'we.' I assume this is your client's representative?"

"Cal."

Fenway leaned back in her chair. "Did you have a schedule?"

"We were meeting on the beach at two o'clock."

"That's two a.m.? You were supposed to meet Mr. Cahill?"

"He said he'd be there, yes."

"What happened?"

"I—" Butler stopped, glanced at the recorder in the middle of the table. "Look, I need assurances from you."

"If you're involved in this murder, Mr. Butler—"

He held up both hands. "I didn't know anything about a murder. Stop the recording."

Dez glanced at Fenway, who nodded. Dez reached out and hit the stop button.

"No one is supposed to get hurt when I make my runs. Picking things up in one place, transporting them to another. The less I know, the more they trust me. The more they trust me, the more work I get."

"And your clients trust you."

"That's right. They see me in here talking to you, I'll be selling my boat and going underground. If I live that long."

"I thought you said no one was supposed to get hurt."

"Don't treat me like I'm stupid, Coroner. I've dealt with the kind of people my clients are. I stay out of their way. I don't have questions; I don't ask people's names. I show up on time—not too early, either. I look the other way when people are loading up the boat, and I keep my head down so I don't run into any trouble. Stay under the speed limit. When the sign says, 'no wake,' I don't make a wake. These people have a business to run, and so do I."

"But you knew who Seth Cahill was."

"He introduced himself to me." Butler gave a small smile. "I told him I didn't want to know who he was, and I didn't want him to know who I was."

Fenway paused. "How long did you wait for Cal last night?"

"What do you mean, how long did I wait?"

"That's the deal, right? Cal would go with Cahill and Jericho, then you'd wait at the beach until he came back."

"Not last night," Butler said.

"What happened last night?"

Butler knitted his brow, then looked up. "The kid—Matt?"

"Mathis."

"He was the only one to show up. Half hour late, too."

"What time was that?"

Butler licked his lips, as if debating whether to answer the question. Finally, he spoke. "A little after two thirty in the morning. Cal didn't like it. He thought the kid was trying to pull something."

"He said that?"

"They argued. Me, I was standing off to the side."

"Smoking."

"Well, yeah."

"What happened?"

"Cal told the kid to leave the merchandise," Butler said. "Then Cal got some supplies, a sleeping bag, some other stuff, headed out with the kid. Probably to make sure he wasn't going anywhere. I had to put the merchandise back on the boat myself. Went and docked."

Fenway shut her eyes and the contents of Unit 112 flashed in her mind. "What color was the sleeping bag?"

"Uh—blue, with gray stripes."

The same as the sleeping bag in the unit. "Do you remember any of the other stuff he took?"

"A red-and-white cooler. A gallon of water, too."

"A lantern?"

Butler furrowed his brow. "Not that I remember. I wasn't paying close attention."

Fenway nodded. Calvin Banning was the squatter in McVie's original rented unit. Maybe his fingerprints would come back with more information. "Where did you dock? Estancia Harbor?"

"I don't like going in there when I have a shipment on board."

"Where did you go?"

"Friend of mine has a dock. Left the boat there for the night."

"Where was this?"

Butler smiled. "You asked me where I was between ten and midnight. You have your answer—I was on my boat with Cal. Arrived on the beach after he was already dead. Doesn't matter where I docked."

"We'll need to confirm your alibi."

Butler shook his head. "Then talk to Cal, not anyone at the dock."

"So when did you go back to pick up your friend Cal?"

"He stayed. Gave me a call and said Seth never showed. Said he was sticking around."

"Where did he sleep?"

Butler shrugged. "I didn't ask."

"Right, because you don't want to know."

"Can't tell the cops something I never heard."

Fenway rubbed her forehead. "Let's suppose Cal stayed onsite at the storage facility, but the next morning, he left. Where do you think he would have gone?"

Butler suppressed a laugh. "We're not friends, Coroner. I don't know anything about him. How would I know where he'd sleep?"

Fenway sat back in her chair and folded her arms. Mathis Jericho had withheld important information, and Fenway hadn't yet located Calvin Banning. They were at the top of her list of suspects.

A big problem with Banning: the timing was off. Calvin had been on the boat with Butler between ten and midnight—in fact, if Butler was to be believed, until two thirty. But time of death wasn't finalized yet.

And Seth could have been at the facility when Cal arrived, and he could have told Cal that the storage facility was off-limits. Cal might have killed Seth out of anger, or, if Seth Cahill couldn't be relied on to store the illegal drugs, perhaps Cal saw him as a loose end who knew too much.

Mathis Jericho was a different animal, though. He might have thought he didn't need Seth Cahill. If Cahill no longer owned the storage facility, maybe Mathis planned to keep the storage units full of morpheranyl when necessary, going behind Tyra Cahill's back. Or maybe Mathis had figured out another solution to the storage issue, but needed Cahill out of the way.

Either way, Fenway was glad she and Dez would question Mathis Jericho again.

———

Fenway walked into the coroner's suite, Dez following, and Sarah's head popped up from behind her monitor.

"Morning, Sarah."

"Check your email," Sarah said. "Seth Cahill's credit card charges, activity on his checking and savings accounts."

"Have you seen them?"

"He was a spender," Sarah replied. "A couple of hundred every three or four days at Bruno Zipper's."

"That new craft cocktail place on Fifth?"

"With the terrible music and the line around the block, yes." Sarah turned to her monitor and clicked her mouse. "All kinds of stuff like that—if it was *en vogue*, he was spending money on it. Two months ago, new titanium wheels for his Corvette at fifteen hundred a pop. The next day, Seth bought one of those online DNA testing things from Genome Genius."

"That's the expensive one with the three-day turnaround?"

Sarah nodded.

Fenway scoffed. "I *wish* our DNA testing was that fast."

Sarah scrolled onscreen. "There's more. Leather moccasins. Six hundred dollars at a record shop."

"How did he pay for all that?"

"Lots of cash deposits," Sarah said, her finger on the monitor. "I got a copy of some of the pages in that ledger. Kind of hard matching up the payments, because he kept the deposits under ten thousand."

"No automatic trigger for the Feds," Dez said.

Sarah nodded. "But we *did* total everything that made it into his accounts, everything he spent, and compared it to the ledger. The totals are fairly close, but the last few months, they're off by about five thousand dollars."

"He probably kept some of the cash. Easier to launder money if you spread the cash around."

Sarah shook her head. "I mean five thousand the other way. He's deposited about five thousand dollars more than what's listed in his ledger."

Fenway rubbed her chin. "Could he have been skimming from the people who were paying him? Keeping more money than he wrote in the ledger?"

Dez leaned against the counter. "Dangerous and stupid." Her phone dinged and she looked at the screen. "Well, well. It's a text from Callahan. Look who just showed up for his shift at Cahill Warehouse Storage."

"Mathis Jericho?"

Dez touched her nose and pointed at Fenway.

"Sarah, can you fill out a warrant application for Mr. Jericho's car?"

"Sure. And I was behind Judge Solano at Java Jim's. He's in early. I'll have it ready for you in ten minutes." Sarah sat at her workstation and turned her attention to the monitor.

"What are you hoping to find in his car?" Dez asked Fenway.

"I don't know of anyone else who could have picked up the shipment last night from the *Ariel,* do you? With any luck, we'll find evidence of morpheranyl in his car."

"And then we arrest him?"

"No—we convince him to tell us the whole truth." Fenway stretched. She needed another cup of coffee.

CHAPTER TEN

Ninety minutes later, Dez and Fenway pulled the red Impala up to the numeric keypad in front of the gate at Cahill Warehouse Storage. Dez rolled down the window, the foggy chill of the morning blowing into the car. Fenway gave the number to Dez, she punched it in, and the gate opened. Mathis's car sat in the employee area on the right-hand side. Fenway ran her finger along the edge of the folder on her lap.

"Office?" Dez asked.

"Let's drive around," Fenway said. "Mathis does maintenance and landscaping. I bet he's out here."

Dez nodded. "I still can't believe Judge Solano signed the warrant without an affidavit."

Fenway shrugged. "I think it'll hold up in court."

"Ha—let's hope it never comes to that."

As they rounded the corner of Building A, Mathis, dressed in beige cargo shorts, a white T-shirt, and a Los Angeles Dodgers baseball cap, pulled weeds from a planter next to the fence. He looked up as the Impala rounded the corner and narrowed his eyes when he saw Fenway and Dez.

The Impala slowed to a stop six feet from the planter, and Fenway got out with her folder.

"Good morning, Coroner," Mathis said, his voice flat. Bags under his eyes.

"We've got a warrant to search your car, Mr. Jericho."

His jaw dropped open. "My car?"

"That's right." Fenway cocked her head. "Remind me again where you were late Monday night, early Tuesday morning."

He squinted. "Monday night?"

"That's correct. The night Seth Cahill was killed."

"My apartment. Asleep."

Mathis Jericho's lies were at least consistent. Fenway cocked her head. "You sure you weren't near Puerto Avila beach?"

Mathis hesitated. "I'm not sure where that is."

"By the Vista del Rincón turnoff. There's a beach there, perfect for a catamaran coming from Mexico to anchor for an hour or two."

Mathis's expression hardened for a moment, but his face was otherwise inscrutable. "I'm not sure what you're talking about."

"You have a wetsuit?"

Mathis paused. "There's nothing illegal about owning a wetsuit."

"You know how to scuba dive, right? You were an instructor."

"Nothing illegal about that, either."

"All right." Fenway hooked her thumb over her shoulder toward Mathis's car. "Meet us at your vehicle. You got your keys?"

"Let me see the warrant."

"Sure." Fenway took the warrant paperwork out of the folder and handed it to Mathis. He took it, his hands shaking slightly, and began to read. He likely found the legalese inscrutable. Mathis flipped the first page over, then began to read the second page. He blinked three or four times, then handed the set of paperwork back to Fenway. His mouth turned down at the corners, but he nodded.

Dez made a three-point turn on the asphalt between the buildings, and Fenway followed a few steps behind Mathis Jericho on foot.

A few moments later, they arrived at Mathis's navy blue sedan. It could have been the same car Fenway had seen on the road near Portico Inlet early in the morning, but she couldn't be positive.

"Open the trunk," Fenway said.

Mathis reached into his pocket lethargically, his mouth twisted in regret. He pulled out a key fob and pushed a button. The trunk of the sedan popped open, the lid flinging itself upward and stopping at a sixty-degree angle to horizontal.

Fenway leaned over the open trunk. What a mess: empty Coke cans, fast food wrappers, a gym bag, a dirty beach towel. The bottom of the trunk had a rubberized weatherproof liner. Fenway leaned over further; a tiny patch of white powder was in one of the square crevices near the left taillight. She looked closer; another small patch of white two-thirds of the way on the right side.

Fenway straightened up, careful not to make contact with the powder. "I see a white powder on the liner, Mathis."

He was silent. How was Mathis so calm about the powder in his trunk?

She bobbed her head toward the Impala. "I've got an MTS kit in the back of the car. You know what that is?"

Mathis was quiet.

"We'll go over your trunk with this little vacuum cleaner. We only need two milligrams of powder to run the test—and I can see there's plenty. We mix it with water in a little test tube, we put a morpheranyl strip into the mixture. One pink line is a positive. That holds up in court—California vs. Washburn, if you want the history."

"I know what an MTS kit is."

"That's great, Mathis. So you know what the lab results will be. It'll go easier on you if you give us a statement now, rather than making me fill out hours of paperwork to get a lab report."

Mathis hesitated. "These are dangerous guys."

"Was Seth skimming money off the top?"

Mathis frowned and looked into Fenway's eyes. "If Seth was

stealing money, he didn't tell me about it. But I don't think Seth would do that. He knows how crazy these people are."

Fenway cocked her head. "You think they killed Seth?"

Looking down at the dirt in the planter, Mathis bit his lip.

Fenway cocked her head. "Are you afraid of them?"

Still no answer.

"If you cooperate, we could take them off the street. You wouldn't be in danger."

"I'm not sure you can do that."

"Then how about this?" Fenway asked. "The MTS kit can stay in our car."

Mathis paused. "Immunity for anything I say."

"Regarding the drug deals? I can ask the A.D.A. about immunity in exchange for your testimony." Fenway studied his face. "But not for murder. Did you kill Seth Cahill?"

"No!" His eyes went wide. "I'd never—"

"Because maybe Seth was stealing from you. Or maybe you wanted to take over Seth's business. Morpheranyl is quite lucrative. Four hundred million per shipment, by my calculations."

Mathis scoffed. "No way. Not that much. Not even close."

"But still a lot, right?"

Mathis was quiet.

"Come on," Fenway said. "Let's go into the station where we can have a conversation."

———

Dez drove them to the sheriff's office, but the interview room was taken. Fenway decided to improvise and sent Dez back to her desk before taking Mathis Jericho into the break room. More informal. Maybe he'd be more willing to talk.

Mathis wandered around the edge of the empty break room, stopping for a few seconds at the vending machine, then took a seat in one of the plastic chairs at a corner table.

Fenway tapped her card to the payment mechanism on the vending machine. After a beep, she tapped a button, then bent down and retrieved a bag of chips. "You want anything?"

Mathis slumped in his seat and folded his arms.

"You sure?"

He hesitated. "I think I saw a chocolate and peanut butter thing in the third row."

Fenway tapped her card to the machine again. After Fenway got the candy bar, she walked to the small table and Mathis reached for it.

Fenway pulled it away. "The truth."

Mathis hesitated, then nodded. She dropped the candy bar into his outstretched hand.

"How did you get involved in the morpheranyl trade?"

"I was only working as a scuba instructor for a few hours a week," Mathis said. "My main gig was at the sandwich shop down the street. Man, what a crappy job. My manager kept messing with my hours, but what else could I do? The scuba place wasn't even cutting paychecks half the time."

Fenway leaned back against the vending machine.

"Every so often, these two guys would come into the sandwich shop. An older guy who smokes weird cigarettes, and a tall, skinny, wiry guy. Not every week, but at all hours. Sometimes I worked the overnight shift, and they'd come in at two, three in the morning."

"How long was this going on?"

Mathis scratched his head. "Maybe six months. You remember there was a fire in those warehouses over on St. Ignatius Street?"

Fenway frowned. "When was this?"

"Two or three years ago."

"Ah, that explains it. Before I moved here." She pushed herself off the vending machine and took a seat across from Mathis. "So what happened?"

Mathis pressed his lips together. "So this warehouse on St.

Ignatius Street—I think they stored their Nyllie there. But the place burned down, then suddenly they had a storage issue."

"They talked about it in front of you?"

Mathis shrugged. "I've worked in the service industry long enough to know that sometimes workers behind the counter don't even register as real people."

Fenway nodded. Nurses, too—she remembered a few incidents when she worked at the clinic in Seattle.

"So I say, hey, there's a guy who owns a storage place down the road."

"Seth?"

"Right. He was in my scuba class. Anyway, the tall skinny one—that's Cal—he gives me a look like he's about to tell me to shut up. But the older guy, he had this white scraggly beard, like he was in some commercial for fish sticks—"

"Stephan Butler?"

"I never heard his name," Mathis said. "He told Cal to hold his horses. 'Maybe the kid can help us.' So Cal says, 'He doesn't know what he's getting into,' so I went back to making their Italian Club, but the old guy asks me to set up a meeting with Seth. Tells me when the two of them will be back."

"No way to contact them?"

Mathis shook his head. "They come to you, not the other way around." He tore the candy bar open and took a big bite, chewing with his mouth open. Fenway opened the bag of barbecue chips and put one in her mouth.

"Next time Seth has a scuba lesson," Mathis said through his chewing, "I tell him what time they want to meet, and then the day after the three of them met, Seth asks if I want a job at the storage place. It paid an extra three bucks an hour, more hours, and I wouldn't have to work overnights." Mathis paused. "Well, not at first."

"So you didn't know you were trafficking morpheranyl?"

Mathis put the candy bar down on the table and stared at it for a moment. "I kept my mouth shut. I figured if I didn't ask questions, they'd be able to trust me. Plus, I didn't want to know."

"Not a defense that will hold up in court."

Mathis shrugged. "Little late for that now."

Fenway took another chip out of the bag. "But you got more involved in the business." She popped the chip in her mouth and chewed.

"Yeah."

Fenway crinkled the bag of chips. "So as a former scuba instructor, are you the one who takes the morpheranyl out of the containers attached to the hulls of the *Ariel?*"

Mathis spun the half-wrapped candy bar around on the tabletop. "I mean, yeah, when the *Ariel* came along the beach, I'd be the one in the water. Seth wanted to learn, but he didn't have the knack for it."

"When we go through that ledger," Fenway said, "will we see a percentage of the sales go to you?"

Mathis shrugged. "You might see a percentage of sales go out. I don't think you'll see my name."

Fenway steepled her fingers, then leaned forward. "You showed up alone early Tuesday morning at Puerto Avila."

Mathis was quiet.

"I heard that Cal and Stephan didn't want to do business with you unless Seth was there."

He pushed the candy bar a few inches away. "I tried to find him. Had to decide if I wanted to show up alone or show up late. I showed up alone."

"Did the meeting go well?"

"Well—uh, not exactly. They asked where Seth was. When I said I didn't know, Cal said I better not be trying to trick him. I was like, what's to trick? You drop off the product, Seth and I store it, Venn picks it up when he's ready to process it—"

Fenway flinched and Mathis's eyes widened.

Anton Venn. Kingpin in the Central Valley. Fenway hadn't

thought his business extended to the coast. She took a normal breath, trying to make it seem like he'd said nothing out of the ordinary. Maybe Mathis wouldn't notice that she'd heard. "And you get paid, you give Cal and Stephan their cut?"

Mathis gave a dry chuckle. "If only it were that easy. No, Cal always stuck around until V—" He coughed. "Until the product got picked up. *He* got the money and gave Seth the, uh, storage fee."

"Thirty thousand dollars."

"For a big shipment, or if they need to store it a week or two, yeah."

"Thirty thousand is a lot of money for a storage unit."

"They lost over three million in product in the St. Ignatius fire. The Cahill storage facility has sprinklers, fire alarms, the whole thing. Gates with electronic monitoring, and an owner willing to put his ass on the line. That was peace of mind, and I think Seth was a good salesman. Able to convince Cal that peace of mind costs some money."

Fenway rustled the chip bag. "But that peace of mind went away."

Mathis grabbed the candy bar, pulled the wrapper down a little, and took another bite.

"When did Cal find out that Seth lost the storage facility to Tyra?"

Mathis swallowed. "Seth didn't want to tell him. We talked about the situation a couple of weeks ago after they picked up the last shipment for packaging."

"So it's not clear to you whether Seth told Cal that the storage facility would no longer be available for morpheranyl?"

Mathis shook his head.

"When did he tell you?"

"Uh—he didn't, really. I mean, I knew that he and Tyra were getting divorced. The walls in the office aren't thick enough to cover up their arguments. I knew Tyra asked for the storage business—she'd put in a lot of the investment, and Seth needed the money."

"Even with thirty-thousand-dollar payments every few weeks?"

"What do you think kept the business from going under?" Mathis said. "Seth worked it so that he spread those payments out into a few services to fake customers. Or that some storage units were rented that didn't get rented. Some of the storage unit numbers in the computer—fully rented—don't exist in the buildings."

"And Tyra never caught on?"

Mathis shook his head. "Seth was careful. He made everything look legit."

Fenway clasped her hands together and spoke carefully. "Mathis, you didn't just get three dollars an hour more when you came to work here. You got a cut of those 'storage fees' Seth got. You were the diver. Seth couldn't have done it without you."

Mathis stared at the top of the table.

"I bet he didn't give you anywhere close to half."

Mathis shrugged. "Yeah, you're right. But what was I gonna do? I couldn't make that kind of money anywhere else. Yeah, I had to work eight or ten hours three or four nights a month, and yeah, it's not fun going out into the Pacific in February, but I made good money, and like I said, I couldn't get it anywhere else."

Fenway bit her lip. So far, Mathis had cooperated. Maybe that would all change with Fenway's next question.

"What if you wanted to cut Seth out of the equation?" Fenway said.

Mathis frowned. "What?"

"The divorce agreement kicked Seth out of the storage business. Tyra's taking over. The way I see it, the morpheranyl trade can keep going as long as there's a diver to take the drugs from the blister to someone's car. Seems to me like Seth is not only keeping most of the money, but he's the least vital part of the whole business."

Mathis grinned. "I don't think you've ever done business with these guys before."

"Why do you say that?"

"Because they didn't trust me. They trusted Seth." He took another bite of the candy bar, then spoke with his mouth full. "Seth knew the accounts. He had the econ background. They saw me as an assistant—nothing more."

That was true. Fenway had pointed out that they didn't want to do business with Mathis when he showed up without Seth. "You might not have known that."

Mathis started laughing and put his hand over his mouth.

"What's so funny?"

"You seriously think I killed Seth to take over his business? How would that work? Without Seth's storage units, I don't have anywhere to put the Nyllie."

"You could rent another storage unit."

Mathis looked as if Fenway had insulted his mother. "Are you kidding? The storage places all close by nine o'clock in this town. And they've got cameras I can't turn off. No way."

"It doesn't take up much space," Fenway said. "A spare room in your apartment."

"Are you kidding? My roommate would kill me. If the people in charge of the Nyllie didn't kill me first."

Fenway looked thoughtfully across the table. He may have been right about not having other storage options, yet he picked at the corner of the candy bar wrapper. He was hiding something.

"Did Tyra know about Seth's business arrangements?" She remembered the look of utter confusion on Tyra's face when Fenway showed her the ledger—but maybe Tyra had great acting talent, and she and Mathis *were* working together.

"I don't know if she found out about Seth storing the drugs."

Fenway sat back in her chair and thought for a moment, her chin in her hand. Had Tyra discovered that the illegal storage of morpheranyl propped up the storage business? Had she found out after she'd already taken control of Cahill Warehouse Storage? She and Seth could have fought over a number of things: getting the drugs out of the storage facility, misrepresenting the viability of the business during the divorce proceedings, not to mention his infidelity. Any of those might anger her enough to kill her ex-husband.

If Tyra found out about the morpheranyl, she'd have a terrible decision to make: either go out of business or keep the operation going. Maybe she'd want to replace Seth in the operation. That might be amenable to all involved except Seth: same location, same deal, no finding a new place. Tyra had the business background that Mathis didn't.

Mathis had said nothing, of course, but he might be purposely misdirecting Fenway.

Neither Mathis nor Tyra would have to pull the trigger, so to speak. If Tyra could replace Seth, that meant that Seth was expendable. But Seth would have been a loose end: his knowledge of the morpheranyl business, the identity of the players, and the operational logistics would make him a liability. Killing Seth would make sure he couldn't talk. Tyra and Mathis could plan to cut Seth out of the business, install Tyra as the new storage representative, and be sure that someone else would see that Seth was killed.

"You ever talk to Tyra about the business?"

Mathis shook his head. "I remember one day, right before Thanksgiving, we had Channel 12 on the TV in the office, and the news showed a special story on how there'd been forty morpheranyl deaths that year. A new record for Dominguez County. And Tyra—man, maybe she'd been drinking or what, because she starts swearing, yelling, breaking things."

"Breaking things?" If Tyra had a history of violence, Fenway might look more closely at her.

"Just a cheap plastic clipboard—she raised it over her head and slammed it down on the counter so hard it broke in half. But I've never seen her like that before. After the clipboard broke, she stared at it for a while. It felt like an hour. Then she went into her office and slammed the door."

"Did you ever find out what got her so upset?"

"No."

"You think the morpheranyl report triggered something? That Seth kept the business afloat with something illegal and she couldn't get out from under it?"

"Maybe." Mathis shrugged. "Like I said, I heard them fighting. The occasional screaming match where one of them says something about the business—or Seth hooking up with another woman. But otherwise, I don't know what goes on between the two of them."

"Tyra didn't talk about it after she broke the clipboard?"

"No. I went out and fixed a sprinkler head, came back in, and knocked on her office door. Asked if she was all right. Tyra asked me to stay late. Said she had to go downtown for something—she wouldn't tell me what. Happy Thanksgiving to me."

"Where was Seth when all this happened?"

Mathis put the candy bar down on the table. "He told me he was out of town."

Fenway arched an eyebrow. "Does that mean he was with Miranda Duchy?"

"He didn't tell me in so many words, but I assume so. Pretty obvious that he and Miranda were together. Come on—a conference for storage vendors the week of Thanksgiving in San Diego? It's like he thought Tyra was stupid."

Maybe that's why Tyra lawyered up. Seth had not only brazenly humiliated her with Miranda Duchy, but he'd possibly tricked her into giving him money for his half of a business that would fail without the illegal activity to support it.

"One more thing," Fenway said. "We were reviewing the video footage from Monday night and early Tuesday. The storage facility has cameras all around."

Mathis was silent.

Fenway cocked her head. "Yeah, you already know that we saw a whole lot of nothing. Seth turned off the cameras, didn't he?"

Mathis rolled his shoulders like his muscles were too tight. "We turn them off on shipment days. Can't have either of us on camera bringing Nyllie into the storage facility."

Of course. Seth wouldn't have to hide or destroy evidence that hadn't been captured in the first place. "Final question," Fenway said.

Mathis's eyes glazed over.

"We ran into the *Ariel*'s captain on Belvedere Beach this morning," she said.

Mathis flinched.

"From what you've told me, he and Cal wouldn't trust you with the Nyllie. But it seems they trusted *someone* with it last night." She tilted her head. "Do you know anything about that?"

He shrugged. "Nope. Those guys must have figured out another place to store the Nyllie."

She asked a few more questions, but Mathis was running out of steam.

"Okay, we're done for now," Fenway said. "Thanks for your cooperation. I can take you back to the storage facility."

Mathis popped the rest of the candy bar in his mouth, then stood and went to the door of the break room, leaving his wrapper in the middle of the table. Fenway threw it in the trash.

Tyra and Mathis were the top two suspects right now, at least in Fenway's mind.

But those in the morpheranyl business couldn't be overlooked either. Maybe the killer had simply patched up a loose end.

Or maybe Seth's murder was meant to send a message.

Fenway walked out to the parking garage, Mathis following close behind her—then stopped in her tracks.

"What's wrong?" Mathis said.

"My car. It's still in the parking lot at Puerto Avila beach. Come on, I'll ask someone else to drive you back."

CHAPTER ELEVEN

After asking Deputy Brian Callahan to take Mathis back to the storage facility, Fenway called Dez to take her to get her car. A few minutes later, they met at the Impala and got in.

Fenway relaxed in the pleasant warmth of the car, the fog having burned off during the Mathis Jericho interview. The sun shone brightly, though the ocean breeze still had a hint of chill in it.

Dez started the engine, rolling down the windows, then switched the car off. "Mathis give you anything?"

"Too much." Fenway ran a hand through her hair. "I'm swimming in potential suspects and motives and illegal activities."

"Let's hear it before we get on the road."

"Seth and Mathis were taking kilos of morpheranyl from the *Ariel* and storing it at Cahill Warehouse Storage. Then someone from the Venn organization would pick it up—"

"Wait—Anton Venn?"

"I assume. Mathis got a little freaked out when he realized he'd said the name *Venn*, so I didn't get confirmation he meant *Anton* Venn. But who else? He wasn't talking about Venn diagrams." She leaned back in the seat. "Someone from Venn's organization picks up the drugs when everything is ready for packaging."

"Think that's what the ledger tracks?"

"A safe assumption. I don't think Mathis had any idea about the ledger. But if we can determine what he got paid, we could cross-reference those payments with stuff in the ledger."

Dez stared out the windshield across the parking lot.

"What is it?"

"I don't like the idea of asking the A.D.A. to give Mathis immunity. Last year we had fifty-two morpheranyl deaths in Dominguez County. If we can tie these shipments of morpheranyl to any of these deaths, we can charge Mathis with manslaughter. That'll give us leverage."

"Leverage to use against whom? Anton Venn? We wouldn't know he's involved with this if Mathis Jericho hadn't said something. Mathis wouldn't have talked otherwise."

Dez looked at Fenway sideways. "Oh—you haven't okayed immunity with the D.A."

"I didn't promise him anything."

"You left the testing kit in the car. You didn't even take—"

"We both know the warrant was signed without a supporting affidavit—and I don't want to gamble on whether it'll get thrown out if we find the killer, and this goes to trial. Mathis gave us a ton of information, and as far as the courts should be concerned, the warrant had nothing to do with it. I don't want some defense lawyer making a 'fruit of the poisonous tree' argument. Right now, there's a warrant hanging over Mathis's head that we simply didn't execute."

"But if—"

Fenway held up her hand. "If vice wants to use the warrant, they can. If the DEA wants to get involved, they can. My job is to find who killed Seth Cahill, not arrest a kid who drove a trunkload of drugs twenty miles a couple times a month."

Dez shook her head. "Did you at least read him his rights?"

Fenway scoffed. "Are you kidding? And scare him off? I got information."

"What if he'd confessed to killing Seth Cahill?"

Fenway paused. "Then I would have reassessed the situation. But I didn't expect him to confess."

Dez shook her head. "Yeah, yeah, all right. Maybe I would have done the same thing. But it's a gray area."

"Duly noted." Fenway cleared her throat. "Okay, lots of suspects. Seth hid facts from everyone. From what Mathis said, I don't think Tyra knew about Seth's illegal activities until recently. Maybe after she took control of the business. The Nyllie dealers and transporters may not know Cahill Warehouse won't be available for storage in the very near future—and if Seth told them, he only told them a week or two ago."

"Or maybe even the night he was killed." Dez knitted her brow. "So everyone he lied to is a suspect."

"Right." Fenway held up an index finger. "Okay, so Cal—that's Calvin Banning—isn't the trusting type. He might have gotten mad at Seth for screwing up his business processes."

"Makes sense."

"Mathis did most of the work, though." Fenway held up a second finger. "He got in freezing water late at night, pulled the kilos of morpheranyl from the storage containers on the bottom of the hulls, and schlepped them into his car. He might have thought he deserved a bigger cut of the storage fees."

"Is that borne out by the evidence?"

"Not yet. But maybe there's something in the ledger. Easy enough to check." Fenway pressed her lips together. "Calvin and Stephan did business with Seth and Mathis. Mathis told me they wouldn't do business without Seth. Calvin trusted Seth, not Mathis."

"According to Mathis," Dez pointed out.

"Right, so let's take that with a grain of salt. We still have the problem that Seth lost access to the storage business because of the divorce settlement.”

“So that eliminates Mathis as a suspect?”

“Not necessarily.” Fenway’s ring finger joined the other two fingers. “A couple of possibilities. Either Tyra is pissed off when she finds out about Seth’s dealings with the morpheranyl dealers, or she decides to replace him. She still has Mathis—maybe she offers a bigger cut to him—”

“In exchange for killing him?”

“No, he’s not the one who brought down the hammer. Once the drug dealers realize Seth is a liability, *they* kill him. Tyra and Mathis don’t have to touch him.”

Dez crossed her arms in the driver’s seat. “Theories without evidence?”

“We have to start somewhere.”

Fenway’s phone buzzed. She took it out of her purse. McVie.

r u making it back 4 breakfast?

Oh—definitely not. Already ten-thirty. She texted back.

FENWAY

Sorry, I can’t.

I’m surprised you’re not already at the Pilates appointment

MCVIE

Been here 4 an hour

Next to Hula Shack

Sure u dont want 2 join me for Portuguese sausage & eggs

FENWAY

Can’t today but you have fun - some of us work for a living

. . .

Dez glanced over at Fenway. "Is that Craig?"

"Yeah." Fenway blinked. She'd meant her last text to be playful, but did it come across as snide? She sent a smiley-face emoji to take the edge off it.

Dez harrumphed, starting the car again. "Not that it matters, but I told him he's an idiot."

"For leaving? You wouldn't do the same if Megan was your daughter?"

"She's seventeen. Megan's already decided she's moving a thousand miles away. Craig being five miles down the road won't change anything. In fact, it might drive a wedge between them." Dez checked the rear-view mirror, took off the emergency brake, and put the car into reverse. "Put your seatbelt on."

"Right, my Accord is still in the Puerto Avila parking lot."

"Later. Right now, we're heading to San Miguelito. Autopsy on Seth Cahill. Michi texted me right after you called."

"Oh. Yeah, that's more important."

"Plus," Dez said, texting from her seat, "Michi knows the captain who runs vice in San Miguelito. If anyone knows about the ins and outs of Anton Venn's morpheranyl trade, it's him."

Forty minutes later, they pulled up to the county offices in San Miguelito. Dr. Michi Yasuda met them in the lobby, and she kissed Dez's cheek, then blushed.

"Coroner Stevenson, excellent to see you again," Dr. Yasuda said, the color fading from her cheeks. "I've got Mr. Cahill on the table if you want to take a look." She glanced at Dez. "Captain Alvidrez is already here."

Dr. Yasuda turned and rushed through the door on their left, and Fenway ran to keep up. Dez fell a step behind as they turned the corner and went down the stairs, Yasuda arriving at the bottom half a flight before Fenway.

A moment later, they were in the morgue, a steel table with a body covered by a sheet. A Latino man, about six feet tall, wiry and dressed in the black San Miguelito officers' uniform, sat on a high stool about five feet from the steel table.

"Have you met?" Dr. Yasuda said, snapping on a fresh set of latex gloves and putting on a surgical mask.

Fenway turned toward the man. "Coroner Fenway Stevenson from Dominguez County."

"Of course. Steve Alvidrez." He raised his gloved hand. "I'd shake your hand, but I'm already gloved up. I've been running a task force with Sheriff Donnelly for almost a year. Nice to meet another member of the team."

Fenway nodded, pulling a medical mask over her nose and mouth. "Good to meet you, too."

"Just wanted to show you the wound," Yasuda said, grasping the top of the sheet and pulling it down. The body of Seth Cahill lay under the sheet, on its stomach. Michi took a bullet probe, long and straight, and pointed to the wound on the back of Cahill's skull. "I believe Dez—Sergeant Roubideaux—mentioned this wound could have been made with the claw end of a hammer." Michi took the probe away and put it back on the tool tray next to the steel table. "I believe the weapon is, specifically, a framing hammer."

"What's the difference between a framing hammer and a regular hammer?" Alvidrez asked.

"Commonly twenty-eight or thirty-two ounces, whereas a generic household hammer is less than half that. More importantly, however, is that the claw side of a framing hammer is flat, not curved, and a flat claw definitely created this wound."

"Can you narrow down the weapon any more?" asked Fenway.

"Given the raw edges of the wound, I can't say how heavy the hammer was, or who the manufacturer might be. McCrate Industries, Brosius, and Lemoine Steel all make multiple framing hammers that would potentially match this wound. As such, it's also hard to determine the height of the assailant. I'd say between five foot six and six feet tall, but without knowing the position of Seth Cahill's body during the assault, I wouldn't put much stock into that estimate."

"You can buy these hammers at most hardware stores?"

"That's correct," said Dr. Yasuda.

Fenway grunted. Tyra Cahill, Mathis Jericho, Hope Dunkelman, George Pope, Calvin Banning, and Stephan Butler were all in that height range. Maybe even Miranda Duchy. The only person who didn't fit the height profile was Isabella Chan.

"We believe Seth Cahill did business with Anton Venn's cartel," Dez said.

Alvidrez shook his head. "Not to say that this death is entirely unrelated, but it wasn't a message or a business disagreement. Not from Venn, at least." He stood and stepped closer to the corpse. "Venn's cartel likes Glock 19s. You'd see a nine-millimeter in the heart and another between the eyes."

"You're sure?"

"I'd love this to be a Venn hit. We thought we were close to nabbing one of their lieutenants back in January. Set up the deal with one of our guys, but when we showed up, no evidence. I think someone tipped them off."

"My theory is that a confidential informant didn't stay confidential," Dr. Yasuda said.

The lines around Alvidrez's eyes crinkled. "However we got burned back then, *this* isn't a Venn hit. If Mr. Cahill had attacked one of Venn's lieutenants or employees unexpectedly, perhaps you'd see this as a result of self-defense or a counterattack in the heat of the moment. But if you're thinking Venn planned to take Mr. Cahill out, this isn't how they'd do it."

Dr. Yasuda nodded. "Sorry to waste your time, Captain."

He shook his head. "Not at all. It's helpful to know that Anton Venn's influence now extends all the way to the coast. It's not good news for us, but I'm glad we're aware. Makes the task force with Sheriff Donnelly that much more important."

Dr. Yasuda turned to Fenway. "The killer is right-handed, although that describes eighty-five percent of the population."

"Anything else? DNA? Under his nails? Clothing transfer?"

"Nothing like that, unless you count the scuff marks on the backs of his shoes." Yasuda pulled the sheet away from Cahill's left arm. "I saw that his pinkie and ring fingers were at a slightly odd angle. A scan showed healed fractures of the pinkie and ring finger on his left hand. If I had to guess, it might have been three to four months ago. From the looks of his hand, a professional surgeon set the broken fingers."

"What kind of break?" Fenway asked.

Yasuda's eyes danced. "Exactly the right question. A rotational injury. As if someone twisted the fingers on purpose."

Fenway glanced at Alvidrez. "Would that be the type of injury caused by someone in the Venn cartel?"

Alvidrez's brows knotted above his mask. "Yes, I've seen it before."

"But the injury occurred so long ago, we can't conclude it had anything to do with Mr. Cahill's murder."

Fenway nodded. She wondered if the morpheranyl that Seth Cahill had stored in his facility had been the same morpheranyl that killed Scott Behrens and the other people who had died of the overdose.

Dr. Yasuda frowned. "Cahill... Cahill."

"What is it?"

Dr. Yasuda stepped to the counter, took a glove off, and flipped through the paperwork on her clipboard. "Ah, yes, here. Tyra Cahill, spouse."

"Ex-wife," Fenway said. "The divorce was finalized a week or two ago." She stared at the back of Yasuda's head. "What about Tyra Cahill?"

"I recognize the name."

"We know her corpse didn't show up on your table, though, right?"

"Oh, of course not. The name rings a bell, that's all. Maybe I ran into her at a social event."

Dez guffawed.

Dr. Yasuda looked up at her, wide-eyed.

"Oh, come on," Dez said. "You haven't been to a social event this millennium."

"Are you suggesting I ran into her in the morgue?"

"If you remember where," Fenway interrupted, steering the conversation back on track, "let me know."

"Certainly." Dr. Yasuda cleared her throat. "Would you like to go over the body with me?" Her eyes sparkled. "Make sure I didn't miss anything?"

"Need me for anything else, Michi?" Alvidrez asked.

"No."

"Thank you for your time, Captain," Fenway said.

"I'll walk you out." Dez stood from her stool and hurried to the door.

When they had left, Dr. Yasuda grinned. "You have now witnessed the real reason Dez didn't run for coroner," she said. "My wife acts tough, but she doesn't have the stomach for autopsies."

The two of them closely examined the body but found nothing of note. No bruising, no recent injuries, no tattoos or, besides the Y-incision that Dr. Yasuda had made on the chest and sewn up the day before, any notable scars.

"I was hoping to find something that would push me in a more specific direction," Fenway said. "Did your team get anything from the rug?"

Dr. Yasuda pulled the sheet all the way up again. "The lab results will be back in the next week or so. Are you expecting anything out of the ordinary?"

Fenway shrugged. "The rug from Cahill's office is missing, and I'm pretty sure it's the one used to wrap up the body."

Dr. Yasuda paused. "Wouldn't that suggest the murder occurred in the office?"

Fenway pulled off her gloves and considered this for a moment. "I suppose it's possible," she said, "but I saw no signs of a struggle in the office. No blood spatters, either."

Dr. Yasuda moved the tools off the tray into a shallow tub. "Murder with the claw end of a framing hammer suggests no premeditation," Dr. Yasuda said.

"Sure."

"Therefore, if the murder did not occur in Mr. Cahill's office, where the rug lay, someone knew enough about the office layout to retrieve the rug and use it to wrap the body."

Fenway nodded slowly. "An excellent point." She paused. "Someone who knew the facility well—that would be Mathis Jericho or Isabella Chan, and of course Tyra Cahill."

Yasuda's forehead wrinkled.

"Still can't think of where you recognize Tyra Cahill?"

"No. It feels like the answer is right on the tip of my tongue." Dr. Yasuda gave Fenway a pained smile. "I'm sure I'll think of it at three in the morning."

"The people involved in the drug deals might know about the rug in Seth's office, too," Fenway mused. "I imagine they've been to the facility to drop off and pick up the morpheranyl. And I bet Seth took them into his office to pay him or to discuss negotiation terms."

"It's possible." Dr. Yasuda walked to the hazardous waste bin and disposed of her gloves. "Although Mr. Cahill's corpse isn't providing a wealth of clues, it appears you have no shortage of murder suspects."

Fenway puttered around the work area, helping Dr. Yasuda clean up. A few moments later, the door to the morgue opened and Dez popped her head in.

"Fenway? You all finished up?"

"Yes."

"Body's about to go back in the drawer," Dr. Yasuda said. "Sure you don't want to take a look?"

"I'm good." Dez walked into the room and turned to Fenway. "That was Deputy Salvador. Let's head back."

"Why?"

"Miranda Duchy wants to file a restraining order against Tyra Cahill."

CHAPTER TWELVE

"Against Tyra?" Fenway asked. "What for?"

"Miss Duchy says that Tyra stopped by her house about an hour ago."

"Not a good idea for Tyra, but that in itself isn't illegal."

"According to Miss Duchy, Tyra was threatening her," Dez said. "Apparently, Tyra dumped about thirty cardboard boxes all over the front yard."

Fenway chortled. "All of Seth's boxes he was supposed to take with him last night. Now she's giving everything to the mistress." She paused. "But we don't take applications for restraining orders. Duchy has to go online. Form CH-100. Or she needs to talk to her lawyer."

"Miranda Duchy is, uh, not content with filling out forms online," Dez said dryly. "Nor with talking to a mere sheriff's deputy."

"Aha. She wants to speak to the manager."

Dez chuckled. "Salvador said she could handle it, but I thought we could use Duchy's insistence as an excuse to interview her."

"Mark interviewed her, but yeah, you and I should talk with her, too. Especially now that we know more."

"And you saw Mark's notes—Duchy didn't provide a good alibi. Out for a drive, she said."

Fenway nodded, then turned to Dr. Yasuda. "You okay here?"

"I'll be fine," said Dr. Yasuda. "I'll see you at home, Dez."

"You'll shower before I get back, right?"

Dr. Yasuda rolled her eyes.

Fenway and Dez left the morgue and walked up the stairs at a much more reasonable pace than they'd come down. They stopped in the lobby.

"She says she'll shower," Dez muttered, "but I bet she's gonna shower *here*. This place smells like formaldehyde and blood, and she'll get home and still have the morgue stink on her." She shook her head. "I'll meet you at the car." She turned and walked down a hallway with a sign that said "Restrooms" with an arrow.

Fenway stepped out of the lobby into the parking lot and took her phone out. She texted Melissa.

> Anything on the camera footage yet?

Three dots—Melissa was typing back. Fenway walked to the Impala as she waited for the text to appear. A ding.

> I got Patrick to cross-reference the dates and times of Seth Cahill turning off the cameras at the storage facility and disconnecting his Corvette's SafeBoard security system

> The dates all match—the times are all within ten minutes of the systems turning off

So Seth hadn't just turned off the cameras; he'd been taking pains to hide all evidence of the drug transactions and transport.

The Impala chirped as it unlocked, and Dez appeared with the key fob in her hand. "Ready to go?"

They got in.

Fenway tapped the phone app on her screen and called Sarah as Dez started the engine.

"Hey, Fenway," Sarah answered. "Did the body tell you anything?"

"Only that the murder weapon was a framing hammer, and we're looking for a right-handed killer."

"So, no."

"Add it to the report anyway. Also, I need you to look into something. You might need Patrick's help."

"Sure," Sarah said.

"A will. Life insurance. Anything like that. Did Seth Cahill leave anything to anyone? Did he have any beneficiaries to his life insurance?"

"Anyone who'd benefit from his death."

"That's right." Fenway paused. "You know how to fill out those IT forms so Patrick gives you the right info. I may have taken him to dinner at Dos Milagros, but he still won't process my requests if I don't fill out the forms the way he wants."

Sarah paused.

"What?"

"He talks all the time about when you took him to Dos Milagros. I think it was the highlight of his year."

"Are you kidding me? We talked about how duck tongues have bones that explode when you cook 'em."

"A little grace, Fenway."

Fenway blinked.

"What do you mean, a little grace?"

"Oh, Fenway, you're not stupid. You're often very compassionate. You made me feel welcome in the office. But you're not doing the same for Patrick."

Fenway bit her lip. Patrick was infuriating.

But more infuriating was that Sarah was right.

"I'll work on it," Fenway mumbled.

"And I'll work on Seth Cahill's beneficiaries."

"Thanks."

It took twenty minutes to get back to Estancia and another five to drive to Sycorax Hill and pull up in front of Miranda Duchy's house. On the way, Fenway filled Dez in on all the information she'd gotten from her interview with Mathis, and what little she had gleaned from the body after Dez had left the room.

"We meeting Celeste there?"

"No. Salvador said she didn't feel she could do anything else. She's taken the statement, but Duchy will be waiting to talk to someone 'in charge.'"

"Celeste will be the one in charge before too long."

"How's the process going?" Dez looked out of the corner of her eye at Fenway.

"I asked HR for a status update yesterday. They should have all my interview notes."

"You're not thinking about giving the job to Callahan, are you?"

Fenway looked at Dez out of the corner of her eye. "He's a good guy, but he doesn't have the head for detective work. He's still a little green. Really showed when I interviewed him."

"He has more service years than Celeste."

"The years haven't un-greened him." Fenway frowned. She checked her email. Nothing from HR. Her morning had started at three o'clock and she'd barely been in the office. She promised herself she'd call HR as soon as she got back.

Miranda Duchy's house was just as ostentatious as Fenway's father's house, but on a smaller scale and without acreage. Still five or six times as big as the square footage of Fenway's apartment, but not quite a third of the size of Nathaniel Ferris's oceanfront mansion.

Still, there were faux-marble columns going up twenty feet and a stone façade surrounding two ten-foot-high double doors. Fenway sighed. She and Dez got out of the Impala, which Dez left in the circular driveway.

A wide expanse of well-manicured lawn ran between the front porch and the sidewalk, and in the middle of the verdant grass sat five stacks of moving boxes of varying sizes. A few of them said "Seth" in a scrawl.

"Tyra's handiwork," Dez said.

Fenway and Dez strode up to the double doors.

Fenway reached out and rang the doorbell—a PorchRight camera doorbell. Miranda Duchy may have had impressive Doric columns, but the presence of the cheap PorchRight suggested no expensive camera-based security system around the house's perimeter.

A pale-skinned white woman answered the door, perhaps five or six years older than Fenway. Her blonde hair had a touch of auburn —an expensive color treatment, if Fenway had to guess—and she was elegant and gorgeous, dressed in a simple asymmetrical blouse with one shoulder exposed, and expensive-looking designer jeans in a deep denim blue.

"Miranda Duchy?"

The woman nodded. Whatever Fenway expected, Miranda Duchy wasn't it. She supposed she'd thought Miranda Duchy would be twenty years younger than Seth Cahill, maybe a little trashy. Not older, not elegant.

"Coroner Fenway Stevenson." She motioned to Dez. "And Sergeant Desirée Roubideaux."

"I could tell the deputy thought I was being silly," Duchy said, "but I don't feel safe with Seth's ex-wife being so confrontational. I know it's only a piece of paper, but I think a restraining order—at least so she can't come to my house—would work. Tyra doesn't seem unreasonable. Perhaps she'll see that coming to my house and screaming isn't rational."

"Can you lead us through what exactly happened?" Fenway asked.

"I was working from the office, near the back of the house," Duchy began. "I was on a conference call when the bell rang."

"Did you answer the door?"

"No, it's usually a delivery," Duchy said. "When it's not a delivery, it's a salesperson or a teenager selling chocolate bars to send their basketball team to some tournament in Arizona."

"So you didn't get the door."

"Not at first. But the bell rang twice, then three times, and then I heard pounding on the door. I excused myself from the call and looked at my phone—I've got one of those doorbell camera apps— and I could see Tyra, slamming her open palm against the door."

"You answered the door when she was so clearly agitated?"

"Uh—no. I needed to get back to my call," Duchy said. "Tyra isn't exactly my friend, but until today, I wouldn't call us bitter enemies. Seth and Tyra—their romance had run its course. They'd been separated twice before and had gotten back together. But it was clear Seth was simply going through the motions, and after a few months of knowing each other, both Seth and I had to admit we'd fallen in love. He was a client of my previous employer; that's how we met. When I left my husband and started my new job, Seth and I started seeing each other romantically. I'll admit the timing wasn't ideal, and I can understand that Tyra feels wronged. I'd feel the same in her situation. But I never thought she'd be so hostile."

"My understanding is that Seth had agreed to take his belongings from the house that he and Tyra used to share, and that he had failed to do so on multiple occasions."

Duchy folded her arms. "Unfortunately, that sounds like something Seth would do. Just to push Tyra's buttons."

And that didn't scream 'red flag'? But Fenway kept her mouth shut.

"But look—leaving all those boxes on the lawn like that? And screaming at me? That's uncalled for."

"I understand that it's not an ideal situation." Fenway gave Miranda her best sympathetic face, Sarah's words about compassion ringing in her ears. "But try to understand—Tyra was grieving the loss of her marriage. Now she has to grieve her ex-husband, and their recent divorce must make her feelings rather complex."

"I'm sure that's what you think is going on—" Then Miranda stopped talking.

Fenway pressed her lips together. What was that supposed to mean? For a second, Fenway thought Miranda implied that Fenway and Dez took Tyra's side because they were all Black. Ganging up on Miranda. Fenway studied Miranda's face. Were her cheeks reddening?

Then Miranda sniffed and put her hands on her hips, all trace of embarrassment gone. "I understand there are a host of good explanations *why* she behaved in an abusive and irrational manner, but her actions are affecting me. This isn't acceptable—I don't care who she is or what excuses she gives you."

Dez nodded. "We can point you to the form to apply for a restraining order. You can fill it out online, but you'll have to make the trip into the sheriff's office in order to get it processed."

Miranda nodded. "I expected as much."

"I noticed you have one of those doorbell cameras. Would you mind letting us see the footage of Tyra coming here?"

"Yes. You can see the threats for yourself. Let me get my phone."

Duchy pushed the door closed as she disappeared into the house.

"What do you think, Dez?"

"I think someone isn't processing their grief very well. Her therapist will have a field day."

"I mean, how do you think we should transition this into an interview?"

Dez shrugged. "Let's watch the footage. We might be able to slide the conversation from where Tyra is to where Miranda *was*."

"Right."

After a moment, the door opened again. "Okay," Duchy said, out of breath. "I've cued it to where they show up."

Fenway raised her eyebrows. "They?"

"She came with a man. White guy, gray at his temples, mustache and goatee. New boyfriend, maybe?"

Or maybe an old high school friend—Miranda's description sounded like George Pope.

Duchy tapped the screen and the footage started. She turned the screen so Fenway and Dez could both see it.

The camera showed the same SUV that George Pope had driven the afternoon that Fenway found Seth Cahill's body at the storage unit. The SUV pulled up in the circular driveway. A white man got out of the passenger door—Fenway had to squint before she could make out George Pope's features—and the rear tailgate popped open and raised to its full open height.

A Black woman appeared, her back to the camera. She turned; it was Tyra Cahill. She hefted a box out. George Pope hurried to the back of the SUV and took the box from Tyra, then rested it on the bumper and put another box on top of it. Tyra traipsed over the lawn and pointed for Pope to set the boxes down at her feet. Between the small speaker on Duchy's smartphone and the distance from the doorbell, they heard no audio.

This went on for ten minutes as Tyra and George pulled more than twenty boxes from the back of the SUV and put them on the grass, with Pope placing the boxes less and less neatly on the lawn as the minutes ticked by.

Then Tyra came up to the doorbell and rang. She stood directly in front of the doorbell camera, her light blue blouse all that could be seen. Her voice boomed, even over the tinny smartphone speaker. "Hey, Miranda, come get my ex-husband's shit!"

She stood in front of the camera for what seemed like an awkwardly long time. She reached out and rang the doorbell again.

"Miranda! I said get your shit! You wanted him—well, now you can take what's left of him!" An edge crept into Tyra's voice—not anger exactly, but displeasure. Exasperation. But her voice cracked on *what's left of him*, and for a brief moment, Tyra's lip trembled.

Then she stepped forward, her face out of the camera frame, and banged on the door loudly.

Nothing was visible onscreen for a full three minutes except for Tyra's blouse, every thirty seconds or so another knock. It felt like an hour.

Finally, Tyra backed away from the door a couple of feet, though she still took up most of the frame. A man's voice behind her— George Pope, it sounded like, but Fenway couldn't see him. The voice was too far away to be distinct.

"No, I'm sure her car is in the garage. She's home, I can feel it."

Another unintelligible string of syllables from Pope.

"This isn't my *job*, George. He promised me he'd take all his shit, but these boxes have been in my living room for a month."

George spoke again. "You've returned them now, but..." Then his voice got quieter, and Fenway couldn't understand anymore.

"She's home. I know she is. If we leave those boxes there and someone steals them, it's her own damn fault."

Pope said something else.

"Yeah, fine, I guess you're right." Tyra slumped her shoulders. She walked off the porch—then turned and hurried back onto the landing, where she extended both middle fingers right in front of the doorbell camera. "Chicken shit," Tyra yelled. "Homewrecker chicken shit. *You're* the reason he's dead."

Suddenly George appeared at her side, taking her elbow, pulling her away.

They walked back to Tyra's SUV. Tyra started to walk to the driver's side, but George stopped her, leaned close to her ear. Tyra stopped, nodded, and the rest of the fight went out of her. She let George lead her to the passenger door. He opened it for her, and she got in. George went around the back of the SUV, stopped and pinched the bridge of his nose and took a deep breath, then walked to the driver's side. A moment later, the engine started, and the SUV drove out of the camera eye.

Miranda Duchy tapped the phone screen to stop the video.

She raised her head, a triumphant look in her eye.

Fenway cocked her head. "What do you think this proves, Ms. Duchy?"

"It's clearly a threat," Duchy said.

Fenway blinked. "I didn't hear Tyra make any threats."

"She called me a 'chicken shit.'" Miranda bristled. "She wanted to fight me."

Fenway bit her lip. "I didn't hear her challenge you—"

"Of course, she didn't say that directly." Miranda scoffed. "But it's like when organized crime families say, 'I'll take care of him,' and everyone knows 'take care of' means 'kill.'"

Fenway raised one eyebrow.

"She called me a coward," Miranda insisted, "to lure me into a fight. How *else* could it be interpreted?"

Fenway shifted her weight from foot to foot. She glanced at Dez's face, but Dez stared impassively back as if to say, *You're doing great, no need for me to intervene.* So she turned back to Duchy. "I'm not sure the judge will interpret Tyra's words that way. If not, you won't get a restraining order."

"If she didn't threaten me, what would you call it?" Duchy folded her arms.

"An angry ex-wife delivering her ex-husband's belongings."

"She came over specifically to create an excuse to fight me. I don't want her to come over anymore."

Fenway shook her head. "Tyra wanted Seth to take those boxes, and Seth *agreed* to take the boxes." Fenway looked Miranda in the eyes. "If I review their divorce paperwork, will I find out that a written agreement includes a date when Seth will remove his belongings from the house?"

Miranda looked at the ground.

"You might not have *wanted* his stuff—"

"No. It's all hideous."

"—but if the judge said they're his, then Tyra is responsible for giving them to Seth. Or, in this case, bringing his belongings to where Seth lived." Fenway crossed her arms. "Even if Tyra planned to lure you into fighting her, she was following the divorce agreement."

"Seth is—" Miranda Duchy's face, taut and tense, suddenly crumpled. She bowed her head and squeezed her eyes tight. Her shoulders began to shake.

After a moment, Dez cleared her throat. Fenway looked up at her, and Dez motioned with her head toward Duchy.

"I'm sorry," Fenway said, taking a step closer to Duchy, and suddenly Duchy leaned against Fenway, body wracked with sobs. "Hey," Fenway said, "hey, hey. It's—" She swallowed hard. She'd been here, too. After Fenway's mother died, so many people—friends, former co-workers, neighbors—had stood awkwardly in the room as Fenway sobbed and tried to get herself under control.

Duchy shifted her weight after a moment, then wiped her eyes delicately with the back of her hand. "Sorry," she gulped. "I—I don't know what came over me."

Fenway patted Duchy's shoulder. "You've been through a lot."

Duchy took a deep, shuddering breath, straightening up and stepping back from Fenway. "Tyra's right. This is all Seth's stuff. And I didn't want him to bring it here."

Fenway stood in silence for a moment. The buzz of insects in the flowerbed next to the front porch.

"I guess I don't need to file a restraining order." Duchy finally said.

"I can see why you'd want to," Fenway said, "but you're right. A restraining order won't accomplish much, and it'll heighten the tension between you and Tyra."

"She's not a bad person," Duchy mumbled.

Fenway stole another glance at Dez, but again couldn't read her. "Is there somewhere you can store these boxes?"

"Uh," Duchy said. "Yeah. I've got a storage shed around the side. My ex used to keep his tools in there. Lawn mower, that kind of stuff. I've got some shelving, but it's empty. I told Seth to put his stuff in there until I figure out where to put everything." She looked up at Fenway, a question in her eyes she was reluctant to ask.

Fenway blinked hard. She didn't want these words to come out of her mouth, but they were coming out anyway. "Would you like some help carrying the boxes back there?"

Dez groaned faintly.

"Oh!" Duchy said. "Yes. Very much. I'm afraid I'm not very handy."

Don't need to be handy to carry boxes—but then Fenway admonished herself. Miranda Duchy had just been through a trauma. Even though she'd been cheating with a married man, Fenway reminded herself that she and McVie had started their relationship under— well, questionable circumstances. She pressed her lips together. *You never know what people are going through.*

Fenway stepped back, then walked over to the lawn and picked up one of the smaller boxes. "Lead the way."

"Around the corner." Duchy walked toward the side of the house—and Fenway stepped in front of her and handed her the small box. She hurried back to the lawn, grabbing a larger box—oof, this one was heavy—and followed Duchy around the corner of the garage. Dez followed a few steps behind, a medium-sized box in her hands.

About ten feet past the corner of the garage, a storage shed, about ten feet wide by five feet deep, stood on a concrete pad next to the house. Miranda Duchy grabbed the handle of the barn-style door and pulled it to the right. The door slid smoothly—the shed looked expensive and was made of solid wood, maybe oak—and Miranda placed the box in front of her.

"Might be better to put that in the corner," Dez said.

Miranda nodded and pushed the box with her foot so it moved closer to the corner—but not in it. She obviously thought Fenway and Dez would do all the work for her.

Fenway stepped into the shed. A shelf of tools stood on the left, all the way against the edge of the shed, and plenty of room for the boxes, if they stacked them properly. She carried the large box to the rear of the shed and placed it snug against both corners. There were a few more large boxes which should go next to—and on top of—this one. Maybe Dez could put down her box a few feet to Fenway's left.

"Dez, how about you put your box against the back wall in the center?"

No response.

"Dez?" Fenway turned around.

Dez held the box in front of her, staring at the shelving unit against the leftmost wall.

"Dez?" Fenway repeated.

She followed Dez's eyes to the second shelf from the bottom. A box of motor oil, a coil of rope—

And a framing hammer.

The claw end was covered in blood.

CHAPTER THIRTEEN

Miranda Duchy sat on the cream-colored sofa in her living room. In front of the sofa, an oval glass coffee table sat on a large Persian rug—with a somewhat similar design to the rug in which Seth Cahill's body had been wrapped.

Fenway stood on the opposite side of the coffee table from Duchy. Dez, several feet away, leaned on the archway between the living room and the dining room, her phone out. Fenway suspected she was texting someone at the sheriff's office. In Dez's left hand, an off-white opaque evidence bag encased the hammer.

"I don't know *how* that hammer got there," Duchy said. "It's not mine."

Fenway held up her hand. "Let's start on Monday evening, Ms. Duchy. Five or six o'clock."

"Okay." Duchy's voice shook. "I got back from the spa at about five-thirty. Seth was home, and he and I went out to dinner."

"Where?"

Duchy took a deep breath, steadying her voice. "Maxime's, that French place over on Fourth Street."

Ah—Fenway's father's favorite restaurant. Delicious, though a distant second to Dos Milagros for her. "About what time did you get there?"

"Seth made reservations for six fifteen."

"How was your—how was Seth?"

"Fine."

Fenway arched an eyebrow. "I mean, how was he acting?"

Miranda screwed up her mouth. "I guess he wasn't fine. I mean, he was chatty and laughing, but I could tell he was nervous."

"About what?"

"Probably about seeing Tyra later. He told me he had to pick up his boxes. But I could tell he didn't want to do it."

"Do you know why he didn't want to pick up his boxes?"

Duchy hesitated. "No."

"Ms. Duchy, we'll be talking to the staff at Maxime's. What will they say?"

Duchy closed her eyes, then opened them. "We had a mild argument. Hardly raising our voices."

"What was the fight about?"

"I told you—going to Tyra's."

"No," Fenway said. "Give me specifics."

"Oh. Uh... Well, he said he wished he didn't have to go. I told him that if he didn't want to go, he shouldn't. Then he said Tyra would be mad, and I told him I couldn't stand walking on eggshells when he talked about her."

"How did Seth take that?"

"Not well." Miranda bit her lip. "I mean, the divorce was final. He didn't owe her anything else, did he?"

"Alimony?" Fenway asked. She knew the answer, but did Miranda?

"No—in fact, she paid him. He sold his half of the storage business for far less than it was worth. They both agreed. Tyra got the business and kept the house."

"How did he respond when you told him you didn't want to walk on eggshells around him?"

Duchy paused. "He told me he needed to finish things. That's when I told him their divorce was final."

Oh. *Finish things.* Maybe Seth meant getting the boxes from Tyra, or maybe he was referring to the last shipment with Calvin Banning and Stephan Butler. Or maybe Miranda knew about Seth's side hustle.

"Then what?"

Duchy shifted her weight in her seat.

"Then what, Ms. Duchy?"

"I left."

"You left? By yourself?"

"That's correct."

"You had arrived at the restaurant together, but you left him there?"

"That's right."

"Did you drive home?"

Duchy shook her head. "We'd come in his Corvette. It's a cliché, middle-life crisis, blah blah blah, but—"

"How did you get home, Ms. Duchy?"

"I took a FlashRide."

Fenway nodded. She could check the rideshare company's records—and the doorbell camera to confirm. "When did Seth get home?"

Duchy leaned back and put a hand over her eyes.

"He didn't?"

"No."

The last time Miranda Duchy saw Seth Cahill was in the restaurant after an argument—one so bad that Duchy had left.

"If you got up in the middle of your meal to leave, Ms. Duchy, I wouldn't call that a mild argument."

Duchy's hand still covered her eyes. "No, I guess not."

Fenway cleared her throat. "What time did you get home?"

"I didn't look."

Not a problem; FlashRide's records would show the time. "Was it dark outside?"

Duchy shook her head. "Not yet."

Sunset had been about eight thirty on Monday night.

"Did you stay at home?"

Duchy paused.

"You can show us the video footage from your doorbell if you don't remember."

"I took the SUV out and went for a drive."

"A drive." Too late, Fenway heard the skepticism in her voice.

"I didn't know what time Seth would be home, and I didn't want to see him. I wanted to turn up my music and be alone."

"Where did you go?"

"I drove down to Vista del Rincón. I thought maybe I'd watch the sun set over the water. But halfway through my drive, I realized I'd get there too late. The sun was already setting."

"So, what did you do when you got to Vista del Rincón?"

"Nothing—I mean, I didn't go there. I kept driving. Turned off Ocean Highway near Tierra del Verano, drove some of the frontage roads back to Estancia. Thought about going up to my cabin, but I didn't want to drive on those roads in the dark. I ended up pulling into Le Platine."

"The five-star hotel over where Estancia Canyon meets Dover Drive?"

"I wanted a drink."

Thirty-dollar martinis at the hotel bar there—her father had once bragged about it. "Okay—so do you remember your bartender?"

"Well, no. The bar had closed early for a business event. Some CEO networking thing. They wouldn't let me in."

"Did you argue with anyone?" Fenway pressed her lips together. "Did you see anyone? Talk to anybody? Maybe get a valet?"

"Look, I told this to the detective yesterday. I simply turned around and got back in my car."

"Sometimes going over your tracks again can jar a memory loose," Fenway said. "Run any red lights? Did you have to stop for gas anywhere?"

Duchy brought her other hand up to her face. "No."

Fenway paused for a moment. She had no good way to segue into a discussion of the murder weapon, so she dove in headfirst. "So, about the hammer."

Duchy sat upright again and placed her hands in her lap. "I told you, I don't know anything. I've never seen the hammer before."

"Did Seth own a hammer like that?"

"I don't know."

"Did you put the hammer there?"

"No!"

"Who else had access to your shed?"

"My ex-husband. But Dave took the padlock when he emptied it out."

"When?"

"A little over a year ago."

"You never bothered to lock it up again?"

Duchy crossed her arms. "That shed wasn't my responsibility. I didn't keep my stuff in there. I didn't think about the shed after Dave left."

"That's awfully convenient," Dez said from across the room, still staring at her phone and tapping on the screen.

Fenway cocked her head. "So you think you're being set up?"

"Well, *I* didn't put the hammer in the shed." Miranda dropped her hands back to her lap. "I might have had an argument with Seth, but we were happy together. We were planning a wedding."

Fenway stole a glance at Duchy's left ring finger. A big, sparkling diamond, the classic round cut. Maybe two carats. The two women locked eyes for a moment. The ring looked expensive. Unless it was fake, Seth had paid at least twenty thousand for it. Probably much more. The drug storage business was lucrative.

"We'd already set a date—soon, in August. People say it's fast, but we've been seeing each other for over a year."

"So you didn't see Seth after you left Maxime's?"

Duchy shook her head.

"And you didn't see his Corvette after that, either?"

Another shake of the head.

"You know where we can find his Corvette?"

"No."

"Any idea what he was doing at the office last night?"

"Only that maybe he didn't want to see me either. Going to the storage place would give him something to do."

Fenway glanced at Dez as if to say *Did I miss anything?*

Duchy stood suddenly. "You think I killed him."

"I never said that. We're gathering evidence, Ms. Duchy." But the hammer matched the murder weapon—and had blood on it. Pretty good evidence.

Duchy took a step toward Fenway. "It sure *sounds* like you're accusing me. I can see it in your eyes, Coroner." She pointed at Fenway aggressively with her index and middle fingers together. "Maybe you're too high and mighty to have an affair with a married man—"

Fenway tensed.

"—but that doesn't mean I killed him. I *loved* him." She took another step forward—

—and Dez shot to Fenway's side, hands facing Miranda. "I'll need you to take a step back, Ms. Duchy."

Duchy bristled and drew herself to her full height. But then her eyes lost their fire, and she dropped back down on her heels, took a step backward, then plopped onto the sofa. "I—I apologize."

Dez nodded. "Now, listen, Ms. Duchy, you may be telling the truth—"

"I am—"

Dez raised her voice. "You need to let me finish."

Duchy dropped her shoulders. "Sorry."

"But domestic partners are most commonly the perpetrators of violence against the victim. We're doing our job."

"I don't have a motive, though," Duchy said.

Dez inclined her head. "You sure about that?"

Duchy opened her mouth, then blinked a few times. "Oh—well, yes, last week, Seth changed the beneficiary on his life insurance policy."

A moment of silence.

"From?" Dez asked.

"From Tyra to me," Duchy whispered.

"That's right. According to our research, the policy is for two million dollars."

Duchy lowered her gaze to the floor.

A few moments passed in silence, then Dez's phone buzzed in her hand.

Dez glanced at the screen, tapped for a moment, then lowered the phone. Fenway turned her head toward Dez, and Dez gave a small nod. Another piece of evidence? Whatever it was, Dez didn't want to discuss it in front of Miranda Duchy.

Fenway pointed at the rug under her feet. "A rug very similar to this was in Mr. Cahill's office at the storage facility. It looks expensive."

"Uh—yeah. I had that Persian rug in here, but the room overpowered it. I needed a much bigger rug." Duchy gave Fenway a forced smile. "Besides, the imagery on the old rug failed to align with my goals."

"The—imagery?" Fenway looked down and noticed for the first time. The design wasn't lifelike, but crimson and wine-colored flowers—or were they upturned leaves?—covered the rug under her feet.

"Persian rugs have intriguing symbolism. The flower at the center of the old rug was a peony. It represents power."

"And you didn't want to manifest power?"

A shy smile on Duchy's lips. "I thought I did. But I really

wanted prosperity."

"So these leaves symbolize prosperity?"

"Not leaves, Coroner, tulips. And yes, tulips represent prosperity." She paused. "I wonder—is it possible to get that rug returned to me? Tyra may own the company now, but that rug is my property, even if you found it in Seth's office."

Fenway frowned.

The killer would know that Seth's body had been wrapped in the Persian rug. Was this a masterful piece of misdirection, or did Duchy honestly not know?

"I'm not sure how you would go about that," Fenway said, "but right now, I'm concerned with piecing together what happened the night of Mr. Cahill's—" She paused and inwardly swore at herself. "On Monday night."

Duchy paused. "I'm not sure what else I can tell you."

Fenway nodded and motioned to Dez with her head. "We'll be right back, Ms. Duchy."

Dez followed Fenway out of the living room, through the dining room, and into the front hallway.

Fenway craned her neck; Duchy was out of sight, and if they kept their voices low, out of earshot.

"You got a message on your phone?"

"From Mark. Judge Solano signed a search warrant for Miranda's house and vehicles."

Fenway nodded. Duchy had been fairly open with them; if she knew about the warrant, she'd likely call her lawyer and say nothing else. "So what do you think, Dez? Think Miranda did it?"

Dez knotted her brow. "She doesn't have an alibi. She has an emotional motive for arguing with him—if she didn't think he'd get over his ex. Plus two million other reasons."

"And she's in possession of the murder weapon." Fenway rubbed her forehead. "Still, she invited us into the shed where the hammer sat in plain sight. That doesn't strike you as odd?"

"I learned a long time ago not to use a criminal's stupidity as an excuse for their innocence." Dez paced in a small circle. "I texted Mark to look into her finances."

"So if it's not Miranda leading us right to the murder weapon, what's bothering you?"

Dez scratched her temple. "Whoever killed Seth Cahill would have had to drag his body, wrap it in the rug, and move the body into the storage unit." Dez hooked her thumb over her shoulder toward the living room. "Would Miranda Duchy even be able to move Cahill?"

"Not a big guy," Fenway said. "A hundred fifty pounds, tops."

"And adrenaline can account for a lot."

"We'll need to see the footage of the doorbell for Monday night, too."

"Covered by the warrant. Sarah worked fast."

Fenway nodded. She didn't think she'd ever be able to get as effective of an assistant as Rachel, but she'd been wrong: the hyper-competent Sarah ran circles around all the other assistants.

"Do we have enough to arrest Ms. Duchy now?"

Dez nodded. "The evidence is circumstantial, but it'd be enough to get an indictment. Means, motive, opportunity—all there."

"But besides the hammer, no physical evidence. And if Duchy can show that the shed didn't have a lock…"

"We'd get our arrest, but no conviction. The D.A. might not want to go to trial. I'd feel better with something more concrete—her financials could give us a stronger motive."

"What are we hoping to find with the warrant?"

"We put down that we're looking for evidence of the crime. Any bloodstained clothing, towels, clean-up, any stains or drips in Duchy's SUV."

"That's a little vague."

Dez shrugged. "That kind of head wound means a lot of blood. Something's bound to turn up."

"The warrant covers the vehicle too?"

"Yes."

Fenway blinked. "Judge Solano?"

Dez smiled. "That's right."

Fenway pressed her lips together. Solano gave the police a lot of leeway when asking for warrants—but she'd been overturned on appeal six times in the last year.

"We're also looking for any signs of struggle in the house," Dez said.

"But it's likely that the murder occurred at the storage facility."

"Likely, but not yet conclusively," Dez said. "If we find something here, then that makes a conviction easier."

Fenway stared down at the floor.

"You don't think it's Miranda," Dez said evenly.

"I do not."

"Why not?"

"Because she asked for the rug back."

A crease between Dez's eyes. "Part of her plan. She asked for the rug to make it seem like she didn't know that the body had been wrapped up in it."

Fenway pursed her lips. "I don't think Miranda Duchy is that good of an actor. Trying to throw us off her trail by pretending not to know about the rug wouldn't have occurred to her, either."

Dez gave a stiff nod. "But no one else has the murder weapon on their property."

Fenway paused. "Plenty of people have motive, and they all knew about Seth and Miranda. Easy enough to hide the hammer in an unlocked shed."

"Doorbell camera. Easy enough to confirm."

"Plus," Fenway continued, "Seth was involved in the morpheranyl trade. Calvin Banning might have wanted to keep his storage unit available and gotten angry when told no."

"Or Mathis Jericho might have killed him to take over and get a bigger cut of the profits."

Fenway paused. "What if Tyra found out about the drugs?"

Dez cocked her head.

"If Tyra found out that the storage business only stayed afloat because of Seth's illegal activities, how do you think she'd react?"

"She'd be pissed off."

"Right. She negotiates a good deal to buy the business, has to pay *him* alimony, then finds out the business will fail if it goes legit?"

"Do you think she knew Seth had replaced her with Miranda as the beneficiary of the life insurance policy?"

Fenway thought for a moment. "Maybe not. It's possible she thought she'd still get that two million dollars."

"One problem with Tyra as a suspect: she has an alibi."

Fenway folded her arms. "Her best friend from high school? That alibi's not necessarily airtight. I figure that Hope Dunkelman could have helped drag Seth's body into the storage unit. If Tyra found out about Seth's storage of the drugs, she might have known that Seth turned off the security cameras, too."

Dez peered over Fenway's shoulder into the living room; Duchy hadn't moved from the sofa. "Motive and opportunity—yeah, other people have those. But we can't ignore the hammer—covered in blood—found on this very property."

Fenway nodded.

"I agree that this isn't perfect, Fenway, but we've got to follow the evidence. And right now, all the evidence is pointing to Miranda Duchy."

"This feel right to you?" Fenway asked.

Outside, a car approached and slowed. Sergeant Mark Trevino serving the search warrant.

"We'll know more after the lab work and the finances come back." Dez clicked her tongue. "Let's see if we can match the blood to Seth's, if there are any fingerprints on the hammer, and if we can find any receipts connecting Miranda to the purchase of a similar hammer."

Fenway's phone buzzed. She pulled it out. "Speaking of lab work..."

"Michi?" Dez asked.

"Yep." Fenway tapped the screen and held the phone to her ear. "Good afternoon, Dr. Yasuda."

"Good afternoon, Coroner. Do you have a moment?"

"Just about to serve a search warrant."

"I'll make it quick. I remembered where I recognized the name *Tyra Cahill.*"

"Oh—at this time of day? I expected a call at three in the morning."

"Very funny." Dr. Yasuda cleared her throat. "I'm sending you a copy of the paperwork. You remember we talked about the deaths from morpheranyl right before Thanksgiving?"

"Right—yes. We were talking about Scott Behrens. I have a contact who knew him."

"I also thought of Scott Behrens."

Fenway furrowed her brow. "Why is that?"

"The person who identified his body? Tyra Cahill."

CHAPTER FOURTEEN

Fenway opened the door of the coroner's office and Sarah Summerhill's face popped up from behind her monitor.

"Oh, I didn't expect you back for another couple of hours." Sarah tilted her head. "Wasn't Mark serving a warrant?"

"Yeah. Dez and Mark are there. No sense in all of us taking up space." Fenway hadn't waited for Mark's arrival, instead taking a FlashRide from the Duchy house down to the Puerto Avila beach parking lot to pick up her Accord.

On the way to the beach, she'd peppered the driver with questions about how the company tracks riders and trips—until he turned up the radio and made it clear he didn't want any more conversation. Fenway put her elbows on the counter, about three feet from Sarah's workstation. "Can you do some research for me?"

"Sure."

"Check with the rideshare companies. See if anyone got picked up or dropped off at the storage place—or anywhere in, say, a two- or three-block radius—on Monday night or early Tuesday."

"Sure." Sarah clicked the mouse, then looked at Fenway. "Taxis too?"

"Yes. They take cash, so that might be a way our killer hid their trip."

Fenway walked into her office and dropped her purse on the desk, then turned and took a few steps toward Sarah's workstation. "Also, I discovered that Tyra Cahill, the ex-wife of our murder victim, identified a body from a drug overdose death in November."

Sarah blinked. "Coincidence?"

"Maybe not. Our murder victim stored that same drug at his storage facility."

Sarah nodded. "And that's too much of a coincidence."

Fenway hesitated. "Murder weapon found at our victim's girlfriend's house. The girlfriend doesn't have an alibi, and they were fighting a few hours before the murder. But even so, Tyra identifying the body of someone who died from the same drug her ex stored? Yeah, too much of a coincidence for me."

"What does Dez think?"

"Dez rightly pointed out that we have no evidence implicating anyone but the girlfriend."

Sarah chuckled. "But you're not buying it."

"Maybe I'm a natural skeptic," Fenway said. "Tyra Cahill identified the body of Scott Behrens. Why did *she* identify his body?"

"Uh—I have access to the files. I can look."

"Please." Fenway approached the desk and started pacing in front of it.

"You have access to these records on your laptop, too."

"Humor me?" Fenway looked at Sarah. "She'd have to be a relative, right?"

"Most of the time, yes." Sarah started clicking the mouse, then typed on her keyboard. "Okay, Scott Behrens—twenty-one years old."

Fenway squeezed her eyes shut and tried to remember the backgrounder she'd been sent. "Tyra is—um, let's see, thirty-seven. That would have made her..."

"Sixteen at Scott's birth."

Fenway nodded. "And Scott Behrens—"

"Adopted," Sarah said, not taking her eyes off the monitor. "By Rebecca and James Behrens. Oh—they both died in an auto accident fifteen years ago."

"When Scott was eight?"

"Looks like it. Hold on."

That would explain the teeth, the foster system. Scott Behrens had fallen through the cracks. "So Tyra Cahill is Scott Behrens' birth mother? Or an older sister? Or maybe a long-lost cousin or something."

Sarah shrugged. "I don't have access to the adoption files—or, if I do, I need to figure out where to find them."

"But Scott Behrens stayed local."

"He did."

"If Tyra Cahill identified his body, she must have known about him."

"I can only assume."

Fenway tapped her chin. "How long do you think Tyra and Scott were in contact?"

"Long enough for her to be contacted when the authorities found his body. He must have changed his emergency contact information somewhere."

"Maybe it's time I called on Tyra's bestie." Fenway wondered if Hope Dunkelman would be any more helpful than Tyra.

———

Walking to her car, Fenway pulled her phone out and called Melissa de la Garza.

"Afternoon, Coroner."

"Did you get the hammer yet?"

"It's on the way here. We'll do the blood test—I'll put a rush on it. We can get the type fast."

"I'm actually more concerned about the fingerprints."

"Oh—you didn't hear?"

"Hear what?"

"I assume Kav would have told you. Looks like the handle was wiped clean."

"It looks like the—" Fenway scratched her head. "Why would Miranda Duchy wipe the handle but not clean the blood off the hammer?"

"I don't know. Some people have a fear of blood."

"No, that doesn't make any sense." Miranda had said she was being framed. If she'd been the murderer, she'd have cleaned the entire hammer, not just wiped the handle of fingerprints.

Of course, maybe Miranda had wiped the handle of the hammer just to make it *look* like she'd been framed. It would be a pretty brilliant maneuver. Perhaps Miranda was someone many people underestimated.

"Text me as soon as you know any more, okay?" Fenway arrived at her Accord and unlocked it.

"Sure, Fenway. See you later."

———

As Fenway turned off Tres Arboles Road, she navigated a dip stretching between two five-foot-tall brick columns, standing like mini-tower sentries at the entrance to Estancia's Prospero Park neighborhood. A sign at the edge of the park proudly proclaimed:

Welcome to Prospero Park
The cloud-capp'd towers, the gorgeous palaces,
The solemn temples, the great globe itself…
We are such stuff
As dreams are made on

Prospero Park was beautiful, if surrounded by elitism and arrogance, and it buffered the mini-mansions on the west side from the working-class duplexes and apartment complexes on the east. Fenway navigated her Accord through the labyrinthine streets bordering the park, every so often sneaking an envious look at the much-shorter bike trail that went straight through the center of the park.

She finally came to the end of the zigzagging road, turning left on a quiet oak-lined street named Rodrigo Avenue, bordering the southern edge of Prospero Park.

Three houses from the corner on the right sat the ranch-style craftsman house. Behind the beautiful, gnarled coastal live oak next to the street lay a tidy front yard with a drought-resistant garden of pea gravel, manzanitas, and snapdragons. Fenway pulled her Accord next to the curb, next to the coastal live oak, and walked the winding path toward the front door. The front door opened as she approached.

"Coroner?" George Pope asked.

"Hello, Mr. Pope," Fenway said. "Is Ms. Dunkelman home as well?"

"Oh—I'm afraid not. She took Tyra out to buy flashlights, batteries, gallons of water."

"To prepare for the storm?" A fleeting thought: how old were the batteries in Fenway's flashlight?

"Yes," Pope replied. "I think they're heading to the mall, too. A little retail therapy, as she says. Take her mind off everything that's happened."

"I see." Fenway rubbed her chin. "Well, perhaps you can help me out."

"Oh, I don't know. If you were looking for Hope—"

"Were you on your way out?"

"Yes. Running an errand."

Fenway paused. "You have five minutes?"

Pope blinked, as if weighing the importance of the errand against helping the coroner with a homicide investigation. He looked up and down the street. Fenway followed his eyes, but nothing; a man washed his car two houses down.

Pope shrugged. "I suppose so. Why don't you come on in?"

Plants filled the foyer: fiddle-leaf figs, century plants, and ferns. Pope walked into the living room and motioned to a fabric-covered sofa in a dark blue next to a side table. "Can I get you anything? Coffee? I've got a nice tea blend I found at the farmer's market."

"Nothing, thanks." Fenway looked at the sofa but remained standing. "This shouldn't take too long, I hope."

"All right," Pope said, hands on his hips. "What did you want to know?"

"Tyra had a relative I didn't know about. A baby boy adopted when Tyra was sixteen."

Pope's eyes widened, but then he averted his eyes.

Aha.

"George." Fenway crouched, trying to get into Pope's line of sight. "You and Hope knew Tyra back then. Did she have a baby?"

Pope swallowed hard, then looked up at the ceiling. His chin trembled, and he cleared his throat. "Yeah. She, uh—she had a rough time of it."

"I imagine. Being a pregnant teen isn't easy." Fenway remembered a couple of her classmates from her own high school years—one whose father kicked her out. "You were all friends back then, but did you know her when she was pregnant? Had you started dating Hope at the time?"

"Oh—well, yes. That's not what I meant, though. I meant what happened before this past Thanksgiving. Only a year after getting back in touch with him after two decades, then losing him like that." He screwed up his mouth. "You know she wanted to start the process of adopting him?"

"You can adopt someone when they're in their twenties?"

"Sure. At any age."

"I didn't know that."

"No, not many people do. After his adoptive parents died, he went into the foster system, then aged out. A year later, Scott reached out to the agency to see if he could find his birth mom. And that's when Tyra got the call."

"That must have been a surprise."

"Yeah, when Tyra put him up for adoption, she thought she'd never see him again. She was ecstatic to find him." Then Pope's jaw tightened. "Right after Halloween, Tyra wanted to invite Scott to join them for Thanksgiving, but Seth wouldn't hear of it. He actually got pissed off. Then a couple weeks later—the Monday or Tuesday of Thanksgiving week—Scott was found in an abandoned house. He'd been dead a couple of days." He coughed, circled his shoulders. "No one should die like that. Devastating. Tyra was beside herself—she had to identify the body. And right after that, she served Seth with divorce papers."

"Sounds like you were pretty close to it."

"Yeah, well, my wife has been best friends with her for over twenty years. I hear all the good stuff, all the bad stuff, all the venting about Seth..." Pope trailed off.

"Anything specific that Tyra said about Seth?"

"Now, look," Pope said, "Tyra had nothing to do with his death."

"How do you know?"

"Because Hope and Tyra were together the entire time you've asked our whereabouts."

Fenway paused. Yes—that was the problem. Hope stayed with her the whole time. Did Tyra blame Seth for Scott's death? Would Hope have gone along with a plan to—

The realization hit Fenway like a smack to the side of the head. Seth Cahill's murder hadn't been premeditated. Instead, a spur-of-the-moment crime of passion. Had Tyra been holding a hammer, maybe Hope helping her replace a picture on the wall, or putting up a new shelf, when Seth showed up? Was Seth angry about his argument with Miranda and started taking it out on Tyra, and had she had enough of it?

And had Tyra looked at Seth and blamed him and his morpheranyl storage business for the death of her son? After Seth had told her that Scott couldn't spend Thanksgiving with them? After Seth wanted her to ignore Scott when he had no one else? Did Tyra feel guilty for giving her son up for adoption, thinking she was giving him a better life, only to discover he'd been orphaned at eight years old to a life in the foster system?

Had Tyra snapped?

And after an enraged swing of the hammer, had Hope helped Tyra drag his body out to the Corvette, driven it to the office, wrapped his body in the Persian rug in Seth's office, and left it in a vacant storage space?

That would explain a lot.

That would explain why Tyra was adamant about not giving Fenway the first space she saw onscreen—because she knew Unit 176 held Seth's dead body.

That would explain how Tyra could have an alibi—yet still commit the crime.

And Tyra had gone over to Miranda's house later, angry about the boxes that were still in the house. Had she sneaked around the side of the house and hidden the hammer in Miranda's shed?

That made sense. It made more sense than Miranda acting on her own. And it made more sense than Miranda leaving a bloody hammer in a nearly empty shed on the side of the house.

Now if she could only prove it.

"You said Tyra first met Scott after he aged out of the system. Was he trying to establish a relationship with her? Maybe he asked for money?"

Pope opened his mouth, then closed it.

Uh oh. Fenway had gone too far.

"Coroner, what does this have to do with the murder investigation?"

"We're trying to cover all avenues."

"Is Tyra a suspect?"

"We want to eliminate her. These defense attorneys, they'll ask us if we knew the victim and the ex-wife were at odds, and we need to be able to say we followed up on all those leads—even if we don't think she's guilty."

"But she has an alibi."

Fenway took a breath. How did she want to play this?

But Pope saw through her. "Oh—you don't *believe* my wife? You don't believe we spent the entire night with Tyra?"

The wheels spun in Fenway's head. "A defense attorney would ask why we believed Hope. She and Tyra have been friends for twenty years, like you said. And the lawyer would have a good point —why *wouldn't* your wife lie for her best friend?"

"Don't you have any other suspects?" Pope fumed. "What about that girlfriend of his? She had an affair with him for months, maybe years. As soon as he divorces Tyra, he changes his insurance policy and leaves Miranda everything?" His nostrils flared as his voice rose. "Have you searched her properties? His storage facility? The drugs stored there?"

"How do you know about Seth changing beneficiaries?"

Pope rolled his eyes. "He told Tyra. Tyra told Hope. I *told* you, they've been best friends for decades." He crossed his arms. "If you don't think Miranda Duchy is a suspect, has it occurred to you that one or two of Seth's drug dealer friends might have gotten a little greedy?"

Fenway pounced. "Drug dealer friends? What drug dealer friends?"

Pope hesitated. "Everyone has a pretty good idea what Seth was up to."

"Who told you this?" Fenway narrowed her eyes. "Is it something else Tyra told Hope? Did Tyra know about Seth using the facility to store morpheranyl? When did she find out?"

Pope scowled. "I don't believe this. Seth gets involved with drug dealers, known killers, and you're laser focused on my wife's best friend." He walked to the door and opened it. "I think it's time for you to leave."

Fenway nodded and stood. "I apologize, Mr. Pope. Thanks for your time."

Pope turned his head away from her as Fenway walked out the door.

She looked up at the sky. Clear blue. The literal calm before the storm.

———

Fenway had her mobile phone in her hand as she got to her Accord. She tapped Sarah's number.

"Hey, Fenway."

"Are you all prepared for Alonso?"

"The tropical storm? Yeah. Fresh batteries in my flashlights. Got an electric lantern, pantry items. You?"

"I've been helping McVie pack. I haven't thought about it."

"I bet McVie's all ready. He's probably got a camping stove and portable propane tanks."

"Assuming he hasn't packed them yet." Fenway cleared her throat. "I called because I need Hope Dunkelman's phone number. Her mobile."

"Oh. Yeah. Hang on."

Sarah put Fenway on hold, and Fenway started the engine. A moment later, Sarah came back on and told Fenway the number.

"Can you text that to me?"

"Sure. And one more thing—Miranda Duchy's financials came in. Looks like she's not as well-off as she appears. A lot of credit card debt, a second mortgage on her cabin."

"And yet her boyfriend is driving a Corvette." Fenway thought of the life insurance policy. Two million dollars would go a long way to ease the financial pain. "Can you email me the details?"

"Sure, right after I send you Hope Dunkelman's number."

"Thanks, Sarah."

Fenway ended the call, then pulled away from the curb and her phone dinged. She opened her messages and tapped on the phone number. It rang twice.

"This is Hope Dunkelman."

"Ms. Dunkelman, hello. This is Coroner Fenway Stevenson. Do you have a moment for a few follow-up questions?"

"Sure. When are you thinking?"

"Now, if you're not too busy."

"Oh—well, now isn't the best time for me to come to the sheriff's office."

"You don't have to come down," Fenway said, her mind racing. "I can come to you."

A short laugh. "I'm shopping right now."

"That's fine. Where are you?"

"I'm at Las Cruces Mall."

"Fantastic—I'm only about five minutes away. Have you eaten yet? I could buy you lunch."

A pause. Snippets of conversations in the background. Definitely the mall. "I'm sorry. This isn't a good time. I can come by the sheriff's office at, say, four o'clock?"

Fenway tapped her fingers on the steering wheel as she took the on-ramp to Ocean Highway. What had Pope said? Retail therapy—with Tyra. Maybe Fenway could insist on seeing her now, but if the two of them were still together, would she be able to get what she needed out of Hope with Tyra right there?

Well—maybe. She wouldn't be able to ask pointed questions about their supposed time together on Monday night. Not with both of them there. But she could ask about their past—and about Scott Behrens.

Or maybe that wouldn't be a good idea. Asking about Scott—Tyra's dead son—in front of both of them in a public place? Might be too much for Tyra emotionally. That could trigger a protective response from Hope—and if Hope agreed to give a fake alibi for Tyra, she'd protect her from uncomfortable questions.

"Four o'clock is fine. I'll meet you in the lobby."

Fenway ended the call, then smacked her hand on the dashboard. George Pope would almost certainly warn his wife about the kind of questions that Fenway wanted to ask. If Hope Dunkelman showed up at four o'clock, it would be a minor miracle.

Fenway got off at the next exit. She hadn't eaten lunch yet and her stomach rumbled. She pulled into an All Access Burger parking lot, then turned into the drive-through behind several other cars.

Ugh. All Access Burger. Had it come to this?

But while a mediocre fast-food restaurant wouldn't get any top marks from her taste buds, it would afford her some time to process the next step of what she could do.

The cars ahead of her pulled forward, and she drove her Accord next to the speaker. The All Access menu looked mouthwatering. Whatever the salary of their food photographer, it wasn't enough.

"Ortega Dream Burger, zucchini fries, and a medium Coke."

She hated herself as the words were coming out of her mouth. But the photo made the burger look delectable. The zucchini fries picture: crispy, golden breading.

She knew the execution would be nothing like the promise. The Ortega chile would be too soft, oily, sliding off the bun along with the rest of the condiments, making it likely she'd get mayo all over her blazer. More like an Ortega Nightmare.

And the zucchini would be either overripe and limp or unripe and flavorless.

Fenway pulled forward, with a single car ahead of her before the window. She drummed her fingers on the steering wheel.

She took a step back in her head. The connection between Scott Behrens and Seth Cahill's murder had been strong in her mind. But weren't there other possibilities?

Mathis Jericho was a player in the morpheranyl scene—like Calvin Banning. Jericho had a tenuous alibi at best. In fact, no alibi. He'd said he tried to save the shipment meeting on the beach when Seth Cahill hadn't shown up. But maybe the reason he hadn't shown up was because *he* had smashed the claw end of the hammer into Seth's skull.

And Jericho knew that his extra money was about to dry up. Did Jericho blame Seth for that? Did he blame Miranda Duchy? If he blamed them both, maybe he killed Seth and hid the bloody hammer in Duchy's unlocked shed. Best of both worlds—could Mathis Jericho hatch a clever plan like that?

Fenway rubbed her chin. Perhaps she should have taken Jericho into custody when she'd had the chance? Maybe she should have gotten the container of the white substance—morpheranyl, presumably—into evidence. That would have given her the option to take Jericho into custody.

She shook her head. No—she knew the warrant was flimsy, and any competent lawyer could get everything Mathis said excluded—and that meant everything they'd found since. Dez had been right that not taking the powder was a gray area, but she'd done the right thing.

And Mathis Jericho was still a suspect. How valuable was Mathis Jericho to Anton Venn and his cartel? Fenway knew Jericho was a simple pawn in the morpheranyl chess game. And would getting Jericho off the street make any difference? Without Cahill Warehouse Storage, Jericho wouldn't be a player much longer. Not without proving his value to the higher-ups.

Fenway's best bet was to get Jericho to turn on Banning or Butler or anyone higher up in the organization.

Stephan Butler had probably moved his boat by now. As much information as Butler had given them, he could still use his boat to bring morpheranyl into Estancia. In fact, he held as much responsibility as anyone for the spate of deaths around Thanksgiving.

Though if Stephan Butler wouldn't import the drugs, someone else would take his place.

Fenway shook her head. Those kinds of thoughts led to complacency, and she couldn't afford to get complacent.

Butler, Banning, Jericho. They all knew that the police had

discovered the boats coming in with the drug shipments. Fenway assumed they'd concluded the police were aware of Cahill Warehouse Storage. So they probably wouldn't be making any more appearances at the facility. They'd go somewhere else: up the coast, down the coast, over the mountain pass east of Calexico.

A honk behind her. Fenway snapped to the present, drove up to the window, and exchanged a debit card charge for a messy burger and zucchini fries. She drove the car around the corner of the building and parked in the shade on the far side of the lot, windows rolled down.

Just as she suspected. The squishy burger had too much juice from the chile, oil, and globs of mayo. The zucchini fries looked almost as good as the picture. She bit into one: crunchy, bland, unripe. After swallowing a few bites of each until her stomach stopped growling with hunger, Fenway got out of the car and threw away the half-eaten burger and zucchini fries in the fast-food bag.

"I should have gone back to Dos Milagros," Fenway grumbled as she turned on the engine.

Where to now? Maybe back to the office. Spend some time researching suspects. Maybe Scott Behrens, too; his adoption files might be available now that he was deceased. She might have access to his birth certificate and other information. Yes, she could give that job to Sarah—who would no doubt be faster and more thorough.

Fenway jumped in her seat. What was she thinking? McVie might have been available for lunch. She frowned. She was miffed that McVie put other things before their relationship, but here she was, totally absorbed in a case. The two of them only had a few more days together before he left for Colorado, and instead of calling him and going to a shrimp ceviche stand on the beach, she sat in the baking-hot parking lot of an All Access Burger eating a craptastic lunch by herself.

At least she hadn't eaten enough to ruin her appetite. And

McVie owed her a nice dinner tonight—they could go late, after Mark's retirement party at Winfrey's.

Besides, if they went to Maxime's, Fenway could ask the waitstaff about the argument between Seth and Miranda.

Her phone rang. An 805 number she didn't recognize.

"This is Coroner Fenway Stevenson."

A pause.

"Hello?"

"Hi, Coroner." A tentative woman's voice, worried, almost breathless.

"Who is this, please?"

"It's Isabella Chan."

She'd hardly talked to Chan the day before; no wonder she didn't recognize her voice on the phone. "Oh, hello, Ms. Chan. How can I help?"

"I—I don't know if you can. I had to contact someone."

Fenway's heart leapt into her mouth—did the drug organization think Mathis and Isabella knew too much? Were they trying to kill them? "Are you in danger?"

"Oh—no. No. I—look, Mathis has been a little distracted lately. Hasn't been doing all the landscaping work he should have."

"It's not uncommon for people who are grieving. Even if Mathis didn't seem that close to Seth." Fenway frowned; surely Isabella wanted to talk about more than this.

"He didn't show up for work today, either. Taking another day off after a late night, I'm sure."

"Miss Chan, what does this have to do—"

"Sorry, I'm getting there. There's a little walkway between Buildings B and C, and we have a few junipers that have gotten overgrown. One of them is over six feet tall."

"Junipers?"

"It's becoming a hazard. So I took pictures of the junipers."

"Why would you take pictures of them?"

"I wanted to send them to Mathis. Tell him we're all sad about Seth, but he still has to do his landscaping work."

Great, just what Fenway needed: to get in the middle of a petty employee squabble.

"And that's when I saw it," Chan finished.

Fenway paused. "Saw what?"

"Blood. A bunch of blood splattered on the wall. You can't see it from the walkway, but if you get closer..."

"Stay in the office, Isabella. We'll be there shortly."

CHAPTER FIFTEEN

Deputy Celeste Salvador was the first one at Cahill Warehouse Storage. Fenway drove her Accord up behind the cruiser. Celeste was striding up to the office door.

Fenway threw the car into *Park* and got out of the car. "Celeste!"

Deputy Salvador stopped and nodded. "Coroner."

So formal.

Oh.

"I'm sorry," Fenway said. "I've been so busy with this investigation. But I haven't forgotten about you. I've emailed HR for updates. I'm just waiting for their response. But listen, Celeste, you're at the top of my list."

"You haven't *talked* to HR yet?"

Fenway's heart dropped into her stomach, taking up uneasy residence next to the Ortega Dream Burger. "I submitted most of the paperwork weeks ago. I'm sure everything will be fine as soon as they give me an update." She hoped. "But things have been busy. And the HR specialist leaves early."

Deputy Salvador pressed her lips together.

"I'll make it a priority," Fenway said.

"You know, Dez says you're a pretty good boss."

"Oh." Fenway felt the color rise to her face. "I appreciate that. I think she's a pretty good sergeant, too." A smile touched the corners of her mouth. "Even if she *is* a pain in the ass sometimes."

"The one thing she says is that you don't like doing paperwork."

"Heh. Who does?"

"Yeah, but you're late with it."

Fenway paused. True, she didn't always hand in her reports on time, but she usually handed everything in within a few days of the due date. "I don't know—I mean, I'm not perfect, but I don't have stacks of unfiled paperwork on my desk or anything."

"Except when it comes to replacing Sergeant Trevino." Salvador looked at her feet. "Just saying—you've had a while. And now whoever you choose won't have the benefit of getting trained on the job by Mark."

"No. You're right." Fenway swallowed hard. "I've been remiss, and I apologize."

Salvador smiled—despite herself, it seemed. "Dez also said you're the first boss she's had who can admit when you're wrong."

"Don't fool yourself, Celeste. Lots of people can admit when I'm wrong." Fenway began walking toward the office. "Let's make sure we cordon off the area. You called CSI?"

"Melissa is on her way. But if we think Seth Cahill died on Monday night, those bloodstains have been there almost forty-eight hours."

"Right." Fenway paused. "Has anyone tried to contact Mathis Jericho?"

"Mark is trying to reach him now," Salvador said. "His phone rang and went to voicemail."

They opened the door to the office and Isabella Chan stood behind the counter, the color drained from her face. "Thank God," she said. "Thank God."

"Ms. Chan, would you mind showing us where these junipers are?"

"I didn't touch anything."

"I'm not saying you did," Fenway said. "We need to tape off the area."

"Will we have to shut down again?"

"I don't know yet."

Chan clenched her teeth, then smacked her hands on the counter. "I'm sick of this. First, Seth gets killed, and I had to be the one to see his dead body. Now I find blood all over the wall on the side of Building B, and I—"

"Miss Chan," Deputy Salvador said forcefully, "please take us to the walkway you're talking about. Now."

Chan folded her arms, then took a deep breath and put her arms at her side. "Sorry. It's been a rough week."

"I know," Salvador replied.

Chan came out from behind the counter, shoulders slumped. She hadn't put on makeup, and she wore sweats instead of the smart blouse and tailored trousers she'd worn the day before. "Follow me." She exited the office on the rear side, following a path into the storage unit buildings.

Striding across the asphalt, sneakers a blur, Chan must have wanted to get this over with. Fenway and Deputy Salvador followed her.

After a moment, Chan turned right. There seemed to be nothing at first. Then, a narrow opening between the two buildings came into view. The three of them walked between the buildings, single file, and the gap led into a wider area with junipers and a small ironwood tree on each side of the walkway.

"There." Chan pointed.

Nothing but the thick fronds of junipers were visible.

"Behind the right side of those branches."

Fenway squinted and saw a stack of lumber on the ground under the junipers: short flat boards, maybe three feet long, and two-by-fours that were a foot to two feet long. A small plastic toolbox sat next to it.

Fenway handed a pair of blue nitrile gloves to Deputy Salvador, snapped a pair on herself. Then she stepped to the right of the greenery area and pulled the thick juniper branches away from the wall.

Chan was right. A splattering of blood on the wall—only a few dried droplets were visible, but enough that Fenway suspected this might be the spot where Seth Cahill had been attacked.

She looked at the small stack of wood, too: more blood had landed there.

"The spray went this way," Fenway said in a low voice to Deputy Salvador. "Cahill stood about five-six, so if his head came to here—"

"Right-handed killer, correct?" Salvador asked.

"That's right." Fenway was impressed; Salvador had done her homework and read the M.E.'s report.

"We'll have to wait for CSI to make the determination," Salvador continued, "but a blow with the claw end of a framing hammer could have caused this blood spatter pattern." She dipped into a crouch. "Do you think this will tell us anything about the height of the assailant?"

"Let's wait to hear what Melissa says."

Salvador nodded, pulling the thick juniper branches at the bottom. Her glove came away with a small smear of mostly dried blood on it. She showed her palm to Fenway.

"Ick," Chan said.

"Ms. Chan, do you know if this walkway is commonly used?" Fenway asked.

"Mostly by employees," she said, her eyes on the junipers.

"So—you, Mathis, Seth, Tyra?"

"And when Seth and Tyra have their friends here," Isabella said. "They'll cut through here to get to the back of the property or whatever."

"Seth and Tyra had friends on the property? What for?"

Isabella shrugged. "I don't ask. Seth has this one friend, a tall, skinny white guy. British or Australian or something. I've only seen him once or twice. Kinda creepy."

Hmm. Maybe Calvin Banning.

"And Tyra's friends?" Fenway moved herself between Isabella and the junipers.

That snapped Isabella out of it—she lifted her eyes to meet Fenway's. "You interviewed them before. Hope and George."

"Are they here a lot?"

Isabella tilted her head from side to side. "A couple times a week, maybe. They're pretty tight."

"All three of them?"

"Yeah." Isabella scoffed. "That's weird, right? Hanging out at a storage unit?"

"Maybe."

"I don't know what George sees in Hope, frankly." She leaned forward. "You know, I think they're only together because George thinks he owes her."

"He owes her? For what?"

"We all went out for drinks after work," Isabella said. "Hope met us at Winfrey's, and she drank a little too much and started talking about how George got into massive debt in one of his businesses when they were still dating. I guess Hope's family bailed him out—financially, I mean. He had terrible credit for years." She gave Fenway a half-smile. "George didn't want to be thought of as a gold-digger, I guess."

"Uh-huh." Fenway leaned forward to get a better look at the wall—and Isabella craned her neck, trying to steal a glance over Fenway's shoulder.

"Ms. Chan, would you be so kind as to wait for us in the office?" Fenway asked.

Chan didn't move.

"You don't want to miss any customers."

"Sure. Of course." Chan stepped away, then hurried down the walkway out of sight.

Salvador stared after Chan. "You don't think she had anything to do with Seth Cahill's murder?"

"No." Fenway considered a moment. "No," she said again, this time with more finality. "Seth Cahill weighed one-fifty or so, but Isabella is five-foot-nothing. She couldn't have dragged his body into the storage unit." Fenway blinked. "Besides, she's the one who assigned me Unit 176. If she'd killed Seth Cahill, she'd have wanted to keep me out of there. And she would have washed the blood off the wall here when she found it."

"Which way is Unit 176?"

Fenway pointed forward, away from the office, farther down the walkway.

Deputy Salvador turned in her crouch and examined the concrete, then tilted her head and squinted.

"Fibers from the Persian rug?"

"Right." Salvador pointed the way they'd come. "I saw on the video that the Persian rug—the one wrapping up Cahill's body—lay on the floor of Seth's office. So I'm thinking that the killer met Seth Cahill in his office, then Cahill walked out here with him. And the killer took advantage of this area. Look." Salvador pointed to the walls. "No cameras."

"Cahill had turned the cameras off."

"Maybe our killer didn't know that. Or maybe this felt like a safer place to commit murder. So the killer attacks Cahill, smashes him in the back of the head. The blood splatters all over the bushes, and the killer doesn't realize a bunch of the blood went through the branches and got on the wall."

"That follows." Fenway was impressed. Salvador would make a great replacement for Mark.

"I don't know if the killer planned this. The back of a hammer —that suggests a crime of passion or opportunity."

"Or both."

"But not lying in wait. Not premeditation."

"I don't know." Fenway looked back and forth along the

concrete walkway. "This suggests someone who knew the facility well. Maybe someone who suggested coming this way."

Salvador pursed her lips.

"And," Fenway continued, "the killer knew the Persian rug's exact location. Knew it would be easier to drag the dead body wrapped up in a rug." She pointed to the ground. "No blood on the ground. If Seth's body had been dragged—or moved at all—without being wrapped up, blood would've dripped all over the concrete."

"Unless the killer—or a maintenance person—washed it off."

Fenway pressed her lips together. "Possibly."

"And remember, it rained early Tuesday morning."

"Not enough to clean off blood spatter from the wall."

"Probably not," Salvador said, "but let's see what Melissa has to say." She cocked her head. "You're thinking something."

"She's got motive," Fenway said, "but I'm thinking it's less and less likely that Miranda Duchy did this. She knew Seth had the Persian rug in his office, but I don't buy her wrapping the body up and dragging it to Unit 176."

"Is it a long way to the unit?"

Fenway turned and walked down the walkway. Twenty feet later, the walkway ended—right into the asphalt, with the back gate across the blacktop, only a dozen yards away from Unit 176. She turned back. "No. Not far at all."

"So maybe Miranda Duchy *could* have done it."

"She had the financial motive." Fenway shook her head. "But I don't believe she'd do that. Even a crime of passion. Why take the hammer back home?"

"People do crazy things. Maybe she was in shock."

"And she invited Dez and me into her shed where the hammer was sitting on a shelf in plain sight."

"If Miranda was in shock, maybe she put the hammer in the shed and forgot she did it."

Fenway tilted her head. "Do you really believe that?"

Salvador thought for a moment. "Not really. The evidence points to Miranda, but I'm not sure I trust it."

"Me neither." Fenway bit her lip in thought. "But the blood spatter, the murder location—if this is indeed where the killer attacked Seth Cahill—I'm thinking the killer knew this place a lot better than Miranda Duchy did."

"Someone who knew this facility? Are you thinking Mathis Jericho?"

"Especially since we can't find him. He doesn't have an alibi, he isn't answering his phone, and he's in charge of maintenance. There must be twenty framing hammers he has access to. Plus, his gravy train was about to run dry. Means, motive, opportunity."

Salvador was quiet.

"Or Tyra," Fenway said.

"Tyra? But—didn't we uncover that the life insurance money went to Miranda, not Tyra?"

"That's right, and Miranda is in a lot of debt. But the motive might have been personal."

Salvador tilted her head. "Personal?"

Fenway told Salvador about Scott Behrens and how he had reconnected with his birth mother after twenty years. And then how the same morpheranyl that Seth Cahill had stored illegally might have been responsible for Scott's overdose. "If she blamed Seth for her son's overdose, maybe it was still a crime of passion. Just not for money."

Salvador pointed at a spot on the concrete walkway. "Red fibers. Looks like they might be silk."

Fenway took out her phone and took a picture, first a wide shot, then a close-up.

"And another here."

Deputy Salvador, still crouching, scooted down the walkway and continued to find fibers—most of them a dusky gold or navy blue color, which had been two of the dominant colors of the Persian rug Cahill had been wrapped in—and Fenway followed.

She tapped and pinched the phone screen to take pictures, zooming in and out. She took out an evidence baggie and began picking the fibers up with gloved fingers. Should she put them all in separate bags? No, she didn't have enough. Better to put them all together than to leave them out another night—or even another hour.

A dusky gold fiber had stuck to the edge of the wall when the walkway narrowed at the edge of the buildings. The asphalt met the walkway, only thirty or forty feet from the corner of the Building C —where Unit 176 stood.

Celeste stood and drew herself to her full height. "So we know the way the killer came."

"Seems so."

"And the killer probably worked alone."

Fenway cocked her head.

"The murderer wouldn't have dragged the rug on the ground otherwise." Salvador thought for a moment. "Unless the second person didn't want to get their hands dirty, or if they were incapacitated. But my money is on the killer working alone."

Fenway nodded. Deputy Salvador kept proving why she was the right choice for the detective position. Fenway would call HR as soon as she could to make sure the process was still moving forward. Salvador might get promoted to sergeant within a couple of years.

Salvador looked up. "The Corvette's still missing?"

"Yes."

"They've checked the local airport lots?" Salvador paused. "Don't Corvettes come with tracking devices? SafeBoard? Something like that?"

Fenway nodded. "But it's not responding. Our IT specialist thinks someone disconnected it."

Salvador blinked a few times. "Okay—let's try to recreate this killing. Maybe an hour before and in the aftermath."

"Sure." Fenway started walking around the building, back to the office. Salvador followed. "We already know that Seth Cahill got here at a quarter after ten, then turned off the cameras at 10:18."

"Was anyone else here?"

Fenway thought back to her earlier phone call with Melissa de la Garza. "No one else was on the property when Cahill turned the cameras off."

"The killer had to arrive after 10:18, then."

"And we think Seth turned off the cameras because he didn't want the cameras recording his receipt of the drugs."

"So anyone involved in the drug transaction would have shown up after the cameras were off."

"And we can't rule any late-arriving person—or people—out. We're pretty sure Mathis Jericho—the maintenance guy—was here, and he might have wanted to take over Seth's business." Fenway shook her head. "But we're looking for a guy named Calvin Banning. He travels on the ship that smuggles the morpheranyl into Estancia, and then oversees the handoff and the placement of the drugs in storage—or that's what I've been able to piece together."

"But right now, our lead suspect is Miranda Duchy."

"Yes. She says she was driving back and forth to Vista del Rincón during the time in question. No one—at least, no one so far—can place her in any of the places where she said she'd been. Not to mention the murder weapon being found at her house."

"Pending the blood analysis."

"Right."

Salvador frowned. "And she knew Seth had a rug in his office?"

"She gave it to Seth. Asked for it back, as a matter of fact."

"That's bold." Salvador folded her arms and stared at the ground in thought. "And would she be able to drag Seth's body from the middle of the concrete walkway into Unit 176?"

Fenway scrunched her nose. "Probably. Dragging a one-hundred-fifty-pound dead body in a forty or fifty-pound rug? Miranda could have done that."

"It's not that far. A hundred feet, tops."

"True."

They reached the office, and Fenway reached out for the handle, then she stopped.

"What is it?" asked Salvador.

"We put out an APB on the Corvette, and it disappeared. That's strange."

Salvador nodded. "I thought the same thing."

"We know Seth drove the Corvette the night he was murdered. So the killer would have had to get rid of the car."

Salvador spread her arms wide. "I would imagine several units within this facility are large enough to store a vehicle."

"I was thinking the killer might have driven it somewhere else, then somehow gotten a ride back." Fenway rubbed her chin. "But if the Corvette is hidden here, no need for a ride back."

"And if the car isn't hidden here," Salvador said, "how did the killer get the Corvette *out* of the facility? It's not like the cameras will magically turn back off."

Fenway squinted. "They would if the owner of the facility was the killer."

"Tyra?"

"Right."

Salvador nodded. "Or Miranda might have known how to do it. She and Seth were sneaking around for, what? A year?"

"I know the physical evidence points to her, but Miranda Duchy wouldn't even carry a heavy box to the shed. She doesn't strike me as the kind of woman to get her hands dirty."

"When it comes to extramarital affairs, maybe you'd be surprised at how dirty your hands can get." Then Salvador stopped, took a sharp breath as if to say something else, then thought better of it.

Oh no. Dez wasn't the only one who knew Fenway and McVie had a dalliance before the divorce. How far had that knowledge spread?

And maybe Deputy Salvador didn't have the context that McVie had found out his wife had been carrying on a yearlong affair of her own.

Fenway shut her eyes tight. *Celeste doesn't care that you and McVie have a past. She wouldn't want to work for you if she did. Focus, Fenway. You're in the middle of a murder investigation—with a woman who might very well be your next detective.*

"Oh," Fenway said. "Tyra Cahill is gonna *love* us."

CHAPTER SIXTEEN

<hr>

"I've tried three different judges," Sarah Summerhill said, "and none of them will touch it."

"But it makes sense," Fenway insisted. "The Corvette *has* to be there."

"It doesn't, actually," Sarah said.

Fenway paused and took a step back from the counter. "But how else could the killer have hidden the Corvette? There are fourteen storage units at Cahill Storage big enough to fit a Corvette."

"And at least thirteen of them have no reason for the Dominguez County Sheriff's Department to enter. Which means, without a compelling—"

"Come on, Sarah, I expect that kind of argument out of Migs."

"Migs is someone else you'll need to replace. I imagine you'll have a hard time getting a decent legal assistant in here, and Migs will have his pick of employers by the end of the summer. Maybe sooner."

"Oh—right. I've gotta get over to HR and ask them what the next step is for backfilling Mark's position."

Sarah's eyes widened. "You made your decision?"

"I was leaning toward Celeste, and after her insights today, I'd be foolish to choose anyone else."

Sarah nodded. "I agree. What did *she* say about your idea to get a search warrant for fourteen storage units?"

"She didn't think it would work." Fenway folded her arms. "But I don't think storage units should have an expectation of privacy. Don't storage units fall under the same fourth amendment exception if there's a murder?"

"Dunn vs. Commonwealth of Virginia," Sarah said. "Just the opposite. No blanket search warrants for storage facilities. Law enforcement must treat each of the units as if it were an apartment or other domicile. Even though no one lives there. You're right—if you knew which storage unit belonged to the deceased, you could search that specific storage unit. But not every storage unit in the facility."

Fenway took a step back, thinking. "Yeah, you're right. I didn't think it through."

"But maybe it doesn't matter." Sarah cleared her throat. "Put yourself in the shoes of the killer. Would you want the Corvette on the property? With the police sniffing around for days? I'd bet five bucks that the Corvette's somewhere else."

"I don't know—if it were me, I'd leave the Corvette at the storage facility if I could. It's the best way to buy a day or two of time. There's the problem of the killer needing to get back to the facility. Taxi drivers might recognize your face. The FlashRide app would track your location." Fenway shook her head. "No, it makes the most sense to leave the Corvette there. Whether it's found in a day or a week or a year."

Sarah put a hand up. "Wait—maybe the killer put the Corvette in an empty unit. If that's the case, Tyra Cahill essentially is the owner. You could get a warrant to search those."

Fenway shook her head. "They're all rented. All the units big enough, anyway."

"Are they really?" Sarah said. "Maybe something to ask Tyra

about."

Fenway nodded. "Unfortunately, she's lawyered up. I can't attempt communication with her."

"Unless it's through her attorney," Sarah pressed.

"I can ask." Fenway drummed her fingers on the counter. "Besides, she doesn't look nearly as guilty as the woman set to receive two million dollars from the life insurance policy who had the murder weapon in her shed. Tyra Cahill isn't worried about explaining why she told me I couldn't take possession of Unit 176."

"What if," Sarah said, "it's true that all the storage spaces big enough to hold a car were full? Or if the killer simply didn't think of it? What if the killer drove the Corvette away?"

"They'd have to get back to the storage facility if they had their car there."

"I requested info from the rideshare companies," Sarah said. "Nothing near Cahill Warehouse Storage on Monday night."

"So maybe we ping the taxi services. Or maybe they caught a ride with a friend." A friend like Hope Dunkelman was to Tyra Cahill: besties for two decades.

"I'll check with the taxis."

Fenway screwed up her mouth. "But where would they take the Corvette? It's a flashy car. Sure to get noticed."

"We've found missing cars before abandoned at long-term airport parking. Callahan has checked some of the popular lots."

"Any hits yet?"

Fenway shook her head.

"So what about private garages?"

"Like private parking garages?"

"I mean one-car or two-car garages at houses or apartment buildings."

Fenway cocked her head. "Well, Mathis Jericho doesn't have a garage space at his apartment complex. And I don't think Calvin Banning or Stephan Butler have any in Estancia—well, maybe they do. Where would I even start?"

"What about Tyra Cahill?"

"She has a garage. I guess she could have put Seth's Corvette in there."

"And you checked Miranda Duchy's garage?"

Fenway nodded. "Yes, when Mark served the search warrant. We found only the SUV in the garage." Then Fenway blinked and stared down at the counter.

"What is it?"

"Hang on a sec." Something in Fenway's head rattled around. Miranda had been driving. She'd wanted to go to Vista del Rincón, but the sun had already set. She wanted a drink at the fancy hotel bar, but found it closed for a private event. Then she wanted to drive...

"Up to her cabin," Fenway mumbled.

"What?"

"Miranda Duchy. She has a cabin. She said she wanted to go up there but didn't want to drive in the dark on winding roads."

Sarah nodded. "Let me search the land use records in the county."

"San Miguelito County, too."

Sarah adjusted her chair and turned to her screen, tapping on the keyboard in front of her.

"Can you tell me if you find something?"

"Of course."

Fenway went into her office and woke her PC. She sat down heavily in her chair and let out a sigh. A glance at the clock in the corner of her monitor: still over an hour before Hope Dunkelman's arrival.

A flash in the bottom corner of her screen. Weather alert. Tropical storm Alonso was a little weaker than before—the Pacific waters were cold, after all—but if the meteorologists were right, it would still be destructive.

She opened her email. A message from Melissa: the footage from the security company for Cahill Warehouse Storage. The company uploaded everything to the cloud, posting a dozen links, with three-hour increments of the footage from Monday and Tuesday. Fenway scanned the email again.

> *Hi Fenway,*
> *My report with timestamps is attached. I couldn't find anything suspicious on this footage. Maybe I missed something. Can you be my second set of eyes on this?*
> *—M*

Fenway opened Melissa's report, moved it to the side of her monitor, then clicked on the *9 PM-Midnight* link. Six screens, all going at the same time. She glanced at the front of the office and gritted her teeth: three of those stupid Tailwhip electric scooters were parked on the sidewalk. Even though the county ordinance prohibited people from riding scooters on sidewalks, many would still do it. She took out her notebook, opened to a new blank page, and uncapped a pen from her pen cup.

Fenway didn't see anything that wasn't in Melissa's report.

She turned her attention to the other buildings, particularly Building A, which housed Unit 112—where the squatter had left the sleeping bag and other material. None of them had activity; only the blue-white bulbs in modern-style sconces on the buildings provided any light at all.

Two minutes. Nothing. Fenway fast-forwarded. Even with the sped-up video, no changes were visible on the screen.

And now, the Corvette. It pulled into the driveway with the timestamp of 22:15:21—10:15 PM nearly on the dot. Fenway glanced at Melissa's report—there it was. Seth Cahill leaned out of the Corvette's driver's-side window and tapped a number on the keypad. The gate slid open, and Cahill impatiently drove in as soon as the gate allowed enough room, swung the car into a parking space, then hurried out of the Corvette before the gate opened all the way. At 22:18:33, the screens all went dark.

Fenway fast-forwarded the rest of the video: blank screens for the rest of the three-hour section. She closed the file.

Oh—she should have talked to HR today. She clicked over to her email; still nothing. The specialist was probably gone for the day, but it wouldn't hurt to try. She picked up the phone and dialed Debbie Farzan's desk. It went to voicemail.

"Hi, Debbie," Fenway said after the beep. "This is Coroner Stevenson. Just wanted to make sure we're moving forward on the backfill for Sergeant Trevino. I sent an email or two and haven't heard back. Let me know next steps." She paused for a moment. "An email update is fine, thanks."

She hung up the phone, wiggled and stretched her fingers, then opened the *Midnight-3 AM* link. Blank screens for the full three hours. Same with the *3 AM-6 AM* link. Finally, the *6 AM-9 AM* link: the cameras came on at 07:47:11—almost eight o'clock the next morning. The cameras had been off for roughly nine-and-a-half hours.

Fenway double-checked the timestamps in Melissa's report, then scanned the videos. No sign of the Corvette. Mathis Jericho's compact sedan sat in the space next to the office entrance. A few minutes later, Jericho exited the office, ran his hand over his face, and walked to a maintenance shed in another screen, unlocking the shed and removing a few small gardening tools: a trowel, a small hand cultivator, and a mini-tiller. Melissa had noted this as well— *Mathis Jericho retrieves tools from the work shed,* along with the correct timestamp.

Hmm. The mini-tiller resembled a hammer, but with three narrow claws on one side and a thin, flat blade on the other. Could that have been the murder weapon instead of a framing hammer? Fenway squinted—no, not even close. Besides, Seth Cahill had already been killed.

Maybe the framing hammer had been taken from the shed a day or two before. She had neglected to ask Mathis Jericho—or Tyra Cahill, or anyone from the storage facility—if they'd been missing a framing hammer. Maybe Mark or Dez had been more pointed with their questions. Of course, Mathis and Tyra were two suspects, so expecting the truth was folly.

Sarah knocked on Fenway's open office door.

"Come on in," Fenway said, not taking her eyes off the screen.

"You have a guest," Sarah said.

Fenway looked up. Piper Patten stuck her head into the room.

"Hi, Piper! What's up?"

"I need to shuttle some office stuff to McVie's storage unit, and I rode my bike in today. Can I borrow your car? Just for a couple of hours?"

Fenway nodded. "Sure, I'll be here for a while."

"Thanks."

"McVie can't take the office stuff himself?" asked Sarah.

"He's still following his client's wife. Didn't get anything incriminating at Pilates, so the client's paying him double to tail her a few extra hours."

Fenway shook her head as she took her keyring from her purse and removed the Honda key. Some people *really* wanted to catch their spouses cheating. She tossed the key to Piper, who caught it with one hand.

"Thanks. It'll be back in your spot by five."

A thought occurred to Fenway. "Hey, Piper, hang on a sec."

"Yeah?"

"I'm working on a case with a bunch of security camera footage," Fenway said.

"You got the footage from the storage facility?" Sarah asked.

"Yep. *Fascinating* stuff." Fenway turned back to Piper with a droll smile. "Piper, you still keep up with all the latest technology on machine-assisted identification?"

"Even more so now, since I work for McVie. What do you need?"

"Is there any technology that could help us find a framing hammer in these videos?"

Piper cocked her head. "A—a framing hammer? What do you mean?"

"There's a tool shed onsite, and one of the cameras is focused on it."

"And we think it's—" Sarah began.

"—important to the crime," Fenway finished. Of course, Piper could connect the dots. Maybe Fenway was getting too close to revealing details, but if anyone was familiar with this technology, it'd be Piper.

"I think I understand," Piper said, turning her eyes to the ceiling, almost as if she were counting tiles. "If you can find the hammer in the video footage before the murder, but then the tool shed people can't find it after the murder, then you can prove it's the murder weapon?"

"Something like that." Fenway scratched her head. "But did the hammer disappear two days ago or two months ago?"

"You could train one of the expensive software tools to do that." Piper tilted her head. "But why not ask the employees if they're missing a hammer?"

"Because all the employees are suspects."

"But," Sarah said, "they're not *all* the killer. Unless you think the three of them are all in on a little conspiracy."

Fenway paused. A conspiracy was possible. Tyra and Mathis might have intended to take the drug storage business away from Seth—and if the divorce and subsequent sale of the storage business to Tyra wouldn't crowbar Seth away from it, maybe the hammer claw to the back of the head would.

Tyra had known about the drug storage, but not for very long. And Isabella Chan didn't appear to be involved in the slightest. Fenway shook her head. "Not likely. Not with what we've found so far."

"So one of them might lie about the hammer, but not all of them."

Fenway nodded.

"There are a couple of forensic analysis tools that could help," Piper said. "But they're not cheap. And it might take a while to roll out and start using."

"Never mind," Fenway said. "Thanks anyway."

Piper left the room, and a moment later, the sound of the suite door opening and closing.

"Even if you find the hammer on the video," Sarah said, "it doesn't prove that was the murder weapon. I'm not sure you could use it in court."

"Is that why you want to ask the employees first?"

"Well, that and it would save us the trouble of finding and installing a new piece of software."

"But it's possible that the only person who ever saw or touched the hammer was Mathis Jericho."

Sarah shrugged. "Ask all the employees first, before you analyze the weeks of footage."

Fenway sighed. "And then dig through two months of footage until we find the hammer on video."

"My friend Jax was so envious when I got this job," Sarah said. "They thought it'd be so glamorous. Five hundred hours of video footage to sort through." She batted her eyelashes. "I'm ready for my close-up, Mr. DeMille."

On screen, a white Honda Civic pulled into the driveway of the storage facility, avoiding the two Tailwhip scooters on the sidewalk. Fenway noted the timestamp. Isabella Chan leaned out of her window and opened the gate. She parked next to Mathis and went into the office.

Fenway leaned back in her chair. "I might be looking at this footage for a while."

Sarah nodded. "Door open or closed?"

"Closed, I guess. And I'm expecting Hope Dunkelman at four." Fenway smiled. "If her husband doesn't convince her not to come."

Sarah furrowed her brow.

"I asked him too many pointed questions earlier," Fenway said. "He knows I think Hope is giving Tyra a false alibi."

"Ah. Hell hath no fury like a husband defending the honor of his wife." Sarah's tone had a sardonic note. "I'll tell you when you've got ten minutes left."

"Make it twenty," Fenway said, stretching her arms above her head. "That'll give me time to grab a latte at Java Jim's before I head to the sheriff's office."

"Gotcha." Sarah closed the door behind her, and Fenway turned back to her video feeds.

She stared at the front entrance and the driveway for a few seconds, then blinked. Something seemed off. What was it?

She stared harder, got nothing, and shifted in her chair.

Maybe the killer had hidden the Corvette in a storage unit and came back to drive it away. She turned the video on fast-forward—about 3x speed still allowed her to view the details of the footage. Mathis tended to a dead bush in a planter near the entrance. He went to the office, then brought out two fluorescent light tubes.

"Dispose of the dead light tubes properly, young man," Fenway muttered. "Hazardous waste is everyone's problem."

Over the next three-plus hours of video—only about ninety minutes viewed on high speed—ten vehicles went in and out. About thirty minutes in, a U-Move-It van drove in, and its two occupants loaded the contents of a unit in Building E.

Then Mathis Jericho walked from the office to the storage shed, unlocked it, and pulled out a small toolbox, a drill, a tool with a wooden handle—Fenway squinted, but couldn't tell if it was the framing hammer they'd found in Miranda Duchy's shed—and several short pieces of wood. He turned and walked toward the walkway between two buildings—the same walkway that Isabella Chan had shown her the day before. The toolbox and wood looked identical to what Fenway and Deputy Salvador had discovered.

About five minutes later, Mathis left the walkway between the buildings, without any of the tools or wood, and hurried over to the office. He left the office a minute later, following a man who went inside another storage building across the parking lot. Maybe a customer in need of help. Mathis must have forgotten all about the wood and the toolbox.

Fenway and Deputy Salvador had found the toolbox underneath the junipers. But there had been no tool with a wooden handle, framing hammer or no.

But Seth Cahill had almost certainly been murdered next to the junipers at the concrete walkway between the buildings. And if Mathis *had* taken the framing hammer there, then the killer had probably picked it up and used it as the weapon.

A few SUVs and crossover wagons unloading boxes or furniture out of the backs of their vehicles.

Then Fenway saw herself onscreen drive McVie's Highlander up to the front. She frowned. No Corvette. No one going into a unit that looked like it could hold a car.

Fenway yawned and looked at the clock on her screen. Three thirty. Close enough for her to finish out the video review. She looked at the timestamp—only about an hour left on the video, but the other law enforcement representatives would show up on the recording soon enough. She paused the video, saved her location, then exited the web browser.

She stood from her chair and reached her arms toward the ceiling, feeling a satisfying crack between her shoulder blades. Maybe she'd be surprised and Hope Dunkelman *would* show up for the interview. Then she'd listen to what Hope had to say about Tyra's whereabouts—Fenway could ask some questions to catch Hope in a lie.

She opened her office door. Sarah glanced up. "It's not quite time."

"I'll head over to Java Jim's early. I reviewed most of the video."

The door to the suite opened, and McVie walked in, holding a small brown paper bag. Dressed in board shorts and flip-flops, he smiled when he saw Fenway. The tips of his ears and his nose were pink from the sun. He walked into Fenway's office, and she shut the door behind him.

"Rough day at work?" Fenway asked, giving him a hug in greeting.

"Nothing's going on between the wife and her Pilates instructor," McVie said. "Or the wife and her surf instructor, although he got handsy behind the beach shack with another woman."

"Your client will be pleased," Sarah said.

"We'll see about that," McVie said. "I got us in at Maxime's at eight."

Fenway grinned. "Did you read my mind?"

McVie shrugged. "Probably."

"I can interview the waitstaff there. Two birds with one stone."

McVie rolled his eyes. "Why is it that one of us is always on the clock?"

Fenway smiled. "Keeps us on our toes. It's good timing too—we can go to Mark's retirement party first."

"Speaking of which—" McVie pulled out a small flat wrapped box from the paper bag and placed in on Fenway's desk.

She narrowed her eyes. "What is that?"

"You haven't had time to go get Mark's gift, right? I drove by HomeCreate and figured I'd save you some time."

"Gift card?" Fenway asked.

"A hundred bucks. Figured that'd look good coming from his boss."

Fenway blinked. "Wow—thanks, Craig. Really—really thoughtful."

"No trouble at all."

With a dopey grin on her face, she reached out and took his hand. "Want to run over to Java Jim's with me? I need an afternoon latte."

"Sure. I could use some energy to pack some stuff up." McVie drew a small circle on the carpet with his foot. "Don't suppose you'd keep me company this afternoon."

"And pack the boxes when you complain you can't get every-thing to fit?" Fenway asked.

McVie blinked. "I—I don't do that."

"They call that *weaponized incompetence,* Craig," Fenway said, a sweet smile on her face. "And if you weren't leaving for a year, it'd bug me a lot more than it does. But no, I can't pack for you—"

"Keep me company—"

"I can't do it tonight, not with the interviews for my investiga-tion and the retirement party. But I promise I'll meet you at Winfrey's for Mark's party by six thirty, then we can go to dinner." She stepped behind him and held the door open. "You didn't already pack all your nice clothes, did you?"

"I have a button-down shirt, slacks, and a decent pair of shoes." McVie walked through the doorway, Fenway letting the door close and following him. "Don't worry, I'll be presentable."

The afternoon had grown warm, and Fenway had to remove her blazer as they took the concrete path to Java Jim's. Fenway got her latte iced. McVie ordered an iced tea.

Fenway stepped back from the counter and took in McVie. She was still attracted to him, just like at the beginning. But more than that, she liked his company, too. Part of her wished she *could* watch him pack boxes as they riffed on their jobs and the latest dumb TV shows, rather than her going across the street to the sheriff's office to wait for Hope Dunkelman to try to catch her in a lie about Tyra's alibi.

McVie caught Fenway's gaze out of the corner of his eye. "Oh, don't give me that. I'm secure enough in my manhood to order a big pink drink if I want. I'll ask them to stick an umbrella in it if—"

"No, no." Fenway shook her head. "I don't want to stay at work and do an interview. I wish we didn't have to go to Mark's retire-ment party, either. Not that I don't want to say goodbye to Mark—"

McVie sighed. "I know."

"We don't have that much time left."

"You make it sound like I'm crossing the River Styx."

Fenway cast her eyes down. "It's a long way."

"It's a two-hour flight."

"It's a different time zone."

McVie nodded. "Yeah."

The barista called *Joanne* and Fenway grabbed her iced drink from the counter. "Okay, I gotta head to the sheriff's office. You can get another girly drink when I see you at Winfrey's at six thirty."

"It's a deal."

————

Fenway walked into the sheriff's office building and almost ran into Sheriff Gretchen Donnelly in the empty lobby. With the storm coming, the deputies must be on patrol, not in the office.

"Ah, Coroner," Sheriff Donnelly said.

"Sheriff."

"I saw you booked the interview room."

Fenway nodded. "Possible witness in the Seth Cahill case."

Donnelly nodded, but didn't meet Fenway's eyes. "With the murder weapon found at the victim's girlfriend's house, are we sure that's a good idea?"

"We haven't matched the blood yet."

"It's type A-negative. Same blood type as the victim. Only six percent of the population."

"It's not enough to convict." Fenway tried to catch the sheriff's eye, but the other woman stared resolutely at the bottom of the door behind Fenway.

"Given Ms. Duchy's financial status, we're worried she's a flight risk."

"So bring her in for questioning. I know we can't ignore the murder weapon found at her residence, but I've got several more leads to follow."

"I'm worried Ms. Duchy has already disposed of evidence at her cabin," Donnelly said.

Fenway rubbed her left shoulder with her right hand. She was too young to get aches and pains like this. "Miranda said she didn't want to drive those roads in the dark."

"But maybe she did." Sheriff Donnelly paused. "Not that far of a drive. The cabin still technically sits within the Estancia city limits."

"Yeah, well, so does the Cactus Lake Motel, but only the post office calls that Estancia." Fenway paused. "Where is the cabin?"

"Just on this side of the Hutash Bridge. Off Cactus Lake Highway and the Windkettle cut-off."

Fenway cocked her head. "Oh. That *is* closer than I thought. Only, what, ten or twelve miles?"

"From here? Yes."

But taking the back roads would be a long, winding drive. Yes, Fenway could understand why Miranda wouldn't want to make the drive in the dark.

But Donnelly had a point: Miranda Duchy had plenty of time to kill Seth Cahill, take the Corvette, and drive to the cabin.

"You need to specify what you're looking for if you request a warrant," Fenway said.

"And that's just it—I'm not sure what sort of evidence she would have hidden."

"Seth Cahill's Corvette, for one." Fenway pressed her lips together. "You've got a murder weapon. You didn't see the blood spatter, but it would have gotten on the killer's clothes. So search for bloody clothes, bloody shoes—any evidence that Miranda was there when Seth was killed." She put her hands on her hips. "You've got a motive. And you've got no alibi. So why is Miranda Duchy still at home? Don't you have enough to arrest her?"

"According to ADA Pondicherry," Donnelly said, "we have enough to arrest her, but we don't have enough to convict her. Not even if the blood is a match for our victim."

"We could do a drive-by of the cabin."

"I had Brian swing through there this afternoon. Nothing."

"No Corvette?" Fenway asked.

"No."

"What'd he look for?"

Donnelly folded her hands. "I told him to be on the watch for anything out of the ordinary."

"What did he find?"

"Nothing. No signs of life."

"Did he knock on the door?" Fenway asked.

"Yes."

Fenway nodded. A good guy and a decent deputy, Brian Callahan nevertheless often skimmed over details. "Can you ask Deputy Callahan to send me his write-up of the visit?"

Donnelly furrowed her brow. "I'm not sure he should prioritize—"

"He's got to write it up anyway, doesn't he?"

"Of course." Donnelly smiled. "I'll tell him to get it to you as soon as possible."

"If I get any other ideas, Sheriff, I'll let you know."

Fenway walked through the lobby as Sheriff Donnelly exited. She glanced up at the clock above the reception desk: already 4:06. No sign of Hope Dunkelman. She went to the door of the interview room and opened it. The table sat empty, the lights off in the room, the chairs on either side of the table pushed in all the way.

This wasn't how she wanted to spend her Wednesday evening.

She waited another fifteen minutes for Hope Dunkelman to show up. She got some water from the cooler. Fenway debated getting a bag of chips from the vending machine—but no, she wanted to save her appetite for the Pheasant Normandy special at Maxime's. She walked back out to the lobby. No sign of Hope.

She walked out the front door and crossed the street, back to her office. Sarah looked up as she entered.

"That was a short interview."

"Hope never showed up. I'm sure her husband told her I was looking to undercut Tyra's alibi."

Behind Sarah, Dez stared at her screen.

"Afternoon, Dez."

Dez raised a hand in greeting, not looking at Fenway.

"Phone records," Sarah said.

"Whose?"

"Seth Cahill's. We found a whole bunch of unregistered phone numbers."

"To be expected when one does business with drug dealers."

"True."

Behind her, the door to the coroner's suite opened, and Deputy Brian Callahan walked in.

"Coroner," he said, nodding.

"Afternoon, Brian."

He held a folder out. "Sheriff said to make sure you got my report on Miranda Duchy's cabin."

"Oh—thanks." Fenway took the folder from him and opened it.

A printout of the form—something he could have easily sent in email, or a link to the form on the system. Fenway glanced up at him; Deputy Callahan stood there expectantly.

"Something else I can do for you?"

"Yes, if you have a moment."

Fenway motioned to her open office door. "Let's go in here." She led the way, Callahan at her heels. Fenway closed the door softly behind him as he took a seat in front of her desk. She walked to her desk chair and sat, placing the folder on her keyboard.

"I haven't heard anything about my application for detective since our interview."

Fenway paused. "We're in the middle of a murder investigation."

"But Mark—"

"Sergeant Trevino," Fenway said.

Callahan stopped, blinked twice, then continued. "But Sergeant Trevino will only be here until the end of the month. In fact, an active investigation provides a unique opportunity for a new hire to get on-the-job experience."

Fenway leaned forward, her elbows on the table. Callahan made a good point. She opened the folder in front of her.

"You went by Miranda Duchy's cabin?"

"I did." Callahan indicated the paper. "Gret—uh, Sheriff Donnelly said you wanted this right away."

Fenway read.

2:17 p.m. Drove to 13328 Hutash Road. Parked vehicle in driveway. No signs of residents. Rang doorbell and identified myself as sheriff's deputy. No response. Rang twice more and identified myself twice more. Returned to vehicle and departed at 2:21 p.m.

Fenway frowned. Only four minutes? "Did you take any photos?"

Callahan sat back in his chair. "I did not. I saw nothing out of the ordinary."

Sheriff Donnelly had used that phrase too—common enough, Fenway supposed. "No notes as to anything on the porch. Window coverings? Is there a garage?"

"I believe I saw a covered carport behind the house."

"Was there a car there?"

"I didn't have a warrant."

Fenway frowned. "Was it behind a fence?"

"There's no fence on the property."

"But you could see the carport?"

Callahan looked up and to the left, focusing on nothing in particular. "The side of it, yes. I couldn't see inside the carport from the angle I was at."

Fenway blinked. "Walk me through this, Deputy. You couldn't see inside the carport?"

"Not from where I parked my cruiser," Callahan said. "And not when I walked up to the door."

"But surely you walked as much of the perimeter of the house as you were comfortable with?"

"As I said, Coroner, I didn't have a warrant."

Fenway ran a hand over her face. "There's no fence. The driveway is public access. Maybe the carport is visible from the road. You are aware that we're looking for the victim's Corvette?"

Callahan was quiet.

Why didn't he think to walk along at least the front of the house to check everything?

"You spent all of four minutes at the cabin," Fenway said.

"Obviously, no one was home."

Fenway sighed. "Look, Brian, you did everything by the book, okay? But we're looking for specific evidence."

Callahan's face fell and his eyes dropped to the desk. "But—but, look, Coroner, everyone is saying that you don't think Duchy did it."

Wow. Word traveled fast.

"That doesn't mean I want our sheriff's deputies to cut corners. I've been wrong plenty of times. I don't need the evidence to fit my theories."

Callahan was quiet, but his upper lip curled for a split second, then his face went impassive as he looked up. "You're absolutely right, Coroner. Let me make it up to you. We'll go back there first thing tomorrow."

"Tomorrow?"

"Well—" Callahan scrunched his nose. "Our department has to be careful about overtime. My shift ends in about ten minutes."

"Alonso is supposed to make landfall tomorrow."

"Yeah, but I have to follow my boss's orders on overtime."

Fenway closed the folder and stood. "Thanks for getting this report to me promptly. And you make an excellent point about needing someone in this role sooner rather than later. I'll talk to HR to see what the holdup is."

Callahan nodded stiffly. "I appreciate the time, Coroner."

He closed her office door a little harder than he needed to.

CHAPTER SEVENTEEN

"Dez, can you take me over to the Hutash Bridge? I lent my car to Piper."

Dez still stared at her monitor. "Let me guess—McVie is too busy to pack up his office, so she has to—"

"Yes, yes, all the women in McVie's life are doing his grunt work for him. I'll be barefoot and pregnant within the week."

Dez chuckled. "Don't let this become a habit, girl, that's all I'm saying."

"So can you take me?"

"I'm digging through Miranda Duchy's phone records. I can go in maybe an hour."

Fenway glanced at Sergeant Trevino's empty desk. "Is Mark around?"

"He's in San Miguelito. He's following up on Scott Behrens's medical records."

"Oh—sounds like *someone* believes me that it's not Miranda."

"No," Dez replied, "it sounds like *someone* had to pick up some material for Randy's costume at Villa House Theatrical Supply before his retirement party tonight and needed the excuse to be out in that direction."

"Ah. Well, two birds with one stone." And yeah—Mark's retirement party. A sense of relief that McVie had gotten the gift card, sitting wrapped on her desk.

"Brian could take you—he left a couple minutes ago. You could still catch him."

"Uh—I'm actually following up on something I think Callahan might have overlooked."

That broke Dez's concentration, and she glanced up at Fenway, who shrugged.

"Then ask Celeste," Dez said.

"I've made up my mind, by the way. I'm hiring her to backfill Mark."

"Will wonders never cease," Dez said. "You better tell HR first thing tomorrow."

Fenway startled. "I've sent emails. I left a message this afternoon. It's hard enough to hire someone when I'm in the middle of a murder investigation—the least they could do is reply to an email." She stood. "I'll walk over there right now."

"You've missed her. Debbie leaves at three thirty."

Of course—Celeste had said that yesterday. "Why so early?"

"She gets in at seven and takes thirty minutes for lunch."

"Sometimes I miss being an hourly employee," Fenway muttered.

"Isn't Celeste off in a half hour? She doesn't say no to overtime."

"I didn't think Callahan did either. But he said the department is cracking down."

Dez frowned. "Wow, you and Rachel haven't been talking, have you?"

"No, but we're having a girls' night after McVie leaves."

"Be that as it may, Rachel and Brian have been dating for six months. Tonight's their anniversary. I think he's taking her to that fancy new bistro in P.Q. after Mark's party."

Ah. That would do it. That's why Callahan had been too distracted to spend more than two minutes at the cabin. And why he didn't want to take another hour or two to drive Fenway to the cabin.

Fenway considered this; Sheriff Donnelly might not like to spend the extra money, but Fenway could propose pulling Deputy Salvador's overtime from her own budget. A little creative accounting could make it work.

"Thanks, Dez." A pause. "Anything useful from Miranda Duchy's phone?"

"Nothing to report."

"Okay. Keep me posted."

Dez turned back to her monitor and Fenway went into her office, sitting at her desk. She sent another email to Debbie Farzan, asking the HR specialist for the status of Mark's backfill and the requisition. Since she hadn't gotten a response before, she dug the requisition number from the hiring system, referencing it in her email. She hit *Send*. There. She should have an answer the next day.

Next, she called Deputy Salvador.

"Hey, Fenway." Oh, good. They were back on a first-name basis.

"Hey, Celeste. Would you mind taking me to check out a suspect's second house?"

"If you've okayed it with the sheriff."

"I'll call her. The overtime can come out of my budget."

A pause. "You thinking about Miranda Duchy's cabin by Hutash Bridge?"

"I am."

"Callahan already did a drive-by this afternoon."

"I have the report on my desk." Fenway opened her mouth, closed it again, and thought about what she wanted to say. "There's a carport in back of the cabin."

"You think someone parked the Corvette there since Brian did the drive-by?"

"Uh—sure."

Deputy Salvador sucked in a breath through her teeth. "Are you telling me that Brian didn't check for a car in the carport?"

Fenway hesitated. "I'm not telling you that."

"But that's what happened."

Fenway was quiet.

Salvador exhaled, low and long. "Okay. I can pick you up in front of the Coroner's Office in ten minutes."

"Deal."

Fenway ended the call.

She looked at the clock on the corner of her computer screen. If they headed out there in ten minutes, she could be there and back by six and still make it to the retirement party at six thirty. She'd call the sheriff on her way to meet Deputy Salvador.

Fenway put the PC to sleep and left her office. She went to the supply cabinet, grabbing several sets of blue nitrile gloves and evidence baggies.

"Heading out, ladies," she said.

Sarah stood. "Just one thing before you go."

"Sure."

Sarah leaned across the counter. "I got Mark a sterling silver pen and pencil set and a two-hundred-dollar gift card to Walleye & Claw."

"That seafood restaurant on the wharf?"

"Yes, you think it's overpriced, but that's where Randy proposed to Mark. It's their favorite place, and you *will* shut up about the quality of their seafood tonight at the party." Sarah smiled sweetly. "Your name is on the pen and pencil set, and 'from all of us in the coroner's office' is on the gift card. Four hundred ten dollars and thirty-two cents total. I'll send you my cash app info for your share, if that's most convenient."

Yikes—over four hundred dollars? But Sarah was a lifesaver— these two gifts were a lot more thoughtful than a home improvement gift card, as kind as McVie's gesture had been. "You'll have it tonight."

Fenway exited the coroner's suite and walked down the hall. She had to call Sheriff Donnelly to make sure Deputy Salvador could take her—still seven minutes until Deputy Salvador would pick her up. She pulled her phone out and brought up Donnelly's number—

Fenway startled. Hope Dunkelman and George Pope appeared right in front of her, looking harried and out of breath.

"Coroner—I'm glad I caught you," said Dunkelman. "Sorry for being so late. They said you'd be over here."

"That's all right." Fenway smiled, but her mind raced. Could she discuss what she needed to with Dunkelman in the next seven minutes?

"George told me that you thought I lied to give Tyra an alibi," Dunkelman said.

Pope avoided eye contact, but Fenway let him off the hook. "Well, 'lied' is a strong word. I wouldn't be doing my job if I believed everything people told me, right?"

Hope gave Fenway a sad smile. "No, I guess not." She turned to George. "Why don't you wait in the car?"

"We've got to pick up the generator by six. I want to get it in the garage before the storm hits."

"It'll just be a minute."

George nodded stiffly and exited out the front of the building.

Fenway paused, then broached the topic herself. "It's merely due diligence, Ms. Dunkelman. I don't want to open old wounds, but if we arrest someone else and we don't explore Ms. Cahill's possible motive—"

Hope Dunkelman's forehead creased. "I don't want it to come out in open court, for sure. But look, Tyra was with me the whole time—from nine forty-five until I drove her back to our house, and then until the next morning." She set her jaw. "And you wouldn't believe what the three of us went through in high school when Tyra got pregnant."

"I'm sorry—the *three* of you?"

"Everyone abandoned Tyra except George and me." Hope

folded her arms. "Honestly, I expected George to dump me once he knew I planned to support my best friend through the pregnancy. Tyra and I did birth classes together instead of me going to parties or out to the movies. I'm lucky George stayed with me. What other sixteen-year-old kid would stick around?"

Fenway looked up and down the hall. "Do you want to go where we have a little more privacy?"

"I really can't stay long."

"Did you come to tell me something specific?" Fenway paused. "Was it about Scott Behrens?"

Hope flinched. "Oh. You know about him."

"That he was Tyra's biological son? Yes."

Hope grimaced. "I guess you think Tyra wanted revenge—that she blamed Seth for Scott's overdose."

"After discovering Seth wouldn't let Scott come to Tyra's Thanksgiving dinner? Yes, that crossed my mind."

"Seth knew she'd gotten pregnant in high school and put the kid up for adoption. When Scott reached out to Tyra a couple of years ago, it put a strain on their relationship for sure."

"And did Tyra find out about Seth storing the morpheranyl?"

Hope paused. "Not at first. In fact, not until about halfway through the divorce proceedings."

Finally an answer. "Halfway through?"

"How do you think Tyra came out of her divorce with everything tilting in her direction?"

"She told Seth she'd go to the cops?"

"I'm not sure, but Tyra told me she'd found out about his drug business."

"How did she find out?"

"Maybe someone on the inside told her—"

"Like Mathis Jericho?"

Dunkelman shrugged. "She's not dumb. She can put two and two together. After she confronted Seth, he stopped contesting most of what Tyra asked for in the divorce. More than anything, she wanted him out of her life." She scoffed. "I think George and I were angrier at Seth for the drugs than Tyra was."

"But Seth stayed in the drug business."

"Tyra insisted he was getting out of it. Seth told Tyra everything would stop this past weekend—the drug storage, the people staying in the units, everything. I guess the shipment was delayed. Not that Seth kept Tyra in the loop."

"No wonder Tyra didn't want to give me Unit 176," Fenway said. "Because Seth was using that space. Off the books—probably intending to store the morpheranyl. And that's why Isabella didn't know it was taken." Or she knew his dead body already lay on the floor inside the unit—but Hope didn't need to hear Fenway's alternate theory.

Hope nodded. "That kind of thing happened all the time. Seth would mark some unrented units as 'reserved.' Tyra finally figured out that Seth was doing something shady."

"She knew about Unit 176 on Monday night?"

"I don't remember the number she said," Hope said, "but she was complaining about the unit on the phone with us."

"I appreciate you coming in," Fenway said. "You've given me valuable information. But it doesn't prove that you and Tyra were at her house during the time of the murder."

Dunkelman thought for a moment. "Can't you track our cellphones?"

"Sure, but you could have left your cellphones at Tyra's house and left to commit the crime."

Hope blinked. "Both of us? You mean—like, we both killed him?"

The Persian rug fibers on the concrete walkway—no, only one person had dragged the body in the carpet. "We're still gathering evidence. But like I said, we need to cover our bases."

"What can I do to convince you that we never left the house? Not until, like, eleven-thirty—and then we drove back to my house."

Fenway blinked. "I can ask our tech people if there's a way to be certain. You might have to give us your phone. Or Tyra might."

"I'll testify in court," Dunkelman said. "I have nothing to hide."

"But Tyra does," Fenway said. "She won't answer questions without a lawyer. I assume it's because she's not sure about her legal liability since she owns the storage facility where criminals have been storing morpheranyl." Fenway paused. "But it could be because she killed her ex-husband, too."

"I'll testify that she stayed with me all night," Hope said.

Fenway nodded. "I appreciate that."

Dunkelman looked behind her. "I should get going."

"Just one more thing."

"I really must go—"

"Even if Tyra didn't blame Seth for Scott's death, maybe someone else did? Her parents? Maybe the father?"

"The father?" Hope shook her head. "A college freshman visiting Estancia on spring break. He told her he went to Stanford. He'd given Tyra a fake name. She figured it was pointless to try to find him. I would imagine he never found out about her pregnancy."

Oof. A rough spot for a teenager.

"You didn't meet this guy?" Fenway asked. "I thought you two were best friends."

Hope rolled her eyes. "My parents took me down to San Diego to visit my aunt. I remember being ticked off the whole week—spring break of junior year and I'm stuck with my parents. Six weeks later, I find out my best friend is pregnant."

"I'm sorry."

She pointed a finger at Fenway. "Don't you dare judge her. An older guy, at least nineteen or twenty, took advantage of a sixteen-year-old girl. Maybe he lied about being a college student. It happens all the time. No one ever gives a shit about the guy. He got Tyra drunk. These days, he'd get arrested for sexual assault." She dropped her hands to her sides. "All our friends abandoned her. It was like that book we read in American Lit senior year—that woman with that red letter around her neck?"

"Scarlet, not red." Fenway nodded. "Her name was Hester Prynne."

"Right. No one gave a damn what happened to the father of Hester's kid. They wanted to make sure the whole town shunned Hester. That she knew everyone thought she was a whore." Dunkelman spat the last word.

Fenway nodded; she felt no need to point out that the father of Hester's kid died at the end of the book. "What about Tyra's parents? Maybe they wanted revenge for the death of their grandchild?"

Hope guffawed. "Are you kidding? They acted like the pregnancy never happened." She folded her arms. "And besides, they moved to Phoenix to be near their *other* daughter and her kids."

Fenway exhaled. So Scott's father and grandparents—those were a couple of dead ends.

"I'm glad you were there for her." Fenway hoped she sounded as sincere as she felt.

"Yeah, me too. George and I were the only people who treated her like a human. And that includes her parents."

Fenway nodded.

"I really have to go," Hope said, casting another furtive look over her shoulder.

"Have a good evening, Ms. Dunkelman."

———

The cruiser's tires crunched on the gravel as Fenway and Deputy Salvador pulled up in front of the cabin.

Not what Fenway had in mind for a "cabin": no logs or stone walls. It didn't look rustic. Just a relatively small stucco house, single story, with woods surrounding the clearing.

"Doesn't look like anyone's home," Salvador said.

"Pull to the right," Fenway said, pointing to the side of the driveway.

And from the passenger seat, Fenway saw it: the very corner of a red sports car tucked into the carport, half-hidden by the house.

"That's it," Fenway murmured.

"The Corvette?" Salvador put the cruiser in *Park* and killed the engine.

"Not a hundred percent sure, but it looks like it from here. And it's red." Fenway unbuckled her seatbelt. "Come on, let's go look."

Salvador nodded. "You've got gloves?"

"Just restocked." Fenway handed Salvador a pair, then pulled a pair on herself.

The two of them walked toward the carport. The more the sports car came into view, the more it looked like a Corvette. Then she saw the license plate: the same as the APB they'd posted the day before.

"Radio it in," Fenway murmured.

Salvador got on her radio and informed the dispatcher they'd found the missing Corvette.

They were twenty feet away from the rear bumper when Fenway elbowed Salvador. "The windows are down."

"Yep. Weird."

"Who leaves the windows of an eighty-thousand-dollar sports car down outside? Especially with a tropical storm coming?"

"A murderer," Salvador said.

Fenway nodded, took another step, then sucked in air through her teeth. "There's someone in the driver's seat."

Salvador already had her hand on her holster. "This is the sheriff!" Salvador called. "You're in a stolen vehicle! Come out with your hands up!"

No movement.

"Sir!" Salvador barked. "I said, step out of the car with your hands up!"

Still nothing.

Fenway took a step closer. A blur in front of the head of the Corvette's occupant.

Fenway's stomach leapt into her mouth.

"Wait for backup?" Salvador whispered. "Do you think he's dangerous?"

"I don't think so," Fenway said. "That blur around his head?"

Salvador gulped. "Flies."

The deputy was right. Not a swarm of them, but enough, especially out here in the woods on a warm day.

Fenway had seen corpses before—many of them. Cut them open on metal tables, lost patients in the hospital, seen plenty of overdose deaths. Some whom she'd encountered in her time as coroner had been dead for a day, two days, sometimes more. But the more she saw, the less it affected her, of course. Working the jobs she did, first as a nurse in Seattle and then a coroner here in Dominguez County, had exposed her to enough where she didn't have to suppress the urge to vomit. But she'd never completely gotten used to dead bodies. And seeing the cloud of flies around the body in the driver's seat didn't help.

They stood stock-still for a moment that seemed like an hour. Fenway steeled herself and took a deep breath. "You ready?"

Salvador nodded.

Fenway took the driver's side of the car, while Salvador went around the passenger side. They both crept closer until they stood even with the side windows.

Deputy Salvador's hand dropped off her holster. "That's Mathis Jericho."

CHAPTER EIGHTEEN

SIXTEEN, SEVENTEEN, EIGHTEEN BRICKS OF OFF-WHITE POWDER. Most probably morpheranyl. Ten of the bricks had been stacked on Mathis Jericho's lap. The other eight were around his feet. Both doors were wide open as Fenway and Deputy Salvador examined the car and the corpse.

"There might be more in the trunk," Deputy Salvador said.

"There's trunk space in the front of the Corvette, too." Fenway closed her eyes. "Check there." Mathis Jericho hadn't been killed by Calvin Banning or Stephan Butler. They would have taken their morpheranyl with them; they wouldn't have left it to throw law enforcement off the scent. This was too valuable—maybe hundreds of millions in street value, and likely worth over a million to both Banning and Butler as cogs in the larger drug machine.

Maybe Fenway hadn't identified all the players in the drug game. Someone could be between Banning and Anton Venn who controlled everything on the distribution side. Maybe that person got sick of the back and forth with Seth Cahill. Maybe Mathis Jericho had gotten too greedy, trying to take Seth's business for himself. Jericho had possibly killed Cahill and had pissed off the wrong drug dealer.

Fenway opened her eyes again.

But then why store the Corvette at the second residence of Seth Cahill's girlfriend?

Fenway supposed whoever had killed Mathis knew Miranda Duchy was the lead suspect in the Seth Cahill murder. Throwing more evidence there, to put law enforcement on the wrong track.

But no, that didn't make sense. If Mathis's murder had been a drug-related killing, it would have made a statement. Everyone who looked at Mathis's dead body would get the message. But this? With Mathis sitting dead in Seth's Corvette—and with the car essentially hidden in the carport at Miranda Duchy's cabin?

No. This was something personal.

Salvador knelt at the side of the car, then stood, a round key in her gloved hand. "I found this in the footwell."

Fenway nodded. "Looks like a key to a storage unit at Cahill Warehouse. We should bag that up and check if that's the missing key to Unit 176." She leaned forward, swatting the flies away from Mathis's face. Ligature marks, lower on the neck than a hanging would indicate.

"Strangled," Fenway said.

Deputy Salvador nodded. "I saw the marks."

Fenway carefully attempted to move Mathis's limbs. No—they didn't want to move. "Full rigor," Fenway said. Eight to twenty-four hours.

Salvador stepped over to the driver's side door behind Fenway.

Fenway pointed at a white discoloration on the dead man's face. "Blanching. That narrows it down—he's been dead eight to twelve hours. Killed sometime this morning."

"Didn't we expect him to make another drop of the drugs this morning? Or late last night?" Celeste peered over Fenway's shoulder. "Mathis was Seth Cahill's right-hand man. Tried to make a stab at climbing up the drug business ladder and stepped on the wrong set of toes?"

Fenway shook her head. "Maybe that's what the killer wants us to think. But in all the murders tied to drug gangs and cartels that you've studied, is this what you'd expect?"

Salvador drew herself to her full height and shook her head. "No. Usually more public than this. Or at least, where cartel people can see it."

"Right. Because if the cartel or the drug dealers had done it, it would have been a warning."

"And they wouldn't have left the drugs behind." Salvador squinted as she stared at the dead face of Mathis Jericho. "But this is *too* on point, isn't it? I mean, Miranda Duchy said she'd been framed. Now we find Seth's second-in-command garroted in Seth's car—at Miranda's second house?"

Fenway pressed her lips together. "Surely we've had eyes on Miranda Duchy since she emerged as a suspect."

"She only emerged today," Deputy Salvador said. "You didn't talk to Duchy until what, eight or nine o'clock this morning? By then, Mathis could have been dead three or four hours."

"But that doesn't make any sense." Fenway scratched her chin. "The best way to throw people off the scent isn't to plant the murder weapon in your own yard and hide the missing car in your own carport. Especially if you can't provide an alibi for the first murder."

Salvador nodded. "I agree with you. But—"

"But?"

"Let's say Duchy killed Seth Cahill, but screwed up. She left the murder weapon in her shed; she never established a decent alibi. I mean, the claw of a framing hammer? That's not premeditated. Let's say Seth did something to piss her off. He's still in love with Tyra, he met somebody new, or she wanted the insurance money. She lashed out, killed him with the hammer, dragged his body into Unit 176.

Suddenly, we were all over her, and she'd left some truly boneheaded clues for us to find. Maybe Mathis contacted her, asked her where he could continue storing the drugs or said he saw her beating Seth over the head and maybe asks for blackmail. What better cover than to kill him and continue to make it look like she was being set up?"

Fenway bobbed her head from side to side. "I suppose it's possible."

Salvador took a step back. "I don't think we have a choice, Fenway. I think we have to bring Miranda Duchy in."

"ADA Pondicherry doesn't think we have enough to convict."

"But that was before we found Mathis Jericho's body and the Corvette on her property. Besides, we can hold her for forty-eight hours before we decide whether to arrest her." Salvador shook her head. "It's not up to me," she said, "but the bloody hammer found in her shed, the missing Corvette at her second residence, and the victim's right-hand man dead in the missing vehicle? Maybe the evidence is circumstantial, but I can't see any reason Donnelly would allow her to continue walking free."

"Maybe she's got an alibi for the death of Jericho. You're a couple of steps too far ahead."

"Maybe," Deputy Salvador conceded. "But the standard for charges isn't reasonable doubt. It's a reasonable basis for believing the defendant is responsible for the crime. And in my opinion, we've met that standard."

Fenway couldn't argue with that.

"In the meantime, we can look for more evidence." Celeste slowly walked around the car, looking at the fenders, the hood. Maybe searching for telltale scratches in the paint or dings. She reached the passenger door and cocked her head.

"What is it, Celeste?"

Deputy Salvador pointed. "Two indentations in the leather. Like two little blunt objects had pushed into it."

Fenway looked at the passenger seat, then all around the

passenger area. She pointed below the glove compartment. "Scratches," she said. "And they look fresh."

Salvador nodded.

"I think the killer put something in this seat when they drove it from the storage facility here."

Salvador furrowed her brow. "Was that Mathis? Or someone else?"

Fenway shook her head. "Maybe CSI can shed some light on this when they get here."

———

Once Melissa de la Garza and the CSI team arrived, Fenway would have left Deputy Salvador at the cabin to go pick up Miranda Duchy, but they'd come in one car. By this time, Piper had sent Fenway a text: she'd parked Fenway's car back in the parking garage and given the key to Sarah, who likely put it on Fenway's desk.

Fenway had gotten Dez on the phone, and consulted with ADA Pondicherry, who reluctantly agreed that Miranda had to be brought in, though he didn't want to officially place her under arrest until they had more concrete evidence—or if Duchy insisted on leaving.

Dez and a sheriff's deputy had taken a confused and somewhat belligerent Miranda Duchy into custody, and she'd given Fenway an update: Duchy had gone into an interview room, where Dez had read her her rights. Duchy had promptly declined to speak with law enforcement without a lawyer. Apparently, Duchy's lawyer, who specialized in intellectual property, had contacted one of his friends in criminal defense. That sounded not only expensive but intimidatingly competent.

Fenway sighed as she ended the call and walked to Deputy Salvador, standing between the carport and the cabin with her arms folded.

"Good work today, Celeste," Fenway said.

A small smile. "Thanks."

"Have you started searching the cabin yet?"

"Sheriff said to wait for a warrant. She's heading out here, said she'd be handling it personally."

"I guess this is getting high profile."

Deputy Salvador nodded.

"What is it?"

Salvador opened her mouth, closed it, then took a quick breath. "I applied for detective in your office because I want to grow my career. And because when I've worked with you, you seem like a boss who'll have my back. I talked to Dez and Mark."

"Oh." Fenway's face grew hot. "I appreciate that."

"But things have changed in the sheriff's office since Donnelly took over. All the deputies, we used to be tight. But we don't have each other's backs anymore." Salvador glanced around, seeing no one paying attention, and took a step closer. "I think Donnelly's coming out here to take credit for this," she said in a low voice. "Eighteen bricks of Nyllie, a dead man found in a murder victim's car—you watch. She'll spin this into a win for the sheriff's office, and she won't even mention you." She paused. "Or me."

Fenway nodded. "You want an exit strategy from the sheriff's office."

"And you're one of my exit strategies, yeah."

Fenway's phone rang in her hand again. She looked at the screen: 7:17 PM—

Oh no. McVie. She was supposed to be at Winfrey's forty-five minutes ago. "Sorry, Celeste, I have to take this—"

Celeste nodded and turned away as Fenway hit *Answer*.

"Hi, Fenway." Craig's voice, smooth, soft.

"I'm sorry," Fenway said. "I'm late."

"Not many people at Winfrey's. Mark hasn't even shown up yet."

"Not surprising. He's an introvert."

"That could explain why he's not here—but why aren't you?"

Fenway hesitated. "There's been another murder. I'm at the crime scene."

More silence.

"So I'll have to cancel. Not only for the retirement party, but for dinner too. I'll have to take a—" She almost said *rain check,* but there would be no rain checks. McVie was leaving too soon.

"I get it," McVie said, a little late. "It comes with the job."

"It's not like I'm *trying* to convince killers to murder people before you leave."

"And I'm not trying to get my demanding client insist that I follow his wife around every second of every day." He exhaled loudly. "I wish we had more time."

"I wish you didn't have to leave," Fenway said.

McVie stopped.

"I mean," Fenway said, "I know you have to. Your daughter comes first. I just wish—I want you here."

"I didn't have any control over where Amy got her job. And you saw how hard I tried to convince Megan to live with me her senior year."

"Yeah." Did she know how hard he tried? He'd said he did, and Fenway knew herself how unshakable teenagers could be. She knew Megan's boyfriend dumped her and her friends had kicked her out of their social group.

"I wish you could come with me."

Fenway stopped. This felt like a trap, and McVie didn't play games like this. She frowned. What was he doing?

Then she took a deep breath. She hadn't been in therapy for a few months—not since Dr. Tassajera—but she'd learned enough to at least intellectually understand that maybe it wasn't about her.

"I wish we could be together," Fenway said carefully. "I wish I could have my career, and you could have a daughter who could get through this shitty time in her life, and that you and I didn't need to be apart to get everything we wanted."

Would voicing those thoughts make her feel better?

No, it didn't. Instead, one thought reared its head: why *did* they need to be apart to get everything they wanted? This was Fenway's first relationship that had lasted more than six months. And he was fourteen years older. And why couldn't McVie and Megan get by with video calls online? Why did he have to pick everything up and move four states away—abandoning his business, abandoning his support system, abandoning *her?*

"It's too late to cancel our reservation, isn't it?" Fenway said.

"Don't worry about it. As sheriff, I got called away at the last minute, too. All the time." He paused. "Want me to come to your place and wait for you?"

Yes. She wanted that very much. "You don't have to."

"I want to."

"I hate to have you wait for me when you've got so much going on. Maybe I can see you tomorrow?"

"Client's wife isn't headed to the beach tomorrow," McVie said. "Maybe we can get that breakfast at Jack and Jill's."

"We'll see how the murder investigation progresses," Fenway said.

"Right, right, of course." He paused. "I miss being sheriff."

"Me too." Oh—that had come out so fast that Fenway hadn't had time to assess the impact of those words.

"I mean, it'd be dicey, what with you and I dating. But at least we'd work together again."

Fenway closed her eyes and remembered the flutter in her chest when she worked with McVie on a case. Trying to keep the heat level between them on a low simmer. And failing from time to time.

"It wouldn't be a bad thing if you were home when I got there," Fenway said softly.

"Duly noted," McVie said. "I'll make some more storage runs. See you tonight."

Fenway tapped *End* on the call—then Sergeant Mark Trevino appeared at her side.

"Mark!"

He smiled. "This sure beats some stupid retirement party, doesn't it?"

"Why aren't you at Winfrey's?" Fenway's hand went to her mouth.

"I'll let you in on a little secret," Mark said. "I'd rather be here processing a murder scene than forcing myself to smile at a crowded bar while Randy tries to get my co-workers to tell embarrassing stories about me."

"People are there. I just got off the phone with Craig."

Mark theatrically looked around. "Looks like most of the people I work with are *here*."

"Well, Craig did say it was lightly attended."

"Randy's keeping the party going," Mark said. "He told me he's about to make a speech and buy a round of shots."

"He won't be mad at you?"

"Randy's glad I'm retiring." He looked at Fenway out of the corner of his eye. "Although I'm happy to come in on a contract basis and train my replacement." He cocked his head, his eyes questioning.

Fenway leaned closer to Mark and lowered her voice. "I'm offering it to Celeste."

A smile came over Mark's face. "That's great. She's smart. And a quick thinker. When does she start?"

Fenway furrowed her brow. "Bureaucratic hiccups, I think."

"Yeah, we have a lot of those." Mark's face grew serious. "Sheriff Donnelly has hired a lot of people. Maybe she'll be able to help you navigate the red tape."

"She won't be ticked off that I'm taking one of her best deputies?"

Mark shrugged. "Not if she's a decent manager."

"Is she?"

Mark shrugged, then straightened up. "So we've logged the bags of morpheranyl into evidence. Melissa checked them for fingerprints."

"Wiped clean?"

"You'd think, wouldn't you?" Mark said. "And yes, most of them were, but we've got about five or six usable prints off a couple of the bags."

"Maybe the killer messed up," Fenway said.

"It's possible," Mark said. "I've seen this kind of thing before, though. The person we're looking for uses gloves, maybe doesn't wipe the bag off first. So maybe we'll get the prints of the person who packed the baggie—"

"Or maybe the person who loaded it into his car in the first place." Which would likely be Mathis Jericho. But still worth a shot. "Thanks, Mark."

He started to turn away, then snapped his fingers and spun around. "Almost forgot to say what I came over here to tell you. I accessed Scott Behrens's birth certificates and some of his medical records."

"Anything of note?"

"Only that Tyra Cahill left the father's name blank on the birth certificate."

Fenway nodded. "That tracks with what Tyra's BFF told me. Some college kid who got her drunk and gave her a fake name. Apparently, the guy never talked to her after that one night. Never realized he had a kid out there."

Mark nodded.

Fenway sighed. "I looked for an alternate motive, but I can't find one. I thought maybe Mathis wanted to take over Seth's business, and so he killed him. But now that he's dead—"

"Mathis might still have killed Seth Cahill." Mark's brow furrowed. "But then who killed Mathis? I read the report—the death doesn't have any of the hallmarks of a cartel killing."

Fenway tapped her forehead, and a thought sprang to mind. "Not the cartel. Maybe someone else who wanted to take over the business."

"Like who?"

"Like Tyra Cahill."

"Tyra?" Mark blinked. "Take over the illegal business that resulted in the death of her son?"

"Wouldn't the ultimate revenge be to kill the business from the inside out?" Fenway asked. "Or maybe Tyra thought she could make an extra two hundred grand a year that used to go to Seth. Money tends to soothe a lot of emotional wounds."

"But..." Mark scratched his chin. "I suppose that would explain some things."

"And who better to pin the murders on than the 'homewrecker' who stole your husband?"

Mark tapped his foot. "*That* part makes sense. But Tyra killing the one person who can make the dives to the bottom of the boats to get the morpheranyl?"

"Divers can be hired," Fenway said.

"True."

"And the fact that our victim had recently made the girlfriend the new beneficiary of the life insurance—"

"Icing on the cake," Mark said. "Oh, I guess, that's the one thing I'm missing about my retirement party. The cake."

Fenway laughed, then knotted her eyebrows together.

"What is it?"

"Mathis's death really threw my suspect pool for a loop."

"At least Mathis is no longer a suspect," Mark said.

"I still feel like I'm missing something."

"Evidence," Mark replied.

Fenway nodded. "Yeah. Tyra being the killer is a good story, makes a lot of sense, but with nothing to back up that story..."

Mark scratched his chin. "Didn't you say that Tyra knew about Seth's illegal activity?"

"Hope Dunkelman said that, yeah. So did her husband. But Tyra has an alibi, remember?"

Another bolt of inspiration hit Fenway. "We can get around

Tyra's alibi by naming Hope Dunkelman as an unindicted co-conspirator. I think she may have lied about Tyra's whereabouts."

"So get Dunkelman to walk back the alibi," Mark said. "You'd be surprised who'll crack when their freedom is on the line." Mark rubbed his chin. "Maybe you can figure out how to disprove the alibi. Threaten Hope with prosecution unless she turns."

Fenway put her hand on her hips. "One thing I can do is subpoena their phone records. Maybe Tyra and Hope were smart enough to leave their phones at Tyra's house while they went out and committed murder, but maybe they weren't. And if their phones were on, I can figure that out." She paused. "Only problem—only one person dragged the body. At least that's what the evidence suggests."

A smile touched the corner of Mark's mouth. "Maybe Hope drove to Cahill Storage and waited for Tyra, thinking they'd hash something out. Tyra killed Seth, wrapped his body up, dragged it into Unit 176, and then walked out to Hope's car, disheveled, maybe some blood on her. Hope cleaned her up and calmed her down before they go back to the Pope-Dunkelman residence."

"That *is* a good story, Mark. Maybe you should start writing the plays Randy stars in."

"We'd be a hell of a team." Mark put up an index finger in front of his chest. "But if you find that the phones never left Tyra's house, there's no way Hope will change her story."

"Maybe we can find Hope's vehicle on camera," Fenway said. "Running a red light or driving past an ATM."

"There's still a lot of police work to do."

Fenway grinned at Mark. "You'll miss this, won't you?"

"Of course," Mark said. "I'll be thinking of you and Dez—and maybe Celeste—every day when I wake up at ten o'clock and have a mimosa."

Fenway grinned, then raised her phone and tapped the screen. "Maybe I can get someone to get a judge to sign the phone paperwork tonight."

———

One of the deputies drove Fenway back from the Hutash Bridge, and she entered her office, grabbed the key from her desk where Sarah had left it, and finally walked in the door of her apartment at 9:27 P.M.

The door swung all the way open. The apartment was warm despite the air conditioning.

"No boxes," Fenway said dumbly.

McVie looked up from the kitchen counter. "Oh, good," he said.

Fenway felt a rush of affection toward McVie. "You've been busy."

"Made it in only four trips. Done in a couple of hours. Landlord did the walkthrough, and I'm getting all my security deposit back." He came around the counter and started to wrap his arms around Fenway.

"Hold on, hold on," Fenway said, ducking under his arms. "I've got murder scene all over me. Let me take a quick shower and put some sweats on."

"Well, hurry up about it."

Fenway dropped her purse on the kitchen table. "Thanks, Craig."

"For what?"

"Coming over tonight. I'm glad you're here."

McVie grinned.

She turned and began to walk down the hall—then the scent hit her nostrils: baked apples and sweet onions. "Did you cook?"

"Ha," McVie said. "We couldn't cancel the reservation, so I got our food to go. And it's keeping warm in the oven."

"Pheasant Normandy?"

"For you," McVie said. "I got a ribeye."

"What a surprise."

"I would have gotten the scallops, like you recommended last time, but I worried they'd dry out in the oven." He grabbed a dishtowel from the counter. "Hurry up and take your shower. When I hear the water go off, I'll start plating."

"You'll start 'plating,'" Fenway said, a smile crossing her lips. "Look at you, fancy."

"And we can figure out when you can take some vacation. I'd like you to come visit. And I'll fly back here, too."

"Really?"

"We should shoot for once a month," McVie said. "Maybe we won't have a lot of vacation time, but with long weekends here and there, we can make it work."

Fenway grinned. "Don't say stuff like that when I still have guck all over me."

"I could join you," McVie suggested.

"Then our food will *definitely* dry out."

"Maybe it would be worth it."

Fenway turned with a smile and went in the bathroom to turn the shower on.

PART 3
____

THURSDAY

CHAPTER NINETEEN

Six o'clock came early. Fenway swung her feet onto the floor, turned the alarm off. McVie rolled over, facing away from Fenway, and exhaled, a muted snore escaping his lips.

She padded out to the kitchen and looked out the front window.

The sky shimmered with pink and lavender, almost like a sunset. A perfect morning to take a cup of coffee out on the tiny porch—if only there weren't so much to do before the storm arrived.

Fenway took a quick shower, wrapped herself in a towel, and went into her bedroom, gently shaking McVie awake.

"You need to shower?"

"I'm moving a few pieces of furniture today. I'll shower when I'm done." He sat up in bed and rubbed the sleep from his eyes. "You have time for Jack & Jill's?"

"Not really, but it's still early. I guess if we hurry." Fenway looked at McVie. "You worried about the storm later?"

"Alonso is weakening by the hour," McVie said. "But I left my flashlights and my camping stove out of the boxes. And I picked up a few gallons of water yesterday to be on the safe side. We might lose power for a few hours, but I doubt it'll be any worse than that."

"Will the storm be bad enough for you to postpone leaving tomorrow?"

McVie smiled sadly. "I can always hope." He stretched his arms over his head. "I'll get dressed. We can take two cars."

Twenty minutes later, they were out the door. McVie looked up at the sky.

"Yeah, the storm is coming today," he murmured. "I can tell by the sky."

"It's beautiful."

"You never heard, 'red skies at night, sailor's delight; red skies at morning, sailors take warning'?"

Fenway blinked. "Maybe. Not really a lot of boat owners in the neighborhood where I grew up."

McVie followed Fenway's Accord out of the apartment complex's parking lot. Fenway stifled a yawn as she turned onto Estancia Canyon Road and tapped her phone to play her funk playlist. That would get her blood moving.

A little over five minutes later, they parked next to each other in the Jack and Jill's parking lot. They got out of their cars. The light breeze off the ocean felt refreshing.

"Were you listening to the radio?"

"Uh, no. My funk playlist."

"Yeah, well, the weather report said Alonso will make landfall further north than they thought."

"Closer to us or further away?"

"Closer." McVie frowned. "How are you on batteries?"

"I'll get some today."

"Pick them up at the grocery store before work. I'm afraid people will start buying them out of stock." He shook his head as they walked toward the entrance. "This is a shitty time for me to be packing and moving."

Fenway agreed, though perhaps for different reasons.

She checked the clock above the counter when they walked in. Not quite seven.

The ruthlessly efficient server brought their eggs and toast within a few minutes, and McVie paid the bill by twenty after.

After McVie signed the receipt, they walked out of the restaurant to find the wind had picked up. They kissed goodbye in the stiff breeze, standing between their two cars, Fenway tasting the smoky flavor of bacon on McVie's lips. Fenway wrapped her arms around McVie and gave him a squeeze, holding it for an extra couple of seconds. He squeezed back.

As Fenway drove to the office, the muted purples and dusky rose colors, more suited to a sunset, glowed in the sky. Eerie.

Fenway opened the door to the coroner's suite a few minutes past seven thirty.

"Oh, good," Sarah said, standing behind the counter. "I knew you had a late night. I thought you wouldn't get in for another few hours."

Fenway blinked. "What happened? Was there a third murder?"

"The way Sheriff Donnelly is talking, you'd think so."

"Donnelly? What's her—"

Oh no. Fenway hadn't talked to Donnelly about moving Celeste's overtime to the coroner office's budget. She'd gotten waylaid by Hope Dunkelman.

"Celeste put in for overtime," Sarah said.

"We had a murder last night. *Everyone* got overtime. There must have been six deputies of Gretchen's there."

"Donnelly said you overstepped your bounds."

Fenway rolled her eyes. "Oh—come on. Is this about Gretchen asking Brian to do a drive-by on the cabin, then me taking Celeste?"

Sarah nodded. "Ah, there's the context I needed. Now some of her comments make more sense. She said you should keep in mind that Celeste doesn't work for you."

"Ugh." Fenway pursed her lips. "I'm in the middle of a murder investigation, and I've got a ton of stuff to deal with. And Gretchen wants to get all territorial."

Fenway put her elbows on the counter. "Did we get any judges to sign off on the warrant for the phone location info?"

"It's not eight o'clock yet. Plus, with the storm due to arrive this afternoon, a few of the judges cleared their dockets."

"Then maybe they'll have more time to sign warrants."

"As soon as I get a signature, I'll let you know." Sarah clicked her mouse. "One thing that did come in—the three rideshare companies you asked me to look into? No pickups or drop-offs at Cahill Warehouse Storage. The last ride took place over a month ago."

"Hmph."

"Based on yesterday's events, I requested everything near Hutash Bridge, too. I hope they'll get back to me this morning."

"Taxi companies?"

"The two local companies are checking their logs, looking for people who paid in cash. No luck yet."

"Thanks." Fenway turned, then stopped. "Oh—Sarah, how bad do you think this storm will be?"

"First tropical storm to hit California in years. And the last one hit south of L.A." Sarah shrugged. "They say it's got a fifty-fifty chance of making landfall in Dominguez County. And the ocean here is cold enough that Alonso is losing speed. I think we might just get a whole lot of rain."

"In June—here, in Estancia."

"Crazy, I know. We're usually lucky to get half an inch the whole month."

"If you hear things are about to get bad, go home. Or go somewhere safe."

"Will do."

Fenway unlocked the door to her private office, walked in, and put her purse on her desk. She signed into her laptop and turned to the window. The blinds were closed, and she reached out to turn the stick to open them. The parking lot stared back at her; not a great view, and the eerie pinks and lavenders still shone in the sky, casting an uneasy pallor over her office.

She turned back to the computer and typed in her password. The browser window appeared, with the paused footage from Tuesday afternoon on six different virtual screens, from the back corner of the building to the front gate with the two electric scooters parked on the sidewalk.

Fenway narrowed her eyes.

Two electric scooters.

Weren't there three?

She sat at the desk, grabbed the mouse, and brought up a new window. She had to type in the URL and log in to the security footage website again. Then she clicked on the link for Monday night from 9:00 PM to midnight, when Seth Cahill arrived—just before he turned off the cameras.

All six screens came online. The timestamp: 21:00:00.

The left bottom screen showed the front of the facility with the gate closed. Streetlamps were on, the camera setting at low light.

She counted the Tailwhip scooters. One, two, three.

The cameras had been off for nine hours.

Someone had driven Seth Cahill's Corvette from the storage facility to Miranda Duchy's cabin—and left it there. That person had to get back somehow. No bus routes went out there, but if FlashRide and the other rideshare companies didn't have any record of anything—

Hang on.

The indentation in the passenger seat near the headrest. The scratches on the plastic above the footwell.

An electric scooter could have done that.

Fenway opened another browser window and brought up an online map of Estancia.

Four miles from Hutash Bridge to Cahill Warehouse Storage. Those scooters topped out at fifteen or twenty miles per hour, but if the killer had murdered Seth Cahill, put the scooter in the passenger seat, driven to Miranda Duchy's cabin with the Corvette, then taken the scooter back to the storage facility so they could pick up their car, that would explain a lot. And it might have only taken a half hour to ride back. Perhaps a little harrowing on the downhill mountain roads, but doable.

Fenway stood and strode to Sarah's desk. She looked up.

"I need to get usage records from Tailwhip."

"The electric scooter company?" Sarah asked.

"Yep. And if we need those phone warrants signed, who's available?"

"Judge Azurra. He's thinking about canceling most of his docket for the day because of the storm. If you want him to sign anything, do it in the next hour." Sarah pressed her lips together. "He's a stickler for privacy rights, but we've got all the T's crossed and I's dotted, but I'll double check the phone record warrants before I give them to you. We don't have much of a choice of judges today, anyway."

Fenway looked skeptical.

Sarah shook her head. "I promise, after I check everything, he'll sign them."

"I know. Sometimes your competence is scary." Fenway grinned. "Okay, I'll call Tailwhip while you finish up the warrants. Then, when I'm out tracking down Azurra, why don't you look through the Estancia High yearbook? See if Tyra Cahill had other classmates connected to this case."

"That sounds an awful lot like busy work."

"It might not lead to anything, but Hope said Tyra lost a lot of friends when she got pregnant. And she said Tyra didn't blame Seth for her birth son's death. But maybe we'll find something that makes the puzzle pieces click into place."

"Maybe," Sarah said. "You owe me Dos Milagros for this."

Fenway chuckled. "Don't threaten me with a good time."

She went back into her office and closed the door, then found the Tailwhip customer service number online. After navigating their system and waiting on hold for ten minutes, she got a manager on the phone.

"Tailwhip, this is Vivian."

"This is Coroner Fenway Stevenson with the Dominguez County Coroner's Office. I need some scooter rental records."

"Certainly," Vivian said. "Now, I'll need to verify your identity. That usually takes one to three business days."

"One to three days? Is there a faster way?"

"Well, if you download our app..."

Fenway rolled her eyes.

———

After downloading the app, entering her credit card information—because of course Fenway's records request required that she sign up to the Tailwhip service—Sarah dropped the phone record warrants on Fenway's desk. It took ten minutes for Fenway to walk the warrants over to Judge Roland Azurra's office.

"This is the Seth Cahill case?" he asked.

"That's correct, Your Honor."

"We don't have someone in custody for that already? Gretchen told me they made an arrest last night."

"That's true, Your Honor."

Azurra raised an eyebrow.

"Due diligence, Your Honor."

"Due diligence?"

Fenway took a breath. How much should she say? What the hell—she'd put it all out there. "There's another theory of the case."

Azurra grunted. "Is there?"

"Yes." Fenway leaned forward in her chair. "Our victim was paid to store drugs—specifically, morpheranyl—at his storage facility. The ex-wife of the victim gave up a baby for adoption at sixteen and recently reconnected with him as an adult." Fenway paused.

"The adult son died from a morpheranyl overdose about seven months ago."

"And the conflicting theory of the case is that the victim's ex-wife blamed him for her son's death?"

"That's correct—or, at least, that's what we think the defense might try to say. And if we haven't explored this possibility, that could create reasonable doubt in the jury's mind."

"Gretchen is confident she got the right person."

"The existing evidence suggests we *did* get the right person, Your Honor," Fenway said. "It's hard to argue you're innocent when both the victim's missing car and the murder weapon are found on your property. But isn't it worth discovering if our case has a hole in it?"

Azurra tilted his head. "If you think the ex-wife is a legitimate suspect, I see how her phone records are relevant. But"—he glanced at the warrant paperwork—"Hope Dunkelman?"

"Ms. Dunkelman is Tyra Cahill's alibi, and this will either confirm the alibi or cast doubt on it. Ms. Cahill had the means, and if she blamed her ex for the death of her son, she's got a motive. Plus, she was angry at Miranda Duchy for the affair with Seth. I don't want Duchy's expensive defense attorney to plant this theory in the jurors' minds and for us not to have an answer."

A smile crept over Azurra's face. "That's a lovely story, Coroner. But I think you believe we have the wrong person in custody."

Fenway couldn't suppress her grin. "I'd love to be proven wrong."

Azurra cackled. "Now I *know* you're lying." He pulled the warrant paperwork toward him and looked over the pages for a moment, then signed it and handed it back to Fenway. "Happy fishing."

———

Fenway gripped the warrant paperwork folder tightly as she exited the City Hall building to go back to the Coroner's Office—then she stopped. Yes, Fenway had the investigation in full swing, but neither Miranda Duchy nor Tyra Cahill would talk without a lawyer. She could be doing other things, but since she was already by City Hall...

She turned around, went back in the door, walked down the hallway to the administrative area, and opened the door of Suite 130, Human Resources. HR had consolidated into this section of the City Hall building right after the new year, and the woman who had replaced Lana Cassidy—after the infamous shooting incident— was nice enough, if a little scattered.

A dark-haired woman with an olive complexion, schoolmarm spectacles and a thin, white cardigan over her shoulders looked up from her computer. "Oh, hello, Miss Stevenson! How can I help you?"

"Hi, Ms. Farzan," Fenway said. She took a breath and began. "I meant to call you this morning. I wondered what the holdup was with Mark Trevino's backfill."

"Of course." Debbie gave Fenway a disapproving look over the top of her glasses. "When were you planning to start looking at the candidates?"

Fenway blinked. "Looking at the candidates? What do you mean? I've gotten three applications and I've made my decision. I asked for a status update."

"And I sent you the status update yesterday and asked—" Debbie cocked her head. "I don't believe I have anything in the system. Hold on just a moment." She turned to her computer and began clicking the mouse. "In fact, I emailed two weeks ago to see if you didn't want the position filled."

"I do—I most definitely do." Fenway bit her lip. "I don't under-stand where the disconnect is. I've been adding the interview notes into the system. I hoped we'd be ready to make an offer."

"An offer? I don't even have the first steps of the backfill complete."

Fenway furrowed her brow as Debbie tapped on the keyboard again.

"Now, Sergeant Trevino helped you out by filling in the first two forms that you need to get this process started."

Fenway's shoulders relaxed. "I'll miss Mark." Then her brows knitted. "Wait—Mark filled out the forms online? What forms?"

Debbie pointed at her computer screen. "The backfill paperwork. Here—you're listed as the supervisor. We've had the job posted on the website and on the job board for—let's see, six weeks now. Minimum is thirty calendar days, so we're all good there." Debbie grinned at Fenway. "I wish all my outgoing employees made it this easy."

"I'm glad Mark was so helpful." She lifted her chin hopefully. "So, where are my interview notes?"

It was Debbie's turn to look confused. "You haven't even logged into the system."

"No, that's not true—I submitted the job req a few weeks ago. I've done three interviews. Have you not received *any* of my notes?"

"They're certainly not in here." Debbie cocked her head. "I am equally surprised. You haven't received any of the emails stating that you need to move the hiring process forward?"

"None." Fenway felt her heart rate speed up. She thought there was a bureaucratic hiccup—not that she was this far behind. "I don't understand what I did wrong. I know I made some mistakes when I hired Sarah, but I thought I'd done a better job—"

"Sarah?"

"Sarah Summerfield. My assistant."

"Hold on—you used the system that you used to hire Sarah Summerfield?"

"Sure."

Debbie closed her eyes for a moment, then opened them again.

"You can't use the same system for hiring administrative and support staff that you use for hiring law enforcement officers."

Fenway blinked. Oh no.

"Log into the law enforcement officer hiring system," Debbie said, "and go to the section of the job boards that says, 'Hiring Manager Access.' Then enter your username and password—"

"Just my regular system name?"

"No, no, the law enforcement hiring system credentials." Debbie tilted her head. "You should have received the training from Human Resources when you joined."

Fenway shrugged. "I jumped right into an investigation when I started." *Plus, the former HR manager tried to kill me.*

"Well," Debbie said, "if you can dig out that email with all your credentials, you'll have to log in. Then you go in and score all the candidates." She frowned. "If you never signed up for the law enforcement hiring system, that might explain why you haven't received any of the email updates."

"Can you check to see if I'm in the system?"

"It will take me a minute," Debbie said, staring at the monitor and tapping the keyboard.

"I've got time," Fenway said, though it wasn't true. The investigation wouldn't wait. But then, she didn't want to lose out on hiring Celeste Salvador just because she didn't have the right credentials in the hiring system.

"Yes, here it is—oh, dear."

"What?"

"Your name was changed in the system, but the email address is wrong. It should be *fstevenson,* but instead it's *hwalker.* Who is that?"

"He was the coroner before me."

"But you should be getting his email. It automatically forwards to you for a year."

Fenway smiled. "I've been here fourteen months."

Debbie clicked on the keyboard, read the screen, then frowned.

"I'm so sorry, Miss Stevenson. It looks like you've entered notes for three candidates in the administrative hiring system, not the law enforcement hiring system."

"Can you move them over to the law enforcement system?"

Debbie stifled a sigh. "The fields are slightly different, but I'll make sure they're moved over. I feel terrible. Someone should have trained you properly."

"Well, I'm glad we caught it," Fenway said calmly, though her heart pounded in her ears. "It's just three candidates. Hopefully, we can get this back on track."

"Oh," Debbie said, primly putting her hands in her lap, "you are required to score *all* the candidates, not just the ones you interviewed."

"All the candidates?" Then Fenway closed her eyes. Of course. The job had been posted for six weeks. There must be candidates who applied to the law enforcement hiring system—the *correct* hiring system. Fenway sighed. "Okay, how many are there?"

"Well, as of this morning..." Debbie turned to the computer, clicked a few times, then pointed at the screen. "Thirty-one."

"Thirty-one?"

"That's correct."

"But—but I've identified who I want to hire."

Debbie winced in sympathy, meeting Fenway's eyes. "I've only been in this role six months, but we must follow the rules. Often, they have to do with the union or with laws written for public employees. I'm afraid we can't change the rules due to our miscommunication."

Fenway exhaled and put her hands over her face. "Thirty-one."

"Plus the candidates you've already interviewed." Debbie pressed her lips together. "The form for candidate evaluation is pretty straightforward, but I must warn you, it's a bit time-consuming."

"Just what I need when I'm reviewing the applications of three dozen people."

Debbie's eyes turned toward the monitor again. "Well—let's see what we can do." She tapped the keyboard. "I can run a few algorithms and if the applicant doesn't meet the minimum requirements, we can disqualify them without the full evaluation."

Fenway hesitated. She remembered when the clinic closed in Seattle, how desperate she was for work, and how she hadn't gotten anyone to respond to her job applications. Was it algorithms like the ones Debbie suggested that kicked her out before she appeared as more than a series of ones and zeros to the hiring organizations?

Debbie was the only one in the office, but she looked around conspiratorially, then lowered her voice. "Can I ask—who did you want to hire?"

"Oh—Deputy Salvador. One of the top scores on the detective exam, and I've been in the field with her. She's great. Fast learner, quick thinker, everything I want in a detective."

"Ah yes—here she is. Applied online." Debbie paused. "But—there's an issue with her application."

"I know, I know, she's not at the level of a sergeant yet. But I expect her to get there in another year or two." Fenway smiled at Debbie. "She's an exemplary employee, too. Surely that counts for something."

Debbie paused and looked at the floor.

"Are you saying that her prior performance holds no weight?"

"On the contrary. It's one of the few things that could affect her score compared to more experienced candidates."

Something about Debbie's word choice: *affect her score.* Not *improve her score.* "Is there something you're not telling me, Debbie?"

Debbie looked up at Fenway with wide eyes. "Deputy Salvador was just written up. Insubordination."

CHAPTER TWENTY

"Insubordination?" Fenway asked from the open doorway of Sheriff Gretchen Donnelly's office. Fenway's voice was calm—the rage simmered under the surface, but she could hear the pot lid clinking.

The sheriff looked up from the paperwork on her desk and narrowed her eyes. "Shut the door."

Fenway closed the door, resisting the urge to slam it. She wanted the walls of the building to shake.

"I told Celeste no overtime." Donnelly stood and walked to her bookshelf, taking a binder out. "Not two days after we have that conversation, she's staying late at the storage facility. And then she puts in another four hours last night when she drove you to Hutash Bridge. Where I come from, disobeying a direct order is insubordination."

"I asked her to do that. I was planning to tell you I'd allocate her overtime to my budget. But I got pulled away by a suspect interview."

"Yes, well, you *didn't* allocate Sandoval's overtime to your budget. And don't get me started on the red tape if we attempt to change the cost center number after the fact."

"Changing the cost center requires just two forms—and that's on me, not Celeste. Besides, the overtime is justified. We found another murder victim!"

Donnelly set the binder on her desk, but remained standing. "Why don't you explain that to the Board of County Supervisors when I'm hauled in there for going three million dollars over budget?"

Fenway hesitated—three million dollars for a county as relatively small as Dominguez County was hefty. She put a hand on the back of the guest chair in front of Donnelly's desk. "The voters put you here for a reason, Gretchen."

"The reason is, McVie handpicked me." Donnelly leaned forward. "And I'm not stupid. I'm *not* Craig McVie. He would go a couple million over budget and smile his easy smile and go in there, and charm Alice Jenkins and let Barry Klein get just enough of his complaints out there so he felt he was being heard." Donnelly raised out of her chair and pointed at Fenway with two fingers, half-standing. "Well, guess what? Alice and Barry aren't around anymore, and the new people they have in place are former accountants. They want murders solved between eight and five." She glared at Fenway. "Tell me, why don't *you* have to deal with the politics I do?"

Fenway blinked.

Oh no. Could it be...

Donnelly scoffed. "You may not have the same last name as your father, but the specter of Nathaniel Ferris is still strong in this county." She shook her head. "You don't realize all the interference he runs for you, do you? He's happy to suggest cuts for the sheriff's office, but the coroner's budget isn't touched."

"Then I'll take one of your problems off your hands," Fenway said. "Celeste scored high on the detective exam. And if you're worried about all the overtime she's pulling, then rescind the write-up so I can hire her. Make her overtime my problem, not yours."

"Just like all the murders in this county. Your problems, not mine."

A sharp tone in Donnelly's voice put Fenway on edge. She chose her words carefully. "It's literally my job description. I'm the coroner. My job is to investigate *all* deaths outside of a home or hospital."

"And my job is to write up my employees when they disobey direct orders."

"What—" Fenway almost said, *what's your problem?* But that would have been extremely unhelpful. "I'm sorry this is a bad situation," she said instead. "I want Celeste to work for me. You have a problem with her overtime. It's a win-win."

Donnelly's gaze softened, and she sat back down in her chair. "Solution-oriented as always, Coroner."

Fenway wasn't sure if that was sarcastic or not, but she let it slide.

Donnelly steepled her fingers and looked at Fenway over the top of her hands. "What do I get out of it?"

Fenway blinked. "What do you get out of it? I just told you, it's a win-win. You get rid of an employee who was giving you budget issues."

Donnelly folded her arms. "I need something more than that."

Fenway paused, then nodded. "I can't make up for the shortfall, but once she's reporting to my department, I'll transfer *all* of Celeste's overtime into my budget. At least for this quarter—I don't think we can go back further than that."

"Something more," Donnelly repeated.

Fenway blinked. "Like what?"

Donnelly put her hands down on her armrests. "You've shown that you're a savvy, intelligent woman. I'm sure you'll figure something out—and I'll bet you figure it out soon."

Fenway pursed her lips. What did that mean?

Hold on—no.

Was Donnelly asking for a bribe?

Where in the world did Donnelly get the idea that Fenway could afford a bribe? Oh, of course. Fenway's father was rich.

A bubble of rage grew again in the pit of her stomach, but she tamped it down. She always thought she could trust Gretchen Donnelly, but no more. Should she reach into her purse and start recording this conversation on her phone?

Hang on—was Donnelly recording her, trying to catch her *offering* a bribe? While her nemesis, Dr. Barry Klein, was no longer mayor, Fenway knew she still had enemies. But California was a two-party recording state. Donnelly couldn't use any of the recording unless Fenway agreed to it—not without a warrant.

Fenway nodded, her head spinning, doing everything she could to keep her face neutral. "All right, I'll give it some thought. Thanks for your time."

Fenway opened the door, using every ounce of self-control not to scream.

She turned down the corridor and was heading toward the front doors of the sheriff's office when a voice called out. "Coroner!"

She turned at the low, somewhat familiar voice. There, hurrying down the row of cubicles, was Captain Steve Alvidrez.

"Glad I caught you, Coroner."

"Everything all right?"

"Better than all right." His face broke into a grin. "The eighteen wrapped bags discovered at the cabin belonging to Miranda Duchy?"

Fenway tilted her head. "Has that already gone through the lab? It hasn't even been twenty-four hours."

"I know a guy." Alvidrez winked. "You were right, Coroner. It's morpheranyl. Matches another batch of Nyllie that the Riverside County Sheriff seized two weeks ago. That narrows down where we search for the packaging and distribution center."

"That's good news."

"There's better news. You should talk to a certain someone in the drunk tank."

Fenway tilted her head. "The drunk tank? Did Tyra Cahill get blind drunk and cause a disturbance?"

Alvidrez shook his head. "What would I care about the victim's ex-wife? No—this is someone who could take down the Nyllie dealers in SoCal."

Fenway furrowed her brow.

"Calvin Banning."

———

Fenway walked over to the jail, Captain Alvidrez following a step behind her. The windy morning was getting humid and hot, and she broke out in a light sweat underneath her blazer. She and Alvidrez showed their identification to the guard, signed in, then they waited in an interview room on the right side of the hallway past the metal detectors, with a metal table and three uncomfortable plastic chairs.

The door opened, and a guard walked in with a tall, thin man in front of him. The man had pale skin, but his face was ashen, his eyes were bloodshot, and he walked with a little uncertainty.

"Calvin Banning?" Fenway said.

Banning shifted his eyes to Alvidrez, a look of mild disgust on his face, then his gaze turned to Fenway. Although she was sitting down dressed in a blazer and trousers, Banning's eyes raked over her, and she felt like she had to take a shower.

"Have you dropped from heaven, love?" Some kind of British accent, maybe from the northeast. Geordie, perhaps. Not quite Scottish. She'd seen a patient from Newcastle in the clinic in Seattle, almost an identical Geordie accent. Like her former patient, Banning was a long way from home.

Alvidrez bristled. "That's enough, Mr. Banning. Our coroner is investigating the death of the guy who's been storing the Nyllie for you."

"Not our Nyllie, mate."

"The bad news for you, Mr. Banning, is that a thumbprint belonging to you was found on one of the Nyllie bricks."

"Had nothing to do with it, did we." The end was a question spoken like a statement—and used the Newcastle way of referring to himself in the plural.

"How did your prints end up on it, then?"

A smile came over Banning's face. "I say by sorcery."

Fenway rolled her eyes. "Mr. Banning—"

"Yes, love?"

"You don't understand. That Nyllie brick was discovered near a dead body. With seventeen other Nyllie bricks, by the way."

Banning shifted in his chair—losing track of that many morpheranyl bricks might have rattled him. He frowned. "A dead body? Whose dead body?"

"Mathis Jericho."

Banning's eyes widened, but only briefly—then his face returned to leering impassivity. "Is that name supposed to mean something to us?"

"We're aware that you, Seth Cahill, and Mathis Jericho would meet. Maybe once a month, every six weeks. There'd be an exchange of money and a storage locker at Cahill Warehouse Storage would magically become unavailable." Fenway suspected this scenario was true—and if she could read the look on Banning's face correctly, it was.

"There's no crime in meeting your mates," Banning said.

"If you're storing drugs, there is," Alvidrez said.

"Are we under arrest?" Banning said.

"For drunk and disorderly, yes," Alvidrez responded. "And with your fingerprint on the Nyllie brick, and given where we found it, I bet we can find a prosecutor who can make a case for possession with intent to distribute. And that'll keep you locked up until we figure out whether we want to charge you with murder."

"I didn't hurt no one," Banning said.

"I've got a corpse in the morgue with two rotational fractures to the fingers of his left hand that suggests differently," Fenway said. "Twisting your fingers until they break? That would hurt."

Banning looked down at the table, not meeting Fenway's eyes. "Weren't us."

A lie. Fenway blinked. What had Dr. Yasuda said? His fingers had been broken three to four months before. Was that timeline important? She couldn't know for sure.

"It was two fingers the first time he said no," Fenway said. "What was his punishment this time, when you found out he'd lost the storage facility outright? And what was Mathis Jericho's punishment for asking to take over for Seth?"

"It were nae—" Banning said, then clamped his mouth shut and crossed his arms.

"It wasn't like that?" Fenway said. "You'd allow someone to simply walk away?"

Banning raised his head and looked from Alvidrez to Fenway, this time without the leer, then shook his head incredulously. "Haddaway and loss yasel—you're nae wanting us. Thinking we'll turn, is that it?"

Fenway leaned forward and stared Banning in the eye. "I'm the coroner. I only care about solving murders. If you killed Seth Cahill, I don't care if you're the biggest lieutenant in the Venn cartel—I want to put you away for murder. But if it wasn't you, I want you to tell me what you know."

"This Jericho fellow," Banning said, leaning in toward Fenway, his eyes open and pleading. "Nine-millimeter, yeah? Two in the heart, one between the eyes, like?"

Fenway rubbed her forehead. Banning wasn't trying to hide the truth this time. He was describing a Venn cartel's murder-for-hire. Banning didn't have the facts of how Jericho died. He might be responsible for dozens of overdose deaths in Southern California from morpheranyl, but he wasn't responsible for Mathis Jericho's death.

Fenway shot a quick glance at Alvidrez. The captain winced—if Banning had talked about who'd be responsible for contract killings, maybe that could solve other murders up and down the California coast. She paused. Would this be the break that Alvidrez needed for other cases? And was there an opportunity for Banning to talk about who might have committed other murders?

Fenway tried to keep her disappointment from showing. This might be good for Alvidrez, but Banning's possible identification of a hit man had no bearing on the murders of Seth Cahill or Mathis Jericho. Unfortunately for Fenway, Banning had started opening up to her. She'd have to follow this through.

"Two in the heart and one between the eyes," Fenway replied. She was deliberately misleading him, but in some cases, maybe the end justified the means.

Banning's mouth turned into a snarl. "That's not right," he said. "You send a message, you do it for accountability, yeah? Mathis were just a kid. He weren't hurting no one." He bowed his head. "Had no clue they knew who Mathis were."

"Sounds like you have a pretty good idea who was responsible?"

Banning turned his tongue over in his mouth a couple of times, leaning back and staring at the ceiling. Finally, he slapped his hands on the metal table. "If Mathis was supposed to be a message, then we're a dead man anyroad."

"We can get you protection," Alvidrez said.

"In prison? Not bloody likely."

"Maybe not in prison," Alvidrez said. "I can ask the D.A. to set you up with a new life."

Banning folded his hands and stared at them for a long time. Finally, he lifted his face to Fenway. "What do we have to do?"

"Let's hear what information you have," Fenway said.

"And what if you don't like what we have to say?"

Fenway shrugged. "You think if you don't say anything to us, you'll be safe if you go back into general pop?"

Banning chuckled softly. "You're a right straight talker. Pretty, too. Shame we're opposite sides of the law."

Fenway was silent for a moment. There was nothing she could say; it was all up to him. A minute went by, each second feeling like an hour.

"There were a bloke out of the San Fernando Valley," Banning began, speaking directly to Fenway.

Fenway looked at Alvidrez. He was rapt with attention. Fenway needed to get back to the murder investigation—but the way Banning was speaking so emotionally, directly to her, she didn't think she'd get out of there for a while.

———

An hour later, after Alvidrez had called the D.A. and set up the first steps of witness protection, Fenway stepped out of the interview room. She took a deep breath—handing Banning off to Captain Alvidrez was no simple task. But Banning had no information on either murder.

She looked at her phone. A message from Dez.

> Patrick Appleby wants to see you

Fenway put the phone back in her purse and walked past the guard and the security station, and out of the jail.

The morning was still warm, but instead of the eerie pink and lavender, now dark gray clouds covered half the sky.

Some of her friends who had gone to college in the South were fond of a joke: if you don't like the weather in Houston, wait fifteen minutes. But California wasn't like that. With the morning so sunny and clear, rarely would the sky change so dramatically. With the sky this gray, the weather would often become chilly, even in summer.

But the air was still warm—and humid. Fenway wished she'd brought an umbrella this morning as she stepped into the crosswalk toward her workplace. Hopefully, Alonso wouldn't make landfall in Dominguez County. Still, heavy rain was certain.

The IT department was in the same building as the coroner's office, down the corridor. She considered stopping for a coffee at Java Jim's—but with an hour spent discussing the Venn cartel's hit man from San Fernando Valley, Fenway couldn't justify getting her caffeine fix.

She opened the door into the IT office. Jordan Daniels, the IT director, was coming out of his office about ten feet behind Patrick Appleby's cubicle. He nodded at Fenway in greeting. "Hi, Coroner."

"Hi, Jordan. Here to see Patrick."

Patrick's back was to Fenway, headphones clamped on his ears. She'd learned to get in his line of sight first, instead of tapping him on the shoulder. She walked around the side of his cubicle, trying to make herself as visible as possible. He looked up, nodded, and removed his headphones.

"Good morning, Coroner Stevenson."

"Hi, Patrick. I heard you wanted to see me."

"I have completed my review of the doorbell camera footage from Ms. Duchy's home. The footage started at 9:02 PM on Monday and continued through the time you and Sergeant Roubideaux removed the boxes from the front lawn on Wednesday." He clicked on his screen. "The camera only records when it detects movement, resulting in seven hours and thirty-three minutes of footage to review."

"You got it done fast."

"There was little of note. Often, it was simply a car driving by. The mail delivery on Tuesday. A package delivery that Ms. Duchy signed for on Wednesday morning. People walking their dogs in front of the house."

"Anyone walking to the side of the garage?"

"Only you and Sergeant Roubideaux."

Fenway scrunched up her nose. "Then that really doesn't look good for Miranda Duchy. Hard for anyone to argue beyond a reasonable doubt that she wasn't the one who put the hammer in her own shed."

"Possibly, but I did note there are no cameras in the back of the house. It's possible someone who knew about the doorbell camera came over the back fence. We could potentially access the doorbell cameras for the houses behind Ms. Duchy."

"I suppose we'll have to do that. Due diligence, right?"

"Correct. However, the assistant district attorney believes there is now sufficient evidence to arrest Ms. Duchy."

Fenway raised her eyebrows. "He's usually pretty cautious."

"If you would like, I could download the form to apply for the doorbell camera warrant and email it to you. Judge Azurra canceled his docket for the day except for a single arraignment at two o'clock."

"Oh—thanks, Patrick. That's very kind. I appreciate it."

He hesitated. "I feel compelled to point out a door from the side of the garage next to the shed."

"Right. Our theory is that Ms. Duchy used that door to take the hammer from the car in her garage to the shed."

"The camera does not cover everything, as I said," Patrick said. "The technology is not flawless. Someone may have been able to trick the camera *not* to activate."

"How would they do that?"

"Movements so slow that the camera would not pick it up. Or keeping out of the camera range until reaching the corner of the house, then staying close against the wall and ducking under the camera doorbell."

"Aren't those cameras wide-angle? Designed with that kind of deception in mind?"

"True," Patrick said. "It's unlikely that someone would have been able to sneak along the front of the house without the camera picking up at least some of their movements." He tapped his chin.

"If the camera were covered and tricked into not activating, perhaps at night—"

"Two people working together?" Fenway said.

"If two people were working together, the first person makes sure the camera is focused on them, and it's easier for the second person to sneak by the camera."

"Right." Fenway nodded. "Thank you for being thorough."

"I'll send you the links to the footage in case you want to review it yourself."

Yes, that's just what she needed for the last two days McVie was in town: reviewing seven hours of doorbell camera footage. Oh, and screening over two dozen applicants for Sergeant Trevino's position.

"You're quite certain," she said, "no one was hanging out around the edges of the screen? Waiting to avoid the camera?"

Patrick thought a moment. "The camera shows that the only people who went around the side of the house from the front yard were you and Sergeant Roubideaux." He ran his tongue along his teeth, debating with himself. "It is possible that the defense will see this and suggest that one of you planted the bloody hammer in Ms. Duchy's shed."

"How? Neither of us is carrying a bloody framing hammer."

"You are both carrying boxes. You could be hiding the hammer behind a box."

"That's ridiculous."

"I make no judgement other than to say the defense might suggest it. Reasonable doubt."

Fenway hadn't considered this possibility, but of course she should have. Half of her was insulted, the other half relieved that Patrick had told her before the defense suggested it at trial.

"Then it's of prime importance we look at the footage from the doorbell cameras behind Duchy's house."

"Remember, Judge Azurra," Patrick repeated.

"Thank you, Patrick."

Patrick turned back to his computer screen and put his headphones on.

Fenway turned and walked out of the IT office. The beige carpet of the corridor stretched in front of her, the next steps toward a light she still couldn't see at the end of this tunnel.

CHAPTER TWENTY-ONE

Sarah looked up from her computer as Fenway walked in. "Anything?"

"Nothing," Fenway said, shaking her head. "Came up empty on the doorbell camera footage. We got one of the drug guys on the boat in custody on a drunk and disorderly. He turned on a hit man who works for the Venn cartel."

Sarah's eyes went wide. "Does he have a death wish?"

"He thought Mathis Jericho had been killed by—oh, look, it doesn't matter. I mean, it *does* matter. Alvidrez is salivating over it. But Banning had nothing to do with our murders. And I don't think he has any information on who did."

Sarah nodded. "Miranda Duchy is getting arraigned right after lunch. Two o'clock."

"Let me guess—Judge Azurra?"

"Good guess."

"I'll need to get more warrants drawn up for the doorbell cameras from the two or three houses behind Duchy's home. Patrick suggested getting Azurra to sign off."

"Assuming they have doorbell cameras."

"It's a well-off neighborhood. Whoever doesn't have doorbell cameras usually has more elaborate security systems in place."

Sarah tilted her head. "Why would Patrick suggest Judge Azurra? The phone records? Yeah, Azurra signed off on those, but doorbell cameras are a different set of privacy concerns. I don't think you have a prayer of getting him to sign those."

Fenway cocked her head. "I thought Patrick was trying to help —" She stopped, then tapped her fingers on the counter in front of Sarah, her mind spinning.

"He's more detail-oriented than that," Sarah said. "Why—"

"I think Patrick doesn't believe that Miranda Duchy is guilty," Fenway said in a soft voice. "And he thought if Azurra sees that I'm still investigating other possibilities, then the judge would be more inclined to be lenient during the arraignment."

"Does he know you got Azurra to sign off on the phone records?"

"No."

"Why wouldn't Patrick say anything to you?" Sarah mused.

"Maybe because he doesn't have proof that Miranda didn't do it."

Sarah motioned with her head toward the door of the coroner's suite. "Go back and ask him."

Fenway paused.

"He won't bite you, Fenway."

"Yeah, okay." Fenway pushed away from the counter as if it were the wall of a pool, then went out the door, back to IT. She opened the door, nodded to Jordan, then stood in Patrick's line of sight until he removed his headphones again.

"Is there something wrong?" he asked.

"You don't believe that Miranda Duchy killed Seth Cahill."

Patrick frowned, placing his headphones delicately on a headphone stand next to his monitor. "It does not matter what I believe. Only what can be proven in a court of law."

"Sure," Fenway said, "but you could help me get to the truth."

Patrick folded his arms. "There is nothing in that footage that will prove Miranda Duchy's innocence."

"Yet you sent me to the judge who's arraigning her this afternoon."

Patrick shrugged. "He's available to sign your warrant."

"Maybe you missed something on the recording."

Patrick shook his head. "I missed nothing. I studied the background thoroughly. Nothing would suggest anyone hid the hammer in her shed."

Fenway tapped her foot and thought for a moment. "All the evidence points to Miranda Duchy. Is there anything you can do to help me out?"

Patrick sighed. "I have been thinking about this all morning. The only thing I could think of was getting the judge to realize that you are not convinced of Ms. Duchy's guilt."

Fenway nodded. "Already done, by the way. I asked him to sign off on warrants for another suspect's phone records." She tapped her fingers on the corner of Patrick's cubicle. "But thanks. And please tell me if you *do* think of anything."

Fenway walked back to the coroner's suite. In the hallway, she could hear the wind pick up outside, and the first taps of rain against the front windows. This would be a great day to snuggle up on the couch with McVie with a cup of hot chocolate—

No, wait, the air was hot—too hot for coziness and cocoa. No good being outside. And the weather would get worse.

Her phone rang in her purse: McVie.

"Hey, stranger."

"This moving stuff is a pain in the ass," McVie said. "Literally. I ran my shin into the corner of my end table while I was stacking boxes. I'll have a big bruise."

"Pain in the leg, you mean."

"You're not taking my injury seriously." McVie chuckled.

Fenway grinned. "Poor baby. Is that client finally leaving you alone today?"

"Fortunately, with this storm coming, his wife is staying home. But I still had to promise I'd get Piper to dig into his wife's financials. See if she's got any secret bank accounts or credit cards that are going to a P.O. box, anything like that."

"I don't know how you stand all the excitement of private eye work after the boring murders we had to solve."

"What can I say? I'm an adrenaline junkie." The sound of a door closing. "Want to grab some lunch?"

"Lunch? Like, go out for lunch? Have you seen the weather?"

"They're downgrading it to a tropical depression."

"What does that mean?"

"Winds lower than thirty-three knots."

Fenway blinked. "Thirty-three knots?"

"A little under forty miles per hour."

"How do you know this?"

"Because when I was sheriff, I worked with the Coast Guard on a couple of cases. Forty miles an hour—yeah, not great, but at least the wind won't destroy any houses."

Fenway interrupted. "Isn't there a flood warning?"

"For South County, and that's only in effect until midnight."

Fenway paused. "I don't think I'll go out to lunch. I want to finish this case and go home before Estancia Canyon Road turns into a river."

"Want me to bring something to the office?"

"Oh—yeah, maybe."

"What do you want?"

"Two tacos—"

"Right, right, Dos Milagros, lengua, extra cilantro, large horchata."

"Get something different for yourself this time. No carnitas burritos."

"Okay, maybe. I'll be there in an hour."

————

She sat in her desk chair, the email from Patrick on her screen. Yes, Patrick was very observant. So, no, he probably hadn't missed anything.

Still, Fenway couldn't quiet the itch in her brain that she needed to see it for herself. She clicked on the link in the email, logged in with the authorization in the email, and steeled herself to watch seven hours of video—at twice the normal speed.

After watching twelve cars drive past, three joggers, two dogwalkers, and a man with a stroller, she yawned widely. Patrick was a good man for fighting through the complete boredom of this.

A knock on the door. Fenway raised her head—it was McVie. She paused the video.

He walked in, placed a white paper bag on her desk—smelling of spices and cilantro—and set down a large Styrofoam cup. "Your meal awaits," he said. He opened the bag and took out two wrapped tacos, placing them on a paper napkin on Fenway's desk.

"Thanks." Fenway grabbed the cup and taking a drink of the horchata. "Where's yours?"

"Ate it on the way. Sorry, I got hungry."

"That means you got a carnitas burrito and didn't want my snarky comments."

"Hey, would I do that?"

Fenway grinned. "Everything okay out there?"

"For now. The rain is picking up, though. I guess you were right —Dos Milagros is closing early. They chased me out of there and flipped their sign to 'closed.' I guess I should send Piper home."

"And maybe don't take anything else over to storage today." Fenway took a bite of her taco.

"Any closer to finding the killer? I heard on the radio that you'd made an arrest."

"I didn't make the arrest. Gretchen did." Fenway swallowed, then lowered her voice. "Hey, close the door, would you?"

"Oh—I didn't realize you wanted to have *that* kind of afternoon. But I'm game. Even with your onion-and-cilantro breath—"

"Not today, cowboy," Fenway said, but grinned.

McVie's face turned serious, and he shut the door. "What's up?"

"I went to HR to ask what the holdup was to hire Celeste as Mark's replacement."

McVie nodded. "It's about time."

"And I found out that Sheriff Donnelly had Celeste written up for unapproved overtime because she took me to Hutash Bridge."

"Where you found another murder victim?"

"Right. And now, because this open disciplinary action is on Celeste's record, I might not be able to hire her." Fenway leaned forward, elbows on the desk. "But then, get this—when I went to talk with Gretchen about it, I think she tried to bribe me."

"What?" McVie's brow furrowed. "That doesn't sound like Gretchen."

Fenway related the conversation between the two of them, from the comment about the board of supervisors' budget concerns to the cryptic comments Sheriff Donnelly had made.

When Fenway was done with her story, the corners of McVie's mouth turned down. "What does that mean, *I need something more than that?*"

"I was kind of hoping you could tell me."

"I've got no idea."

"The only thing I can think of is that she wanted my father to give her some money. I'm not the rich one." She was doing better, of course, now that her father had paid off her student loans. But she wasn't rich.

"And you wouldn't bribe her anyway."

"But Gretchen doesn't know that."

McVie crossed his arms. "If only you knew a private investigator who could get to the bottom of this."

"If only that private investigator weren't leaving the state tomorrow."

"Maybe I can swing by the office and do a little digging."

"You could take the laptop and work from my apartment."

"It's better in the office."

"Not with a flood warning and forty-mile-an-hour winds. I'd rather you stay in my apartment. Wi-Fi and cold beer in the fridge."

McVie crossed behind the desk and kissed Fenway's forehead. "Deal. I'll see you at your apartment. Did you at least get fresh batteries for your flashlights?"

Fenway was quiet.

"Okay. I've got some extras. How much more work do you have here?"

"Maybe not much more. I'll talk to HR, see if I can send the team home in this weather. I haven't been able to find any solid evidence pointing to anyone besides Miranda Duchy."

"Maybe your gut is finally wrong."

"It's been wrong plenty." Fenway shook her head. "But I don't think she's guilty."

"Good luck," McVie said, then stopped. "Never mind. If you have good luck with your case, you won't be getting home early."

Fenway smiled as McVie left her office. As the door closed behind him, her face fell. What would she do when he left town? Would seeing him once a month—if she was lucky—be enough? She liked being with him almost every day. She hadn't ever dated someone this long without the other person getting on Fenway's nerves constantly.

Maybe McVie was a great guy.

Or maybe Fenway was finally learning how to be in a relationship.

She turned her attention back to the monitor and hit *Play*. So much easier to focus on a single recording than having to watch all six camera feeds from the storage unit footage.

Ah, the package delivery. The driver pulled up in the telltale brown truck, brought a box to the door—maybe the size of a hardback novel—and rang the doorbell.

The sound of the door opening, then Miranda Duchy stepped out onto the porch wearing an elegant beige top and form-fitting dark blue jeans. The driver handed her an electronic tablet and a stylus. Duchy switched the stylus to her other hand, signed it, took the package, and went back inside.

Fenway tapped her chin. Was the package something important? Maybe she should subpoena the shipping company to see where it came from. Still, something bothered Fenway. She paused and rewound the footage, looking at the transaction in real time.

Patrick had missed something. He *had* to have missed something.

What was it?

Did someone run from behind the truck? She carefully looked at the scene. Duchy was blocking the left side of the camera, but the edge of the truck was still in view. Fenway squinted, but still saw nothing: nobody sprinting from the rear of the truck to the side of the house.

She went back another two minutes and stared at the footage again. Nothing there. Nothing big, no one sneaking to the side.

Miranda switched the stylus to her other hand and—

Fenway smacked herself in the forehead.

Dr. Yasuda's voice in her head: *The killer is right-handed, although that describes eighty-five percent of the population.*

Fenway hit the pause button onscreen.

Right-handedness might have described eighty-five percent of the population, but it didn't describe Miranda Duchy. The driver had offered the stylus in front of Miranda's right hand. She'd taken it—and switched it to her *left* hand before she signed it.

Miranda Duchy was left-handed.

CHAPTER TWENTY-TWO

Fenway hurried out of her office and stopped at Sarah's desk. "Miranda Duchy isn't the killer," she said.

Dez popped her head up from her workstation. "What?"

Fenway turned. "Miranda isn't the killer. Dr. Yasuda said the killer was right-handed. Miranda's a lefty."

Dez pursed her lips. "And we didn't check that out *before* she was arrested?"

"Maybe we were all blinded by the life insurance policy and Miranda's debt." Fenway paused. "Sarah, have we received the mobile phone location information yet?"

"Miranda Duchy's mobile?"

"No, no—Tyra Cahill's phone. And Hope Dunkelman's phone."

Sarah furrowed her brow.

"Sorry—you're not a mind reader." Fenway gave Sarah a small smile. "If Hope or Tyra's phone location info show that they made a trip to the storage facility at the time of the murder, that should give us enough evidence to arrest one—or both—of them."

"And release Miranda Duchy," Dez said.

"Have the phone companies complied with the warrant yet?" Sarah asked.

Dez walked over to the counter. "We just served the warrant this morning, but the telecoms work fast."

"Patrick didn't mention getting the telecom records when I went over there," Fenway said.

"Did you *ask* him about the phone records?" Sarah tapped in a number on the phone. "Patrick, hi. It's Sarah in the coroner's office. Have you gotten the records from the mobile phone companies? Cahill, Dunkelman?" She paused, then nodded. "Send them over—me, Fenway, and Dez. Thanks. Talk to you later." She lifted her eyes to Fenway. "He's got to log into their system and download the data, but he said he'd send it over within the hour."

"Great." Fenway glanced at Dez. "What do you want to do for the next hour, Dez?"

"What are you suggesting?" Dez responded. "Go to Hope Dunkelman's workplace? Maybe convince her to get ahead of this?"

Fenway shook her head. "I want to find out where her phone was before we talk to her."

A boom of thunder sounded.

"We might not have an hour," Dez pointed out. "Businesses are closing and sending people home. I think they're about to do that with non-essential personnel here."

Sarah nodded. "We got an email about ten minutes ago. We're supposed to leave here at three o'clock."

Fenway shook her head. "I still don't want to confront Hope Dunkelman without the phone records—"

A flash of lightning outside the window.

Fenway blinked.

A thunder crash. The storm was getting closer.

"Dez," she said, "doesn't Anton Venn have a problem?"

Dez blinked. "What do you mean?"

"A storage problem. The same kind of problem we thought of

when we first found out that Seth Cahill had stored morpheranyl at his facility."

"That the people in the organization were mad at him for their storage going away."

"And we thought maybe Mathis Jericho was taking over. Or that Tyra Cahill had somehow agreed to store the morpheranyl after taking over the business."

Dez put her hands on her hips. "But we never answered the question. Where are they storing the morpheranyl now?"

"Right."

Sarah stood. "When Mathis Jericho's body was found in Seth's Corvette, wasn't it surrounded by bricks of Nyllie?"

Fenway nodded. "Eighteen bricks."

"Why?"

"To make it look like Anton Venn was sending a message..." Fenway's voice petered out. Was it? That was an assumption they'd made—that it was a personal motive, and the killer was trying to point to the cartel. "Sarah," she said, "can you call Captain Alvidrez?"

"Sure. Speaker?"

"Please."

Sarah tapped buttons on the landline phone and lifted the console to the counter. Through the phone's speaker, a ring.

"Alvidrez."

"Captain," Fenway said, "it's Coroner Stevenson."

"Of course. What can I do for you?"

"The Venn cartel. They had a problem with where to store their morpheranyl after Seth Cahill lost the facility to his ex-wife."

"It's possible."

"One of our original theories was that someone in the drug business had killed Seth because the loss affected a crucial part of their business."

"Not unheard of. But the murder weapon and the way he was killed? Not a cartel killing."

"So—why not?"

"What do you mean?"

"This is an illegal business worth millions of dollars. Seth loses the storage facility. Why does the cartel keep him alive?"

"I don't know."

"He's a loose end, right? If he can't store their drugs, he knows too much."

Alvidrez paused for a moment. "He did have two broken fingers. Maybe that was a warning?"

"Yet he was still alive—for another four months. And we're pretty sure the cartel didn't kill him."

"Oh," Alvidrez said. "So you're thinking the cartel threatened Seth Cahill, broke his fingers to make sure he found another place to store the morpheranyl?"

"And I think he *found* that other place." Fenway scratched her temple. "The drugs don't *need* to be stored in a warehouse facility, right?" Fenway asked.

"I suppose not."

"Where else do dealers store drugs?"

"Residences, mostly, but like I said, you get neighbors complaining. And trucks can't really show up without drawing attention."

"What about a residence out in the sticks?"

Alvidrez paused. "You mean like Miranda Duchy's cabin?"

"That's exactly what I'm thinking. The road is winding, but it's wide—it's a truck route—all the way to Hutash Bridge."

"I like your thinking," Alvidrez said, "but we found no drugs in the house. Sheriff Donnelly performed the search herself."

Fenway remembered: Donnelly wanted to wait for the warrant, and Deputy Salvador thought she'd steal the credit. "You weren't part of the search team?"

"I was in a training in P.Q. Couldn't get over in time."

Fenway frowned. "She got the warrant awfully fast."

"I didn't see the warrant. But with probable cause, she wouldn't have needed one. Maybe she wanted a warrant to make sure her search was airtight, but couldn't get one?"

"Yeah, maybe Judge Solano was in court." Fenway furrowed her brow. "Still, if there were no drugs found in the cabin, that doesn't mean there hadn't been any earlier."

Alvidrez clicked his tongue. "True, but without a panel truck, I expect it would have been hard to trek everything out of there."

Fenway glanced at Dez. "If the drugs were stored at Duchy's cabin, that would explain why we found an entry in Seth Cahill's ledger, but no sign of drugs stored in either of the storage units."

"Could have been in other units," Dez said.

"Yes, of course—I mean, that was our thought at the time. But I think they'd already moved the storage to the cabin. Cahill was simply meeting Banning at the office for payment. And Banning only stayed in Unit 112 the night of Cahill's death to make sure Cahill wasn't tricking him."

"Let me call Sheriff Donnelly," Alvidrez said. "See what she noted. Maybe she has bodycam footage of the cabin search."

"Thanks, Captain."

"Oh, and Fenway, I want to thank you."

"Thank me? For what?"

"Those eighteen bricks of morpheranyl. Vice hit our six-month target."

Fenway looked at Dez, who shrugged.

"Is this for the SJRD incentive?" Sarah asked.

"That's right," Alvidrez replied. "Donnelly and I submitted the paperwork last night, and we got confirmation about an hour ago. I forgot to tell you when I ran into you earlier."

"That's great," Fenway said.

"The available incentive money isn't as much as last year," Alvidrez said, "but we're getting a much bigger chunk of it, thanks to you and Salvador. Just shy of five million." He sounded both proud and relieved. "It'll be in our account by the end of the month. The Board of Supervisors should be delighted. No more budget shortfall."

"Delighted," Fenway said distractedly.

They said their goodbyes, and Sarah ended the call.

Fenway clenched and unclenched her fists. Donnelly knew about the incentive application. She had written up Deputy Salvador for insubordination, citing a budget issue for overtime she *knew* was going away. Fenway closed her eyes. Not the time to be focusing on interdepartmental personnel issues—their prime suspect in the Cahill murder had been exonerated, and the investigation needed to accelerate.

"That wasn't too helpful." Sarah tapped her fingernails on the counter, then sat down in front of her machine.

"Maybe," Fenway said cautiously, pulling her train of thought back on the investigation track. "If Seth Cahill was using Miranda Duchy's cabin as morpheranyl storage, that might explain a lot."

"Like what?"

"What Mathis Jericho was doing there, for one," Dez said.

Fenway nodded. "And what Seth's Corvette was doing there, too."

Dez grunted in agreement. "Mathis was the last one seen with the hammer, going into the area where the murder occurred. Maybe he's the one who killed Seth Cahill, trying to take over the business for himself, and then Miranda Duchy killed Mathis—in revenge for Seth."

"Did Miranda know her cabin was being used for drug storage?" Fenway asked.

"Let's hold that thought—you're assuming a lot."

Fenway bit her lip.

"You're assuming a lot, Fenway," Dez repeated. "You heard Captain Alvidrez: the sheriff didn't find any drugs or evidence of drug storage."

Fenway pressed her lips together and took a step away from the counter.

Dez tilted her head. "What is it?"

"I, uh—" She glanced at Sarah. Could she tell Dez and Sarah that she didn't trust Sheriff Donnelly?

Well, yes, she could, but for a reason like Donnelly writing up Deputy Salvador? For something that didn't even affect her budget —the poor excuse she came up with? Fenway folded her arms and looked at the floor. There must be a way she could get around the roadblocks Donnelly had put in her way. Dez and Sarah—two smart people from two entirely different backgrounds. Maybe one of them, or both of them, would see something she couldn't.

But trying to block Deputy Salvador from getting hired, while annoying, was no reason not to trust Donnelly when she said she'd found no evidence at the cabin.

"Nothing," Fenway finally said.

Dez stared at Fenway for a long time, then shook her head. "You want to go see the cabin for yourself, don't you?"

Fenway was quiet.

"Out with it, Fenway."

She rolled her options around in her mind, then found a way out. "Patrick said he didn't find anything on the video of Duchy's doorbell cam. And he was mostly right. There wasn't any evidence on the footage itself—except Patrick hadn't heard the killer was right-handed, so he wasn't looking for Miranda Duchy to write with her left hand. Maybe it's something like that. I've been around this case. Donnelly hasn't. She could have been looking for drugs when evidence of the murder was in front of her."

Dez was quiet, tapping her chin. "Maybe."

"I'll be awake all night if we don't check out the cabin." Fenway tapped her fingers on the counter.

"Gretchen got the warrant," Dez said. "Think it's still valid?"

Fenway turned to Dez. "We're going anyway. Dead guy found in the carport. Searching the cabin is probable cause."

"It's been over twenty-four hours..."

"You're okay," Sarah said. "Last year, the California Supreme

Court ruled that the sheriff's department had standing without a warrant. And that was a week, not a day."

"Let me grab my purse," Fenway said. "We'll get the key from evidence on our way out." She looked at the clock on the wall; two fifteen, then she turned to Sarah. "You can check out the phone location info when it comes in, right? Tell me if Hope and Tyra were together?"

"Sure."

Fenway motioned to Dez. "Let's go. I don't want to be out in this storm any longer than we have to."

———

"Give me a second," Deputy Donald Huke said. "The key to the cabin was originally with Ms. Duchy's effects, but it's not there now." He was tall, his beige uniform stretched tight across his chest. He looked a little less doughy and more muscular than the last time Fenway had seen him. Dating Melissa de la Garza was looking good on him.

"You don't know where the key to the cabin is?" Dez asked. Her brow was creased, the way it was when she was in a hurry but trying to be polite.

Dez and Fenway were both dripping wet. The gentle drizzle when they'd left the coroner's suite turned into a downpour when they were halfway to the sheriff's office. Fenway was glad Huke hadn't commented on their soggy state.

"Sheriff Donnelly brought it back earlier. The key's here some-where. Maybe in the wrong box, or maybe not put away."

"Thank you, Donald," Fenway said, shooting a glance at Dez.

Huke disappeared into the back for a moment, then returned with the key in a baggie.

"Here it is."

"Where was it?"

"Box on the shelf underneath. The labels aren't clear."

Fenway took the baggie. "How long before Duchy's arraignment?"

"They pushed it to tomorrow. With the storm and all."

"Duchy's lawyer won't like that."

"She squawked a little, but then the lightning started, so she got quiet pretty fast."

Dez took Fenway in her Impala. Ocean Highway was almost empty, the rain coming down in sheets, turning the midday into a gray dusk. Dez drove about ten miles per hour under the speed limit and took the offramp onto the Windkettle cut-off through a large puddle on the right side that sprayed a sheet of water to the side.

The Windkettle cut-off road was wide, and it began to wind into the hills. The rain lessened, but Dez still kept her wipers on high.

"A panel truck could take this," Fenway said. "Not in this weather, but normally, it'd be easy enough."

Dez pointed to a sign mounted below the California Highway 331 sign. *No Trucks Over 10 Tons*. "On the smaller side of box trucks, but yeah."

"It means the cabin could have solved Seth Cahill's storage problems with the Venn cartel."

Dez nodded.

About ten minutes later, a sign on the right: *Hutash Bridge 500 Feet*. Fenway leaned forward and pointed out the windshield. "That's the cabin."

Dez slowed the Impala and followed Fenway's finger, squinting. "Back from the road a little."

Fenway nodded. "Look at those eucalyptus trees. Not very thick, but there are so many of them, you might not see a box truck from the road."

"Might be the rain."

Dez pulled the Impala up in the front of the driveway, as close to the front door as she could. She applied the emergency brake and gripped the steering wheel. "You ready?"

"We'll get soaked."

"It's ten feet to the front porch. By the time we get our umbrellas open, we'll be underneath the overhang."

Fenway took a deep breath and opened the car door. She hadn't brought her umbrella, anyway.

Dez and Fenway raced to the front porch. The wind blew hard, throwing some rain on their shoes and the bottom of their trousers as they stood under the overhang. Probably would have taken an umbrella right out of her hand.

"Key," Dez said.

Fenway pulled the baggie out of her inside blazer pocket and took the key out. Dez took it out of her hand and put it into the lock—

—but it didn't fit.

"What the hell?" Dez muttered under her breath, turning the key upside down, but it still didn't fit. "Is this the wrong key?"

Fenway pressed her lips together, then spoke. "Donald was in charge of the evidence room—and he wouldn't mess up like that. He's the most detail-oriented person I've ever met. Even more than Patrick."

"I don't know what to tell you, Fenway. The key doesn't fit."

"Maybe Gretchen took the wrong key, but maybe the door was open when she got here."

"Possible." Dez tried the doorknob, but it was locked. "If it was open then, it's locked now."

Fenway's stomach roiled. Why didn't the key work?

Fenway's phone buzzed—and so did Dez's. She looked at the screen, suddenly aflurry with texts:

Severe Weather Alert for ESTANCIA, CA THU 18 JUNE 04:02 PM
Tropical Storm Alonso advisory number 11
A tropical storm warning is in effect from Tierra del Verano north to Point Dominguez

Maximum sustained winds are near 50 mph (80 km/h), with higher gusts
Slow weakening is expected until 9:00 AM Friday June 19
Landfall is expected between 5:00 PM and 6:00 PM between Estancia and Point Dominguez

Fenway's stomach sank. The tropical storm *was* coming to Dominguez County.

Dez ignored their phones. "If Donnelly *had* brought the wrong key, and the door was open and she tried to lock it when she left, do you think she would have told anyone she had the wrong key?"

"Possibly not. But if she couldn't lock it when she left, why is it locked now?"

"Or if it's one of those locks that you can lock before you close the door."

"That would explain it." Fenway's shoes were getting drenched. "It's also possible that Miranda Duchy had a friend come by after law enforcement left to make sure everything was locked up."

"Also possible," Dez said. "Although she'd have a tough time coordinating that from her jail cell."

Fenway looked on either side of the door. Windows, but the shades were drawn. They wouldn't be extracting any information out of this visit.

Fenway's phone rang in her purse. Cell service here: that was always a crapshoot. She took the phone out: Sarah. She tapped *Answer* then turned on the speakerphone.

"Hey, Sarah. You've got me and Dez. And Tropical Storm Alonso in the background."

"I went through the cellphone records for Hope Dunkelman and Tyra Cahill."

"Anything of note?"

"Tyra Cahill's phone location says she never left her house until she went to Hope and George's house—exactly when she said she did."

"I'm hoping there's a 'but' coming."

"But," Sarah said, "Hope's phone shows she didn't go to Tyra's at all."

Fenway knotted her eyebrows. "Not at all?"

"No," Sarah said. "Records show she left home and went to Cahill Warehouse Storage."

CHAPTER TWENTY-THREE

"Hope went *by herself* to the storage facility?" Dez couldn't disguise the disbelief in her voice.

"If she did, she didn't go with Tyra's cellphone," Sarah said.

"How long did she spend at Cahill Warehouse Storage?" Fenway asked.

"According to the records, forty-three minutes."

"That's enough time to argue with Seth Cahill, hit him over the head with a hammer, find the rug in his office, wrap his body, and move it into an empty unit." Fenway lifted her wet feet, one by one, putting them back down into the growing puddle on the porch. "Does Hope's time at the storage facility match the time of the murder?"

"Yes," Sarah said.

"I knew Miranda didn't do it," Fenway muttered.

"We need to contact ADA Pondicherry," Dez said. "Miranda shouldn't spend one more minute in jail."

"You're right," Sarah said. "The ADA is my next call. But look—that's not all."

"The Corvette."

"Right." Tapping keyboard sounds on Sarah's side. "At 10:57 Monday night, Hope Dunkelman's phone leaves the storage facility and goes to—"

"Miranda Duchy's cabin," Fenway finished.

"Right. Less than five minutes there. Then the phone pings off towers along the Cactus Lake cutoff road, then along the back roads until it gets back to the storage facility."

"Where Hope got back in her car." Dez folded her arms. "And Tyra was her alibi."

"That's what it looks like," Sarah said. "You've got a copy of the phone records in your email. Anything else?"

"The cabin was a bust." Fenway looked out toward the Impala; the rain was getting heavier, the wind blew harder. "And this weather is no fun."

"HR asked us to leave," Sarah said. "Essential personnel only."

"Go," Fenway said. "Get home before the roads get too bad."

"And before the power goes out at work," Dez added.

"Right after I call to get Ms. Duchy released," Sarah said. "You two drive safe. I'll see you tomorrow—if we're not underwater."

Fenway ended the call. "We need to get into this cabin. I'd bet twenty bucks the latest shipment of morpheranyl is somewhere in that house. We can go back to evidence, try to get the actual key, then come back—"

"We're not coming back here in this weather," Dez said. "Besides, I assume Deputy Huke went home with the rest of the non-essential personnel. We couldn't get the key from the evidence room, anyway." Dez frowned at the rain, coming down in sheets again. "Let's not stand here—"

"Right."

They both ran to the Impala, trying to get soaked as little as possible. They got in and slammed the doors shut.

Dez gripped the steering wheel, not starting the car. "If Hope drove the Corvette to Miranda's cabin, how did she get back to the storage facility? Did Tyra drive her?"

Fenway paused. "I have another theory."

"Whatever it is," said Dez, "It's gotta match the location information from the phones. Hope went straight to the storage facility. But Tyra's phone didn't leave her house until 11:18 p.m."

"My theory explains that," Fenway said, her phone dinging. It was the location info from Sarah. Fenway tapped the file to open it.

Dez was silent.

"You still don't believe it was Hope," Fenway said.

"The evidence is staring me right in the face," Dez said. "I can't argue with it."

"But your gut's telling you something's not right," Fenway said.

"I don't really believe in that. But—uh, yeah."

"So here's my theory." Fenway looked at Dez. "The scooters."

Dez cocked her head. "What?"

"You've seen those Tailwhip electric scooters that are all over Estancia?"

Dez nodded. "Yeah. Gotta admit, they're kinda fun."

Fenway blinked. "I guess."

"What?" Dez said. "Oh, don't tell me you're one of those pearl-clutchers who think those cute little scooters are ruining the city."

Fenway screwed up her mouth. Not worth explaining the injuries she'd seen in the clinic back in Seattle. "Three scooters on the sidewalk in front of Cahill Warehouse Storage when Seth Cahill turned off the cameras. When the cameras were turned back on? Only two."

"The cameras were off all night, right? Someone else could have taken a scooter."

Fenway tapped her phone screen. "That's why I asked Tailwhip for their usage information for that area."

"You lowered your standards enough to talk to them?" The corners of Dez's mouth curled into a smile.

"Hilarious." Fenway scoffed. "I got their response last night before I went to bed. You know what they made me do?"

"I have no idea. Sing a song about how awesome Tailwhip is?"

"They said if I wanted it within a few hours, they could send it via the app. So I had to download Tailwhip to my phone. And I had to enter my credit card information before I could receive data from the company. They're diabolical."

"Maybe this is the universe's way of telling you to lighten up."

"Not likely." Fenway tapped the Tailwhip app. "Oh—there it is. Came in while we were driving here."

Dez started the engine and turned the defroster on. The rain strengthened, the sound of the drops hammering against the car almost as loud as their conversation. "Did they ask for a subpoena?"

"Nope. Sent the usage information for Monday night." Fenway tapped the screen. "The file's loading. Hang on a second."

"I'm heading back to the office. I don't want to get caught in the hills in this storm."

"Sure."

Dez backed out of the driveway. The file loaded, then finally appeared as the Impala got onto the Cactus Lake cutoff road.

Fenway tapped with two fingers, pulling them apart to enlarge the image. Five rows of information, each with a first column labeled *Vehicle No.* It was weird to think of an electric scooter as a *vehicle*, but Fenway turned her attention to the rest of the spreadsheet.

Three of the rows had no information. One of them had location information about three blocks away from Cahill Warehouse Storage and had been ridden to the bus station. But line 4…

"Vehicle 03046," Fenway read. "Went into standby mode at the corner of St. Ignatius and Thirty-Fifth."

"That's Cahill Warehouse Storage." Dez's eyes showed strain with the difficult driving. The car was staying on the road, no hydroplaning yet, but Dez had a tight grip on the wheel.

"The scooter's GPS shows that it was removed from its location two minutes before Hope's cellphone pings away from the storage facility," Fenway said.

"And it didn't sound some sort of alarm?"

Fenway shrugged. "Maybe Tailwhip doesn't do that. The scooter was activated about twenty minutes later—at the Hutash Bridge. Got the last four digits of a credit card number."

"Name?"

Fenway frowned. "Not on this spreadsheet. Maybe Sarah can find out."

"She went home, remember?"

"Maybe we can catch her."

"HR sent everyone home. Don't be that manager, Fenway."

"No, no, of course not." Fenway startled—she still hadn't resolved the hiring issue. As much as Fenway hated to say it, the hiring process would have to wait. Probably until after the storm passed. "The scooter was dropped off about a block away from the storage facility—maybe right where Hope left her car."

Dez nodded. "So Hope *didn't* get a ride home. She took the scooter."

"Down these mountain roads, too. I wouldn't have pegged her as that type of risk-taker."

"She'd just killed her best friend's ex-husband with a hammer. Adrenaline can do a lot."

Fenway braced herself as Dez turned onto the freeway on-ramp. "Yeah, I suppose."

The Impala went through a puddle, spraying water up and around, and the vehicle floated for a moment. Fenway held her breath, but then the familiar feeling of the tires on the road came back.

"Why?" Fenway asked.

"Why what?"

"Why did Hope do it?"

"Not sure we need to figure that out before we arrest her." Dez looked over her shoulder as she merged onto the freeway.

"Watch out—the shoulder's full of water."

"Got it." Dez changed into the middle lane. "The sooner we can be out of this storm, the better."

"Maybe the two of them were having an affair and he threatened to tell Tyra?"

"Hope and Seth Cahill? We haven't seen any evidence of that."

Fenway shook her head. "There's gotta be something else." Then her eyes widened. "Scott Behrens."

"What about him?"

"That's the motive. We thought Tyra's motive might be revenge for Scott's death. Maybe that's Hope's motive, too."

"You mean," Dez said carefully, slowing down to forty miles an hour as the rain continued to batter the windshield, "We thought Tyra might have killed Seth because she held him responsible for Scott's overdose. Now you're saying Hope killed him—for the same reason? Does that make sense?"

"It's possible," Fenway said. "Hope and Tyra were best friends. The two of them were ostracized in high school after Tyra got pregnant and Hope stood by her. Maybe Tyra fell apart when she learned Scott had died, and Hope got overprotective."

"As a motive for murder?" Dez frowned. "That's a stretch."

Fenway jumped in her seat.

"What?"

"I thought of something."

"Thank God. I thought you saw something in the road."

"Sorry," Fenway mumbled, pulling out her phone. She opened the file on the cellphone location. She scrolled back a few weeks.

"This is interesting," Fenway muttered.

"What?"

"Hope visited Cahill Warehouse Storage a few times a week."

"Not surprising, if she and Tyra were such good friends."

"But here—" Fenway tapped the screen. "For the last six weeks. Every Thursday at eight thirty in the morning."

"Maybe she and Tyra went to breakfast."

"Tyra doesn't work on Thursdays. So even if they *did* go to breakfast together, Hope wouldn't have gone to the storage facility."

Dez raised her eyebrows. "So maybe it *was* an affair with Seth."

Fenway knotted her eyebrows. "I suppose that's a possibility. But maybe..." Ugh. The cacophony of rain on the Impala was almost deafening—it was hard to concentrate. She tapped the phone screen again and went back to her email. She scrolled—there it was. Seth Cahill's bank records. She tapped the email and opened the file.

"Yeah," she murmured.

"Did you find something?"

"You heard Cahill's cash deposits were about five thousand more than what was listed in the ledger?"

Dez nodded. "Yeah, I was there when Sarah told you."

"Right. I think I found the discrepancy."

"Yeah?"

"Every Thursday for six weeks, Hope goes to Cahill Warehouse Storage at eight thirty. On Thursday afternoon—for the last six weeks—Seth Cahill makes a cash deposit of a thousand dollars at the ATM on St. Bonaventure. Well, a couple of times it was nine hundred. Once it was four hundred." Fenway looked up. "That's the missing five thousand dollars."

"Blackmail," Dez said.

"It's not evidence, but blackmail is one reason Hope might have given five grand to Seth."

"And that's motive." Dez exited the freeway, the wind pushing the Impala nearly out of the lane. "Do you want to wait for Sarah to get the name of the person who rented the scooter?"

"I'm impatient," Fenway said. "But yes, we should wait."

A flash in the sky illuminated the world so brightly that Fenway blinked. Almost immediately, a *boom* shook the car.

"The storm is almost on top of us," Dez said.

"Craig says the storm isn't as bad as it could be."

"It's not a hurricane, but it's pretty bad."

Dez navigated around a scooter left in the middle of the street and turned into the office parking garage. Immediately the raindrops slamming against the car ceased. "I don't think Hope realizes she's a suspect."

Fenway swallowed and her ears popped—she could hear herself think again. "She will as soon as Miranda gets released."

Dez was silent.

"I'm right, aren't I? Miranda will get released, and Hope will realize we're onto her."

"She might not find out for a while."

"No," Fenway said, "she might not. But if she does, the storm will provide good cover for her to get away. She could be in Mexico by the time Tropical Storm Alonso lets up."

Dez grunted.

"Sorry. Our safety is more important."

"Two conditions," Dez said. "We're heading to the office and you're checking the credit card info. If it matches Hope Dunkelman, then onto condition number two."

"Which is?"

"Check the weather." Dez pulled into a parking space. "If the experts have downgraded it to a tropical depression, we'll go visit Hope Dunkelman. But if it's still a tropical storm, we're going home."

Fenway tapped her weather app, then clicked on the *Severe Weather Alert.*

Severe Weather Alert for ESTANCIA, CA THU 18 JUNE
05:07 PM
Tropical Storm Alonso Advisory Number 12
Sustained winds at 45 MPH, with higher gusts
Landfall 5 mi NW of Estancia

"Not downgraded yet, but close," Fenway said, turning the phone so Dez could see. "It was fifty miles per hour when we were at Miranda Duchy's cabin."

Dez turned off the engine. "Fine. Let's go in."

The wind whipped through the parking garage, stinging Fenway's eyes. They walked down the ramp, the rain blowing sideways into the covered areas. Fenway and Dez looked at each other at the bottom of the ramp, and Fenway gritted her teeth, then ran through the plaza between the parking garage and the office building. Fenway pulled the door open and the wind nearly tore it out of her hand. Dez grabbed the edge of the door, and they struggled to pull it shut. Finally, they got the door closed, and as it clicked shut, the pressure popped Fenway's ears again.

"We're crazy," Fenway said. She should be in her apartment, cuddled up with McVie. Maybe with the storm, he could postpone leaving for a day or two. She blinked. She needed to catch a killer first.

Dez nodded. "I'm amazed the power is still on."

Fenway nodded and squished her way down the hallway toward the coroner's suite. "Let's hope I can still get that credit card info."

"I'll get paper towels from the restroom," Dez volunteered.

A few moments later, Fenway woke up the laptop in her office. Sarah had sent the notification that ADA Pondicherry had submitted the paperwork to release Miranda Duchy. Given the order of non-essential personnel going home, it wasn't clear if Duchy's paperwork would get expedited, or if they'd wait until the storm passed and everyone was called back.

Fenway closed the email, then opened her web browser and clicked the financial app on the county intranet. She opened the spreadsheet she'd gotten from Tailwhip earlier. She copied the credit card number, then went to her financial app and pasted it, then clicked *Search*.

Mid-Coast Bank
Cards issued: 2
Account owner
Hope Jessica Dunkelman

Fenway looked up as Dez walked in, still dripping, with a large stack of paper towels. "These are terrible, but they're better than nothing."

"Got a hit on the card used for the Tailwhip scooter," Fenway said. "Account owner: Hope Dunkelman."

"So now we wait for the storm to be downgraded." Dez sighed. "I could really go for Java Jim's."

"The coffee machine didn't close for the storm." Fenway grinned. "It even has decaf, so you can keep your wife happy."

Dez mimed a retch.

Fenway's phone dinged; it was a weather alert.

Severe Weather Alert for ESTANCIA, CA THU 18 JUNE
05:16 PM
Tropical Storm Alonso advisory number 13
Sustained winds at 37 MPH
Alonso has been downgraded to tropical depression
The deepest water will occur along the immediate coast in areas of
onshore winds
Surge-related flooding depends on the relative timing of the surge
and the tidal cycle and can vary greatly over short distances

"There's your second condition met," Fenway said to Dez. "So if we want to catch Hope Dunkelman—"

"Yeah." Dez mopped the back of her neck with a paper towel; half of it stuck to her skin. "Maybe we can get something better over at the sheriff's office."

Fenway blinked. "The sheriff's office? Shouldn't we take—"

"We're checking out a cruiser," Dez interrupted. "Ain't no way I'm getting a soggy murderer into the back seat of my Impala."

CHAPTER TWENTY-FOUR

THE PUDDLES WERE GETTING DEEPER ON THE FREEWAY AND especially on the offramp onto Tres Arboles Road. When Dez steered the cruiser through the right turn, past the five-foot tall brick mini-towers, and into the Prospero Park neighborhood, the street dipped. The cruiser muscled its way through four or five inches of standing water, hydroplaning for a moment, then getting back under control. Fenway exhaled in relief.

Although the sun wouldn't set for three hours, the sky was dark, like twilight before it became completely dark. Dez's headlights were on, but the light bounced off the heavy rain, minimizing visibility.

Dez drove carefully, following the streets as they zigzagged next to Prospero Park. Turning onto Rodrigo Avenue, lined with oak trees, Dez narrowly missed a Tailwhip scooter lying partway in the street. The cruiser's tires didn't hold for a moment, and the car slid before Dez regained control. Fenway looked over at Dez from the passenger seat.

"Oh, give it a rest, Fenway. Don't be such a fuddy-duddy."

"Those newfangled scooters are simply a blight on our fair city," Fenway said in her best snooty voice.

They pulled up to the curb next to the ranch-style craftsman house on Rodrigo Avenue. The manzanitas and snapdragons were battered from the wind, and some of the pea gravel had been blown over the driveway.

"That drive wasn't terrible," Fenway said.

"You weren't the one behind the wheel," Dez muttered. "Let's hurry this up."

"It's Thursday, almost six," Fenway said. "With the storm, Hope should be home, right?"

Dez thrust her chin at a beige sedan and an SUV in the driveway; Fenway recognized the SUV that George Pope had driven through the rear entrance of the storage facility. "That's their vehicle, right?"

"Right."

"Estancia's shut down," Dez said. "Everyone was sent home. I bet Hope Dunkelman is at home. *We* should be at home."

"The sooner we arrest Hope, the sooner we can finish this up."

Dez narrowed her eyes: yes, they could go home now. But Dez, like Fenway, hated to let the bad guys get away.

Fenway took a deep breath, opened the door, and rushed out of the cruiser, slamming the car door shut and scampering up the driveway to the front porch. She was soaked again.

Dez, right behind her, was also drenched.

"See?" Fenway said. "Piece of cake."

"If you have gills." Dez stomped, her shoes squishing water out. "Your can-do attitude is pissing me off."

"Happy to be of service." Fenway reached out and rang the doorbell.

A moment later, the door opened. George Pope stood there in sweat shorts and a blue-and-yellow T-shirt reading *Estancia High 20th Reunion.*

"Coroner?" His eyes narrowed in confusion. "It's—it's..."

"Good evening, Mr. Pope. You remember my colleague, Sergeant Roubideaux? From Tuesday—she interviewed your wife at the storage facility."

"Of course." Then his eyes widened, and he stepped back, opening the door wider. "Sorry—where are my manners? Get in out of the storm."

"Thank you." Fenway stepped inside into the foyer, full of fiddle-leaf figs and ferns, and Dez followed. "You don't happen to have a couple of towels, do you? I hate to drip on your floor."

"I'll be right back." Pope turned toward the living room. "Hope? The coroner's here."

"What?" came Hope's voice faintly from the back of the house.

"Bring a couple towels!"

Fenway and Dez stood in awkward silence for a moment, only the sound of water dripping off their faces and clothes onto the tile floor next to two of the century plants.

Pope's eyes darted toward the tile, then back up. He smiled. "Don't worry. That'll clean up, no problem."

Hope Dunkelman appeared, four hot pink beach towels in one hand and a dark green electric lantern in the other. "Oh—Coroner. And Sergeant—uh, is it 'Roosevelt'?"

"Roubideaux," Dez said, holding her hand out. Dunkelman handed her a towel, and Dez patted her face off. Fenway took a second towel and wiped the bottom of her blazer, the worst offender on her person in terms of dripping water onto the floor.

"I found it," Dunkelman said to her husband, holding up the lantern. "In the front of the garage, underneath some boxes. *You* must have put it there after we went camping."

Pope pressed his lips together.

"Sorry," Dunkelman said to Fenway and Dez, setting the lantern on an empty plant stand on Fenway's left. "Can I get you anything? Coffee, maybe, while we still have power?"

"I found a fantastic tea blend—" Pope began.

"Oh, honey," Dunkelman interrupted, with a stern yet affectionate glance. "No one likes that farmer's market tea but you."

"I don't need anything," Fenway said. She cleared her throat and looked at Dunkelman's face: open, helpful. She narrowed her eyes. "Did you hear Miranda Duchy was released?"

"Can't say I'm surprised," Dunkelman replied. "I never thought she was capable of murder."

"Really?" Dez asked. "I'm surprised to hear you say that."

Hope smiled with a trace of bitterness. "Don't get me wrong—I don't *like* her. She cheated with my best friend's husband. But she'd never do the grunt work herself. If she wanted him dead, she'd hire someone. Or something less bloody. Poison, maybe."

Fenway tilted her head. Not what she expected. Hope didn't appear nervous or jittery at all. Fenway toweled the rest of her blazer off and thought for a moment. She'd need a different tactic.

Pope cleared his throat and took the two remaining dry towels from Dunkelman. "Did you have other information for us, Coroner?"

"Yes," Fenway said. She glanced at Dez's face: uncertainty there, too. "We try to cover our bases during investigations like this. We don't want to focus on a single suspect so heavily that we lose sight of alternate explanations."

Dunkelman nodded. "That's why you let Miranda go, right?"

"Correct." Fenway felt like she was treading water—not water, exactly, but thick, sticky syrup. Was coming to their house a mistake? She'd expected Hope to be nervous, cagey. Now Fenway needed to buy a little time to think. She pressed the towel against her trousers. The towel came away sopping wet, but her trousers still stuck to her legs. Probably a lost cause. "In the course of our investigation," she said, "we tracked phone location information and credit card payments."

Dunkelman frowned. "You're allowed to do that?"

"We've got a court order." Fenway tried to fold the towel—and nearly knocked the lantern over. She grabbed it just in time before it fell. "That was close." She set it back on the plant stand. The lantern looked new, but was missing one screw near the bottom. No wonder it was unstable. "Most telecoms and banks cooperate with law enforcement requests. And we have warrants when they don't."

"I see."

Pope stepped forward. "Fresh towel?" He held out his hands: one holding the two dry towels, one empty.

"Thank you." Fenway put the wet towel in Pope's empty hand and took a dry one. "As I was saying—"

"How about you, Sergeant?" Pope asked, stepping in front of Fenway. Dez nodded, taking the last dry towel, swapping her wet one.

"The phone location information was kind of revealing," Fenway said.

"I'll put these in the laundry," Pope whispered, pointing to the back of the house.

Fenway nodded, trying to keep her focus on Hope Dunkelman. "And the location information doesn't appear to back up your alibi, Ms. Dunkelman."

Dunkelman blinked; a curtain of confusion crossed her face. "I don't understand."

"It shows that instead of going to Tyra Cahill's house, you left here and went straight to Cahill Warehouse Storage."

Dunkelman folded her arms. "I did no such thing."

"I'm afraid you only have Tyra Cahill's word to back you up. The telecom records don't lie."

"You must be looking at the wrong number, then. Because both my phone and I were at Tyra's."

Fenway's ears popped again—stupid storm. She shook her head to clear her thoughts.

"We can also show that you spent about forty-five minutes at the storage facility, then drove to Miranda Duchy's cabin near Hutash Bridge. You drove Seth's Corvette there to hide it, and we think the evidence we have will be enough to convince a jury."

Dunkelman scowled. "Again, I did no such thing."

"One more thing," Dez said. "We also believe you murdered Mathis Jericho."

"Who?" Dunkelman's voice came out in a croak.

"Mathis," Fenway said. "The maintenance and landscaping employee at the storage place."

Dunkelman's eyes widened. "Why would I want to kill him?"

"Perhaps he saw you driving the Corvette after you killed Seth." Fenway pressed her lips together for a moment. "Where is your phone, Ms. Dunkelman?"

"I'll get it. It's in my purse. I'll prove to you I wasn't anywhere near the storage facility."

Dez followed a step behind Dunkelman as she stepped into the kitchen, grabbed her purse off the counter, and rummaged through it. She pulled it out, as if triumphant.

"Okay," Fenway said, pulling her own phone out of her purse, waking it up and tapping on the screen to load the telecom file. It took a moment. She set her purse down on the top of the divider between the foyer and living room. "We have your credit card payment for a Tailwhip electric scooter," Fenway continued, "activated at Miranda Duchy's cabin, and ridden back to the storage facility."

Now Hope Dunkelman looked nervous. "You mean to tell me," she said, her voice quavering, "you have my phone's location information that shows me at Tyra's storage place when Seth was killed? And driving Seth's car into the mountains and then proof that I—I rented an electric scooter and drove it back to Estancia?"

"That's correct."

Dunkelman raised her hands to her temples. "This can't be happening."

"I'm afraid it is, Ms. Dunkelman."

"No. It's not me. My credit card was stolen or something. Maybe somebody's trying to frame me. I'm telling you, I was at

Tyra's house for a couple of hours on Monday night before we came here. Before we *both* came here."

Then another puzzle piece clicked into place in Fenway's head. "The screw."

"Sorry?" Dunkelman said.

"We found a screw on the floor of the storage unit where Mr. Cahill's body was found. The head is green—and it matches the color of the lantern." Fenway grabbed the lantern off the side table. "This lantern with a missing screw."

Hope blinked in confusion.

"And your phone?" Fenway scrolled through the telecom information. "Here it is—registered to Hope J. Dunkelman." She read off the number.

A flash of lightning outside lit up the entire house.

Hope Dunkelman's face fell.

But it wasn't guilt or shame from being caught. It was horror—and disappointment.

A crash of thunder.

Fenway took a step back. What had she missed? She closed her eyes.

The missing five thousand dollars. Blackmail—wasn't it?

Isabella's voice in Fenway's head. *George had terrible credit for years.* Then Fenway saw the financial app on her web browser: *Mid-Coast Bank, Cards issued: 2.*

Oh—it might have been Hope Dunkelman's name on the phone and credit card. But she hadn't been the one using them.

Fenway opened her eyes. Hope Dunkelman stood in front of her, struck speechless when she'd heard the phone number.

But George Pope had even less motive than Hope Dunkelman. Maybe the thousand dollar a month payment came from him, not Hope—but why?

Another flash of lightning lit up everything, an eerie glow through the windows of the house.

Fenway closed her eyes again.

The blank space under *Father* on Scott Behrens's birth certificate.

Hope Dunkelman's voice from the day before. *Honestly, I expected George to dump me once it was clear that I was supporting my best friend through the pregnancy…I'm lucky.*

Sarah, sitting at her workstation, going through Seth Cahill's financials: *The next day, Seth bought one of those online DNA testing things from Genome Genius.*

Yes, the expensive DNA kit with the three-day turnaround.

It all clicked into place.

A crash of thunder.

Just as an engine started. Fenway stopped and strained to listen. Was that in front of the house? Was that in the *driveway?* She opened her eyes and stared at Hope Dunkelman.

Dunkelman's face drained of color.

The sound of the engine got quieter—the vehicle was getting further away from the house.

"It's George," Fenway shouted to Dez. "He wasn't putting towels in the laundry. He's getting away."

Realization dawned on Dez's face.

And suddenly, another bolt of lightning and a boom of thunder, instantaneous.

A split second later, a whine, like a hinge needing oil.

Then an ear-splitting crash of metal and glass.

CHAPTER TWENTY-FIVE

Fenway and Dez hurried out of the house just in time to see the beige sedan, headlights blazing, back down the driveway through the sheets of rain.

And a massive branch from the coastal live oak bisecting the cruiser behind the driver and passenger seats. Broken glass covered the wet sidewalk; metal shards stuck up from the police car's roof.

That's gonna be a lot of paperwork.

Then the beige sedan shifted from reverse to drive and shot forward, driving around the wrecked police cruiser and the branch of the enormous oak tree sticking halfway into the street.

He's getting away.

Fenway, getting drenched by the downpour, stared for a split second at the cruiser. No way it was drivable.

The sky was so dark it was almost like nightfall—but there, on the corner, lay her only hope.

A Tailwhip electric scooter.

But there was no way she could catch a car. Those electric scooters topped out at, what? Twenty, maybe twenty-five miles an hour?

But she saw the beige sedan, with George Pope in it, turn onto the zigzagging street next to Prospero Park. Then she saw the central bike path through the park, straight as an arrow, right toward the brick mini-towers and the exit from the neighborhood.

Fenway sprinted toward the scooter through the downpour, her phone in one hand—had she left her purse in the house with Dez and Hope?—and splashed her way across the street to the scooter. She held her phone up in front of her face.

The Tailwhip app immediately appeared onscreen.

Rent Vehicle 03062?
Double-click side button to accept

She double-clicked the side button, and the scooter blinked blue and came to life. Fenway jammed her phone in her inside blazer pocket, pulled the electric scooter upright, and jumped on.

Her mind flashed back to Seattle.

"Like riding a bike," she said out loud.

Fenway shifted her weight forward and leaned into the handlebars. The scooter shot forward so fast, Fenway nearly lost control on the rain-slicked pavement. But she gripped the bars tight and steered into the central path of Prospero Park.

If she was lucky, she could go at top speed through the park and meet Pope's beige sedan on the other side of the park.

And then what?

She didn't know. But she had to try.

The rain was pouring down now, like someone had turned a bucket upside down. She'd heard of rain like this in the southern United States or the Midwest, but not in Seattle, and certainly not on the California coast. She could barely see in front of herself.

Another flash of lightning illuminated the sky.

She was glad the path through the park was straight and flat—

A bump in the asphalt knocked her left hand off, and the

scooter slowed, but she immediately grabbed the handlebar again and leaned forward even more.

Riding without a helmet! the nurse voice in her head screamed at her.

"Quiet, I'm catching a killer," Fenway muttered. She stole a glance to her left, the rain stinging her face. The beige sedan had to slow for a left turn, then again for a hairpin curve. She was gaining.

When George Pope's sedan reached the end of the hairpin curve, she was slightly ahead.

She tried leaning further over the handlebars, but the electric scooter was at maximum speed. Fenway squinted through the sheets of rain. The exit out of the Prospero Park neighborhood was coming up, maybe in a quarter mile. She had seconds to formulate a plan.

An action scene from a movie unspooled in her head: could she jump off and have the scooter fly through the air, smashing through the window of the car and disabling it?

She looked to her left again. The beige sedan was too big to be stopped by the scooter. Even if she could time it properly and make sure the scooter wouldn't stop when she jumped off.

Maybe she could cut in front of the beige sedan. That might give Dez enough time to pursue Pope in Hope Dunkelman's SUV. Which would clearly be better in weather like this than the sedan.

But George Pope had killed Seth Cahill, and he'd probably killed Mathis Jericho too. Maybe because Mathis knew that Pope had killed Cahill. Fenway took a deep breath—and almost vomited when the rainwater went up her nose.

The tail of the scooter wavered and Fenway nearly lost control, but her hands steadied the handlebars.

"Don't overcorrect," she muttered under her breath.

The sedan had pulled ahead of her. Another set of turns for him. She might be able to get ahead again.

Then Fenway got an idea. Maybe it wouldn't work. But George might be scared of pursuit. Maybe he wasn't thinking clearly.

"What the hell," Fenway grumbled. "I can't think of anything else."

She chanced a glance down at the handlebar. Just to the left of the handlebar grip was a round knob-like screen. Would this work the way the Tailwhips in Seattle had?

She tapped the top of the knob, the scooter slowing.

"No, no, keep moving," she yelled.

The knob's screen lit up. Another brief glance down.

A blue light, and a white touch button. Was that it?

She moved her finger over the white button—

Then another bump in the asphalt knocked her hand off the knob. It went dark and the scooter slowed again.

Fenway let loose a stream of obscenities, leaning forward farther. The scooter whined and shot forward again. Another glance to her left. The sedan was ahead of her now. If Pope got to the front gate of the Prospero Park neighborhood before he noticed Fenway on the scooter, all hope was lost. She leaned forward more, scooting her right thumb to the top of the knob. The screen lit up again.

"White button," she muttered.

Her thumb struck home.

A bright LED headlight mounted between the handlebars sizzled on. The cold light reflected back in the heavy rain, blinding Fenway for a moment, but she blinked and looked to her left. The beige sedan was completing the third hairpin turn, its headlights shining directly at the scooter.

Surely George Pope saw her that time.

And the beige sedan sped up. Yep—that did it.

Fenway grinned—and got a mouthful of rainwater.

She coughed, the scooter slowing slightly, and she turned her head and spat. She leaned forward again.

George was out of the twistiest part of the road, and he had a straight shot until the stop sign and the left turn onto Tres Arboles Road.

He accelerated—he wouldn't let Fenway get ahead of him.

"That's right, George," Fenway murmured. "Don't let me win. Go faster."

The beige sedan turned toward the exit—

And hit the five inches of standing water where Dez had hydroplaned earlier.

The front of the beige sedan, instead of steering to the left toward Tres Arboles Road, lost traction and swung to the right.

The right front wheel jumped the curb.

Smash.

The front of the sedan crashed into one of the brick mini-towers and popped back into the road. The right headlight went dark. The engine idled, then died.

Fenway wished she had her firearm.

She slowed her scooter and stopped when she was a few feet behind the rear bumper of the beige sedan. She looked over her left shoulder; headlights on the road to that side of the park. Hope Dunkelman's SUV. Fenway hoped Dez was driving it—or was at least a passenger.

She turned back to the beige sedan. The figure in the front seat was slumped to the side. With the angle that the car had hit the brick mini-tower, it was possible that the airbag hadn't gone off. And George Pope had been in a hurry to get away. He might not have put on a seatbelt. He could be injured. Maybe badly.

She got off the scooter, her phone giving her a beep from her blazer's inner pocket. "I'll take care of you later," Fenway muttered.

She cautiously crept forward, looking for any signs of movement from the driver's side. The sheets of rain made it hard to see, and she blinked hard as the rain dripped off her eyelashes.

"Come on," she muttered. "Give me something."

No movement.

Fenway reached the driver's door. The window was covered with rain, and the downpour kept pounding on the windshield and the driver's-side window. The figure inside—definitely George Pope—sat slumped to the right.

Pope moved his head, then gritted his teeth.

Fenway recognized the movement from the clinic. That was serious shoulder damage. Maybe a separated shoulder, maybe a broken collarbone.

Would the driver's door open?

Fenway took a deep breath and pulled the handle. The door swung out toward her.

"George Pope," she shouted over the sound of the pouring rain, "you are under arrest for the murders of Seth Cahill and Mathis Jericho. You have the right to remain silent. Anything you say can and will—"

"Don't tell Hope," he interrupted.

"What?" She leaned into the car.

"Don't tell Hope."

Fenway stood dumbfounded for a moment, the rain pouring off her. "I think she figured out you're the killer."

His eyes blinked back tears.

Oh. That wasn't it.

"You mean, don't tell her you're Scott's biological father," Fenway said.

Tears started pouring down George Pope's cheeks.

"Is that it?"

"I was a stupid kid. Hope was away for spring break. I—I fooled around with Tyra." He swallowed, his mouth dry. Fenway remembered Hope's version of the story: Tyra had been drunk. "Tyra didn't even like me—not like that. I don't know why I did it. We both swore it would never happen again. And then Tyra discovered she was pregnant."

"And Seth found out." The DNA test—the fast, expensive one. "The Genome Genius."

"Of course Seth found out. I never figured out how he got Scott's DNA to test it, but he did." Pope sucked in a painful breath.

"You found out I was paying Seth, right?"

"Only we thought your wife was making the payments."

"Yeah, well, I fucked up with Tyra in high school, and I fucked up my finances, too. My credit cards are all under Hope's name. Even my phone is under her name."

"She only has the one number listed."

"Her work pays for hers. They manage the account."

Of course.

The SUV, its lights shining through the downpour, came to a stop behind Fenway. "What should I tell her?"

"Tell her I killed Seth. I didn't mean for Hope to take the fall. Tell her you don't know why. Promise me. She can't find out I cheated on her with Tyra."

"That was a long time ago. You said it yourself—you were a stupid kid. What were you, sixteen?"

George tried to push himself up and winced. "It'd destroy her."

"And her husband going away for murder won't?"

Pope turned his head toward Fenway. A cut on his left cheek. His right arm at an odd angle from the rest of his body. "Please, Coroner. You got your murderer. I went over to the storage place to talk to Seth while Hope was taking care of Tyra. But he and I started arguing, and I got pissed off. Really pissed off."

"And you hit him with the hammer."

George closed his eyes and sucked in air through his teeth—he was in pain. He opened his eyes and stared at Fenway. "He wouldn't even acknowledge that *his* drugs had killed someone. Someone that Tyra and I—"

He gulped, a tear rolling down his cheek. "Scott deserved better. I thought he'd have a chance at a better life if Tyra gave him up for adoption."

"And her keeping the baby? Maybe you helping out?" But Fenway knew the answer.

George scoffed, then grimaced in pain. "My parents would have hit the roof. Not only did I get my girlfriend's best friend pregnant, but she was—" George stopped, flicked his eyes to Fenway's face, a sudden intake of breath.

Yep. Because Tyra was Black. That's why George's parents would have hit the roof.

The embarrassment shimmered in George's eyes, and Fenway kept pressing. "So Seth wouldn't talk to you about it?"

"He turned and walked away. Said it wasn't a good time. He kept shutting me down, going back and forth across the property, checking locks on the units, practically running away from me. And then we were going between two buildings, and he finally turned around and screamed at me. He didn't care that my 'junkie kid' had died—and I..."

"Where did you get the hammer, George?"

"It was lying on the concrete. Some lumber, a toolbox, and a hammer. Just lying there. Like the universe was telling me something." George closed his eyes.

"Hey, hey," Fenway said, scooting forward. "You still with me?"

Pope's eyes opened again. "I hit Seth over the head with the claw side of the hammer. It was only once, but it felt—it felt, like I *had* to."

Fenway nodded.

"And then I had to clean up. I got Seth's keys. Figured there'd be plastic sheeting or maybe a stack of moving blankets in the office."

"Or a Persian rug?"

"Yeah." Pope cracked a small smile. "His rich girlfriend's Persian rug."

"Then you hid his Corvette at his rich girlfriend's cabin. Even took a scooter with you."

George looked through the windshield at the rain hammering on the glass. "Riding the scooter back into town, flying down the road at twilight, wind whipping through my hair, knowing Seth was dead, thinking my secret was still safe. Best feeling of my life."

"And how did you get the hammer into Miranda's shed?"

George turned his head slightly to look at Fenway. "When Tyra and I went over to take Seth's boxes to Miranda's house, I snuck around the side of the house while Tyra was yelling at the doorbell. I was planning to dump the hammer in her backyard, but the shed was open. Figured putting the hammer in there would look more convincing."

Fenway blinked. How had she missed that? Oh—while the doorbell camera showed nothing but Tyra's light blue blouse. Pretty lucky that Tyra didn't step to the side.

Not lucky that George Pope hadn't thought of leaving his cellphone at home.

"I'll plead guilty," Pope continued. "Save you the cost of a trial. Just don't tell Hope that Scott—" His voice broke, and he pressed his lips together and cleared his throat. "Scott was my son."

Sloshing footsteps on the wet pavement behind her. Fenway stepped back and to the left. Dez was holding out a pair of handcuffs, her hand resting on her holster.

"He needs to go to the hospital," Fenway said. "He's in no condition for cuffs."

Dez took out her phone, the rain splashing all over. "I'll get an ambulance."

Fenway turned to Pope. "We need to immobilize your right arm, George. Can you hold it next to your body with your left hand?"

Pope grunted. "I'll try."

Another set of footsteps, these faster, a little tentative, a little rushed. Hope Dunkelman, soaked to the skin, pushed past Fenway. "Why?" she wailed. "Why did you do it, George?"

Then she knelt down. "You're hurt." She turned to Fenway. "He's injured. Look at his arm."

"Sergeant Roubideaux is getting an ambulance here as fast as possible," Fenway said. "Maybe a broken clavicle."

"I'm sorry, baby," Pope said. "I didn't mean for you to get involved. I love you. More than anything."

"But why?" Now Hope was sobbing, her tears mixing with the rain.

"Because," Pope gasped, gritted his teeth, then slid slightly to the right, more awkwardly than before. "I went to talk to Seth. Told him it was shitty of him to keep distributing Nyllie after Tyra's son died from an overdose."

"You went to talk to him?"

"You'd gone over to Tyra's. She was upset. And it was all Seth's fault. I couldn't take it anymore." Pope swallowed hard. "But Seth—Seth said he'd always been pissed off that Tyra had a kid before they were together. Said Scott was a—" He coughed, sucked in air. "I don't want to say what Seth called him. But Seth said Scott deserved to die." A sob caught in his throat.

Fenway's eyes widened. How much of this was true, and how much was Pope saying for Dunkelman's sake? She looked in Pope's face. Either he was a fantastic actor, or most of what he was saying was the truth.

"I don't know what came over me, baby." And now George Pope was blubbering. "It was like I left my body. One minute I was following him down a sidewalk between two of the storage buildings, and the next I was holding a hammer covered in blood."

"And you tried to pin it on Miranda?"

"Well, I—" Pope closed his eyes. "I'm not proud of that. What else was I supposed to do?" He opened his eyes again, and met Dunkelman's gaze, pleading. "I thought I'd feel better. But I didn't. Miranda had already agreed to let Seth use the cabin to store the—" He swallowed hard. "And Miranda slept with Seth, even though she knew he was married. Tyra doesn't deserve—" He started sobbing again. "What's wrong with me?"

Hope Dunkelman carefully put her hand on the side of his face. "We'll fight this," she said. "With the right jury—and Tyra knows good lawyers..."

"No," he said emphatically. "I did it. I didn't plan to do it. I didn't mean to kill him. But I was just *so* angry."

"I don't understand," Hope said quietly, tears streaking her cheeks.

Fenway could believe it. Maybe the blackmail had been why Pope had gone to talk to Seth that night. But Fenway suspected the hammer's claw in the back of Seth's head had less to do with the blackmail and more with Seth's callous attitude toward Scott's death.

"We can fight it." Hope set her jaw. "It was the heat of the moment. You were defending your friend." A gleam in Hope's eye. "Did he threaten you? Was it self-defense?"

Pope's lower lip trembled. "No, sweetie. He was an asshole. But he didn't threaten me."

"We can still—"

He shook his head forcefully, then winced in pain. "I won't put you through that."

"But we can win—"

"You're not wasting your life savings on a lawyer when I'm guilty."

Fenway startled—she hadn't finished reading Pope his rights. She wiped the rain from her face and cleared her throat. "George Pope, you have the right to remain silent. Anything you say can be used against you in a court of law..."

CHAPTER TWENTY-SIX

Deputy Brian Callahan stood at the door of George Pope's hospital room when Fenway strode down the hallway with her legal pad. After she'd dried off—again—at her office, she'd written out everything she'd heard George Pope say in the front seat of the crashed beige sedan—except the paternity of Scott Behrens.

She stopped at the door. "Everything okay?"

Callahan nodded. "Sounds like it. We let his wife be with him until he goes in for surgery."

"Not worried about him escaping?"

Callahan shrugged. "Broken collarbone? He's not going anywhere. His wife is a little in shock. Maybe she didn't think he had it in him."

"Thanks, Brian." Fenway knocked and opened the door to the hospital room. George Pope lay on the hospital bed, his right arm in a sling, held tight against his side. Hope Dunkelman sat on his left, holding his hand.

"I have the confession for you to sign," Fenway said.

Pope nodded, trying to scoot himself up in the bed. He yelped.

"Don't do that," Dunkelman admonished. "You had a concussion when you said all those things. It can't be used against you in court. We can fight this, baby."

"I said no." Pope smiled sadly.

"At least let me call Tyra. Get her lawyer to give us a consultation."

"The ADA might be interested in negotiating," Fenway said.

Dunkelman stood up and shook her head. "He's not signing anything today. Besides, the doctor just put him on a drip. Painkillers. He wouldn't know what he's signing."

"It's—" Pope began, but a look from his wife silenced him.

"We'll be here when you're out of surgery." Fenway placed the legal pad on the wheeled hospital tray. "Make any changes you need to."

Pope reached out with his good arm, cringing in pain, and grabbed the legal pad.

"Don't read that." Dunkelman's voice went up an octave. "It'll upset you. You need to rest."

Pope blinked and dropped the pad. "She's right. I'm not signing that."

Fenway flinched; he'd been so ready to confess. "Why not?"

"You wrote that I killed Mathis Jericho."

Fenway clenched her jaw. "I see. You think a jury might sympathize with you for—"

"No!" Pope shouted, then yelped in pain.

Aha. Pope was afraid Fenway would reveal Scott Behrens' paternity. She'd have to talk to him about it later—if the ADA didn't get a confession out of him first.

"Get that paper out of here," Dunkelman said. "My husband isn't signing anything."

Fenway turned her head to look at George Pope. Was that resignation or determination in his eyes?

She thought back to his car wreck. She arrested him for both murders. He'd confessed.

He must have thought that a jury would have sympathy for him murdering the man responsible for the death of his son. But juries wouldn't be so understanding in the murder of the person who'd uncovered the truth.

She shook her head. It didn't matter. Pope had driven the Corvette in which Mathis was found dead. The evidence for Mathis's murder might be circumstantial right now, but they'd find something. Maybe ADA Pondicherry could make a deal for manslaughter instead of murder in the second degree. Maybe Pope would get lucky, and he'd get an offer for the sentences to run concurrently. And besides, Fenway—and Pondicherry, by extension—had a great bargaining chip. Scott's DNA, and what Pope had done with Tyra Cahill, would come out at trial. So Fenway knew there wouldn't be a trial.

Fenway felt a little gross holding that over Pope's head. But Pope was a killer. He'd have to pay for his crime.

"You don't have to sign it," Fenway said, "but the two of you should talk about it. Know what your options are." She looked at Pope. "We know you killed Mathis Jericho, too. Things will go a lot easier for you if we don't have to prove it at trial."

Dunkelman narrowed her eyes at Fenway, then turned back to Pope, who closed his eyes.

Fenway walked out of the hospital. The rain had slowed to an insistent drizzle. She sloshed through the parking lot and got into her Accord. San Vicente Boulevard was flooded a block to the west of the hospital—only the street itself, not the buildings, fortunately. A few inches of standing water covered the bottom of the tires of all the cars parked on the street.

Fenway took a different route to avoid the flooded street. She couldn't get onto Ocean Highway, but she took surface streets to get onto Estancia Canyon Road to get back to her apartment. It wasn't yet eight o'clock when she pulled into her apartment complex.

She opened the door and was greeted with smells of cooked tomatoes and garlic. McVie stood in front of the stove, two bowls on the counter beside him.

"Oh, good," he said, turning his head from the pots on the burners. "Your timing is perfect. Just another couple of minutes." He put down the wooden paddle onto a spoon rest and stepped over to Fenway.

She wrapped her arms around him. "Did we lose power?"

"For only about fifteen minutes, right around five o'clock. I already reset the clocks."

"Thanks."

McVie kissed her forehead. "You're soaked."

"I dried off at the office."

"Why don't you go change while I finish up?"

Fenway nodded, broke from McVie's embrace, and walked into her bedroom. She peeled off her clothes. McVie was right: everything was still damp. Her underwear clung to her body. She wondered if she should take a quick shower, then her stomach rumbled. No, no time for that. But she flitted across the hall to her bathroom and grabbed her towel, drying off. She looked in the bathroom mirror: her hair, which had mostly grown out since her adventure in Los Angeles, was a nightmare of frizz.

She finished toweling off, then went back into the bedroom, tossing her towel in the hamper and grabbing a pair of gym shorts and a tank top out of her drawers.

She walked out to the kitchen. "Now I feel less sticky."

McVie grinned as he closed the oven and turned down a burner.

"Thanks for cooking."

"It's nothing fancy. I didn't think we should go out in this weather—plus, I thought most places would be closed."

"What are we having?"

"You had pasta and red sauce in the pantry, and there was a package of ground turkey in the freezer."

"Did you use the mushrooms in the vegetable drawer?"

"And the zucchini."

Fenway sighed. "Thank you."

"It's no problem."

Fenway walked up behind McVie and traced a line down his left shoulder blade. "You think you should wait another couple of days before you leave?"

McVie bobbed his head. "Not sure. Payback Systems wants me there on Monday."

"But the storm is moving inland—and that's the way you're going. You don't want to catch up to it tomorrow."

"No. But I have to drive twelve hundred miles. If I leave Saturday, that's nine hours on Saturday and nine hours on Sunday. I'll be exhausted on my first day at my new job."

Fenway lowered her eyes.

"I've gotta call movers, too, since I won't be able to drive the U-Move-It truck next week. They didn't have anything on such short notice. So much for saving money on the move."

"Did you cancel the U-Move-It?"

"Not yet." McVie stepped back into the kitchen and lifted a lid on a saucepan. Steam wafted up. "I canceled the vehicle moving company, since I'll be driving the Highlander out instead of the U-Move-It."

"That sucks. It'll be a pain to coordinate everything."

"That's part of the reason I didn't cancel the truck rental. Maybe I'll ask for the day off on Friday and fly back. Payback Systems can't expect to ask me to start a week early without giving me a little leeway."

"Well," Fenway said, "demanding you start early wouldn't be fair or ethical. But they might expect you to do it anyway."

"Really?"

Fenway looked at McVie out of the corner of her eye. "How long has it been since you worked for a private company?"

"What do you mean?" McVie took a colander out from a bottom cabinet—*he knows where all my stuff is in the kitchen*—and set it in the sink.

"Like, outside the public sector."

"Oh." McVie turned off the burner under the bubbling sauce. "Uh—it's been a while."

"Like five years?"

McVie grinned. "Like twenty."

"Oh." Fenway sometimes forgot their fourteen-year age difference. "Right. Well, a lot of companies think they can mistreat their employees. And they set up that expectation the first week you're on the job, so you don't expect anything better."

McVie stirred the sauce for a moment, not saying anything. Then he set the spoon down, grabbed oven mitts, and lifted the pot off the stove, dumping the pasta and water into the colander in the sink. He set the pot back on the stove. "It's only for a year."

"A year of hell," Fenway said.

He shrugged. "If I can survive my year of patrol in Bakersfield, I can survive a year at Payback Systems." He opened the oven, mitts on, and pulled out a sheet pan with garlic bread, golden brown on top. Perfect.

Fenway took a step into the kitchen. "Can I do anything?"

"You've been busy meting out justice. Sit at the table. I'll bring this out in a minute."

She hadn't noticed he'd cleaned off the small table in the dining nook. She stepped back, hung her purse—the only thing that hadn't gotten thoroughly drenched—on the corner of the chair.

"Any more news on the Celeste situation?"

Fenway closed her eyes. "No."

The sounds of McVie dishing out food. "Want a beer?"

"Absolutely."

The sound of a can popping, the cabinet opening, the pour of beer into a pint glass. "Are you sure," McVie said, "there's no more news?"

Fenway paused. "What have you heard?"

"Only that your capture of those eighteen bricks of Nyllie led to a windfall for the department. So now Gretchen shouldn't have any problem with Celeste's overtime."

"Ah." Fenway stretched her arms above her head. Usually, after she'd caught a killer, her body would relax. But tonight, her shoulders were still tight. "Turns out Gretchen already knew about the incentive money when she wrote up Celeste."

McVie walked to the table, a flat bowl full of spaghetti in each hand, two pieces of garlic bread on top of each bowl, a fork sticking out of the pasta in each. "Then why did she do it?" He set the bowls down on the table.

Even though the sauce was from a pre-made jar, the aroma made Fenway salivate. She must have been hungry. "Maybe to flex power over me."

"Maybe it was the 'I need something more than that.' She might have thought this was the way to get you to give her what she wanted."

"But she needs to be less cryptic. And since my mind went immediately to a bribe, I'm not sure what her endgame is."

"I've been thinking about it most of the afternoon, too," McVie said. "And I don't have anything. Nothing that doesn't scream bribe."

Fenway twirled her fork, then lifted the spaghetti and sauce into her mouth. "Mmm."

"I added some garlic and onions, too. The jarred stuff doesn't always have enough of that."

"Whatever you did," Fenway said with her mouth full, "It's really good."

They ate in silence for a moment, Fenway crunching the garlic bread, McVie taking a swig of his beer.

"You okay?" McVie asked.

"Sure." Fenway swallowed. "Why?"

"Because you caught the bad guy. An innocent person was released from jail. You usually feel better about your wins."

"It could be because I don't feel like I really did anything to stop the flow of morpheranyl into the county." She picked up another forkful of pasta.

That wasn't it, though. Something didn't sit right with her. Something about Mathis Jericho's murder.

She chewed and swallowed. "But maybe Captain Alvidrez will get lucky with the information Calvin Banring gave us."

"Calvin who?"

"One of the guys who was on the catamaran with the kilos of morpheranyl attached to the hulls." Fenway chewed. "I suppose we at least disrupted operations a little. They won't be able to use the *Ariel*. Probably not a long-term solution, but if it means less morpheranyl, I suppose that's something."

"Yeah." McVie chewed and swallowed. "You beat yourself up too much."

Fenway chortled. "That's rich, coming from you."

McVie grinned. "Yeah, I'm as bad as you. Doesn't mean you shouldn't listen to me."

Fenway nodded.

Her phone buzzed in her purse.

"Don't get it," McVie said.

"If it's important—"

"Yeah, yeah, okay."

Fenway pulled her phone out of her purse. It was a text—from Sheriff Donnelly.

> Congratulations on solving the two
> murders

Fenway knotted her brow.

"What is it?"

"Text from Gretchen."

"You got a text from Gretchen?"

"Yeah," Fenway said. "She's never texted me before."

"What does it say?"

"'Congratulations on solving the two murders.'" Fenway glanced up at McVie.

"Why do you think that's weird?"

"Because I've never gotten any recognition from her about solving cases before. Why now? And why, after she told me she needed something from me?"

"Maybe Gretchen is trying to get better at communication." McVie rubbed his chin. "I've heard she hasn't been the best manager of people since the election. She could be giving you an actual compliment." He raised his eyebrows. "You know, some people I know are terrible at accepting compliments."

Fenway pursed her lips. "Do you think she still wants something from me?"

McVie took another bite. His plate was over half empty. He chewed thoughtfully. "You could go ask her."

"I suppose." Fenway took one last bite and sat back in her chair. She yawned widely.

"You've had a long day. Let me clean up."

Fenway opened her mouth to argue—but he was right. She was exhausted. And she'd been riding full speed on one of those stupid electric scooters.

"I feel bad," Fenway said. "It's your last night in town. We should do something." But as soon as the words were out of her mouth, she realized how impractical that was.

"If you haven't noticed, Estancia just experienced a hundred-year storm," McVie said.

"Yeah, yeah. Everything's closed."

McVie grabbed Fenway's empty plate along with his, stood up from the table, and walked into the kitchen, placing the dishes in the sink and turning on the hot water.

Fenway yawned widely. "Your last night in Estancia and you're cleaning up after me."

"After everything you went through at the storage unit? It's the least I can do." McVie opened the dishwasher and loaded the dirty plates and silverware into it. "Besides, I think a night in with you checks all my boxes for a perfect last day here."

PART 4

FRIDAY

CHAPTER TWENTY-SEVEN

Fenway walked to the HR department at City Hall as soon as she arrived at work on Friday morning. She'd said a tearful goodbye with McVie as he'd driven off in his Highlander to the storage facility to get a few boxes of his essentials, including an air mattress and bare-bones kitchen items. He'd have a long way to go before stopping in Las Vegas for the night.

Her head was awash with memories of their last kiss, with the lingering smell of his cologne on her skin, with the sun reflecting sometimes painfully off the wet streets. Sixth Street was no longer flooded. The power was still out in a few areas, but the emergency was over. And fortunately, no casualties—at least, not in Dominguez County.

Entering Suite 130, she spied Debbie Farzan at her desk and caught her eye. Debbie smiled, rose halfway out of her seat, and motioned Fenway over.

"Hi, Debbie," Fenway began. "I wondered—"

"I heard about the close call last night." Debbie's voice brimmed with excitement.

"What?"

"The big oak tree falling on the police car!" Debbie's hands fluttered. "You were so lucky you weren't inside! You could have been killed."

"Oh—" Fenway hadn't given it a second thought. Nor, apparently, a first thought. "I guess it didn't seem so dangerous at the time."

"Still," Debbie said, "I'm not sure I could do what you and Sergeant Roubideaux do."

"I appreciate that," Fenway said, taking a seat in a guest chair in front of Debbie's desk. "Now, let's talk about replacing Sergeant Trevino."

Debbie smiled. "I don't know what you said to Sheriff Donnelly, but she removed the insubordination write-up on Deputy Salvador."

"So, what do I need to do to get Celeste an offer letter?" Fenway asked.

"I was able to import the interview notes from the three candidates." Debbie arched an eyebrow at Fenway. "Good questions, by the way."

"Thanks." Fenway shook her head. "I guess I'm not sure what I need to do next."

Debbie turned back to the screen. "I got your email address corrected in the system, and I sent you the hiring system login credentials. You have thirty-one external candidates to evaluate based on their applications and résumés, but if you don't like a candidate, simply reject their application. If you reject all but Deputy Salvador, we could have an offer letter out to her by Monday." Debbie winked. "Maybe this afternoon, if you hurry."

She grinned. This was the best news about the hiring process she'd heard all week. "With my latest investigation closed," Fenway said, "I can give this top priority."

"I get notified when applications get approved and denied," Debbie said. "I'll keep my eyes peeled."

Fenway stood. "You've been very helpful. Thank you."

"Couldn't have done it without the sheriff removing her write-up," Debbie said, "so I think you should thank yourself."

Fenway nodded, her insides roiling. What had she done? Or more importantly, perhaps, what had Sheriff Donnelly *thought* she had done?

She exited Suite 130 and walked down the corridor in a daze. She stood for a moment in the City Hall lobby.

Did she want to know?

Let sleeping dogs lie, right?

Fenway paced in a circle. She should go back to her office, go onto the online application tool, approve Deputy Salvador for the position, and be done with it.

But there was still a foul taste in her mouth.

She shook her head, walked out of City Hall, and turned toward the sheriff's office.

———

"Coroner Stevenson!" Sheriff Donnelly said, pushing herself up from her desk.

Fenway stood in her open doorway. "I heard you rescinded your insubordination write-up on Deputy Salvador."

"I did, I did," Donnelly said. "It seemed silly when we don't have an issue with overtime anymore. And like you said, it was a win-win situation."

Fenway nodded, hesitated, then stepped into Donnelly's office and closed the door.

"What's going on?" Donnelly said.

"You said yesterday that you needed something from me," Fenway said. "And I had no idea what that was."

Donnelly smiled, but her eyes turned down at the corners with suspicion. "You know the pressure we're all under to keep the county safe. You got my text?"

"I did."

"Great. Then it's all settled."

"I just—" Fenway began. How should she continue this conversation? "I wanted to understand what—" She almost said *what settled it*. But that might put the sheriff on the defensive.

Donnelly chuckled and sat back down. "I was happy to see that you made an arrest in the murder investigations."

"Sure," Fenway said.

Sheriff Donnelly stared at Fenway for a moment. Fenway stared back, discomfort creeping up her spine, then broke eye contact with the sheriff. Donnelly put her elbows on the table and steepled her fingers. "I thought you'd be happy I removed all the obstacles for you hiring Celeste. We'll be sad to lose her, of course, but it's clear that she's too motivated to stay at the rank of deputy."

Fenway blinked. Donnelly wouldn't give her any clue about what it might be. Fenway had been silly to expect an explanation, right? But she didn't think that McVie's handpicked successor would be involved with anything shady.

She couldn't let it show on her face.

Fenway smiled. "Thanks for your time, Sheriff. Glad it all worked out."

"Take care," Donnelly said as Fenway opened the door.

A polite farewell—or a warning?

———

As Fenway walked back across the rain-slicked street and through the plaza, she racked her brain. What was Sheriff Donnelly hiding?

What made Donnelly so happy? The arrest that Fenway had made? Or the exculpatory evidence Fenway had found that had freed Miranda Duchy?

Hmm—maybe that was it. Perhaps Gretchen Donnelly and Miranda Duchy were friends. Were they former sorority sisters or business partners? Fenway would need to look into that.

She rubbed her forehead. But maybe she'd get Piper to investigate a possible connection between Duchy and Donnelly. Something outside the walls of the county government where Donnelly couldn't track the searches that were made.

The knot in her stomach returned. Mistrusting Sheriff Donnelly felt terrible.

She entered the coroner's suite.

"Congratulations, Fenway!" Sarah said from behind her counter.

Fenway managed a smile. "Thanks."

"My mother would be worried sick to hear about you speeding on that scooter in the middle of a tropical storm."

"Tropical depression," Fenway said, grinning. "Don't make it sound cooler than it was."

"It was pretty cool."

Dez stood. "Everything okay, Fenway?"

"Great."

"So—about Mark's role—"

"On it right now," Fenway said. "Just worked all the kinks out with HR. We'll have an offer letter this afternoon if I can get everything done."

"About time."

"I agree." Fenway walked into her office, shut the door, and took a deep breath. She sat in front of her keyboard, signed into her computer, and launched the hiring manager app on the intranet.

Her phone dinged. A text from McVie.

had 2 take care of last minute stuff

want 1 more lunch at dos Milagros b4 i go?

is 12:30 ok?

Fenway texted back.

Yes please. I miss you already. See you at 12:30.

She found the login information that Debbie had emailed her, and she spent the next two hours going through all the applications. She approved Deputy Salvador's first. Some applicants were terrible, but she read a couple of decent applications: one from San Miguelito and one from San Diego. Not as good as Deputy Salvador, though. She reread the application of Brian Callahan and confirmed that he wasn't right for the job either.

Fenway finally hit *Submit* on the last application.

She glanced at the clock in the bottom right corner of her screen. 11:15. She had plenty of time to find Deputy Salvador and tell her the good news.

———

"You what?" Fenway said.

Deputy Salvador folded her arms and leaned back in her desk chair. "I tried to tell you, Coroner."

"Bureaucracy doesn't move that fast." HR didn't have the right email, and Fenway hadn't even known about the second hiring system. But her stomach dropped. She should have been more on top of things.

"I understand," Salvador said through gritted teeth. "So when I got that write-up, I thought it killed my chances in Estancia." She rested her elbows on her desk. "I was waiting to respond to my other job offer until I found out whether I'd get Sergeant Trevino's job. After that? Called and accepted. They emailed the offer letter, and I signed it electronically."

Fenway closed her eyes. "You don't know what I had to do to get the insubordination report removed from your record." The whole truth: Fenway *herself* had no idea what she had to do. But she knew whatever it was, she had done it.

Or wait a second: maybe she hadn't.

"When did you give your resignation letter to Sheriff Donnelly?" Fenway asked.

"About thirty minutes ago."

"Two weeks' notice?"

Salvador shrugged and pointed to the box on her desk. "Donnelly wants today to be my last day."

"Why?"

"I wouldn't tell her where I'm going."

"Where *are* you going?"

Salvador shook her head. "I'm sorry, Coroner, but I'm not saying. That insubordination write-up put a bad taste in my mouth. If I say anything, I'm afraid it'll get back to Donnelly and she'll poison the well at my new job."

Fenway closed her eyes. Anger coursed through her veins. But anger at herself more than anyone else.

And she'd just rejected the other applicants in the system.

"Okay," Fenway said. She stuck out her hand. "Congratulations on making detective, and I wish you luck—wherever you're going."

Salvador stood and shook Fenway's hand, staring her in the eye.

"If you don't like it there," Fenway continued, "give me a call."

"Will do." Salvador's eyes told a different story. Maybe she didn't want to be anywhere near a sheriff like Donnelly or a coroner who couldn't figure out how to navigate the hiring system. It had taken almost six months to replace Rachel with Sarah, after all.

"I'm sorry I missed out on the opportunity to hire you," Fenway said.

"Me too."

Fenway turned and walked out of Salvador's cubicle.

———

McVie was already seated at a high-top table when Fenway walked into Dos Milagros. Two drinks sat on the table.

"Hi, Craig." She pulled him off his stool, to his feet, and embraced him in a hug.

"I'm sorry I'm leaving."

"It's not that." Fenway squeezed him tighter. "Well, yes, it *is* that. But it's also that I just found out Celeste accepted another job. She won't be replacing Mark."

"What? Where is she going?"

"She won't tell me—and I don't blame her." Fenway broke from his embrace and sat on the other side of the high-top from McVie. "Donnelly tried to screw with her career, so she doesn't want Donnelly calling her new job and, uh, 'poisoning the well,' is how she put it."

McVie frowned. "Sounds like I really messed things up when I recommended Donnelly for sheriff."

Fenway shrugged. "Not sure how you could have known."

He shook his head. "She's smart. Detail-oriented. Saw things during investigations no one else would see—you know, not just the evidence that *was* there, but the evidence that wasn't. Know what I mean?"

Fenway furrowed her brow.

"For example, if she was investigating a robbery, she'd look for things that the suspects did—and also things that the suspects *didn't* do. One suspect called his grandmother every morning at nine. The day after his grandmother's house got burgled? No call. Gretchen jumped all over that."

"Like the guard dog who doesn't bark at the intruder."

"Exactly."

Fenway blinked. Had she really missed something so obvious? "Hang on." She took out her phone and pulled up the phone location information. There was Hope's phone—the one George used—at Miranda Duchy's cabin on Monday night, when he'd confessed to driving the Corvette there.

But George's phone pinged around Prospero Park on Tuesday night and Wednesday. Nothing near Miranda's cabin—or near Mathis's corpse.

She grimaced. George Pope had killed Seth Cahill. He hadn't

killed Mathis. But in order to keep his paternity of Scott Behrens a secret—and the fact that he'd cheated on Hope when he was sixteen—George Pope might plead guilty to a murder he hadn't committed.

She tapped the screen and brought up her text messages and reread the strange text from the sheriff:

> Congratulations on solving the two
> murders

Odd thing to say. Not "solving the case" or "catching the killer," but instead "solving the two murders." Fenway felt a knot in her stomach.

Sheriff Donnelly knew George Pope hadn't killed Mathis Jericho. And Fenway had enabled someone else to take the fall.

What was she going to do?

McVie cleared his throat, snapping Fenway back to the present. "I ordered for you. Two lengua tacos, large horchata." He tapped the drink on Fenway's side of the table. "We're number fourteen."

Fenway couldn't tell McVie about her revelation—he was a civilian now. She forced a smile onto her face. "I'm glad I get to see you one more time before you leave."

"Yeah, I had to grab something from my safe deposit box, and the bank didn't open till ten. I put the last box in the Highlander about thirty minutes ago. I only have one more important thing to do before I leave. Figured we could have lunch before I do it."

The woman behind the counter placed two baskets down. "Catorce."

"That's us." Fenway hopped off her stool, walked to the counter, and grabbed the two baskets. Could she even eat with her stomach doing somersaults? Should she get back to the office immediately? She grabbed the tray and turned around.

McVie was in front of her.

Down on one knee.

Holding a diamond ring between the thumb and forefinger of his left hand.

Fenway blinked and took a half-step backward, almost spilling the baskets of food.

But McVie didn't notice. "Fenway Stevenson, will you—"

CAST OF CHARACTERS

Fenway Stevenson: A former nurse practitioner with a master's degree in forensics, she moved to Estancia in April. Fenway has a rocky (but improving) relationship with her father. Appointed to fill out the coroner's term, she decided to run for election—and won. Her official four-year term started January 1.

Her family

Nathaniel Ferris: The richest, most powerful man in the county, the oil magnate founded and owns Ferris Energy. After his wife took away the then eight-year-old Fenway to Seattle two decades ago, he threw himself into his work, but had hardly seen or talked to Fenway in the twenty years before she came back to town. Four months ago, he took a bullet for Fenway and recently awoke from a coma.

Charlotte Ferris: The former beauty pageant winner

married Nathaniel a decade ago when she was 25 and he was 50—the weekend of Fenway's high school graduation.

Co-workers and law enforcement personnel, past and present

Sergeant Desirée "Dez" Roubideaux: A detective in the coroner's office, Dez has worked for the county for more than twenty years. She's a dedicated, determined investigator despite her wisecracks.

Craig McVie: The former sheriff of Dominguez County, he lost the mayoral race in November. Recently divorced from Amy, he's now a private investigator. He and Fenway officially started dating after the election.

Sergeant Mark Trevino: The other detective in the coroner's office, Mark is on the cusp of retirement.

Deputy Celeste Salvador: A young, bright sheriff's deputy. She recently passed the detective exam and has applied to replace Mark after his retirement.

Piper Patten: Formerly in the county's IT department, this willowy redhead is a whiz at forensic accounting and data gathering. She helped Nathaniel Ferris prove his innocence in a murder case, and now works for McVie.

Melissa de la Garza: A CSI tech from neighboring San Miguelito County, de la Garza's team is a shared forensic resource with Dominguez County.

Donald Huke: An uptight, by-the-book rookie deputy in the Dominguez County Sheriff's Office.

Sarah Summerfield: The newly hired coroner's assistant.

Rachel Richards: Fenway's former assistant, she was promoted to be the county's youngest public information officer in a century.

Deputy Brian Callahan: Another sheriff's deputy, he has

also applied for the detective position in the coroner's office—and he's dating Rachel.

Captain Steve Alvidrez: The head of the vice squad in San Miguelito County.

Dr. Michi Yasuda: Dez's wife is the medical examiner in San Miguelito County, whose morgue houses many victims from Dominguez County.

Roland Azurra: A Dominguez County judge.

Debbie Farzan: A Dominguez County human resources manager.

Patrick Appleby: An IT specialist for the county, he assists with computer forensics and information gathering for investigations.

Jordan Daniels: The IT director for the county, he's Patrick's boss.

Sheriff Gretchen Donnelly: The new sheriff who replaced McVie when he ran for mayor.

Suspects, witnesses, and persons of interest

Seth Cahill: The former owner of Warehouse Storage Solutions, he's found dead on his former property.

Tyra Cahill: Recently divorced from Seth, she received the business in the settlement.

Mathis Jericho: A Nidever University dropout, he's the maintenance and landscaping specialist for Cahill Warehouse Storage.

Isabella Chan: An office assistant at Cahill Warehouse Storage.

Miranda Duchy: The former mistress of Seth Cahill, she was his official girlfriend at the time of Seth's passing.

Hope Dunkelman: Tyra Cahill's best friend since high school.

George Pope: Hope's high school sweetheart, her now-husband owns his own business.

Stephan Butler: The owner/operator of a local whale-watching business who has often used the Cahill's storage facility.

Calvin Banning: This shady figure often accompanies Butler on whale-watching trips.

Zoso: A well-connected low-level drug dealer whose penchant for the pills he uses doesn't interfere with his eyes and ears; he has helped Fenway out on a few cases in the past.

ACKNOWLEDGMENTS

Many thanks to my cover designer Ziad Ezzat of Feral Creative and Jamie Sanfelippo, who keeps my newsletter, social media, and other marketing activities sailing smoothly.

Special thanks to the Wordforge Novelists group in Sacramento, whose comments and guidance are, as always, invaluable. Shout-out to the Just Write Milwaukee and Shut Up and Write Milwaukee groups, who have welcomed me and given me encouragement, support, and community in my adopted city.

Thanks to my early readers, including Dana Luco, Nicole Prewitt, and Devin McCrate, as well as Beverly Ange, Michelle Damiani, Blair Semple, Dr. Christina Bellinger, Dr. Monique Koll, and Gavin Ralph. Your attention to detail and your areas of expertise helped immeasurably and made this book much better.

To my wife, my children, and my mother: I'm deeply grateful for your continued encouragement and support.